THE KING'S COWBOY

COWBOY PRINCES #3

MADELINE ASH

The King's Cowboy

Copyright ©2021 Madeline Ash

All rights reserved.

Cover design: Dominic Brown

ISBN-13: 978-0-6485809-9-7

SERIES ORDER

While The King's Cowboy can be read as a standalone, this series contains a significant overarching royal plot, so I recommend starting with Her Cowboy King.

Her Cowboy King #1

Her Cowboy Prince #2

The King's Cowboy #3

For Dominic
I'll never belong anywhere else

Please be aware that this story contains descriptions of anxiety, past violence/trauma, and references to past homophobia experienced by a main character.

BEFORE

Anxiety ruined Tomas Jaroka.

Nothing new there.

He woke in a sweat, convinced he wasn't going to survive breakfast let alone moving across the world with his brothers. It had all happened so fast. The sudden deaths of his uncles and cousin. The reality of his father's poor health. The plan for Tommy and his brothers to fulfil the duty that had landed at their feet like a ball with nowhere else to roll.

The small kingdom of Kiraly was eager to meet them, speculating about the new royal family, calling them the Lost Princes. That nationwide interest shot Tommy's nerves through the rafters, and Mark and Kris both knew it. Mark had already tried to talk him out of the whole thing, but Tommy had lied through his teeth and sworn he'd cope.

He was going with them.

He sat up—and alarm greeted him at the sight of his packed bags. God, he was really going with them.

I'm really leaving Jonah.

Within minutes, he burst out of the homestead to visit his neighbor. He shouldn't have put it off yesterday. His palms juddered down the sides of his shirt as he crossed the south field.

The early sun cupped his jaw, and the crisp morning air filled his lungs a little too fast.

It was the second-worst day of his life.

Jumping the dividing fence, his foot caught on strung wire and he stumbled. He'd *never* stumbled over Jonah's fence. He'd jumped it since he'd been tall enough—and climbed it before then. When Jonah had moved next door as a boy, his sweet, huggable heart had been inexplicably drawn to Tommy—who'd been quiet and reserved, even at five. Their fast friendship had held firm in the twenty years since.

Tommy stopped. He couldn't do this.

Couldn't tell Jonah how he felt.

Couldn't end their friendship when Jonah was forced to admit he didn't feel the same.

Yet Tommy couldn't keep pretending. This wasn't friendship; it was unrequited affection, and it'd been cutting him apart for years. Pretending to be platonic felt like holding a polite dinner conversation while ripping into his leg with a steak knife just out of sight.

"Enough of this," he muttered, and hounded himself across several acres of hay field, past the barn with the baler and tractors, and up the gravel track to the house that Jonah had bought from his parents when they'd left town.

Tommy's heels thudded against the wooden front steps and porch, and before he could talk himself out of it, he hauled open the door and let himself in. The entrance opened directly into the living room, but he moved into the hallway beyond, with its various adjoining rooms, and waited for a sign of life to poke its head out of the bedroom.

"Jonah," he called.

There was a moment of silence. Then bare-heeled footsteps sounded from the end of the hall where it opened into kitchen and dining area. *Christ.* Nerves shoved his stomach against his spine; fear seized the muscles lining his throat. The sensations were familiar from all the times he'd almost confessed his feelings over the past few years.

No backing out this time.

Except—

A young man appeared at the end of the hall. Lean, coquettish, wearing nothing but blue jeans and fluffy, blow-dried hair.

Not Jonah.

The sight lodged brutally in Tommy's chest.

"Hey," the man said with a curious smile. He gestured with a piece of toast, at home, casual, as if he had breakfast here every morning. "Jonah's just in the shower."

In the shower.

Because this man's scent is all over him.

Because they've been fucking.

Because Jonah doesn't feel the same.

Winded, Tommy stepped back, raising an apologetic hand. "Bad timing."

Panic twisted in his gut. He could hardly try again later. The private plane was just hours away. Bad timing was all he had.

The man said, "You can just wait here," a second before a bang came from behind the closed bathroom door on Tommy's right. There was the thudding of a short sprint, the rattling of a loose handle, and the door flew open. Jonah shoved his head out to look at the stranger, his dark hair wet and dripping onto his bare shoulders. The shower was still running—he hadn't stopped to grab a towel.

Mortification lit the base of Tommy's neck as a darker heat shook loose lower inside him.

"Was that—" Jonah cut off as his gaze landed on Tommy. He flushed, pulled his shoulders back behind the door, and then squinted as he tried to focus. "Tommy." Something about his abashed pink cheeks and scrunched eyes was unbearably gorgeous, and it was a small mercy Jonah wasn't wearing his glasses or he'd have seen the appreciation running wild over Tommy's face. "I didn't know you'd be over."

Tommy took a step back. "I didn't mean to interrupt."

"Oh no, you haven't," Jonah said and then winced.

"This is Tommy?" The man at the end of the hall shifted in interest.

Jonah whipped his head around, hair flinging droplets onto Tommy's arm, and said urgently, "Please don't."

The stranger raised a shoulder and disappeared into the kitchen.

Jonah turned back around and forced a smile, his laugh lines carving deep. *Jesus, those lines.* Like cheek-deep parentheses, turning his mouth into an aside, a moment of clarification, when really, Tommy's stumbling heart knew it contained the entirety of everything worth knowing.

Jonah said, "I'll be out in a second, okay?"

Only a fool would admit romantic feelings with Jonah's lover in the house. Yet Tommy couldn't leave without shattering their lives with a completely different truth.

"Don't rush on my account," he answered and practically hurled himself out the door.

On the porch, he tasted metal when he belatedly noticed the guy's backpacker travel bag dumped to one side. *Faultless timing, Tommy.* Ten out of fucking ten.

With his blood pounding like an aggrieved fist against a wall, he took the steps and focused on the gate at the end of the long driveway. *There and back.* He'd do a lap while he waited—he had no chance of standing still.

He *knew* how Jonah hooked up. Sage Haven didn't exactly have a thriving gay community, so tourists were Jonah's only hope at connection. The men would stay for a night, a weekend at most, and then move on. Jonah had once confided that when the right man finally came along, they'd share their first kiss and first orgasm on different days.

"Maybe a date or two in between," he'd said to Tommy with a crinkle-eyed smile. "I can dream, right?"

Right, except Tommy had done nothing *but* dream. Too aware that his confession would end their friendship—things would be too awkward after that, too painful—he'd kept it secret just to keep Jonah in his life.

Now he had no choice. His royal duties wouldn't tolerate the distraction of long-distance yearning. He wouldn't have the resources to pretend at friendship, not anymore. Not when it meant fighting something that felt like the formation of the universe between his lungs—all while Jonah just carried on.

He had to end this.

With a hand pressed to his chest—as if that would keep him intact—Tommy strode, unblinking, toward the gate. It was the horizon. It was slow, steady breathing. It was the count of ten. *There and back. Just once. There and back.*

Then he'd tell Jonah he was leaving for good.

"Tommy!"

His pulse spiked at Jonah's clear voice and the front door banging shut.

"Tommy, wait!"

No. *Jesus, I can't do this.*

"Honestly, Tom, wait for me, will you?"

Jaw tight, Tommy halted at the desperate edge in Jonah's voice and turned as Jonah jogged down the front steps on bare feet, his hands working to close the buttons of his jeans. A damp shirt was plastered to his chest, covering slender shoulders that were deceptively good at heavy lifting and abs trained to share the load, while the scoop neck revealed the narrow wings of his collarbones. Add shower-damp hair and lips swollen from

5

another man's kisses, and pain pinched in Tommy's chest. He memorized every detail, possessive of these last moments no matter how they ached.

"That was awkward." Jonah sounded off as he stopped in front of him. His smile, usually as bright as a suncatcher, was strained. "Sorry."

Tommy gave a nod, but when the world around him tipped with it, he latched onto a grounding technique for panic attacks. Count down from five using the senses, starting with things he could see—*go*.

Jonah. The brown warmth of his eyes framed by lashes long and thick and dark. His tanned skin. His angular jawline that played right into the hands of masculine beauty ideals, and the concern breaking into a frown on his lips.

Four things he could touch. That curl of soil-dark hair slipping around Jonah's ear and the drip of water on the lens of his black-framed glasses. The now fully wet shirt that Tommy imagined adjusting, unsticking from his friend's chest to set the shoulder seams right. And Jonah's hand, steady and safe, sliding into his pocket as his stance shifted.

"You okay?" Jonah asked, his head tilting.

Three things he could hear. His own pulse thumping in his ears. The echo of that man saying, *Jonah's just in the shower,* offhand, and yet so intimate it hurt. And the swan song of Jonah's voice. The last time he might ever hear it.

"Tommy?"

This wasn't helping.

Two things he could smell. Sweet shampoo and spring grass.

One taste. *Regret.*

"Tommy." Jonah's brows kinked in earnest. "Seriously. What's going on?"

"Nothing." His mouth was dry. *I don't want to do this.* "Everything."

Jonah caught his shoulder and let it go just as quickly. "You can tell me."

Tommy's throat closed. *Can I?*

If only Jonah wasn't good all the way down. Kind and honest and pure. A loud world hushed to its simplest arrangement. Jonah had the wings of an angel—and no idea how they made Tommy's heart fly.

And Tommy had lied to him about everything that mattered.

"Is it about Charlie? He's alright, you know?" Jonah gestured back toward the house. Then an idea seemed to strike him. "You should come in and have toast with us!"

Right. That explained why Tommy had woken with the sense that breakfast wanted him dead. "You're kidding."

Jonah looked like he wasn't quite sure. His gaze lowered to the gravel underfoot. "He's hitching out of town this morning. He was at the bar until close last night, so we just—"

"Sure." Tommy held up a hand. Please, God, let his raised brows look embarrassed, not wounded. "I don't need the details."

Jonah paused. Then he grimaced around another smile. "You didn't knock."

"I never knock."

A flicker at the window betrayed Jonah's one-nighter was watching on. "Maybe start?"

Tommy's embarrassment hid behind denial. "It's not going to be a problem again."

"What does that mean?" Puzzled, Jonah narrowed his eyes. "You all right?"

Tommy shoved his trembling hands in his back pockets. "I have to tell you something."

Jonah scanned his face with a frown. "You're worked up."

Because I'm losing you.

On the actual worst day of Tommy's life, he'd watched Jonah die.

Tommy had believed so completely that he'd lost Jonah, the trauma of it had dropped an anchor deep enough inside him that he *remembered* it happening. The grief. The reality of surviving without him. The irreparable rift it had caused in the arc of his life. He'd thought he'd never again ride with Jonah in the back hills or help him bale hay; never catch his laugh or unwind in his silence or feel steadied by his constancy.

But Jonah had survived their attack. And all those losses had lingered on the sidelines until today.

"We're leaving," Tommy pushed out on a dry whisper.

Jonah didn't ask him to define *we*—the pronoun was an unwitting side-effect of Tommy being an identical triplet. "Leaving what?"

"Sage Haven." Stress slicked Tommy's hands. He'd hardly left this small town in Montana since returning from college almost four years ago. "We're going to Europe."

Jonah blinked at him. "You're what?"

"We're going to Europe."

"Yeah, but that doesn't—" Jonah gave a small laugh. It was the kind of laugh that preceded understanding but was first in line to get the joke. "What are you talking about, you goose?"

"We're going to Europe. Classic instance of saying exactly what I mean."

Smile slipping, Jonah swallowed. "Don't get sarcastic. You're not making any sense."

Tommy ran a hand over his aching chest. "Yes. I am."

For a few seconds, Jonah just stared. Then he shook his head. "I don't understand."

"This was never supposed to happen." They hadn't planned on ever setting foot in that place. He and his brothers were never supposed to matter. "But we're going overseas, leaving in a few hours."

Jonah stepped away abruptly. He collected several drips

from his neck with a confused swipe of his hand. "But that—how long will you be gone?"

Pain locked inside Tommy. He forced the word out. "Indefinitely."

"Indefinite . . ." Jonah stilled with the kind of frown that hinted at panic. He held Tommy's gaze. "Remind me what that means again."

"Without a fixed end point."

"Stop it." A tremor entered Jonah's voice.

Tommy rolled his lips together, fighting a swell of alarm.

"Explain this properly," Jonah said, pointing a finger at the ground, "because I don't understand what's happening."

"We have family over there." The words stuck in Tommy's throat. Something pressed against his breastbone from within, solid like a shoulder, hot like a slick, bloody death. "They died. The whole family, all together." The balcony they'd been dining on had collapsed in an architectural tragedy. "And we're moving over there to take their place."

"No." Jonah's voice rose. "I don't believe you. You boys would never leave the ranch. You'd never leave—"

"We have to," Tommy cut him off, quiet and frantic as his body purged the truth in a clammy sweat. "We have to leave because we're royalty. My uncle was the king of a small country called Kiraly. He died in an accident with the others, and now we're the only living heirs to the throne. Our last name isn't actually Jacobs. It's Jaroka. Look it up—it's real, and they're dead, and that means Mark's going to be king."

Jonah stared.

Tommy couldn't feel anything from his battering heart down.

"Um." Jonah's face had turned red. "It sounded like you just tried to tell me that you're a prince."

The air thinned in Tommy's lungs. His hands shook in his pockets.

"No." Distress was in the hand Jonah plunged into his hair—in the half-step he took toward Tommy. "You're not allowed to go quiet. Not now."

"I—I'm sorry I never told you."

Jonah breathed hard as he waited, eyes wide.

"Dad was raised over there, but we were born here." Sage Haven had always been their home. "We've never even visited Kiraly. It means nothing to us. That's why I never told you. Because it hasn't mattered."

Except deep down, it was because it *shouldn't* have mattered—it was pointless to want to embrace his status when it meant nothing to Mark and Kris—so Tommy had buried his own interest in silence.

"Mark and Kris haven't told anyone either," he said, voice unsteady. "We decided years ago we didn't want to be treated differently. We wanted normal lives."

"Oh." Jonah ducked his head and slid a hand around his opposite bicep, right over the tattoo he'd gotten with Tommy at eighteen. Their left arms both held the same inked text, intended to prove that Jonah was as much a part of Tommy's life as his brothers. Now, that fact thrashed like a lie in their silence. Jonah looked up as he murmured, "But you're not normal."

"No," Tommy answered softly.

"No." Jonah shook his head, features breaking, and Tommy felt it like a quake along the fault line of his sternum. "I want to think you're lying to my face about this, but that look in your eyes is frightening me because it's your honest look. And if you're not lying right now, that means you've lied to me our whole lives about something that doesn't make sense."

Tommy swallowed hard. The problem was that it *did* make sense. He'd always been acutely aware of the royal blood glinting in his veins, the pulse of prophecy calling from a life he could scarcely imagine but desperately wanted.

He'd never been allowed to want it before. Even now, hounded by anxiety, it was an impossible thing to crave. The thought of living among hundreds of palace staff was enough to overwhelm him, let alone a basic duty like giving a public address. But striving for it might be the only way to get past the heartbreak that was closing in fast.

"You could have told me." Jonah's voice was fractured. "Just me. I came out to you years before anyone else. You could have told me that in return. We could have kept each other's secrets."

Shaking his head, Tommy said, "I couldn't have told you I was a prince. You'd have treated me differently."

Insult flashed across Jonah's face. "Oh, because obviously I wasn't terrified you would treat *me* differently. I told you I was *gay*, Tommy. In this town. I was fourteen. I trusted you. You should have trusted me."

"You're right." It came out strangled. Was he really about to do this? "But I have to leave. Mark and Kris need me. Unless—"

The early spring morning seemed to slow around him. His skin stung, overexposed at how close this question would bring him to his most guarded secret, a kind of cautionary scrape as if he stood on the very edge of a platform while a train bulleted past. It was as close as he'd get when Jonah's latest lover was watching at the window. "Unless," he said again, "there's a reason you want me to stay?"

Jonah's pupils were blown as he searched Tommy's face. Pain creased between his brows, and he asked, "What kind of question is that? Nothing about me could ever be more important than your brothers."

Yes, it could.

"Nothing at all?" Tommy pushed as something collapsed at his core. "Nothing that seems small or silly or impossible?"

In a world where Jonah held secret feelings for Tommy, they'd have risen to the surface at that question. But Jonah just shook his head, eyes still wide, no hint of suppressed affection crossing his face. Not even a flicker. Tommy had known this truth since he'd fallen for his friend after college, but it still knocked the wind out of him.

Jonah didn't feel the same.

Tommy tried not to sway on his feet.

His throat tightened. This was it. No more pretending he wasn't drowning in the rapids of his own heartbeat every time their eyes locked; no more pretending he wasn't taking on water in the agonized rush of Jonah's smile. This was really it. The end.

"I'm sorry," he said. "But I should tell you that I—"

"Fuck off, Tomas." Jonah wiped a hand swiftly under his eyes. "It's too late to be sorry."

Tommy jolted. Jonah never swore. Not once in all his years as a target for hatred had he used words intended to cause harm in return.

The nod Tommy gave was the hardest of his life. "You're right."

A haze of incomprehension clouded Jonah's eyes as he lifted a hand to cover the scar that ran across his throat, puckered and white. He only did that when he felt too vulnerable to stand tall. His other arm circled his middle.

"I have a new life to start," Tommy forced himself to say and stepped out of Jonah's range. "You won't hear from me again. And it would be best if I don't hear from you." Then he was turning, feeling Jonah's stunned stare pressing into his back and knowing this was truly the worst day of his life.

The door opened, and the backpacker called out gently, "C'mere. You all right, mate?"

He didn't hear Jonah's answer.

Tommy would never be all right again.

NOW

1

"Good morning, everyone, and thank you for being here."

Tommy stood at the podium in the palace's press room, fingers curled around the edges of the lectern. Every seat was taken; journalists ringed the back and side walls. They stared at him, waiting, the only sound the murmur of translators repeating his opening words. He'd been warned that every media outlet would want coverage of his first solitary public appearance —his own fault for avoiding media attention for the past four months—but the impact of a full audience still seized his pulse.

It's fine. Stay level. Don't panic.

"The initiative I'm launching today strives to change the national conversation around mental health," he said, voice cool and steady even as his grip tightened around the polished timber. All he had to do was introduce the project he'd personally developed in consultation with government and mental health experts, then Mark would field questions. Less than five minutes. As a starting point to public exposure, it was pretty simple.

Someone dropped a pen. The sound jolted across his skin like an electric shock, kick-starting his adrenaline.

It was a fucking pen. He bit his teeth together. *Don't lose it.*

"My brothers and I are still relatively new to Kiraly," he said, noting the strong presence of palace security dotting the perimeter of the room. Strangely, the reminder that the late royal family had been murdered by a man who was currently missing didn't trouble him. The possibility that his heart might hammer itself to death in front of a live audience?

That sure as hell did.

"But we are not new to close-knit communities. We are not new to the reality of stigma and shame." He paused, drawing back from the microphone to conceal his quickening breath. Mark had done breathing exercises with him offstage, but he'd chewed through that calm just to cross to the podium. "The town where we spent most of our lives had one psychologist. The possibility of being recognized at her clinic stopped many people from seeking help when it was needed."

Tommy had only attended appointments in the years after the attack because Mark and Kris and Jonah had taken turns driving him. He hadn't wanted anyone seeing his truck out front in fear of how they'd label him.

"I have known people," he continued—*such as myself*—"who have suffered greatly from the conviction that they should not *need* help. That having a diagnosed mental illness would reduce their value to society, to their workplace, and to their loved ones."

The room was silent but for the scratch of pens on paper, fingers on keyboards, and quiet translation. They were listening to him, sharing his words. Purpose rippled through him, and for a fleeting moment, he dared to think the diazepam he'd taken earlier might work. His heart could pound, his lungs could labor, but the drug would stop his anxiety peaking beyond control.

It would allow him to finally engage with his people.

And that was a capability he *had* to possess. Delivering this speech was the first test in his attempt to replace Kris—who had been training to replace Mark—as King of Kiraly.

Fair to say their roles had become complicated. Soon after arriving, Mark had fallen in love with Princess Ava, who, for good reason, couldn't bear the media interest that came with ruling a kingdom. Kris had stepped up in secret to take Mark's place—despite being third-born—and had spent the past few weeks working to prove himself worthy before Mark would make the abdication official.

Tommy hadn't taken that well. Having his role in the line of succession skipped had smoked out his hidden desire to ascend. He'd resented what Kris was able to do for Mark even as he'd known that his social anxiety would string him up in the very responsibilities he craved. It had gutted him to accept it was the best plan—until Kris had been violently beaten last week on the city's streets, and just like that, Tommy had to at least *try* to step into his own power.

This latest plan was strictly confidential and wholly contingent on Tommy's ability to handle it. The public still believed Mark would be crowned at the upcoming coronation. Only a select few closest to Tommy and his brothers knew the truth.

And only Tommy knew how desperately he wanted to succeed. Not just to protect his brothers from the duty they felt like a burden, but to sate the quiet need that had grown in him since arriving in Kiraly—an identity-deep pull toward the reigning role.

If I can handle it.

"As a society, we have normalized negative opinions of those who battle mental illness," he said, and straightened his shoulders. The small movement pulled his shirt too tightly, trapping his chest, jamming the top button against his throat. It smothered him. A flush of hot-cold sweat erupted down his back, and he threw a horrified glance to where Mark stood in the wings. His brother's brow creased in concern even as he gave an encouraging thumbs up.

Keep going.

Tommy lifted a finger to find his place on the page. He couldn't feel his hands. "We reflect these opinions in our language. We casually use words like crazy. Insane. Mental." The words hardly made sense as they left his mouth; the jumbling letters made less sense on the page. But the part of him that wanted to lead this kingdom didn't need the script at all. "This stigmatizes mental illness to the point that our fear of being referred to in these terms becomes greater than our desire to get help."

God knew how many times Tommy had called himself a nutcase—the conviction with which he still believed it.

"Encouraging a language shift through public stigma-reduction campaigns, as well as removing barriers for early intervention, treatment, and support, are just some of the ways this program intends to create change on this issue. The collaborative services in this program will—"

A white flare stopped him cold.

Then blinding darkness.

A second later, the other cameras started flashing, sparking sharply in his vision, crackling in his ears. The entire room became loud and confusing and alarming. *Don't panic. It's fine. Keep going.* But it wasn't fine, because there wasn't enough oxygen to get a proper breath. Goddamn it, he *hated* this—hated that his sympathetic nervous system poured adrenaline like a drunk with the wine, and that it would always pour for a crowd. That once the chemical hit, his fight-or-flight response had a life of its own.

"We clearly stated no photos until the end," Philip called out from the front of the podium. Firm, but way too late.

Tommy was already running.

"You going inside or what?"

Tommy turned from the door to Kris's royal suite to find Frankie approaching along the arch-ceilinged corridor. Her red hair was styled in its usual short spikes, and despite the navy-blue uniform she wore as head of palace security, her buckled black boots were far from palace issue. She strode like a badass on a mission, and if he hadn't been so busy psyching himself up to face his brother, he'd have heard her coming a mile away.

Caught out, he asked, "What kind of question is that to ask a member of the royal family?"

She rolled her eyes as she reached him, nodding a greeting at the royal guards positioned against the corridor walls. "No idea," she said, "but since I'm engaged to become a member of the royal family, I guess I'll find out."

"Are you two going public soon"—he paused, cocking a brow—"or what?"

"When he's recovered." She reached for the door handle, then paused, not looking at him. "You feeling okay?"

In her role, she'd be well aware he'd spent the past hour riding out his panic attack inside the secret passages that lined the palace walls. His skin still stung, but at least he could breathe again.

"Fine," he said.

She jerked her head toward the door. "He's been worried about you."

Sounded about right. Kris was ferociously protective of him. "Thanks for getting everyone together."

"Easy." Her green gaze was curious. "You wanted Kris, Mark, and Philip, right?"

With a nod, he opened the door and strode through the sitting room to his brother's bedroom.

"There he is," Kris said loudly the second Tommy entered.

Kris was in an enormous bed, half-covered by sheets and propped up against a pile of pillows. Normally, his features were identical to Tommy and Mark's, but the bruised mess of his face made it difficult to tell beyond the blue eyes and dark hair and brows. He shifted position, looking agitated. Good. At least Tommy's public screw-up had distracted his brother from his injuries—fractured ribs, broken arm, and a stab wound in his side.

Pity it couldn't distract Tommy.

Kris winced and stopped trying to sit up. "Where the hell have you been?"

Tommy moved to stand with his back to the nearest window, avoiding his brother's gaze. The sight of those injuries was a fist-squeeze inside him, trying to wring something out of him he wasn't able to surrender. "There was a meet and greet afterward."

Kris's scoff was pissed. "Funny."

Tommy directed a tiny, cynical smile at the floor.

"It's good to see you've recovered, Your Highness." Philip faced him from where he stood at the foot of the bed with a tense kind of respect. He was tall, thin, and dignified to the bone. He'd dealt with their king-swapping with equal parts exasperation and resignation, and, in addition to being their royal advisor, Tommy and his brothers had recently found out he'd been the long-term partner of their late uncle, Prince Noel, which made him the closest thing to family they had in Kiraly.

In a glance, Tommy took in the gathering. Kris had sunk back into the pillows with a scowl. Mark was sitting in an armchair by the window and caught Tommy's eye with a grim smile. Frankie shut the door behind her and moved to stand beside Philip.

They all looked at him, waiting.

Tommy surrendered his pride. "No one try claiming that went well."

"God, no," Kris said.

"Not the first word that springs to mind," Frankie said as her phone buzzed.

"It wasn't a disaster," Mark said, leaning forward with his hands clasped. "I finished the speech and took questions. Your words were good, Tom. Powerful and quotable."

"Perfect." The bitterness in Tommy's voice was a fraction of that fused to his gut. "The journalists' quotes will all end with, *and then he ran away*."

Mark ran a hand over his mouth with a low hum.

"Could have been worse," Kris said. "At least you made it offstage."

Before losing it.

For Kris, that was an unusually poor attempt at reassurance. His protective streak was so strong it often bordered on suffocating, so the fact that Kris wasn't pretending it was fine— that no one had even *noticed* him bolt from the podium mid-sentence—could only mean one thing.

He didn't expect Tommy to pull off being king.

And giving Tommy false hope would only make it hurt more when he failed.

Tommy curled his fingers into fists behind his back. "Tell me I'm going to succeed," he demanded quietly. "All of you."

The words were scarcely out of his mouth before Frankie said, "Obviously," without looking up from her phone.

Mark nodded slowly. "You will."

"The question isn't whether you'll succeed, Your Highness," Philip said, "but how."

There was a silence in which Tommy shifted his weight and took hold of the windowsill behind him. He clamped onto it, willing the pressure and energy to be enough to stop him from tapping his fingers. Then he made himself look expectantly at Kris.

Wearily, his brother said, "I want you to."

"I can do this." One part of him was utterly convinced of it. "Assuming that King of Kiraly is ultimately a position that needs filling."

They all turned to him, looking confused.

"And why wouldn't it be, Your Highness?" Philip asked, brows creased.

"I want to survey Kirilian citizens." Tommy continued to grip the sill out of sight. "About whether we should abolish the monarchy."

There was a beat of stunned silence.

Then Philip staggered back a step. Frankie caught his arm and lowered him onto the foot of the bed as Philip breathed, "About *what?*"

"It's a critical question."

"It's a dangerous question." Frankie hadn't taken her eyes off Tommy. She looked more curious than alarmed.

Philip pressed a hand to the base of his throat in horror. "Why would you intentionally plant that thought in the public consciousness?"

Kris and Mark exchanged an uncomfortable glance.

Oh, for God's sake. "You two think I'm so desperate to avoid public appearances, I'd prefer to literally dismantle the monarchy?"

"It would be a disproportionate response," Frankie said, voice dry. "But effective."

"It would be absurd," Tommy said coldly.

Mark's frown was heavy. "Tell us what you're thinking then, Tommy."

"Look at Kris." Tommy jerked his chin toward his brother.

"He was attacked in our city. Our family was *murdered* by these people."

That had been revealed after Kris's attack. A group of anarchist extremists had planned the deaths of Tommy's uncles and cousin—and had targeted Kris for the same fate. Frankie had suspected foul play all along but hadn't found proof until last week.

"We've assumed that the attitude of those men is an anomaly," Tommy said. "But what if that attack was a manifestation of the feelings of the majority?"

Philip had sagged against the nearest bedpost, an arm wrapped loosely around it. His face was pale. "Tomas, asking such a thing—"

"I refuse to rule a kingdom that doesn't want a king."

"Yes, but—"

"No, Philip. I don't care what it might look like to ask our citizens that question. Kiraly recently lost its reigning family. Our arrival cut off what otherwise could have been a turning point in the government of this country. Kiraly might well be a republic right now if it weren't for us. And I need to know if that's what the people want."

"And . . . if it is?"

Tommy held his advisor's stare. "I've already answered that."

Philip turned to where Frankie stood beside him and murmured, "Oh my God," over and over until she clamped a steadying hand on his shoulder.

"Mark," Tommy said. "Kris. Tell me what you think. We're in this together."

"It hadn't occurred to me," Mark admitted. "But I agree with you."

"Yeah." Kris's eyelids were starting to wilt. "Me too."

Tommy returned his attention to Philip. "This needs to happen quickly. I want people being surveyed in a week's time. Results back two weeks after that. The coronation is drawing closer—stop all expenses until we've confirmed whether or not it'll proceed."

He received another, "Oh my God," in answer, but it came with a nod, so he let it go.

"I hate to break up the party," Kris said on a sigh. "But I'm tried. And sore. And kind of hungry."

Frankie leaned over the foot of the bed to rub his ankle, and Tommy looked sharply out the window. His brother's relationship with Frankie was still new—too fresh for him to watch without a gut-twist of envy. Throughout their four-year friendship of suppressed mutual attraction, this had always been inevitable.

Not quite the same as falling for his oblivious best friend of twenty years.

Don't—

Instantly breathless, Tommy spun to leave. *Don't think about him.* But it was too late. That heartbreak had long since spread to his lungs, and it was all he could do not to clutch his chest as he pulled the door open.

"Hey, Tommy, before you go," Frankie called him back. "Can you grab the painkillers?"

He stilled, forcing in a slow breath.

"Take it easy, Kris." Mark stood and gave Tommy a smile as he headed out the door.

"They're on his bedside table." Frankie was following Philip across the room. She cast a farewell glance at Kris before catching Tommy's gaze expectantly. "Two capsules. With food. There are sandwiches."

Latching onto the distraction, he crossed his arms. "I thought you were in love with him."

"I am." She halted in front of Tommy as Philip disappeared into the sitting room. She'd never been afraid to blatantly ignore his attempts at evasion. She behaved—it bemused him to realize —like a sister. "But my job's important, and I've got shit to do."

"Fascinating." He kept his expression level. "You might not have heard. I'm the new king."

"Yeah." She cocked a brow and leaned in close. "That's less certain now than it was a minute and a half ago though, isn't it?"

"I'm still in pain here," Kris said from the bed.

When Tommy didn't budge, Frankie glanced at his chest and up again, eyes glinting. "I'll get his meds if you tell me about your shirt."

Alarm sparked at the base of his throat. "Excuse me?"

"This." She reached out and tweaked the soft, sage green fabric at his wrist. "I've never seen you wear it, yet it seems familiar."

He stared at her, not answering, confounded as to how the hell she knew.

"Looks a bit small. Is it even yours?"

He said, "Don't," before he'd consciously decided to say it.

"Anyone?" Kris called weakly.

"It suits you," she murmured. And taking that as a win, she added, "Talk to him, will you?" and closed the door behind her.

The rustle of bedcovers betrayed Kris was shifting around again. When he hissed in pain, Tommy jammed his teeth together and crossed the room to the bed. In silence, he passed Kris half a sandwich from the lunch platter, picked up the packet of painkillers, and read the directions as many times as it took Kris to finish eating. Then he popped two capsules into his palm and picked up the water glass.

Kris accepted both with a grunt. Tommy gazed at the carved cornices until his brother swallowed.

"Tommy," Kris murmured as he handed the glass back. "You won't look at me. You've hardly looked at me in days."

Tommy's neck grew hot as he set the glass within his

brother's reach. There was no point denying it. "It's difficult to see you like this."

For too many reasons.

"Because of Jonah?"

Pain reeled in his chest, and he almost left then and there, but Kris hissed again, and Tommy forced himself to face him. His brother's eyes were closed, his brow creased in pain as he shoved at the pillows beneath him with his unbroken arm.

"Should you be doing that?"

"Should *you* be—" Kris froze with a broken gasp. His face went white. "Oh, God. My ribs just killed me."

Tommy focused on wanting to box Kris around the head instead of the tight pinch in his own throat. "Then stop moving."

"I'm uncomfortable."

"Just—*stop*. Here." Leaning in, Tommy slid one arm behind his brother's shoulders. Taking his weight, Tommy held him up while adjusting the pillows so they lay a little flatter. There. "Now relax."

Kris sighed as he settled down, eyes closed.

It was too familiar—nursing someone whose skin was split and stitched, whose soft noises disguised a far greater pain.

"Tommy." Kris cracked his eyes open. "I'm sorry you've been through this. More than you know."

Tommy couldn't answer—couldn't blink away the image of Jonah recovering in hospital. His brave face. His silent tears. His shadowed smiles, weakened splutters of the light that had always filled him.

"I'm having nightmares." Kris's admission was thick. "I keep seeing the knife. And thinking it might be the last thing I feel."

Tommy stepped back abruptly.

Jesus. The knife had gone right to Jonah's neck. Some of the men had pinned Tommy down as his friend's skin had opened itself to the blade, as his terrified eyes had found Tommy's in a horrific attempt at goodbye. *Fuck, oh fuck—*

"Tommy—"

"I can't be this for you," he said, the words strangled as he stumbled back.

get out of here

"I can't—"

fuck, stop, make it stop

"Tommy!"

Years. It had been years since his last intrusive memory, but as he fled the hospital room and the stricken look on Jonah's face —no, *Kris's* face—the trauma reared up, triggered anew, and sought to swallow him whole.

He ran, stumbling, dodging it as his surroundings spun away from him. Hands against the corridor wall, stark white plaster and palace bluestone, scraping like razors over his palms. People closing in around him, nurses and royal guards, making noises he didn't understand. A door—*his* door—and inside, sagging to the floor, hands and knees, blinking but unable to unsee, unfeel, unexperience the anchor so unbearably heavy inside him. It was dropping too low for him to stomach, tearing through him. Blood, so much blood—

breathe, stop seeing, just breathe

—blood and tears squeezed from the tight ball of his soul, because Jonah was dead. There was no way he wasn't dead—

fight it, please fight it

Jonah—

Jonah. *Jonah.* Kneeling beside him. Close but not touching as he tried to calm Tommy with a distraction technique he'd created. He was saying, "Shhh" on one really long breath, giving Tommy time to find the sound, catch it, cling to it, follow the susurration into whatever word it ultimately became. It was a guessing game, a diversion from his panic, stretched like a rope leading out of the dark, because Jonah could go for twenty seconds, thirty, without running out of breath.

"Shhhoelaces," he would eventually say, or "shhhots of Vodka" or "shhhenanigans."

"Was that your guess, Tommy?" he'd ask. And even though Tommy couldn't answer, Jonah would smile and say, "Here, we'll try another one."

Dully, Tommy registered that he was shushing against the woven rug of his sitting room.

He was okay.

Jonah was okay.

"Jesus Christ," he breathed, and dropped onto his side. Twice in one day. Exhaustion emptied him—a battery drained flat. He lay unmoving, panting, staring at the polished foot of a wingback chair.

It was normal, his psych had once told him, for old trauma to be stirred up now and then. Objectively good to know, but emotionally impractical. It was like saying grief was normal after the death of a loved one. Yeah, thanks, genius, but any advice for a man who couldn't even look at his own brother?

Time.

Once Kris healed, and reminders of his own attack faded again, Tommy would be left alone with the legacy of that trauma —social anxiety.

And Jonah.

Tommy had just let him back into his thoughts; allowed him to settle like the softest hand on his shoulder.

Tommy closed his eyes as anguish tore along his sternum.

For months, he'd blocked the pain of leaving Jonah behind— until last week when he'd caved to the temptation of hearing Jonah's voice again and asked Frankie to let him listen in on a phone call between the two of them. *Great idea.* Jonah had

effectively told her that Tommy wasn't the friend he'd known—
that version of Tommy would never have abandoned him.

"My friend wouldn't have done this to me," Jonah had said
with a resignation that had since kept Tommy up at night. "He's
different now. He's a prince. I get it. And I get that someone like
me has no business being friends with a man like him."

That was how Jonah thought of him.

Not so in love he'd had to let Jonah go—but so superior, he'd
shed their small-town friendship like a snakeskin.

It had resulted in the required clean break, but it wasn't
healing. Sometimes, Tommy couldn't think for missing him,
couldn't speak, as if their separation had stripped him of
language since the only thing worth putting into words was
Jonah.

Jonah.

Jonah, I love you.

It killed Tommy that he hadn't said it—that the unspoken
confession was still balled up inside him. If he lived that morning
over again, he wouldn't leave his feelings bleeding through the
cracks of their conversation. He'd say it outright.

Too late now. He'd wasted years of opportunities, and he
couldn't go back to Sage Haven. A part of him had toyed with
that idea—clung to the possibility that his brothers would suggest
he go home. It had been a nonsensical secret desire, because his
brothers needed him, and Jonah didn't feel the same. And
Tommy wanted to rule.

Besides, Jonah had reconciled himself to not being in
Tommy's life. It would be the peak of selfishness to contact him
just to give a different reason they could never see each other
again.

"There's nowhere to go from here," Jonah had added to
Frankie.

That was their truth. Tommy, lying fractured on the floor of his royal suite, halfway across the world from the man custom-made for his heart. In a world where Tommy had never left Sage Haven, their mismatched affection would still have led to this inescapable conclusion.

There was nowhere to go from here.

2

Kiraly was *incredible.*

Jonah Wood stood outside the central train station, bags at his feet, gaping at the city that rose above him. It was —*wow.* Like a fairytale and a mountain range had a baby and it had grown into a place where people could live. The travel brochure he'd read on the train from Paris had explained that Kira City was the capital of this tiny kingdom—vibrant, open-armed, and outrageously steep. The buildings were huddled close, cozy and cluttered across the mountainside, the honey-toned stone glowing in the afternoon summer sun. Tourists, the brochure stated, tended to stick to hotspots where drinks and dancing ran until dawn, but apparently almost everywhere was safe to explore—the only danger was getting lost.

Kira City locals regard its street map with both fondness and frustration. Cobbled streets and laneways cut haphazardly across the mountain with an abundance of one-way streets, pedestrian-only shortcuts, and flights of steps in place of appallingly steep sidewalks. Be sure to plan half a dozen alternate routes if you intend to drive around. We're not even joking.

"A*maz*ing," he said, stuffing the brochure in the back pocket of his jeans.

He hadn't really traveled before. Just been around Montana mostly, so the fact that he was somewhere *else,* like over the hills and far away, was still blowing his mind.

It smelled different, sounded different. A street vendor was frying some kind of sweet pastry with vanilla and cinnamon he intended to devour the instant he exchanged currency, a guitarist played on the opposite street corner, and a group of women spilled out of the station behind him in a burst of laughter and color and sunhats—a beetroot-red tote bag, shoes of buttercup yellow, and a dress that was as blue as an open sky. The women eyed him as they passed, smiles appreciative, and one doubled back to press a card into his palm.

"Hey there, cowboy," she said, reaching out to tug on the brim of his hat. "Party at mine tonight."

"Oh." He glanced down at it—directions—and gave a startled smile. "Thank you. That's so kind."

Her brows shot up in delight. "You're in character! You do a brilliant accent," she said, and with a wink, darted off to catch up to her friends.

Jonah blinked after her as he slid the card beside the brochure.

There was a lake . . . He turned to look down the slope —*there,* the bright blue-green water glinting in the sunlight. And there, back up the hill, that long line of steps cutting north was called The Scepter. If he walked down to the east, he'd end up in a fancy plaza filled with markets during the day and twinkle lights after sundown, and somewhere in among it all was a nightlife district that supposedly cured visitors of their need to sleep.

Oriented and still waiting, he fiddled with the strap of one of his bags, nervously ignoring the city's grandest attraction. It was the most popular tourist destination and open to the public on Tuesdays, Thursdays, and Saturday afternoons.

The Kiralian Palace.

His stomach dropped as he forced his attention to where it flared like high noon above the city. It was enormous, a huge white-stone structure stretching into the sky, big towers supporting smaller towers on their shoulders like children trying to touch the clouds. His breath hitched as the familiar grip of inadequacy pressed down on the soft underside of his jaw.

He swallowed, not looking away.

The Kiralian Palace is the official residence of the royal family of Kiraly, the House of Jaroka, the brochure had stated. *With its own postcode, it employs more than 850 members of staff, their jobs ranging from housekeeping to security, from catering to the armory. The palace has its own swimming pool, cinema, art museum, concert hall, planetarium, and brewery. It has more than 82 royal and guest bedrooms, 148 staff bedrooms, and 75 bathrooms.*

There was more, but his eyes had kept sliding back to the bold line at the top.

The official residence of the royal family of Kiraly.

"Jones!"

Jolting, he spun around, spotting Frankie instantly in the thin sidewalk crowd. She looked the same as always in her jeans, tank, and chunky boots.

He raised a hand. "Hey, Frankie!"

He'd called her the day Tommy had left. Distraught and confused, he'd expected to find her reeling from the fact that Kris was royalty—expected to deal with the loss of their friends together. But it turned out that Jonah was the only one who hadn't been keeping secrets. She'd thrown a curveball into his confusion by speaking in a different accent and admitting to being from Kiraly—and having returned to the palace to manage the boys' security. She'd sounded truly sorry, and despite the high-level demands of her position, had always made time to talk to him.

She was the only person he'd told about his plans for the future.

Frankie slowed as she neared him, shaking her head in dismay. "Could you look any more like a wide-eyed country boy?"

He held his arms out, grinning so hard his cheeks strained.

She blinked in surprise, then said, "Only you," and stepped into his embrace. Her hug was tight and hard, and it hit him like an egg from a passing car that she was the first person to intentionally touch him since she and the boys had left Sage Haven. Sure, there'd been accidental brushes at the bar, the occasional fingertip to palm when receiving change, but nothing that had sprung from genuine human connection.

Heart stinging, he held on, pressing his cheek against her hair when she tried to pull away.

"Hey," she said softly against his shoulder, relaxing into his hold. "You okay?"

"Sure. Maybe. I don't know." He let go, making himself smile as he shoved a hand into his empty rear pocket. "It's been a weird few months."

"You're telling me." She scooped low and slung one of his bags over her shoulder. Then she staggered to one side. "Son of a . . ." Planting her feet, she pulled a face at him. "Did you pack the whole of Montana?"

No. Just everything he could fit.

"You didn't tell me everyone dresses like a rainbow here." Still smiling, he gathered the rest of his stuff. His bags looked drab against the bright surroundings. "I can't believe this is where you grew up."

"Yeah, well." She sniffed, and her gaze swung to the street

vendor. Her wallet was out before he'd seen her hand move. "Want one?"

He squinted at her in the sunlight. "One?"

With a grin, she bought six pastries to share. "This way. Your new place awaits."

The walk was steep and sweltering, but it was so good to talk to Frankie in person again, and there was so much to see that he hardly noticed his muscles burning. Local traders had stalls of silk scarves and jarred preserves on the sidewalk, pubs dotted every other corner, and the brochure hadn't lied—there were steps *everywhere*, connecting roads and restaurants and disappearing around corners like secrets. Apparently, he'd get a proper tour tomorrow by a guard named Gul, but as they walked, Frankie told him more about Kiraly, pointing out the best cafés and gardens and chocolate shops, and the ornate blue signposts that signaled public drinking fountains. *And*, when they passed two young women sharing ice cream with obvious intimacy, she added that Kiraly was so progressive they taught queer history in schools, so he was free to be as gay as he damn well wanted.

By the time she let him into a building rendered the color of tangerines with a flowering vine spilling over the entranceway, Jonah was in a state of sweaty enchantment.

"I am in love with this city," he declared, dumping his bags on the floor and bending over with his hands on his knees to catch his breath.

"Pick those up," she said, and set off up a flight of stairs. "You're on the top floor."

"Oh my God, *why*?" But he hefted his belongings again and followed. "Frankie, you didn't have to set me up like this." His voice echoed in the stairwell as she powered on ahead of him. Despite the hike from the train station and the bag she carried, she was taking the steps three at a time. "I found a hostel for backpackers online. I could have stayed there."

She emerged onto the third and top floor and shot a hard look back at him. "You are *not* staying in that place."

"I am not staying in that place," he echoed fifteen seconds later as he stepped into the

studio apartment she'd arranged for him.

Oh—this was . . . was there a word for something that managed to be both the cutest and most adult space he'd ever set foot in? Beautifully furnished and high-ceilinged, with sun-filled windows, indoor plants, and lumpy turquoise kitchen tiles that popped brightly against the hanging copper pots. There was a tall, long bookshelf with a ladder running up the front, one of those circle chairs with a yellow cushion that made it look like a scooped-out mango, and the couches were so bloated with stuffing he suspected a weary flop would result in bouncing right off.

Disbelief kept his bags on his shoulders. "I can't afford—"

"Don't start." She set his pack against the base of the kitchen island with a grunt. "I asked you to come, so consider this my thank you. Besides, I'm head of palace security, and you're a personal friend of the royal family. So by extension, it's my job to ensure your safety. This place is safe. If you stay here, I can sleep at night. Got it?"

His attention slid to the orange feature wall beside the large bed in the far corner, and his delight burbled up into a grin. "Got it."

"Right. Take this." After giving him the key and code to the building, she eyed him over. "You ready to go?"

"Almost." He knelt beside his bags, unzipping the largest. "I want to change first."

The corner of her mouth kicked up. "Kris might be a prince, but he still doesn't care how you dress."

"It's not for Kris." He rummaged beneath the top layers. "It's to play it safe. I don't—want Tommy to recognize me." He'd tried to say it casually, but Tommy's name still burned in his throat.

"Oh." Her expression shadowed. "You really don't want him to know you're here?"

Jonah stilled in alarm, staring up at her. "You promised you wouldn't tell him."

"I haven't," she said firmly. "I won't."

"Will Kris?"

"I told him to keep his mouth shut." When Jonah pulled a disbelieving face, she said, "I know, but he can keep important secrets."

Yeah. Like being royalty.

Jonah dug deeper as Frankie asked, "You want to work while you're here, right?" At his nod, she continued. "Cowboy has become a fashion trend, so no one will think twice about the way you dress behind the bar. Paired with the accent, though, they might get curious. Start to ask questions."

"Americans don't all know each other," he said, cocking his head and grinning as if he were sliding beers to Kira City locals. "If I had a free pass at the palace, would I be serving you drinks?"

She smiled a little. "You've rehearsed."

"He reads everything in sight. I can't end up in a paper."

Her brows twitched as she watched him hunt. "Do you even own non-cowboy clothes?"

"Please." His grin widened as his fingers brushed against his newest outfit. "I've been in Paris."

With nothing keeping him in Sage Haven, he'd finally packed his bags. His plan had been simple: travel, find somewhere he could be himself, and settle there to open his own bar. The idea of living in a place he belonged sent a tingle down his spine. He'd arrived in France last week, intending to start his travels there—until Frankie had called him yesterday and all but begged him to take the train across to Kiraly.

Not somewhere he'd intended to visit.

Tommy had made it painfully clear he didn't want to see Jonah again. Aside from the sorrow-hollowed ache in Jonah's chest, visiting a country that Tommy kind of—owned? Or something? Didn't feel right. Like turning up uninvited to a house party and getting away with it by avoiding the host the whole night. Just because Tommy wouldn't know he was here, didn't make it okay.

Except Kiraly had three hosts.

And Kris had asked him to come.

Kris, who'd been badly beaten and needed support from someone who understood how it felt.

"Please, Jones," Frankie had said on the phone, her usual boldness replaced by a low plea. "I know it's not part of your plan. But Kris keeps having nightmares. He's stressed and unsettled, and we need him to get through this, but Tommy could hardly look at him earlier. There's no way they can talk about it together. Kris asked if you'll come instead. Talk with him. Help him process everything."

Of course, Jonah had said yes.

He didn't like it. He didn't want to be anywhere *near* Tommy. He wasn't interested in being hurt again—not by a friend who'd abandoned him without a backward glance, who'd literally refused to stay in touch. *It would be best if I don't hear from you.* The thought of bumping into Tommy made his insides go all hot and cold.

But Kris needed his help.

So that was that.

In the bathroom, Jonah swapped his green-and-white-checked shirt for a loose burgundy scoop neck, and his blue jeans for the new slim-fit black jeans he'd bought before he'd left Paris —they were stretchy and soft, and when he'd faced the shop attendant for a second opinion, the male youth had just stared at

Jonah's ass in the fitting room mirror and nodded. Jonah raked water through his hat-flattened hair, bringing the bounce back, and finally pulled on his old boots.

"Ready," he said, finding Frankie sitting on the kitchen counter typing on her phone.

She glanced up, froze, then smirked. "I thought you weren't dressing up for him."

"They told me this was rich casual," he said with a frown.

"Fair call." She jumped to the floor, jamming the phone in her back pocket. "You'll fit in as a palace guest."

"Okay," he said, running his hands over his thighs. Wow, these were *tight*. "Good."

She led him downstairs and into a waiting car that drove them up the zigzagging streets of Kiraly. Within minutes, he turned away from the window, not because he didn't like what he saw, but because he liked it too much. This city was bursting with life and acceptance, and it made him want to fling himself open and let it all in.

For most of his life, he'd stood at a strange crossroads of identity—gay and cowboy—and very few people back home had told him that was okay. An outraged few had even told him those two roads never met, not in Sage Haven, and that he should know the lay of the land better than to think otherwise.

But they did meet. In *him*. He'd struggled long and hard to figure that out and fought for his sense of self every day since.

That was all he'd ever wanted. To be himself.

And after being in this city for less than an hour, he knew he could be himself here, could flirt without fear here, could kiss a man on the street here, and that was still flooding him with a shock that fizzed wildly in his chest. It was the place he'd left Sage Haven never expecting to find. Now he had—he just wasn't allowed to stay.

Not without Tommy's invitation, not in his heart.

Jonah had no idea how he was supposed to feel about this.

Frankie's quick pace hurried him beneath intricately painted ceilings that were as high as soaring birds. She led him up gleaming staircases and down art-lined corridors and past dozens of people in uniforms moving with purpose. Processing it was like trying to fit the moon into a teacup. He could think the words *this palace belongs to Tommy and Kris and Mark* in the same way he could close one eye and line up a cup with the moon in the night sky. But the reality was never going to actually fit inside him.

Too big—too impossible to believe.

It *tried* to fit, stretching him with the truths they'd kept from him—their wealth and status and history—but it hurt *so badly* and was hardly a whisper of the whole, so he focused on the one reality he could comprehend.

Tommy might appear at any moment.

Jonah pictured him in every room they passed, in every possible second between here and Kris's suite. He imagined glancing into a parlor and finding Tommy sitting beside the window. Tommy glancing up with a frown, catching his gaze in a flash of bright blue intelligence before a member of serving staff firmly closed the door. He imagined Tommy striding around the corner ahead and stopping short at the sight of the friend he'd specifically requested to never see again. Jonah would be too mortified to speak. He knew that already. Tommy might say, *"Jonah?"* and for the life of him, Jonah couldn't decide the tone of his voice.

Jonah's stomach was eating its way past his collarbones by the time Frankie muttered, "Why are you freaking out?"

"He's here." Jonah glanced over his shoulder with the

uncomfortable suspicion he was looking *for* Tommy rather than checking he wasn't nearby.

"Yes, but he doesn't wander around aimlessly. I know exactly where he is." She tapped her earpiece. "Our paths won't cross."

Scanning the corridor in front of them, Jonah bit down on the urge to ask where exactly Tommy was. Then a tremor ran through him and the urge bit back. "Where?"

She arched a surprised brow. "I could show you."

"Will he know?" It came out embarrassingly close to a plea.

"No."

"Yes," he said.

Taking his elbow, she retraced their steps a little before veering up a narrow flight of stairs. Two floors later, they were standing in front of a huge window, looking out at a lush garden that sprawled over more land than the entirety of his and the boys' properties combined back home. His head spun at the sight of the flowerbeds and shrubs and wide stretches of lawn, the hedges and water features and pretty winding paths. There was a glasshouse, and a huge plot of fresh produce lined with fruit trees, and the biggest stable he'd ever seen.

"There," Frankie said and pointed.

He shifted, feeling restless and overly warm like he did right before doing something he didn't want to do. Except it wasn't quite like that at all.

He peered down into a crescent-shaped garden in the shadow of the palace.

And there was Tommy.

Jonah had expected him to look different. Princely. Wearing slacks or a pocket hanky at the very least, but it was just Tommy sitting on a bench, facing the palace, reading. Old shirt, jeans. He was lost in the pages, because he was leaning forward, elbows on his thighs with the document held in front of him, and that position meant he wouldn't hear a word anyone said to him until he'd finished.

Jonah knew that because they'd been best friends.

He grasped the window frame as that truth wrenched in his chest. They'd been friends for almost their entire lives. Jonah had trusted him and treasured him more than anyone and anything—and Tommy had lied to him and left him behind.

The scale of that betrayal was too much—stretching him, hurting him—and now, seeing Tommy just sitting there . . . he shattered like china turning to dust beneath the full weight of the moon.

They'd been *best friends.*

They'd played together, grown together. Laughed and feared and healed together.

And Tommy had walked away.

For a reason. Everything Tommy did had a reason. He'd always been so very smart. Miles smarter that Jonah, to the point that Jonah had often worried Tommy didn't get enough out of their friendship. That his sharp mind and silent pull of authority didn't belong with Jonah or in a small town like Sage Haven at all.

Well. Maybe Jonah did know a thing or two, because Tommy had got nothing from their friendship—and he'd always belonged right here.

You lied to me. Throat thick, Jonah wanted to pound on the window. *Left me. I hate you.*

On his magnificent grounds, backed by uniformed guards, his old friend just turned the page.

Jonah pressed his forehead against the glass as his anger drained into despair. "Tommy," he breathed.

"Maybe that's enough." Frankie's fingers brushed his elbow.

With a jolt, he stepped back.

That *was* enough. He didn't need to feel this way. He'd stay in Kiraly to support Kris through his recovery but not a day longer.

This place belonged to Tommy.

It was time Jonah found a place for himself.

That night, as Jonah lay in bed, he tried to be happy about seeing Frankie and Kris again. Kris, the goose, had almost pulled out his stitches by leaping to his feet to hug him, and Jonah had hidden his grin when Frankie scolded him and eased him back into bed. It was just that Kris must have really missed him—no one could pretend to care like that.

Unless . . .

Jonah sat up as the sheets turned cold beneath him.

Unless *Tommy* could pretend to care and had been pretending their whole friendship? Or, worse, he hadn't been pretending, but Jonah had completely missed the signs. Had Tommy tried to avoid him, or given him strange looks, or tried to make a point with distant moods? Had he told Jonah to stop coming around so often but been too subtle, and like an idiot, Jonah had just kept showing up? The thought made Jonah feel faint, but . . . had Tommy been aching for an opportunity to finally get away from him?

If he had, Jonah had been blind to it.

He'd trusted Tommy more than anyone else.

He'd known, even at fourteen, that if he couldn't tell Tommy his secret, he'd never be able to tell anyone. He still remembered walking home from school along the dirt road that led to their properties out of town, remembered how impossible it had felt to start.

"They're saying he left a note," he'd said, balling his hands inside the sleeves of his baggy woolen sweater, more scared than he'd ever been in his life.

The other kids at school had been talking about the old plumber's death all week. It had both excited and disgusted them —put a gleam in their eyes that had made Jonah sick to his core.

"That he told his wife he was sorry. That he was—" Jonah's voice had fractured a little before he'd forced himself to finish "—gay."

Tommy had nodded beside him, kicking a stick off the road.

Come on, Tommy. Jonah's skin had clammed up. *Give me more than that.*

The internet said you could never predict how a friend or family member would react. He and Tommy had never talked about girls, let alone boys who like boys. Just because they'd been friends most of their lives, didn't mean Tommy wouldn't turn on him—call him nasty names and tell the whole town.

But he just might've been the shoulder Jonah desperately needed to lean on.

"And," Jonah had pushed on, despite wanting to run. "I can't stop thinking about how awful that would be. To live so long denying who I am. Being so ashamed that I never tell anyone the truth. Hating myself so much that it kills me."

Tommy had halted abruptly.

A surge of fear had made Jonah pretend not to notice. *A few more steps and I can run.* Tommy was bigger than him, taller and broader, but Jonah was usually faster. *If I have a head start, he might not catch me.*

"Then don't," Tommy had said quietly.

Eyes hot, Jonah had stopped walking. *Oh, God, he knows, oh, God.*

"It's okay," Tommy had said.

Jonah had started trembling. An identity-deep quake that had made his teeth chatter. "It's not okay." There was a reason the plumber had kept it a secret. Jonah had forced himself to turn around. "Not here."

"Right here," Tommy had said, features serious as he closed the distance between them. "It's okay."

Loosened by his trembling, Jonah's schoolbag had slipped off his shoulder and he'd jerked in fright. "I'm so scared, Tommy. I don't want to be like this."

Pain filled his friend's voice as he'd repeated, "It's okay."

"Don't tell anyone." The thought of other people knowing had made Jonah feel too close to prey—heart jackrabbiting, desperate to hide. He'd camouflage himself as straight for as long as he could bear it. "Not even the guys."

"I won't." Tommy had raised a hand, palm up. "I promise."

And then he'd lowered his arm and waited.

A breeze chilled Jonah's wet cheeks as he'd tried to find the words. *How does anyone do this?* "I can't," he'd said helplessly. "Can you?"

Tommy's brows had flicked up. "You want me to come out to me for you?"

At the phrase *come out,* Jonah had made a noise that was half sob, half hysterical laugh. *Oh God, oh God, oh God.*

"Jonah." Tommy had only hesitated long enough to glance over his shoulder, ensuring they were alone. Then he'd thrown Jonah the lifeline of his steady blue gaze. "I'd like you to know that I know you're gay."

His breath had hitched. "I'm gay."

He'd never spoken the words out loud. Too scared of how wrong they'd sound. How punishable.

But Tommy hadn't punished him.

"I'm gay," he'd repeated with a shaky surge of new power. "I am."

Tommy had nodded, watching him carefully.

"Okay," he'd said, and, unsure how it changed the boundaries of their friendship, had taken a step back.

Frowning, Tommy had reached for his hand—only to grab a handful of Jonah's empty sweater. "Jesus, man," he'd muttered, pushing up the sleeve until his rough fingertips swiped Jonah's fist. "Where's your hand?"

"Why?"

Tommy's glance had been calm and level, a silent command to trust him, and instinctively, Jonah had relaxed at the elbow, uncurling his fingers.

"Jonah." Tommy had gripped him around the wrist like a tether. "Nothing about you could change the fact that you're my friend. I know I don't talk much, but we can talk about this whenever you need. Don't pull away. This"—and he'd tightened his hold—"doesn't bother me."

Jonah's vision had blurred. *How did Tommy know?* Jonah had honest to God believed that no one would touch him again once they knew. That he wasn't made of skin anymore, he was made of gay, and no one would want to touch that, not around here.

He'd run the back of his other hand over his cheek. "Why not?"

With a roll of his eyes, Tommy had let him go and gently cuffed him over the head. "It just doesn't."

"You're not worried that I—" Jonah had stopped, mortified.

Tommy had grown still. "Do you?"

"No." Jonah wouldn't have had the courage to come out to Tommy if he'd been into him. "Everyone knows not to fall for your straight best friend."

Eyes crinkling at the corners, Tommy had picked up Jonah's bag and handed it to him. "Thank you for . . . sort of telling me."

"I don't want a life like that," he'd admitted, and they'd

slowly resumed walking. "I don't want to be ashamed of who I am."

"You have the right to be here, Jonah, and you have no reason to be ashamed."

When Jonah hadn't answered, Tommy pivoted, cutting swiftly in front of him to block his path. Jonah had bumped his forehead against Tommy's chin as Tommy said with quiet determination, "Repeat it back to me."

Sniffling, Jonah hadn't met his stare. "You have no reason to be ashamed."

"Cute." Tommy hadn't moved.

Lips quirking just a little, Jonah had snuck a glance up—and the utter conviction on Tommy's face had drawn out his full smile. "I have no reason to be ashamed."

But it turned out he did.

Not because of his sexuality, but because he'd fallen short of his best friend's worth. Tommy knew him almost as well as he knew himself; he'd learned every flaw and tendency and delight in Jonah's life—and decided he wasn't good enough to keep around.

Their friendship had been perfect cover for a prince laying low in a backwater town.

Now Tommy had stepped up to his rightful place.

And ensured Jonah stayed in his.

3

Tommy would fight for this.

He sat cross-legged on the balcony of the monarch's study, located in the tallest tower of the palace, with a view that pitched his stomach downhill. The dawn breeze was warm in his hair, and below him, the first light of sunrise tipped the peaks of Kira City in gold. To be worthy of this position so high above his people, he would have to be able to join them in those streets. Stand before them, look them in the eye, and listen.

His fingers splayed over his knees, digging in hard.

"Damn it," he muttered, lifting his hands in frustration. Why couldn't he even *think* without anxiety hijacking him? It undermined him at every turn.

He had to fight back.

In the three days since his disastrous speech, he'd come across a new coping strategy. A battering ram of a solution. Just the idea of putting it into practice left him weak, like being occupied by a hundred versions of himself and ninety-nine of them had taken a step back in refusal. Deserted, the wisp of resolve that remained raised its fists to fight.

His anxiety wouldn't win. Not anymore.

He was done with it. *Done.*

If the people of Kiraly wanted a king, he would be that king.

The faint snick of a door closing snagged his focus. Frankie. On a long breath out, he rose to his feet and returned inside, finding her at his desk sorting through a stack of folders.

Apology flickered in her eyes when she saw him. "Were you still meditating?"

"No."

"Good. Security briefings," she said and slapped them beside his laptop. "Your daily news." As curated by PR to keep the royal family's finger on the pulse of current affairs. "And Adam's files."

Adam. His fury leapt like a struck match. Adam had been Mark's manservant—until last week, when Frankie had uncovered his role in the deaths of the late royal family and he'd disappeared without a trace. In the nick of time, too, since he had also been responsible for rallying Kris's attackers, securing his place at the top of Frankie's shit list.

"Any progress?" Tommy sat and drew the folders closer.

"Yes and no." Frustrated, she picked up his stress ball from the desk and hurled it against the nearest wall. It rebounded against his shoulder blade before presumably vanishing into thin air, since she made no move to pick it up. "There's no sign of him, and the anarchists are knuckleheads. They don't even seem to know what anarchism is. The only helpful thing they've told us is that Adam's younger brother used to be in charge."

He opened the top folder. "Anarchists don't have leaders. It's kind of the point."

"Please refer back to the part where they don't know what anarchism is."

Frowning, he scanned their profiles. These men had been all too willing to spring into violence against the crown without understanding the basic principles of their cause? Then they weren't anarchists. More likely, they'd felt undervalued by society and their anger had been exploited.

"Where's Adam's brother now?" he asked.

"Died six months ago. He worked in the mines. There was an accident. Apparently, Adam took over after that, seeing out his brother's plans for the balcony collapse."

Adam had been thrust into a position of power in his brother's place? The parallel put a chill down Tommy's spine as he turned the page. "Do we know much about his brother?"

"Name was Rudy." Frankie jerked her head at the folders.

He flicked to the one marked Rudolph Boller. As he read the incident report and related news articles—*died as a result of injuries sustained underground* and *killed with three others in a flow of muck*—unease hovered over him like a word he couldn't quite remember. His regret was less evasive. Rudy had been a Kiralian citizen laboring underground in mines owned by the crown while King Vinci had kept clean and untouchable in his palace in the sky. It wasn't hard to identify the cause of Rudy's resentment.

A second parallel poked Tommy hard in the chest. *He* was untouchable. He'd disapproved of his late uncle's indifference as a ruler, but from the outside, Tommy was no better. A reclusive prince was one thing, but to ascend as king, he'd have to get used to showing his face.

The resolve inside him wavered; strengthened. He slid the folders aside. "That mining accident should never have happened."

"No." Frankie motioned toward the reports. "How involved do you want to be in this?"

"Not very." He already had plenty to keep him up at night, and the thought of being a target could ensure he never slept again. He needed very badly *not* to be involved. "Deliver key updates as they occur, but you do your job and I'll do mine."

She nodded then leaned a hip against the desk and gave him a half-smile. "I was told you want to go into the city tonight. Who misheard what?"

His mouth went dry. "No one misheard."

Confusion lowered her brows. "You want to give the pool lounge another shot? We can clear it out this time."

Desperately. But he shook his head. "There needs to be people."

She eyed him, seeming torn between calling his bluff and asking if he was sure.

"I'm serious," he said coolly. "I don't need you giving me the option not to be."

"Right." Her expression reset to neutral. "Anywhere in particular?"

Heat crawled along his skin, and he bunched up his shirt sleeves. "Familiarity might help, and I've only been to two places. Since I'm not inclined to go back to the cocktail lounge, that leaves the Bearded Bunting."

"The—" Frankie's eyes bulged.

"That's where Mark had his bachelor party," he said, even as his heart protested fiercely against his rib cage. "And Kris goes there often, so they're used to having a prince in the bar without making a big deal about it. That's right, isn't it? They downplay when he's around. And they're locals, not tourists."

"Uh-huh," she said, voice slightly too high. "Mostly."

"Frankie." He swore under his breath. "Stop thinking I can't handle this. I'm already fighting that battle with myself."

"No, that's not—" She pushed her hip off the desk, tugging at the top button of her royal guard uniform. "Okay. It's a busy venue. Loud and packed. I could line up a private booth?"

"Thank you." Discomfort pushed his attention out a mountain-facing window. The alpine forest rose like a dark green palm tipping Kira City sideways for a better look in the light. "Will you come with me?"

He sensed her pause her button-tugging. "Your guards are good, Tommy."

"Not as a guard," he said, and looked at her pointedly.

She frowned at him.

God. This shouldn't be so uncharted that he needed to say it outright. "As a friend."

Surprise angled her head to one side. "As a what now?"

Not actually sure whether she was teasing, he kept his return gaze level.

"Oh man, you kill me sometimes," she said, and dropped into the chair opposite him with one leg hooked over the arm. "I'd be happy to go, but why don't you take Mark?"

"His worry is too obvious," he said around a guilt flare. "It feeds my panic. I need someone who doesn't appear to give a damn about me."

She blinked, then gave a short laugh. "I'm such a bad person. Okay. I'll go."

"One other thing." Nervous tension had him shifting in the chair. "I'll be going as Kris."

Her eyes narrowed. "Unpack that for me."

With a tightness in his chest, he explained the plan.

It was shaky, but he was desperate. He'd seen his psychologist the day after the press conference, numbly acknowledging a king couldn't break down from panic attacks in public.

Instead of tactfully suggesting he wasn't suited to kingship, the older woman had said, "Who do you know who would cope with this?"

He'd almost snorted and said *literally anyone else,* but self-deprecation had never helped him. Who had the skills and confidence to face any social situation, revel in it, and emerge without breaking a sweat?

Kris.

"Would you consider borrowing the parts of Kris that would cope?" she had asked. "Try them on for yourself in public. You have a rare advantage in that you already look similar enough to be mistaken for him. No one needs to know that it's you. You would lean into his confidence and allow it to transform you into someone who can manage."

As far as ideas went, it was farfetched and foolish—and Frankie's incredulous expression seemed to agree.

"Philip has yet to put out a story to explain Kris's absence from the city," Tommy said to her. "It's been two weeks since his last visit. The locals will be wondering where he is. This could stop speculation."

"It could," she said slowly, frowning.

"I want to try this, Frankie. Without Mark and Kris knowing. I don't want to get their hopes up and then disappoint them if I can't hold it together."

Her brow smoothed a little. "Is there any point in saying you could never disappoint them?"

Considering he'd been reduced to pretending to be his brother in order to be in the same room as other people? "No."

"God, Tommy." She sighed. "I plan to teach you boys self-defense once Kris heals. You wouldn't be more comfortable waiting to go out in public until then?"

He almost laughed. His instincts would always, *always,* choose freeze or flight in response to a threat. Her lessons would make no difference. He shook his head.

"Okay then." She stood. "We'll go to the Bearded Bunting tonight. Together. With you pretending to be Kris and me not giving a damn." Her tone did such a good job of it, she didn't even need to add, *what could possibly go wrong?*

"Thank you."

"Maybe don't say that just yet." Moments later, she'd closed the door behind her.

His fear pounced instantly. *I could say I have to work late. That I've come down with something. That I can't pretend to be someone I'm not.* A stream of shiny, convincing ways to back out —and he ground his teeth against them.

Don't you dare. Avoidance was his favored strategy, and he'd become far too good at it.

He would fight this.

It was long past time.

It proved suspiciously easy to borrow Kris's hat.

Tommy needed it. They both wore black, but his was a darker, bolder shade and Kris's was faded and ageing into gray. Wearing the wrong hat in public could give the game away before it had even started.

It was midafternoon when he knocked on his brother's door in an unannounced detour following a meeting. At Kris's weary call, "Did you forget something?" Tommy stepped inside.

Kris was propped up in an armchair by the window, head resting back and eyes closed. The room was warm, but comfortably so, with the drapes half-closed to keep out the worst of the summer heat.

"No," he answered, and his brother started in surprise.

"Tommy." Kris sat up sharply, his eyes wide. Then he winced, cursed, and said, "Hi. Hello."

"Hey." Tommy frowned at him. His bruises were healing. Good. "Who were you expecting?"

Kris made the face he pulled when he was trying not to pull a face. "No one."

Still frowning, Tommy noted his brother's cowboy hat sitting upside-down on the narrow table between two windows. "I have a favor to ask."

"Anything."

Tommy doubted that. "I want to borrow your hat."

Kris was nodding before Tommy had finished the question. "Sure, Tommy. Whatever you want. Yeah."

Tommy narrowed his eyes.

"You take it," Kris said, still nodding as he looked to his hat. His nod slowed, and he looked pained. "Hey, baby," he murmured to it, and then added to Tommy, "What am I going to do with it? I can't go anywhere."

Huh. Tommy scanned the bedroom. Sheets thrown aside from where his brother had eased out of bed. A few discarded shirts by the walk-in robe—evidence he'd put thought into his outfit. And a demolished afternoon tea platter on the table by his chair, with two empty water glasses. "What's going on?"

"What?" Kris's brows flew up. "Nothing!"

Tommy moved to the table and picked up the hat before flipping it onto his head. "You're not even going to ask why I want it?"

"Yes. Obviously. Why do you want it?"

He smiled. "I'm going to burn it."

Kris winced. "No, you're not."

"Throw if off the tower to see how far it flies."

"It always finds its way back to me."

Tommy angled his head. "Auction it off."

"I'm sure it's for a good cause. I trust you."

"Kris," he said.

"Don't use that voice on me," his brother said a little sulkily. "I was half-asleep. I'm delirious. The painkillers mess with my head. Also, I'm recovering from a concussion."

Tommy just shook his head. Kris was a woeful liar—but if he

didn't explain why he was acting strange, then he likely wouldn't press for an explanation about why Tommy wanted the hat. "Okay." He tipped the brim. "Thanks."

"Yeah." Kris lifted a hand as he sunk back into the chair, his gaze lifting mournfully to the hat. "Have fun, sweetheart."

Tommy huffed out a wry breath as he left.

There'd be nothing fun about it.

The Bearded Bunting was so unlike the bar Jonah had tended in Sage Haven that he was worried he'd lied when he'd told the manager he had appropriate experience. At least three times as big and ten times as loud, it attracted locals who didn't need to be a few drinks in to laugh and shout and sling their arms around the shoulders of strangers. During his first shift, he'd lost count how many people told him he must be new and leaned over the bar to shake his hand. They asked his name over the music, and he tried to catch theirs, and if they teased him about sharing an accent with their princes, he laughed it off and moved onto the next in line. Once the music kicked in and the dancing really started, the energy spread as swiftly as the bass surely did across the mountainside, and Jonah alternated between joyous overwhelm and delirious exhaustion.

He'd staggered home that first night, stone-cold sober and spirit brimming.

These people were *everything*.

And they were everything—every. Single. Night.

Frankie had warned him when she'd helped to line up the job. "It's not a bar for the fainthearted. Quiet nights don't exist."

Who needed quiet?

Jonah pressed a palm to the bar counter during his second shift—what would be a sleepy Sunday back home—and

scanned the room with a grin. How did they do it? Most of
them surely had to have work in the morning, but the room was
packed to the rafters and churning like a kettle stuck on the
boil. Even the booths lining the back wall and spill-over in the
rear courtyard were full. Yet despite the press of bodies, the
mood somehow felt open. Borderless. Like instead of a crowd of
turned backs and inward-facing groups, everyone faced
everyone else.

Dazed and trying to keep up, he poured drink after drink at
the main bar with *three* other bartenders, one of whom
specialized exclusively in cocktails, and when he finally found
himself hitting a rhythm around midnight, he'd never felt so
proud.

It wasn't until Nora—a bartender in her early twenties with
short, bottle-silver hair and a nose ring—sidled up to him for a
chat that he realized they'd momentarily put a drink in every
single hand on the premises.

"I can't go on," he said, collapsing onto his forearms against
the counter.

"You'll get used to it." The reassuring pat she gave his arm
quickly turned into excited smacking. "Ooh, this is your first
time!"

Jonah peered up at her with a frown. "My first shift was
yesterday. You were here."

"No." Rolling her eyes, she jerked her head toward the back
of the room. "I mean serving Prince Kristof. He's just arrived."

He—*what?* Jonah straightened in confusion. Just earlier that
afternoon, Jonah had left him dozing in an armchair by his
sitting-room window. Kris was in no way ready for a night out.

Pushing his hair off his face, Jonah tried to spot him in the
crowd. "Is he okay?"

"How do you mean?" Nora sounded puzzled.

"Uh." Oops. He wasn't supposed to know the royal family—

and very few people knew Kris had been injured at all. Backtracking, he sent her a pointed smile. "You know."

"*Oh.*" She grinned. "Yeah. He's more than okay."

"We talking about the prince?" Milosh breezed past them, a tall, lean, tattooed bartender, pausing just long enough to add, "He's on everyone's to-do list, babe."

Jonah's smile widened. Kris would puff and preen if he heard that. "Yeah?"

"Trust me." Nora's eyes shone. "He's almost as hot as you."

Jonah flushed, and barely stopped himself saying that the boys were way hotter. "Um, thanks."

She laughed. "You can have him tonight. It's only fair. We've all served him before. He's in the back-corner booth. Bit weird, really. He usually sits here at the bar."

"That is weird," he said distractedly, scanning the rear of the room until he spotted the booth on the far end—and met eyes with Frankie.

She was sitting at the front, facing him stiffly, blocking Kris from view. Jonah sent her a frown that asked, *what are you doing here?* She held up her phone, wiggled it, then raised her brows at him.

What? Oh. Jonah tugged out his phone. Whoops. She'd messaged him an hour ago. He'd been too caught up in the chaos of bartending to notice.

He swiped to view.

Jones, I'm sorry. I seriously thought he'd bail. But he hasn't, and now I feel like shit because I should have given you enough warning to cancel your shift. Tommy and I are coming to the bar tonight. Soon. I haven't told him about you. Neither has Kris. If you keep your head down, he won't even

**notice you. I wholeheartedly endorse you killing me
later.**

Wait.

Pressure built rapidly in Jonah's chest, and he wanted to
cover and crack it like a knuckle—wanted to pop it open so his
bloodstream could whisk it away.

But—He read the message again, slowly, as dismay set hard
inside him.

"Everything okay?" Nora asked.

Wounded, he looked up.

Frankie was still watching him, but she'd leaned back in the
booth to reveal the man behind her, sitting as far from the crowd
as possible with his face angled down and his cowboy hat
lowered like a shield.

"Fine," he said as his fingers curled and his hurt turned to
anger.

Tommy was here.

Tommy told himself he was being Kris in a reserved mood. That
was still okay. It got him out of the palace and into the bar without
incident. He'd imagined Kris sliding out of the car and through
the front door like the dance party inside had no correlation with
the end of the world. Security had arranged a private booth at the
back of the barroom, half a dozen steps up from the main floor
and tucked away in the corner closest to the exit. It was dimly lit,
cordoned off by a silk rope, and Frankie had even gone so far as to
bring Kris's guards so they could be seen lingering nearby.
Everyone expected to see Hanna and Peter out with Kris, she'd
told him, so their presence would support the charade.

Seated, Tommy tried to find the soft edges of his breathing as everything else attacked his senses. Hard flashes of a too-hot venue—sharp stabs of voices fighting to be heard. The atmosphere felt geometric, angles and edges and points pressing hard and unforgiving against his skin.

He jolted when Frankie shifted beside him. Etiquette should see her sitting opposite him, but she'd evidently decided that acting as a buffer between him and the crowd was more important than social rules. She leaned in close as she slid her phone into her shorts and murmured, "Remember to be Kris."

The heavy beat of the music vibrated against his palms where he gripped the booth cushion either side of his legs. "Who's Kris?"

She shot him a grim glance as she swiped up a cardboard coaster and started spinning it on her fingertip.

Fastening his attention on the movement, he asked, "What would he do?"

"Drape his arm along the back of the booth." The coaster kept spinning as she glanced toward the bar. "Slouch like he thinks it's sexy. Survey the room. Make eye contact and smile at people—but let's stick with the first few."

"Yeah."

Blowing out a breath, she caught the coaster mid-spin and slapped it down in front of him. "I'm going to get drinks. Kris would use the time to spread out and relax. Beer?"

He nodded and, before he could lose control of the plan, slid his arm along the back of the booth in her wake. *This can't be right.* The position instantly exposed him, perched awkwardly with his spine flush against the leather backing, so he tried to picture his brother's roguish sprawl and attempted to embody the kind of confidence that pushed his limbs far from the protection of his body.

It . . . didn't *not* work. He held the lounging pose for the length of a song, peripherally processing the motion of the dancing crowd with something akin to seasickness. He visualized Kris and tried to copy his mannerisms. The easy tap of his fingers to the beat against the leather. The slow bite and scrape of his bottom lip with his teeth. The occasional cracking of his neck, angling his head to one side, then the other, as if a madhouse bar was the perfect place to start winding down his muscles for the night.

By the third song, Tommy's heart rate was up, and the coaster moved quickly between his fingers, but nothing inside him was escalating. Surveying the room still seemed high risk. Doing okay now was one thing, but what if someone was looking at him? Hemmed in by this many people, all he needed was the wrong kind of eye contact to push him over the edge.

Except—they wouldn't be looking at *him*. They'd be looking at Kris, and his brother could handle that without a problem. Wouldn't think twice about it—would just do it. Just —do it.

So just fucking do it.

Wiping the sweat from his forehead and using the movement to nudge his hat up a little, he flung his gaze out of his dark corner—right as Frankie appeared at the head of the booth and slid back in beside him.

"They'll send someone to take our order," she said, sounding irritated.

Relieved at the interruption, Tommy returned his attention to the coaster. "You'll have to get used to being treated like royalty sooner or later."

"It's not going to be sooner," she said, and then stilled. "Damn it. Zara's here."

Zara. A friend to both Ava and Frankie—and recent girlfriend to Adam. Unwilling to scan for her in this seething crowd, Tommy asked, "How does she seem?"

"Drunk. Messy. Not coping." Frankie cursed as she pressed a

hand over her eyes. "She's refused to speak to me since I broke the news to her last week."

"You told her that her boyfriend murdered the late royal family." Pity joined Tommy's nerves. "I'd probably drink my way through it, too."

Frankie lowered her hand. "I just wish she'd let me—" She cut off, turning sharply toward the head of the booth. "What the hell are you doing? I told you to get someone else to do it."

And a low, clear voice said, "No."

Tommy froze.

That voice. It was the enticing sound that sang to sailors—Tommy would steer his ship against the rocks if it called to him. Yet it was a voice that couldn't be here. *Wasn't* here. Just someone who sounded unbearably like—

Tommy looked up. The world flipped like an hourglass.

Jonah.

Standing at the end of the booth, staring straight at him. In blue jeans, a checked shirt with the sleeves rolled up, and a dishrag over his shoulder. One hand rested on his belt and the other moved to splay on the tabletop with the calm composure of a small-town barman in the chaos of Kira City. Casual, approachable, and every inch a breathtaking cowboy.

What—how was—

Tommy's mind stumbled and fell. Knees grazing, palms tearing, but attention unbreakable on the man in front of him. Jonah. He was *right here.* But—why now? After all this—

Oh.

Tommy couldn't hear over the thundering in his ears. Had Jonah realized what Tommy had been trying to tell him that painful morning? Had he pieced it together with the way Tommy must have always acted around him, looked at him, like he couldn't see straight for the hearts in his eyes?

Shock bolted down his spine. Did this mean—could it really mean—

Hope dazed him as he asked, "Why are you here?"

And Jonah answered pleasantly, "To take your order, Your Highness," and leaned forward in a bow.

To take . . . Tommy's heart lunged, *hating that bow,* but before he could tell Jonah never to do it again, Jonah had turned to Frankie, adjusting his glasses and giving her a small smile. "And yours, ma'am."

Cold understanding rammed down Tommy's throat.

Jonah wasn't here for him.

The music got louder. Sharper. Spikier. It filed his pulse down until both beats seemed to pierce him. Obviously, Jonah wasn't here for him. *There's nowhere to go from here,* he'd told Frankie last week.

And just last week, Frankie had warned Tommy there were things Jonah might not want him to overhear—such as, it seemed, a working visit to Kiraly.

"You knew about this," he murmured to her under the shadow of his hat.

"I'll need a vodka," Frankie said loudly.

"Sure." Jonah smiled at her, laugh lines around his mouth cutting perfect grooves in the light of the bar. That smile was quicksand. Only look at it sideways, Tommy had learned, or he'd sink right in until he couldn't breathe.

Then Jonah returned his attention to Tommy. Expression mild. Amiable. The kind of look he'd give a stranger. "And for you, Your Highness?"

"Stop this," Tommy said, his voice low and hard with horror.

Jonah cut a quick look at Frankie.

"Just give him your order." She was staring at the empty seat opposite her.

No. He couldn't pretend this moment didn't matter. Not after all this time. Somehow, Jonah was standing there, *right there,* like it wasn't the most disorienting damn thing. His hair was shorter, waves cut just below his ears, and he wore the glasses that Tommy had too often imagined casting aside as he nudged Jonah back onto the sheets, couch, grass, anywhere he could press down over him until their mouths met and their hips locked and their—

"Kris doesn't look at strangers like that." Frankie's words were hot in his ear as her finger drilled sharply between his ribs. He jolted and met her fierce glare. "Don't forget why you're here."

Her warning landed a second before the screams started. Loud and sudden. Adrenaline speared through his chest even as his panicked glance at the crowd behind Jonah revealed a group of friends welcoming a newcomer. *It's fine.* Not a threat. Just happy people. *Breathe.* But his hands were slick—his heart pounding.

His eyes skimmed Jonah's an instant before he ducked his head.

"Hey now." The warmth of Jonah's voice bordered on laughter. "Prince Kristof would like a drink over here, and I'm having trouble catching his order. Could I get you all to calm down a bit?"

Their gushing apologies were half-lost to the blaring music. *It's fine, I'm fine.* Tommy had torn the cardboard coaster to pieces before he knew his hands were moving. Kris. He was Kris. And Kris could handle this. He'd find their disruption amusing. Smile at them and joke that it was okay—he was happy to see their friend again, too. And even though the thought of engaging with a group of excited strangers made Tommy's insides roil, they wouldn't even know he was here.

They couldn't look at Tommy while they were looking at Kris.

He raised his head, caught the eye of one of the guys watching him. Lifting the corner of his mouth, Tommy tipped his hat in wry amusement. The guy grinned, nodded, and quickly returned his focus to his friends.

There. Tommy sat back, exhausted, and picked up another coaster. Frankie was right. The way he reacted right now wasn't about him and Jonah or their shattered friendship. It was about Tommy's future as king. The strategy was working. He might not be at ease like Kris was in this place, but he was coping, and that was more than he'd done since arriving in Kiraly. If he revealed to anyone paying attention that their princes liked to swap places, he'd never get away with this again.

"Is that better, Your Highness?" Jonah had turned back around.

Jesus. Alarm tremored down his spine. *I have to pretend I don't know him.*

Tommy inclined his head. His tongue felt thick.

It took all of his self-control to relax against the booth cushion, laying his arm along the back ledge and angling his chin up. Only once he'd drawn his bottom lip between his teeth, praying for strength, did he slide his attention back to Jonah.

His old friend was watching him warily. "And your order?"

"Are you new to Kiraly?" Tommy's voice wasn't steady, but the idle question had Kris all over it.

Jonah's features shuttered, but he didn't look away. "I got here on Friday."

That jutted inside Tommy like a broken bone. Jonah had arrived in Tommy's own kingdom days ago without telling him. Tommy had done nothing to earn the courtesy, but that didn't stop it hurting.

"What brings you to our quaint nation?" He circled his fingertips over the leather booth above Frankie's shoulder, trying to ignore the fast beat of the music passing through it, ignore the ache those screams had put in his chest.

Jonah glanced at Frankie, who raised a shoulder like it hardly mattered now. "A friend was . . . in an accident. I'm helping with his recovery."

Tommy's hands flexed.

Kris.

A flush of heat too close to humiliation ran up his neck. Frankie had already known Jonah was here. Kris had known. Who else? Were they all talking about this behind his back? About how Tommy had thrown away the best thing in his life and wasn't it funny that it was right under his nose?

His throat felt swollen. "Have you already been to see him?"

"You don't have to humor me, Your Highness." Jonah pushed the hair off his forehead, and the light caught on the solid muscle of his forearm. Corded and curving, it flexed where it met his elbow. He was lean, but he was strong. "There's no need to pretend to be interested in me. Please give me your order and your evening can go back to the way you prefer it."

Without me, his silence added.

Tommy almost asked Frankie to leave them—almost asked Jonah to take her place beside him so he could purge that sickening misunderstanding from his mind. But this crowd would know that as Kris's bodyguard, Frankie would never leave him with a stranger.

Okay. So . . . damn it.

He had to figure out what Jonah was feeling beneath that half-decent poker face—within a conversation where they were both pretending to be things they weren't. If Jonah had moved on from their friendship, Tommy would back down. No matter how it would gut him, he'd respect Jonah's intention to help Kris without any contact with Tommy himself.

But if Jonah wasn't over the way they had ended, Tommy would bleed this opportunity dry and his heart along with it.

Angling his hat back, he said, "Yet I'm afraid you do have to humor me. And I'd like to know if you've already been to see him."

And *there,* a flash of hurt.

"Please," Tommy added quietly.

"Right," Jonah said, eyes a little too bright. "Because it's all about you, isn't it?"

"Jones," Frankie hissed.

Back teeth sliding together, Tommy glanced over Jonah's shoulder in time to see Kris's guards exchange a glance, but no one else appeared to have heard.

"Yes, I've already been to see him," Jonah said, eyes on the table.

"I see." It stung that Kris had contacted his best friend behind his back; concealed his presence within the palace itself. The sting intensified at the memory of two water glasses in his brother's room. His strange, almost guilty behavior. It seemed Tommy had missed Jonah that afternoon by minutes. "Is he expecting a long recovery?"

Because I'm going to add another few weeks to the total.

"A month, give or take. I'll leave right after."

A month. Selfish relief flooded Tommy's airways—until Jonah's dark gaze sank to Tommy's body and his mind emptied. *Uh.* His skin prickled; denial became a flare deep in his core. *What's he doing?* Jonah's brow was creased as his gaze stroked over Tommy's left shoulder and down his arm before tracking beneath his throat and across to his other shoulder. *Why does he look like he's checking me out?*

Tommy was built. He knew that. Probably more so since arriving in Kiraly and letting out his nervous energy in the palace gym and on the bridle paths. But Jonah had never looked before.

It was everything Tommy could do not to slide his shoulder blades down and in to better show off his chest.

God. He was more like Kris than he'd thought.

Then Jonah said, "I like your shirt," and looked him dead in the eyes.

Oh.

"I used to have one just like it," Jonah added, lifting a brow in feigned surprise. "I've looked for it everywhere. Don't know what happened to it."

Shit. "Maybe someone else needed it more."

"Well, that's silly." Jonah flicked a glance to where the sage green fabric wrapped taut around Tommy's bicep. "It hardly fits them."

"Maybe it reminded them of you."

Startled, Jonah looked up. His face flushed with confusion even as his eyes burned with blame.

And Tommy *knew*.

Jonah wasn't over this.

"I'll just have a beer, thanks," Tommy said, and forced himself to lean back in the booth.

Mouth tightening, Jonah gave a curt nod. He retreated to the bar without another word.

Tommy watched him go with a fierceness in his chest, his unspoken confession desperate to tear itself loose. And it would —he'd let it out. Jonah might have resigned himself to not being in Tommy's life, but he hadn't accepted it. The wounds weren't sealed; he hadn't laid their failed friendship to rest. In offering the truth of his feelings, Tommy wouldn't cause him a second wave of hurt. Not while the first was still burning right beneath the surface.

He could do this.

"You do look like Kris," Frankie said beside him. "Except I'm the only person who's ever seen that expression on his face."

Curling his hands into balls, he said, "Explain some things to me."

She sighed, twisting to face him. "I invited him," she said, leaning closer to speak beneath the bar noise rather than over it. "We get that you're not in a position to talk to Kris about what happened, but he needs to process this with someone who understands. Jones agreed."

"No one planned on telling me." The roof of his mouth was dry and bitter. "That he was here. In the city. In the palace. Today. This afternoon." Outrage lowered his voice to a growl. "He was in my *goddamn palace* and I wasn't told."

She drew back. "He asked us not to say anything."

His heart split in half, each beating loudly in his ears. "Does Mark know?"

"Not yet. He hates being asked to keep secrets."

Jonah was behind the bar again. He had a bottle of vodka in his hand when another bartender grabbed his elbow to get his attention. The young woman gestured vaguely to the room, then clapped her hands a few times with the beat, nodding as she spoke. Her instructions made sense immediately—the chorus hit and every single person on the floor, bar staff included, raised their hands and clapped with the beat overhead, singing at the top of their lungs.

Jonah joined in, laughing and completely bungling the rhythm, and Tommy thought he might die from loving him.

"What have you told him?" he asked, forcing the words past the lump in his chest.

"He knows what happened to Kris." Frankie leaned in again. "But not who did it or why. He doesn't know there's an investigation. And he thinks Mark is and will remain king, mainly because he doesn't want to talk about you, so it's kind of hard to—"

"Don't tell him." Tommy's desire to be king was too personal,

69

too monumental for Jonah to hear from anyone but Tommy. "Make sure no one else does either."

Jonah was pulling a beer from the tap, the movement easy and familiar, and Tommy wondered whether anything would ever be easy and familiar between them again.

"You miss him," Frankie said, her voice unusually careful. "It's so obvious. None of us understand why you cut him off."

He braced himself. "What did he tell you?"

"That you dropped the royalty bombshell and said he wouldn't hear from you again."

He swiped up another coaster and tore it down the middle. "Since you're our highest-ranked secret keeper, I trust you to keep this one to yourself." He fought a surge of shame and said, "He rejected me."

Sweat broke out down his back as Frankie absorbed that in silence.

Then she said, "Not knowingly, though, right? When I told Jones about Mark and Ava's engagement, he asked whether a princess had caught your eye, too. He doesn't even know you *could* like him."

Tommy huffed. That was the crux of his dilemma. "And how was I supposed to hint over the years that it was possible without actually revealing that I do?"

She looked at a loss. "Well. At risk of making it sound obvious or straightforward, which I'm sure it's not when you're living it . . . didn't you ever consider coming out?"

His face went cold. "As what?"

"As . . ." Shifting, she reached for the alcohol she didn't yet have.

"Never mind." Adrenaline was sharp in his veins, but it wasn't panic. It was exposure. No one had seen this part of him, and he feared how it looked, because he'd never had a clear view of it himself.

"But I *do* mind," she said, and glanced quickly back at the bar. "Haven't you two ever—God, I don't know—drooled over Harry Styles together or something?" At Tommy's flat look, she snorted and added, "Okay, or hot guys in general?"

"There are no hot guys. Or girls. Or anyone."

He could feel her watching him.

"There's only Jonah." Pain lashed him. "There was no one. Then I came back from college and—" It had happened suddenly. An unfamiliar surge as a dormant part of him activated. Jonah had come over to welcome him home. They'd sat on the back steps, just the two of them, telling stories and sharing silence like old times. Except Jonah had started wearing glasses in Tommy's absence, and something about them had reframed his face, drawing unusual attention to his cheekbones and eyelashes. Reframed *him* from a close friend into a man of pulse-skittering smiles and concealed skin, and Tommy had finally, *finally* understood what Kris had meant by being too turned on to think straight. "And he was there like he'd never been before."

"Okay." Frankie cocked a cautious brow at him. "So, in terms of what you'd come out as . . . have you considered you might be demisexual? That's when you only feel attraction to someone if you've got a strong emotional connection first."

It is? Tommy clutched that revelation close, his stomach bundling at the thought of a sexuality that could finally make sense of him.

Then Frankie said, "I don't get how he rejected you."

"I thought if I could—" He stumbled for a distancing word. "—*like* him without him knowing it, then it was possible for him to feel the same. But that day, before I came here, I asked . . . and he doesn't. He doesn't feel the same. And I couldn't do it anymore."

"Yeah." For a brief second, she pressed her shoulder against his arm. "Alright."

Tommy swallowed, heart kicking up as Jonah left the bar with a glass in each hand. "I have to tell him. Now that he's here. Even though he doesn't—" It would cut Tommy's throat open to say it again. "I don't want him hating me anymore."

She didn't look at him, but he sensed her smile. "Look at you, facing them all at once."

So he was—taking control of every thread he'd let loose over the years.

His demons could bite his ass.

"Here we are," Jonah said, appearing at the booth. His eyes were lowered as he set down Frankie's glass. "Ma'am."

"Just so we're clear, if you call me that outside of this context, I'll mess you up," she muttered, and was rewarded with his quicksand grin.

"Your Highness," he said next, and half-extended the beer before noting the shredded cardboard in front of Tommy. "Oh. Uh." He flipped a new coaster into place from the stack in the center of the table. "Here."

"Thank you." Tommy's eyes lingered on Jonah's hand as it moved in front of him. It was steady, the tendons standing out as he put the glass down. Several veins pushed against his skin—how soft would they feel beneath Tommy's tongue?

Jonah withdrew and wiped his hands together. "Give a wave if you need anything else."

"We won't," Tommy said. *Not here, not tonight.* "But thank you."

Jonah's brow lowered. "Have a good evening."

"You, too." And then Tommy extended his hand across the table.

It was a gesture worthy of Kris, casually doing away with hierarchy to acknowledge Jonah's assistance. Yet the moment

Tommy reached out, it snapped their unbalanced power dynamic into place. Because Jonah wouldn't *want* to shake with Tommy—yet he had no power to refuse the hand of a prince.

Jonah's features creased with hurt and confusion, but then that gorgeous jaw slid and he clasped Tommy's hand tightly in a non-verbal *damn you*. His touch twisted deep in the pit of Tommy's stomach, grip hard and *right there,* his skin warm and a little rough, on him, around him, not going anywhere until Tommy let him go.

Breathing in long and slow, Tommy held his old friend's stare and pulled *just enough* to force him to lean closer. Jonah's eyes flashed, pained, accusing, but he had no choice but to let it happen. Tommy drew him in until no one but Frankie could overhear. "Why did you serve us tonight?" Tommy commanded himself not to look at Jonah's mouth. "I wouldn't have noticed you behind the bar. You know that."

"Because, Tommy." Betrayal was dark on Jonah's face. "I deserve to be the one to walk away."

Tommy released his hand abruptly, and Jonah straightened, avoiding his eye but seeming to wait for Tommy to respond.

Tommy didn't. He wouldn't take the power out of Jonah's last words.

With a bitter half-smile, Jonah shook his head before turning and disappearing into the crowd.

Tommy's hand was tingling; the truth in his chest was tearing him apart.

Frankie blew out a breath beside him. "Yikes, man. Now what?"

Now he would give Jonah a night to discover that it didn't hurt any less to be the one to walk away.

It just hurt differently.

4

Jonah could go for months without noticing his tattoo. He'd got it at eighteen, so familiarity had made it pretty much invisible over the years. But ever since Tommy had moved to Kiraly, the letters pricked and itched like his skin was rejecting the ink.

It was just so . . . embarrassing.

And confusing, because it had been Tommy's idea.

Jonah had been talking about their friendship not being as long-lasting or binding as the bond Tommy shared with his brothers. He'd opened his silly mouth because Tommy had been about to move away for college—so had Mark and Kris—and sitting on their couch watching them pack had made Jonah feel all needy and vulnerable, and that fear had finally come burbling out.

"We've been friends since we were five." Tommy had dropped his duffel bag on the living room floor. "Explain where short-term comes into it."

"You'll call them more than you'll call me. And by the time you move back here, our friendship won't be the same, but brothers will always be brothers."

Insult had darkened Tommy's face. "Stop trying to write the future. You're getting it wrong."

"You're identical," Jonah had pushed.

"What the hell difference does that make to keeping in touch?"

"I don't know!" Balled up, Jonah had tightened his hold on his knees. What he'd *wanted* to ask was whether Tommy really had to go. "It's got to mean something that you literally look the same."

With a curse, Tommy had hauled him off the couch to get tattoos to bind them. "Since you think what's visible is more important than what isn't." He'd driven Jonah to the parlor in the next town, and an hour later, they'd both had their upper arms branded in black. A simple font, the letters no taller than the width of one of their fingers.

One word that Tommy had chosen.

Same.

When the ink had been fresh, Jonah had been awed by Tommy's conviction.

Now, as he got dressed for his next shift at the Bearded Bunting, the four letters jeered in the corner of his eye, and he jammed his arm through his sleeve to silence them. How were they the same? Tommy was intelligent and established and real-life royalty. And Jonah was about as bright as twilight, living out of his suitcase, and the only power he'd got from his parents was learning to fend for himself after they'd cut him off the day he'd come out.

Jonah was a nobody.

And he'd hardly slept, so was low-hanging fruit for feeling like garbage. He was useless at being tired. Tommy used to tease him about it, gently, somehow striking the right balance between care and humor so Jonah didn't actually start crying.

Hey, it's the incredible sulk, he'd say. *I wondered when we'd meet again.*

The bar hadn't closed until after five last night, but instead of passing out the second he collapsed into bed, Jonah had rolled around with a head full of Tommy.

Tommy shouldn't have been there. In the city. In public. In the bar. Frankie's second message had explained that he was pretending to be Kris in an effort to manage his anxiety and asked Jonah not to give him away. Not to the guests in the bar or to his brothers. As if Jonah would ever do that. He could lie wounded without having to wound in return.

Though apparently, he was less good at lying wounded *out of sight.*

He'd been desperate to avoid Tommy—right up until Tommy had ruined the Bearded Bunting. Jonah's time at the bar was only temporary, but it was good, so *good* for putting him back together, and then Tommy had appeared, making Jonah bleed bad memories all over his new happy place, and *that wasn't fair.*

So Jonah had gone to take his order—showing Tommy he was there first.

Tommy had lounged in the corner of the booth, spread wide like Kris, yet giving off a severe royal energy that his brothers never could. It had warned everyone in the room not to come any closer; pushed like a firm hand in the center of Jonah's chest. Yet there was something *more* in the glinting stare he'd pinned on Jonah, as if that firm hand was shoving him back, back, back until he couldn't go any farther, and Tommy was moving right along with him.

Tommy had said *stop this* like he wanted Jonah removed from his sight—then said *maybe it reminds them of you* like Jonah was too precious to forget. Tommy had shaken his hand like no one would ever tear Jonah from his grasp—then hadn't even bothered to say goodbye.

Breathlessly confused, Jonah hadn't stood a chance of sleeping.

And now, definitely needing to leave for work before he was late, he forced himself across the apartment while a sick ache pulled low in his chest. As he patted his back pocket, feeling his wallet and keys, he opened the front door.

Tommy stood in front of him.

One hand raised in a fist and his eyes pressed closed.

"No," Jonah breathed, startled, and retreated a step before Tommy knocked on his chest.

Eyes snapping open, shock and something else—something fierce and terrified, like determination to do something awful—burst across Tommy's face.

"No," Jonah said again, and spun back inside. This was—no. *He's going to tell me to leave.* Pressing a hand over his mouth, Jonah escaped to the kitchen island, but like sunlight on the backs of his eyelids, he still saw familiar blue eyes—the intent features of his once-best friend standing in the doorway.

Stupid. Jonah shouldn't have said he deserved to be the one to walk away. Now Tommy would make sure he kept walking.

"Jonah." Tommy's voice was quiet—a light scratch on the back of his neck. Jonah's throat grew swollen at the sound. Tommy had left him. Just . . .

Left him.

"Jonah," Tommy said again.

No. He was too tired for this. It wasn't fair.

There was the sound of boots entering the apartment. A shuffle, and the door closed with a light click. Tommy had come in. It sent a tremor down Jonah's spine.

"Jonah, please."

"How could you?" he whispered at the counter.

The silence between them fell a thousand-miles deep. Then, "Will you turn around?"

Jonah didn't move. "Maybe I should leave instead. Since you hate that I'm here."

"I don't hate that you're here." Tommy's soft voice wasn't quite level.

If only he could believe that. "You do. I saw the look on your face when you realized I'd been to see Kris. Have you decided whether you'll let him live?"

"That's not funny."

"No, it's not," he said, his voice gaining strength. "I was helping him. And you've put a stop to it already. What kind of brother are you?"

Absolute silence behind him.

Until, "What?"

"He cancelled on me this afternoon," Jonah said. "You hate that I'm here more than you care about his recovery."

Tommy's next breath was sharp. "I haven't spoken to him."

Oh. "Well, that doesn't mean it wasn't because of you. He's the reason I'm here." *Even though you should be that reason.* "He knows it. Frankie knows it. If he stops seeing me, I'll have to leave." And Jonah would always remember the humiliation of being used like this. Invited in secret and then pushed out of the way like a child underfoot. "I didn't plan on visiting Kiraly, you know? Not even to see the city. Or Frankie. Or the guys. Even though they're my friends, too. Because I knew you'd hate it. But he asked. Kris asked, and he was allowed to invite me. So—I came for Kris."

"I know."

Jonah's eyes were hot and blurry. "Not for you."

"I know, Jonah." Misery ghosted his words.

"You have a new life now." The heat in his eyes spread to his cheeks. Tommy's presence pressed as heavy as the moon behind him, and it was all he could do to hold himself together. "I didn't want you to know that I was here. I didn't want—" *This.* Because it was hurting. It was hurting so much being alone again with Tommy, because despite everything, it felt *right*. "You told me not to contact you. And I haven't. You can't be angry, because I haven't contacted you even once."

"I'm not angry." But he was *something*. His voice was coarse with it. "I don't hate that you're here. I want you to keep helping Kris. It's—I'd like to explain myself. But not during an argument. And not to your back."

Jonah pressed his palms harder into the counter. "Then maybe you'll never explain yourself. I'm hurt and I'm not going to pretend that I'm not."

Tommy cursed quietly.

Jonah's eyes filled again.

"Okay," Tommy said, and Jonah just knew his eyes were closed. "I'm sorry."

"Are you?" If that was true, he would have called—kept in touch. "You thought you'd never see me again, but now you suddenly have to deal with me. You're not sorry—you're uncomfortable, but you think it's the same thing."

"That's not true." A jagged, almost savage sigh. "I feel disgusted and ashamed about the way I've treated you."

Jonah wanted to ask *then why did you do it* but was too scared of the answer.

"You walked away from me last night," Tommy said, and Jonah flushed with both pride and helplessness. "I understand why. But you don't understand why *I* walked away from *you*. Please. Could you turn around? Please, Jonah."

It was as close to begging as Jonah had ever heard him.

Heart tight, Jonah gave in.

The second their eyes met, Tommy let out a shuddering breath that seemed to come from somewhere deeper than his lungs. He looked exhausted. The skin under his eyes was dark, and that hair shouldn't have left the bathroom.

Sniffling, Jonah asked, "Happy now?"

"Fuck." Tommy's features tightened. That was about as expressive as Tommy got. Jonah found his face like a room after dusk, just before full dark, where any sensible person would have already turned a light on. His expressions were flickers in the gloom, silhouettes of his full feelings. "I've made you cry."

Jonah ran a hand over his wet cheeks. "You make it sound like it's the first time."

And Tommy had the nerve to look like Jonah had just punched him in the gut.

Which probably wasn't the best way to treat royalty.

Eyes widening, Jonah clamped a palm over his mouth and gave a muffled, "Oh, no."

Tommy frowned. "What?"

"I should have bowed when I saw you."

"No." Tommy's gaze flashed like lightning in a blue sky. "Not you. Not ever."

But other people bowed to him.

The hundreds of people who worked for him. The bright, laughing people who called Kiraly home. The smart, powerful people who helped him run the country. They all bowed to Tommy.

To Prince Tomas.

Quiet, sharp-minded, commanding in his silence. The kind of prince whose authority could captivate a crowd without saying a word. Maybe that was why Jonah had always been drawn to him. Why Jonah had glittered inside whenever he made Tommy soften or smile or say something that he'd never tell anyone else. Why Jonah would have done anything for him. Maybe it hadn't been friendship, after all.

Just a beta response to Tommy's command.

There was the faint chime of Tommy's message tone, but he

didn't move. He was watching Jonah, his expression shadowed. "You're looking at me like you don't know who I am."

Jonah's breath caught. "I don't."

That seemed to deliver another gut punch. Tommy groaned —this soft, helpless, *frustrated* sound—and said, "I think it's easier for you to believe you've never known the real me than to accept I've hurt you this badly."

Jonah's throat suddenly felt exposed. Gasping a little, he covered it with his hand.

Tommy noticed.

Lips pinching, Tommy looked like he wanted to move closer, and Jonah couldn't decide whether he wanted him to. It was small, this studio apartment, designed for one occupant, two at most, flowing in and out of each other's space. Even standing with the entrance between them, Tommy's presence got under Jonah's skin. He did that sometimes. When not anxious, Tommy's energy was like a growl—claiming his place in a room like a low-throated vibration without having to so much as move or speak.

He was vibrating now. It thrummed down the column of Jonah's spine.

"Why did you do it?" Jonah kept his hand raised in protection. "Hurt me this badly?"

Tommy half-spun away, but not fast enough to hide the complicated mix of anguish and alarm on his face. A moment later, he turned back and blurted, "Can I take you out?"

Uh. That wasn't—

"To explain." There was a slight wildness to his expression as he looked around. "I don't want to do it here. Like this. When your eyes are still red. When it seems like you have to get to work, and I'm already being called back. I'd like to take you somewhere, and God knows you deserve it. Can I do that?"

Jonah stared. *What?* Tommy was avoiding his gaze, attention locked across the apartment at the front windows. His leg was bouncing, but he wasn't worked up. He didn't have that glint in his eyes.

He was nervous.

"Is it good?" Jonah wished he could ignore the lonely hope that sat up inside him, hands clasped, praying, *please be good.* "The reason you did it? Will I understand?"

Bitterness pulled at Tommy's mouth. "I wish I knew."

"But you *hope* I'll understand?" Maybe it was foolish to push, but Jonah deserved an explanation that cast Tommy in a better light. Jonah *deserved* to have his friend back. "It wasn't because you got nothing out of our friendship?"

Tommy faced him, and oh, God, how could he look so severe and so broken at the same time? "Jonah," he said. "I got everything from you."

Jonah's breath hitched. "Then why did you—"

"Later."

"Okay." It felt like surrendering from a fight he'd never wanted in the first place—only to be blindfolded and pushed toward an encounter he had no way to prepare for. "Yes. You can take me somewhere. Later. To explain."

"Oh." Tommy took a small step backward. "I mean, good. That's good." Then he settled his shoulders and held out a clenched hand as his phone chimed in his pocket again. "This is for you."

Startled, Jonah looked to where something small stuck out the top of Tommy's fist. Yellow and white and blue. Confused, Jonah nudged his glasses up his nose. It was—*oh my.*

It was a little posy.

Shock dazed him. "You brought me flowers?"

"Technically, I picked them." Color stained Tommy's cheeks. "To welcome you to Kiraly. Since I did such an appalling job of that last night."

"Oh," he said, and briefly squeezed his eyes shut. *Tommy picked me flowers.* The short-stemmed blooms were almost completely engulfed by his large hand. "I'm so confused."

"I know."

"I was sure you didn't want me here."

"Last night was weird." Tommy's features pinched. "I didn't like it."

Jonah wrapped a hand around his opposite elbow. "Neither did I."

"I was stuck pretending not to know you, pretending to be Kris. It was a coping strategy . . . I'm sorry for making you shake my hand. I was a prick. I just wanted something about it to feel real." Tommy half-lowered his hand. "I understand if you don't want these."

"No, I—no one has given me flowers before."

"I know."

Jonah eyed them again and frowned. He'd seen the royal gardens—perfectly landscaped, not a leaf out of place. "You *picked* them? Where?"

"In the mountains."

In the . . .

"Wait," Jonah said, holding up a hand. "You're a prince who picks flowers in the wilderness beyond your palace?" At Tommy's frown, Jonah widened his eyes and said, "Wow."

Confused, Tommy said, "Please never say *wow* like that about me again."

"*Wow,*" he said. "You turned into Disney for me."

"I—" Where Tommy would normally have responded with sarcasm, he just blinked and said, "That's how sorry I am."

Oh.

"I would become anything for you," Tommy added, and looked down at his hand, his jaw tight. Something close to dismay flickered across his face. "Jesus Christ. These flowers are awful."

Jonah blinked. "What?"

"No one's given you flowers before, and I bring you these?" Tension tightened his fist, flexing right up his arm. "I have a palace garden. Literally. What the hell? I could've asked the gardeners to make an arrangement. Not this piece of—"

"Excuse me." Jonah took a step toward him. If what Tommy said was true—that he was sorry, that he felt disgusted and ashamed, that he got everything from Jonah—then this was an olive branch. And despite everything, despite fearing it made him a beta groveling on his belly, Jonah would take it in a heartbeat. "That terrible bunch of flowers is my welcome gift."

Or apology gift. He wasn't entirely sure.

Tommy tucked it behind his back. "No, it's not."

"I'll have them, thank you." Jonah held his palm out. "Or am I no longer welcome?"

"Jonah—"

"I'll have them," he repeated, extending his hand farther.

"I'm so bad at this," Tommy muttered, but approached. He uncurled his grip and dropped the flowers onto Jonah's waiting palm. The stems were bent, a little crushed, and the whole bunch was kind of damp. Tommy hadn't even added foliage. "Here, welcome to my country. Have some fucking useless flowers."

"Hey." Jonah almost poked him in the chest. "Language."

Tommy flashed a glance up at him. "Sorry." He stepped back. "There."

Jonah looked down—and covered his mouth with his other hand.

They were pathetic. The tiniest grass flowers, little stars and bells, but they *were* pretty. Tommy would've had to walk slowly, deliberately, keeping his attention low as he scanned the ground for signs of color, ducking when he found one, pinching it at the base and twisting carefully. Maybe even thinking, *I hope Jonah likes this one.*

Jonah ached. "Thank you."

"Jesus." Tommy sounded stricken. "Don't thank me. For anything. For a very long time."

"You can't take away my manners, Tommy," Jonah said mildly, moving into the kitchen and pulling out a glass. He ran it under the tap, tried to make the flowers stand up against the sides, and set it beside the toaster. Super floppy, but very cute. He brushed the underside of a wilting white petal. "These won't last the night. I think you still owe me."

"I'll never *not* owe you."

"Hm." Jonah kept his gaze on the flowers. "That's good. Because I've thought of something else you can give me as an apology."

"Anything."

"A hug."

He didn't breathe in the following silence. As friends, they'd never made a habit of hugging, and Tommy had been reluctant to be touched since late adolescence. He'd grown inward as he'd grown up—and Jonah had sometimes wondered what kind of person would be allowed the impossible wonder of Tommy's willing embrace.

He eyed Tommy sideways, waiting.

"You—" Tommy gave a small cough and ran a hand along the back of his neck, tugging so hard he manhandled his head into looking away. His voice was gruff when he asked, "That's something you want?"

"Are you asking me or the bed over there?"

Tommy looked back at him, his blue eyes mocking.

"Yes." Jonah turned to face him fully. He'd gone months without friends, without neighbors, his heart covered in shadow and his body untouched. Honestly, this felt like the least Tommy could do. "It's something I want."

Tommy took a step toward him, then halted, his face intensely serious. "That's—all you want?"

"Sure," Jonah said, leaning against the sink, but at the almost desperate once-over Tommy gave him, he added, "You don't have to."

"I've hurt you." Tommy's tone was sharp—and his expression became even sharper when his phone started ringing. He rejected the call without even looking at the screen.

"Um." He was a prince with big responsibilities, and someone was clearly trying to reach him. "If you need to answer that—"

"What I *need* is to—" Tommy shook his head before meeting Jonah's gaze. "They can wait."

Jonah tried not to let his pleasure show too obviously.

"If you want a hug," Tommy said, "I'll give you a hug."

But he didn't move, except to tap his fingers against his leg.

"Were you thinking now or . . ." Jonah bit his bottom lip to try keep a straight face.

Jaw sliding, Tommy closed the distance between them, bringing that growling undercurrent right into Jonah's personal space. It rushed down his throat, spread across his chest, a tingling chant of *safe, warm, home.* Tommy was here. Right here, less than a foot away, looking down at him with those unlit features. He swallowed, the restrained movement visible right to the base of his neck.

He didn't move closer.

"Hi," Jonah said. "I'll just wait here until you're ready."

"Smartass." Tommy's eyes were dark as they scanned his face. His breathing was a little fast. "The others think you're this slice of apple pie, you know."

Jonah's cheeks glowed. "With cream."

"I know better."

"You won't tell them. You like being the only one who knows."

"Damn right I do," Tommy muttered, and as Jonah smiled—bait taken—Tommy wrapped his arms around his shoulders and drew him close.

Fully intent on being the huggee not the hugger, Jonah tucked his arms up between them and ducked his head so his cheek rested on the front of Tommy's shoulder. Spending most of their adult lives together had made it easy to forget their size difference. Tommy was half a head taller than him, with wider shoulders and a chest dense with muscle—physical strength to match the powerful beat of his presence, and Jonah closed his eyes, sinking into him.

He smelled good. Better than good. Fresh like the turn of spring, open grassy plains, and windy skies. It was familiar, a scent that had trickled through the boys' homestead in Sage Haven along with coffee and hay and horses.

Jonah had always liked it. He just hadn't known it was Tommy.

Lost in the contact, it took him a little too long to realize that despite his nestling, he was not, in fact, the huggee. Tommy kept his head up, nowhere near Jonah's hair or neck or shoulder. It wasn't that Jonah had expected nuzzling, but who hugged without their chin touching *something*? Even Tommy's body seemed pulled back, tense and rigid, like he'd accepted that Jonah wanted to hug him and if he just stood still, it would all be over soon.

Jonah bit the inside of his cheeks, opening his eyes to stare out the kitchen window. He could be offended. Hurt. If he really was good enough to be Tommy's friend, Tommy shouldn't feel the need to hold back like this. It went against everything they'd just talked about.

And yet . . .

Jonah's chest hitched as the hopeless embrace found the pit of loneliness and dejection that had festered in him since Tommy had left—and purged it in an eruption of laughter. The kind of laugh that came from so far down, his stomach locked and his lungs emptied and no sound came out. His shoulders shook; his torso shuddered because he was laughing too hard to breathe.

"What—?" Tommy pulled back abruptly, holding him out by his shoulders. Then he closed his eyes on a light groan. "I thought you were crying again."

Crying? Jonah sagged as his delight bubbled over into sound and he pressed his forehead against Tommy's chin. "I *should* be crying," he managed. "You're an awful hugger."

Tommy let out a warm huff. "That can't be right. I hug people all the time."

Tommy. Going around hugging people. Just the *thought* . . . When Jonah sagged again, laughing too hard to keep himself upright, Tommy took hold of his upper arms and did it for him.

"I'm glad you're enjoying this." Tommy sounded soft and almost shy in his amusement, and when Jonah finally looked up with a last, breathless chuckle, he found Tommy smiling back.

Oh, *wow*.

He'd almost forgotten that smile. Tommy had many, obviously, from cautious to cunning to completely undone, but this one—*this one*—demanded that Jonah hold his stare, so his smile could say things that Tommy wouldn't dare. And right now, it said: *I've missed you, Jonah Wood.* That smile, softened by the light in his blue eyes, the relaxing of long-held hard lines, and the almost boyish chip in his front tooth from when—

—from when—

—it filled Jonah like a shell, his best friend's happiness the sea that echoed and roared inside him.

Not sure how to handle *that* after four months of

abandonment, Jonah took off his glasses to rub his watering eyes. "Those flowers were one thing. But this? Tommy. You're going to owe me for the rest of your life."

"Called it," Tommy said.

Glasses back on, Jonah gestured between them. "Hug me again."

Tommy froze. "Why?"

"Hey, another hug won't kill you." Jonah laughed. "One day you're going to meet a nice princess and she's going to expect you to hug her better than that."

Tommy stepped back. It was several beats before he answered, and his tone was as flat and hard as a truck bed. "I don't want a nice princess."

True enough, Jonah had no idea of Tommy's type, but *nice* shouldn't have been his first guess. He tilted his head, swiping his hair aside. "A sarcastic one, then."

Tommy's posture locked up. Neck stiff, hands fisting. "That's not what I want."

"Okay." Jonah frowned at his reaction. "What *do* you want?"

"Nothing. It doesn't matter. I don't want to tell you right now."

And *those* were three completely separate answers.

"Alright." Jonah wouldn't push it. Not yet, anyway. "Still. You'll never win over anyone with a hug like that." He was only teasing. It hadn't been *that* bad, and besides, Tommy was a quick learner.

But Tommy turned away, cursing under his breath, and strode toward the door.

Wait—is he leaving? Without warning. Just turning on his heel and—*leaving*. The shock of it snapped through Jonah's chest, sharp and stinging, a painful reminder that a split-second was all it took to be left behind.

"I have to go," Tommy said, setting his hand on the doorknob.

We're leaving.

"My advisor is waiting." His back was turned; his shoulders tight.

I have to start a new life.

"Can we make plans for me to take you somewhere? Otherwise—"

You won't hear from me again.

Tommy had cut off as he'd turned around. "Oh, shit."

Jonah refused to talk through the lump in his throat.

"I deserve that look." Tommy's hand fell to his side, and he seemed lost. "I'm sorry if . . . I was going to say, could we make that plan? Otherwise, I'll end up texting you late tonight and doing this all wrong because I can't wait any longer."

Skin cold, Jonah just nodded.

"Are you rostered on Wednesday night?" The question was cautious, almost gentle as he held Jonah's gaze. "It's hot and you love swimming. We could go to the lake for a swim. I could pick you up at nine. Would that be okay?"

Jonah nodded again.

"Good. Okay, good."

"Tommy," Jonah made himself say through the stinging in his chest. "What would you text me tonight? If we didn't make plans, what would you tell me because you can't wait? You could just tell me now."

Tommy looked stricken as a knock came from the door.

"Your Highness?" A voice called carefully from the other side. "Philip has respectfully requested your presence at the palace."

Discomfort creased the edges of Tommy's mouth as he replied, "One moment, Ny."

As footsteps retreated in the hall, he shook his head and spoke more quietly. "I can't tell you now, Jonah. I'd prefer to get it right."

"Will it change this? Because I like being here with you. I like having you back. I don't want it to change again."

Swallowing hard, Tommy opened the door and said, "I like it, too, Jonah."

There was something so unbearably sad in his voice that Jonah couldn't find the breath to say goodbye. That was answer enough.

It would change everything.

5

That hug.
     That fucking hug.

The memory mocked him, wrecked him.

Focus was beyond him. His dawn meditation had been a lost cause. In his morning meeting with Mark and Philip, he'd been so busy trying to forget the feel of Jonah's hair on his neck that he'd launched into his final instructions for the nationwide survey without once remembering that Mark was technically still king and might want to take the lead. After lunch, he'd reached for the files on Adam's brother he'd been avoiding—unable to shake the sense of knowledge just beyond his grasp—and stared at the unopened folder for almost an hour, lost to the way Jonah's body had pressed against his, lean and firm and impossibly unguarded.

Jonah was just so *good*. Big-hearted. Fearless. Flung open.

As Tommy strode to a midafternoon discussion with his minister for natural resources, mines and energy, he replayed Jonah's little sigh as Tommy had drawn him near; his breath puffing through Tommy's shirt and warming the front of his shoulder.

He'd had no reason to accept Tommy in his apartment. No reason to turn around or take the flowers—yet he'd asked for a hug and burrowed close, sweet as pie and heavy as cream and leaving Tommy's sanity hanging by the tips of its fingers to the edge of the world.

They'd never done that—full body touching. Not since contact had mattered.

It had been torture.

One wrong move could have blown everything. A telltale hard swallow. An inhale that sounded too much like smelling. A shifting hand that, in some cruel trick of nuance, betrayed it wanted a hell of a lot more than what it was taking.

He'd stayed back and shut down—so successfully, Jonah had believed he wanted a princess.

Tomorrow night.

Tommy tore foam chunks out of his stress ball as he took dinner in his study, aiming to map out his post-meeting strategy. Except, Jesus, he was going to come clean *tomorrow night* and had no idea how to do it. He'd never liked anyone before Jonah, or wanted to touch them, or actually touched them, or kissed them, or messed around with them, or slept with them, or found words to tell them how he felt. At almost twenty-six, he had no idea how to admit to his sexually confident best friend that he wanted every bone and breath in his hot, angel-winged body.

Desperate, he resorted to googling *how to tell my gay best friend who thinks I'm straight that I'm in love with him* and got results for gay men in love with their straight best friends. So, points for finding something the internet didn't know.

Also, he was screwed.

He didn't eat.

Didn't write the strategy.

By the time he made his way to Tuesday beer and poker night with his brothers, a sick fear coated the inside of his mouth.

This was a bad idea. They would know something was up. He should ditch it. Walk straight past the private lounge to his own rooms and figure this out—except it was Kris's first night out of his royal suite since the attack. So short of Tommy claiming he was on his deathbed, no excuse would land.

Bracing, he left his guards in the corridor and entered.

The lounge was one of the few palace rooms redesigned to suit him and his brothers. After their arrival, blue and gold wallpaper had been exchanged for off-white, brocade drapes removed for sturdy timber slats, and antique furniture subbed for modern couches, an entertainment unit, and a pool table. Simple, comfortable, and a step closer to feeling like home. Most of the downlights were low, fading out the excess space and illuminating one side of the room. The table had been set up with beer and snacks and poker chips, but instead of finding his brothers leaning back in chairs, drinks in hand, he found Mark lounging on one of the couches, his booted feet on the coffee table, with Kris propped up beside him, looking a little bed-rumpled in a tank, sweats, and bare feet.

They looked up when Tommy walked in, smiles fading at whatever he'd failed to get off his face. *Pretend it's nothing. Sit down at the table.* But his traitorous legs took him past his brothers to the open window where he barely resisted clamping a hand around the ledge. They'd notice the attempt to ground himself—his white-knuckled grip.

"Hey, man." Kris sounded like he was frowning.

"Tommy?" Mark asked in concern.

Warm evening air wafted in. Solar lights glowed along the garden paths below. *How nice. Say that. Say, how nice is this view?*

"How," he said, and faltered, his tongue thick, and considered throwing himself upon the view's mercy.

Distress flushed his skin, and he shoved his sleeves up. What would his brothers think if they knew he got flustered over Jonah? Accepting Jonah's sexuality had been one thing—but Tommy was their brother. Sometimes prejudice only snarled to life when people were confronted too close to home. Jonah's parents had proven that. They'd left town rather than be known as parents of a gay son.

"Tommy, what's going on?" Kris's question was followed by the sound of shifting and a pained intake of breath.

Mark asked, "Has something happened?"

Tommy stared outside, giving himself ten seconds. For years, this truth had sat like a weight between his heart and his mouth, and he'd never known how to push it out. Now, he was on the brink of the biggest confession of his life, and he was coming to the alarming realization that he couldn't do it alone.

He needed the support of his brothers.

Look at you, Frankie's words echoed. *Facing them all at once.*

Tommy lost feeling in his hands as he turned around.

Kris was leaning forward with a grimace, the bruises on his face a light brown–yellow. Mark had a hand on Kris's shoulder to keep him from rising. They were both watching him, intent, waiting.

Tommy kept his features neutral, his body steady—until he said, "I love you guys," and his voice cracked straight down the middle.

"Tom." Mark stood in alarm. "We love you, too."

"What the hell is—come here, Tommy." Kris was trying to stand, but his injuries left him struggling against the soft cushion. He gritted his teeth, inching forward, listing hard to one side. "Fuck. Come *here.*"

Tommy only went because Kris was an over-protective ass who'd tear his wounds open before he'd stop trying to reach Tommy.

Mark sat again, his expression grave as Tommy forced

himself to sit facing them on the coffee table. Kris stayed on the very edge of the couch, close to Tommy, staring right at him.

Carefully, Mark asked, "What's going on?" He nudged Kris in the foot in a silent instruction to give Tommy some space. "Is this about being king?"

"I'll do it." Kris inched even closer. "Okay? Done. All sorted."

"It's not about that." Tommy dipped his head, staring at the carpet between his boots as he said, "I don't know how you're going to react."

"I'll kill them." Kris clamped a hand over Tommy's shoulder. "Who is it? I'll kill them."

Tommy's pulse tripped. "What are you talking about?"

"Whoever's made you feel like this."

A surge of *don't you touch him* had Tommy looking Kris dead in the eye. "It's Jonah."

"Oh. Damn." Kris paused for a beat, angling his head. "I guess I could kill him."

"Kris," Mark warned, then said, "Tommy," in encouragement.

Tommy drew in a swift breath as he glanced between them. "I'm into him."

"Okay." Kris leaned even closer. His expression didn't change as he nodded for Tommy to continue.

Okay?

Disoriented, Tommy replayed his admission for ambiguity. Then he cut a tense look between his brothers. "That's—that's it."

"Oh." Kris exchanged a frown with Mark. "Yeah, we know, man."

They . . . Reeling, Tommy gripped the coffee table on either side of his knees. "You *know?*"

"We thought you knew that we knew." Mark sounded

startled. "It's been obvious for years. You clearly never wanted to talk about it, though, so we didn't bring it up. We thought it was an unspoken brother thing."

Years? They'd known for *years.*

And they were okay with it.

Staggered, Tommy asked on a disbelieving breath, "How is it obvious?"

Kris pulled a face, scratching the back of his head as if he couldn't decide where to start. "The way you look at him."

"The way you smile for him," Mark said, his blue eyes shining.

"The way you say his name like you're petting something soft."

"The way you lean in to talk to him."

"Ooh, so not subtle." Kris's mouth lifted. Not in amusement or jest, but in genuine pleasure. "The way you watch him when he's talking like he's the only person who has anything important to say."

Mark leaned forward, nodding, elbows on his thighs. "And the way your body faces him when he's around, even if neither of you are talking."

Kris grinned wide. "The way you defend him."

"Your tattoo," Mark said, and Kris fist-bumped his shoulder with a victorious, "Exactly! I called it years ago."

And before Tommy could even begin to process that Kris had called it before Tommy had *felt* it, Kris said, "Wait." His smile vanished. "You were worried about how we'd react to—" Kris wrapped a hand around the back of Tommy's neck and drew him in until their foreheads pressed together, recent concussion and bruises be damned. "You think we'd react badly? Jesus, all this time you've been worried about it?" His fingers tightened as he said coarsely, "I love you, too."

"I didn't know." Tommy was finding it hard to speak. How could relief feel so suffocating? "I didn't know."

"Tommy." Mark closed in, sliding his arms around them. His firm grip was grounding on Tommy's upper arm as he added his forehead to theirs. "Thanks for telling us."

"Yeah." Kris angled his face to press his nose against Tommy's cheek. It felt like acceptance. "I should have said that bit at the start. Thanks, man. Now let's take a few deep breaths."

Even though it was for his benefit, and that made him uncomfortable, Tommy gave in and closed his eyes. Mark and Kris inhaled for way longer than he ever could, but he focused his mind on their faces, warm and rough against his, their arms around him, and counted his slowly lengthening breaths.

"There," Kris said eventually, making Tommy want to roll his eyes. Which felt good, like steadier ground. "That's better."

"Not completely." Tommy spoke into their huddle. "The problem is that I don't know how to tell *him*."

His brothers both stiffened.

"Oh," Mark said, grimacing. "Right."

"Shit," Kris muttered.

This time, Tommy did roll his eyes. "I know he's in Kiraly."

"Thank Christ." Kris pulled back in a rush, but he kept his hand on Tommy's shoulder.

"Wait, what?" Mark was frowning as he leaned back, his hand dropping to Tommy's knee. "I thought he was in Paris."

"Paris?" Tommy frowned. "Why would he be in Paris?"

"He flew to Europe last week to start traveling. I spoke to him when he landed. He wasn't planning on coming here, not even for the wedding."

I was never going to come to Kiraly. Not even to see the city.

Guilt tried to push Tommy to his feet—God, he'd separated Jonah from his brothers' friendship as well as his own—but Kris and Mark both tightened their hold on him. Not in restraint, but reassurance, so he let himself be held in place.

"I asked Jonah to come," Kris said, answering Mark as he eyed Tommy warily. "To talk about what happened. You know? Last week. But he didn't want you to know he was here, Tom, and *I* didn't blow it, so I have no idea how—"

"That doesn't matter," Tommy cut him off, not ready to talk about his night out in the city. "He's here, and I want to figure out how to tell him."

They both paused. Then Mark smiled and said, "We'll do our best to help."

"Don't ask me." Kris ran a hand through his hair, nape to forehead, and Tommy made a note to rumple his own hair like that when he next posed as his brother. "I made it clear that I wanted Frankie by accidentally dropping a condom at her feet."

Mark drew back in dismay. "You what?"

"Jesus, Kris," Tommy muttered.

His brother's eyes widened indignantly. "I said *accidentally*."

Tommy ran a hand over his mouth to conceal a smile. "Don't tell me it worked."

"Hell, no. She wouldn't even look at me."

That sounded like the Frankie they knew and loved.

Tommy jerked his knee a little under Mark's palm. "What about you?"

Mark gave a small laugh, shaking his head ruefully. "I told Ava that I liked her while we were at the Bearded Bunting. She said she refused to let me complicate everything and left."

"*That's* why she left that night?" Kris paused to grimace. "Whoops."

Eyes narrowing, Mark shifted to face him properly. "What do you mean *whoops*?"

"I might have told Ava to stop messing with you." Kris looked sheepish. "And, you know, then accused her and her parents of plotting the murder of our family."

"You—" Tommy gaped, then finished with a groan, "Need constant supervision."

"Why do you think Frankie made herself my bodyguard?"

Mark's eyes were closed as he rubbed the bridge of his nose. He was shaking his head but looked close to smiling.

"Okay. Tommy." Kris raised a brow. "What were you *thinking* of telling Jonah?"

"That I—" He broke off, heartbeat suddenly sharp in his chest. "That I love him."

Kris said, "Oh, man, no," while Mark sucked in a quick breath and grimaced.

Taken aback, Tommy looked between them. "No?"

"If you want to scare him away, drop a condom," Kris said, and Mark snorted. "But if you want to give him a chance to get his head around it, start slow."

Slow.

"Yeah." Mark raised his brows in earnest. "You've been friends forever, but this is new territory. Don't overwhelm him all at once."

"Why not?" Frustration edged Tommy's voice. "It won't matter. He doesn't see me like that. And I don't want to regret that I never told him."

"Okay, okay, just . . ." Kris held up a placating hand, nodding slowly. "Entertain the possibility that he could grow to feel the same. Why send him running when you could just open his eyes?"

Tommy frowned at him, then at Mark.

Mark nodded, brows still raised.

"Alright." Tommy shifted as nerves tangled around his middle. "How do you suggest I open his eyes?"

"Tell him you like him." Kris gave a one-sided smile. "That you're *into* him. But not the L-word—not yet."

"Okay." Then he cut Kris a warning look. "Don't tell him when he comes to see you. Or anyone. Either of you."

Kris held up a palm. "We won't."

"Your secret's safe with us," Mark said, then paused, tilting his head. "Still."

Kris grinned and poked Tommy in the cheek. "He'd be lucky to have you."

Gut tight, Tommy turned his face away. "Don't."

"He *would*. Anyone would. And if he doesn't—"

"Please don't say you'll kill him."

"Or accuse him of killing our extended family," Mark added under his breath.

Kris rolled his eyes with a laugh. "God. So many rules." Then he slid his arm around the back of Tommy's neck, pulling him in again. It was irritating—until it occurred to Tommy that his brother was taking advantage of the chance to hold him close, since he usually stayed out of range. "But seriously, Tommy. He'd be lucky. Look at you. You're fierce and stunning and so . . . I don't know—*significant*. I never want to let you out of my sight."

Embarrassment had Tommy looking over his shoulder, as if there was something more interesting behind him. "We look the same, you idiot."

"No," Kris answered with conviction. "You look like you're going to change the world and you always have."

Mark's smile was warm when he said, "I think you'll make a good king, Tommy."

Kris nodded, glancing at Mark and back to Tommy.

Tommy arched a brow. A week ago, Mark had processed Tommy's claim to be king with grave concern and Kris had actively tried to talk him out of it.

"I should have seen it sooner," Mark admitted with a sheepish grimace. "You know what Ava said to me last week after we knew you intended to ascend?"

Tommy eyed him, waiting, strangely nervous.

"She said that out of the three of us, you make the most sense as king."

Instantly, Tommy was shaking his head. "Mark, no. You're so good."

His brother smiled, tightening his grip on Tommy's knee. "Thanks, man."

Tommy briefly placed his hand over Mark's before drawing away.

"Uh. Hello." Kris looked between them. "No one's going to insist that I'd be great? Are we not taking this in turns?"

Tommy caught Mark's eye. They both grinned.

"You're assholes, both of you." But Kris was grinning, too.

"You're a great brother." Kris looked startled when Tommy rested his hand over where Kris still gripped his shoulder. "The best brother, really, because you were going to be king to protect both of us even though it terrified you."

Kris's eyes gleamed and he puffed his chest a little. "I'd do it again."

"Not if we can help it," Mark murmured, and Tommy elbowed him with another smile.

"Hey!" Kris was indignant. "I feel attacked."

Tommy frowned at him. "Too soon, Kris."

"Oh, for God's sake, are we playing tonight or what?"

They played. They teased. They laughed.

And for a while, the thought of admitting his feelings to Jonah didn't turn Tommy's stomach inside-out, because no matter what happened, he would always have this.

6

Tommy hadn't considered that he and Jonah would be as nervous as each other.

Jonah talked from the moment he got into the car—*that street food smells amazing* and *do pedestrians have right of way here?* and *I climbed The Sceptre today and my legs still haven't forgiven me*—but didn't seem to expect Tommy to contribute more than occasional murmurs. Tommy's own nerves were thick in his throat, damp down his back. He stared at the driver's seat in front of him, uncaring of the countryside or the moonless sky outside. The world beyond this chattering man was useless to him.

Jonah kept at it as they parked on the far side of the lake and made the twenty-minute trail walk by flashlight down the alpine slope to the water. On the rocky shore, Tommy fell back a few steps, closing his eyes and tipping his head toward the sky. The air was warm, the sluggish remains of a hot day, and if he tried hard enough, he could almost imagine it was midsummer in Sage Haven.

He wished he'd done it there. Before all this.

Without a royal security team positioned around them,

hiding their curiosity and pretending not to overhear. Without the palace high above them and the past four months of hurt between them. Without Jonah uncomfortable and struggling to brace for an explanation he couldn't predict.

Jonah was standing partway to the water's edge, staring across the lake. Silent now. He could be many things—bartender, tourist, best friend—yet his silhouette was unmistakably a cowboy at rest. One foot was propped on a low rocky outcrop, knee bent, and a thumb looped over his waistband. His head was cocked a little to one side, chin up and shoulders back. A body that was as strong and sure as it was expressive.

Nerves hammering, Tommy moved beside him.

Jonah glanced at him quickly, then away. "It's incredible."

They were surrounded by mountain peaks that in daylight would reflect on the glassy surface but now towered black and eerily flat against the night sky. Opposite them, the lake's northern shoreline was scattered with the golden lights of boats and bars and lakeside parties. Music and the occasional holler travelled across the water, and higher up, the streetlamps and windows of the city and palace glowed like a mythical paradise.

"I can't believe you guys own it all." Jonah looked down and scuffed his boot against the rock.

Tommy frowned. "We don't."

"Rule it all, then."

"We don't exclusively." The inadequacy in Jonah's words bothered him. "Our monarchy is constitutional, not absolute, so we have a parliament. While the sovereign has substantial discretionary powers, most legislative matters are . . ."

Jonah was frowning at him uncomfortably. He wasn't following.

"It doesn't matter," Tommy said, and tried to smile.

"It does matter," Jonah said quietly, and looked away. "Still. You guys own a palace. I can't get my head around that either."

"Well." Tommy hesitated to correct him again, but knew Jonah felt worse when he suspected he was being humored. "Technically, the crown owns the palace."

Jonah made a soft noise of confusion. "How can a crown own a palace?"

Oh, uh . . . "I don't mean a literal crown."

"Then what do you mean?" Agitated, Jonah stepped away from him.

The distance landed hard in Tommy's stomach, and alarmed at how the conversation had derailed, he said swiftly, "It's not important."

"It *is* important." Jonah gestured above the city. "It's your life. And if I can't even—"

"I'll explain it to you." Tommy silently cursed himself. The lake was supposed to provide a calm, private setting—not make Jonah feel stupid. "We'll go through it later, okay? You'll get it. I know you will. But it's got nothing to do with tonight, and I don't know why I'm even talking about it."

Jonah was quiet. Then he gave a half-hearted laugh and said, "Yeah, okay."

There was a long, awkward silence. Water lapped gently; a nightbird called from the trees behind them. Jonah stood with an arm wrapped around his middle, gripping his opposite bicep, with his head turned toward a blacked-out mountain instead of the picture-perfect city that would put Tommy in his peripheral view.

Great. He feels like shit.

So Tommy said, "You look nice."

Jonah turned to him in bewilderment. "What? Me?"

"Uh. Yes. You."

Bravo, Tomas. Much less awkward.

"You've had a haircut," Tommy said, his face burning. "Right?"

"Oh." Jonah lifted a hand to the thick, wavy hair that Tommy had spent years aching to touch. "Yes. When I was in Paris. Part of the new me."

"What was wrong with the old you?" He hadn't meant for his voice to drop, but the question came out low and protective.

Jonah clicked his tongue and looked away again. "I assume that's what you're here to tell me."

Oh. God.

"Are we going in?" Jonah's voice was small. It seemed like a polite way of asking: *Are you going to tell me now or in the water?*

"Yes." The glacial lake drew its water from underground and surrounding creeks, and although the summer sun warmed it, the water never quite lost its chill. "It'll be cold."

Nodding, Jonah started toeing off his boots—totally comfortable stripping to his shorts in front of Tommy and completely unaware of what his half-naked body would mean to him. Do to him.

"I'll meet you in there," Tommy said and stiffly turned away. "I just have to—speak to the guards."

"Why?"

Yeah, *why*, Tommy? Back still turned, he said, "I have to tell them . . . that . . . we're going swimming."

Wishing he could disintegrate into the coarse grit underfoot, Tommy crossed without another word to where his personal guards, Zoltan and Nyaring, were positioned at the base of the mountain track.

"Everything alright, Your Highness?" Zoltan asked, his voice hushed. His solid build loomed in the darkness; a man of deep thought who had recently been promoted to Tommy's bodyguard outside the palace.

"Has it ever been?" Tommy ran a hand over his face as if his mortification would rub right off. "Tell me when he's in."

"I will monitor him very closely for you." Nyaring gave a

small, secret smile and fixed her attention over Tommy's shoulder. She was in her mid-thirties with a sharp reaction time and an even sharper eye for detail. Her South Sudanese accent replaced her *V*'s with *B*'s as she added, "Very, very closely."

"Salacious thoughts about him are punishable by tower duty."

"And here I thought you were being magnanimous."

"No one's magnanimous," he said, and her smile grew a little wider.

"He's shirtless." Nyaring cleared her throat lightly a few seconds later. "Your Highness."

Jaw sliding, Tommy suppressed the desire to glance over his shoulder.

"He's removed his glasses." Her voice stayed low, but her chin lifted as she tried for a better look. "Now he's walking toward the lake with a hand in his hair. It's—well. His arm. It's . . ."

Sculpted and flexing with the movement?

Pretending his heartbeat wasn't falling to pieces, Tommy rubbed the bridge of his nose. "Tower duty it is."

"I'll join you." Zoltan angled his head as he watched Jonah.

Tommy narrowed his eyes. "Are you talking to me or Ny?"

"Is the former an option?" Zoltan's expression remained neutral. "I'll go grab my towel."

Jesus, these two. They knew when he needed distracting. "I'm not sure how this is going to go," Tommy said. "Could you arrange for the possibility that he and I will leave separately?"

They inclined their heads as a yelp came from behind him.

"The water truly is quite cold," Zoltan remarked after a beat.

There was a splash that *absolutely* sounded half-naked, followed by calm.

"He's in the water, Your Highness," Nyaring said.

"Yeah." A tremble passed through Tommy; a moment of unbalance before the fall. "Thanks."

Moving to Jonah's pile of clothes, Tommy swiftly stripped to his shorts. Then he clenched his teeth against the bite of the water and made his way to where Jonah was slowly sculling, his head tipped toward the stars. He looked relaxed, close to content, and regret that he was about to ruin it sliced Tommy as keenly as the chill.

Jonah stiffened at his approach, bobbed under the surface, then set his feet down and straightened, rising farther out of the water than Tommy had anticipated. *Oh, Christ.* The surface lapped against Jonah's nipples, revealing his naked shoulders, the lean swell of his upper arms, the chiseled wings of his collarbones. *Don't look, for God's sake.*

"Tommy." Jonah wiped the water off his face with a slight squint. A droplet lingered to one side of his top lip, and in a different life, Tommy would have reached out to cup Jonah's jaw, tracing his mouth with his thumb, the touch as soft as the air in his lungs. "Before you say anything, I want to apologize for what I said the day you left."

Tommy focused on his friend's forehead. "You said nothing you need to apologize for."

"I did," he said, so sincere it hurt. "When I told you to . . . you know."

Ah. "To fuck off."

Jonah winced with a nod. "I was upset. I didn't mean it."

Shame banded around Tommy's middle at how poorly he'd handled that conversation. "You were allowed to mean it."

"But I didn't. It's an appalling thing to say."

"It's not *that* bad. You could have said fuck off and die. That would have been worse."

"Oh my God, Tommy!' Jonah gave a muffled laugh behind

his hand, but it faded fast. "I didn't mean for you to take it seriously. For you to *actually* leave me alone."

Like a fool, Tommy watched Jonah's hand drop back into the water. It left him staring right at his pecs, and God, his guards were definitely getting tower duty if they'd been looking there. The naked skin was smooth, raised and hard with muscle, and for a dangerous moment, Tommy's need to *have him, all of him* hit with a hard pound too low for comfort. "That's not why I left you," he said roughly.

"It's just—" Jonah raked his fingers along the surface of the lake, stalling. "We're like a peach, you and me. Whole for most of its life, then you go to split it around the middle—in that seam bit that makes it look like maybe it's always been two halves grown together—but when you twist it to pull the halves apart, it doesn't break clean. It goes all mashy and drippy and clings on, leaving huge chunks on each other."

Tommy blinked.

"You tried to twist away from me, Tommy, and you left pieces of yourself behind."

In that metaphor, Jonah had kept the pit and Tommy had torn his own heart out.

Sounded about right.

"Tell me," Tommy said, "which star is the brightest."

Jonah froze, seeming to sense this was it. Then he said, "No." Something close to panic pulled at his mouth. "I don't want it anymore. The reason. Don't tell me. I just want to stay friends."

"We can't," Tommy told him, far more gently than his devastation should have allowed.

"But if we—"

"The star, Jonah."

Relenting on a shaky exhale, Jonah tilted his face to the sky. He turned in a slow circle as the stars painted his features in colorless light.

"That one." Jonah pointed to Mars in the east. "I don't know its name though."

"No," Tommy told him softly.

It took all of his strength to move. To lift his hand out of the water and curl his fingers around Jonah's pointing hand.

Jonah jolted, sucking in a startled breath as he turned to stare at him, eyes wide, and Tommy didn't breathe as he guided their hands to settle over Jonah's chest. He was gripping Jonah too tightly, his thumb tucked in on a strange angle, and his mind blanked at the sensation of his knuckles brushing against the bare skin of his friend's chest.

"It's here." His whole body itched, exposed as Jonah stared at him—pupils so wide, they held the universe above. "Right here."

Jonah's breathing filled the silence, unsteady, falling like the beams of their friendship around them. Shock slackened Jonah's hand; his heart raced against the backs of Tommy's fingers.

Then, a hoarse whisper. "What are you saying?"

"I left you, Jonah, because you're the brightest thing in my life—and it was too hard to not be the same in yours." Jonah's eyes grew even wider, and Tommy belatedly remembered his brothers' advice to tone it down. "Because I like you."

Jonah said, "What."

"I like you."

"You—" Jonah's breathing grew heavier, more ragged. His gaze had slipped to Tommy's chin, glazed and unblinking. *He's overwhelmed. Get out of his space.* Carefully, Tommy withdrew his hand and waded back in the water, watching Jonah's eyelashes beat together as if trying to clear away his confusion. "Are you sure?"

Tommy's chest ached. "That I like you?"

Jonah nodded, his attention still fixed on Tommy's chin.

"Yes," Tommy said helplessly. "I'm sure."

"Oh." Jonah sounded disoriented, almost distressed, and it

tore at Tommy that he couldn't comfort him. "I—I'm not sure what to say."

"You don't have to say anything." *Say you want me. Say I can have you. Please. I want you so badly.* "This is all on me. I'm not asking for a response. You can just—not say anything."

"No, I . . . should. I'm sorry." Jonah's hand was still clutched to his chest. "It's just that I . . ." *don't feel the same.* "I didn't think you . . ." *were going to say anything like this.* "I've never even . . ." *thought about you like that.*

"I know," Tommy said, though his understanding came at a cost. Unvoiced, his devastation swelled, shouting in his head, howling between his ribs. "It's okay."

"Tommy . . ." Finally, Jonah looked up, his features stricken.

It was a meeting of gazes Tommy couldn't handle. Swallowing, he averted his eyes and spoke through the pain clogging his airways. "What I should have told you that day is I'm sorry. I can't feel the way I feel about you and treat you like a friend. You're more than that to me. We—I can't do it anymore."

"Oh my God," Jonah said on a gasp. "This is a lot."

"I know," Tommy managed, and then thought, *now what?*

Jonah drew in a shuddering breath—and startled Tommy by stepping closer.

Oh, Jesus. Tommy's heart wrenched at the familiarity of the movement—an instinctive seeking of comfort, because for twenty years, Jonah had always turned to him for strength.

They both froze.

Tommy thought he might die when Jonah recoiled.

"Oh no, sorry." Jonah's hand flew to his mouth. "I didn't—you can't—" *You can't comfort me when you're the reason I need comfort.* He made a sound of distressed confusion. "Would it be okay if I thought about this alone?"

"Yes. Absolutely. Sure." Instantly, Tommy stepped back. His foot caught on a dip in the lakebed, and he almost lost his balance. "The guards will drive you home whenever you're ready."

Jonah's head moved—maybe a nod, maybe a stunned tremor. "Thanks. Sorry, I . . . thanks." Then he turned away to stare at Kira City.

And that was it.

Shock crept over Tommy as he left the lake. He dressed, limbs heavy from the cold water. His guards didn't speak as he approached, all formality now, switching on their flashlights for the return hike. It would hit him later. The reality of finally, irreparably cutting the bonds of their friendship. His blood would get hot in his ears and his guts would writhe.

But he wouldn't regret it.

It was the last thing Jonah had expected.

His chest was alive where Tommy had touched him; his fingers aching where Tommy had held him. It was getting harder to breathe as something huge and fundamental shifted at his core.

Tommy liked him.

It didn't—Jonah couldn't—how was he supposed to process that? Not by himself in the middle of a lake that felt colder by the second. He needed sugar and a bed to fall apart in, because Tommy? His neighbor of twenty years—the boy he'd wanted as his best friend the *second* he'd met him; the guy who'd helped Jonah pack when his parents had kicked him out; the man who could have literally anyone who caught his shadowed gaze?

Likes me.

Ribs tight, Jonah asked the waiting guards to please take him home. They took the request a little too far—because the man who liked him was also a prince who'd instructed his Royal

Guard to escort Jonah all the way to his apartment door. His skin prickled as they climbed the stairs in silence behind him. They knew. Didn't they? They had to know. Sound carried too easily over water for them not to have overheard Tommy's confession.

You're the brightest thing in my life.

Something hot and electric flashed in Jonah's chest as he pulled out the apartment key. Suddenly out of breath, he missed the lock. And again. Then, with the key in place and his face on fire, he said, "Thank you, enjoy your evening," and closed the door behind him.

He—Tommy had never liked anyone. Never talked about crushing or bedding or loving. Shame ran a fever over Jonah's skin as he stripped out of his damp clothes without turning on the lights. He'd honest to God thought Tommy just hadn't met the right girl yet. He'd *known* not to assume someone was straight until proven otherwise—then he'd gone and done it with Tommy. Not that his sexuality was the real shock here.

It was that Tommy liked *him.*

It meant—Jonah's stomach tumbled to the floor. *It means nothing will be the same.*

Overwhelmed, he tossed his damp clothes over the shower rod and sat on the edge of the bed with the sheet dragged around his shoulders. It *meant* that Tommy hadn't abandoned him because he wasn't good enough. That Tommy hadn't forgotten about him or been embarrassed by their friendship. It meant they didn't *have* a friendship, not like before, because in order to cope, Tommy had needed half a world of distance between them instead of half a room. He needed distance he couldn't close, instead of distance he *could* close, *wanted* to close, but wasn't allowed.

Jonah shivered. He could still feel Tommy's hand holding on like a grappling hook. Could hear his voice pitched low with sincerity as he'd said: *You're more than that to me.*

Flustered and thrumming with nerves, Jonah curled up on his side. What was supposed to happen next? He'd have to . . . make some kind of decision. Right? About Tommy. *Because he likes me.* A decision about how Jonah felt or could imagine himself feeling in return beyond *wow, he was so strong when he held my hand.* Except Jonah had no idea where to draw that line and refused to draw it hastily. Tommy expected a rejection. He wouldn't have cut himself off in the first place if he'd thought there was the chance Jonah felt the same. Which, admittedly, he didn't—but that didn't mean he *couldn't,* and this was too important to not know for sure.

Right?

"Okay," he breathed. How *did* he feel? Starting with his initial reaction.

Shock and disbelief had winded him, but it hadn't been mixed in with dismay or guilt that he would never feel the same. Nothing in him had shied away—nothing had braced to reject his friend outright. So, that was a thing. And now his insides were a mess, tangling and surging with shockwaves and nerves and . . . maybe an incredulous thrill? No one had liked him before—at least, no one he hadn't just met fifteen minutes ago. His hookups had all been meeting points of attraction and opportunity, but Tommy *knew* him. Knew he got sulky when he was tired. Knew he wasn't as sweet and innocent as everyone seemed to believe. Knew no one had given him flowers before. Even if Tommy couldn't hug to save his—

Oh. *No.* With a muffled, "Ahh," Jonah turned and buried his face into his pillow. He'd literally said that Tommy would never impress anyone hugging like that. After Tommy had hugged *him*—the very man he liked and wanted to impress.

"Oh my God," he said loudly into the pillow. "I'm such an *idiot.*"

If only Tommy hadn't made it impossible to tell.

Hurling himself onto his back, Jonah stared at the box of streetlight on the ceiling. How long had Tommy liked him? *Why* did Tommy like him? How much? What kind of like was it? Simple appreciation wouldn't have prompted Tommy to cut him off. *I can't feel the way I feel about you and treat you like a friend.* So how *did* Tommy feel, exactly? Jonah's stomach flipped. Did he think about Jonah when they weren't together? Did he lose his appetite remembering something Jonah had said or the way he'd looked? Did he think of him randomly in the middle of reading, or brushing his teeth, or—

In bed?

Did he—*does Tommy want to sleep with me*? The possibility tugged, drawing Jonah closer, hot and new and uncomfortable and exciting. It was late. Dark and private. Was Tommy lying awake thinking about him right now?

Oh. Jonah sat up so fast, the blood rushed to his head. *Tommy.*

He fumbled for his phone and then blinked against the light of the screen as he typed out a text, muttering, "I really am an idiot," under his breath.

Then he sent: **You're freaking out, aren't you?**

A second later, Jonah thought: *Oh no, I'm naked.* He couldn't text Tommy while naked. Rushing, he pulled on his old jeans and carried his phone with him as he switched on a few lamps and moved into the kitchen.

Milk was heating on the stove by the time he heard the whoosh of a reply.

That doesn't sound like me. Tommy, wry as ever.

I'm sorry I asked you to leave. Jonah leaned against the counter, a heavy weight in his chest. Nerves. All of them, every nerve in his body, clustered beneath his sternum. Tommy had put himself in an intensely vulnerable position tonight—

and Jonah had left him hanging. **I should have said more.**

The milk came to heat before the three dots popped up to show that Tommy was replying. Tommy could think fast—type fast. But he couldn't feel fast. **What would you have said?**

The million-dollar question. **That I had no idea. And I'm going to need time to process.**

I'm sorry.

Jonah flushed, the sensation strange and scratchy beneath his skin. **For thinking I'm the brightest star in Kiraly?**

The world.

Those two words stole his heartbeat—then returned it with a neat thud. **I would say wow, but you told me not to use that word about you.**

Tommy didn't reply. Not while Jonah poured the milk into a mug of cocoa and sugar, switched off the kitchen light, or padded back to the bed.

Please don't freak out. Jonah sat cross-legged with his back against the headboard, mug in one hand, phone in the other. **Just let me get my head around it.**

You're pretending it's okay, but it's not.

Pretty sure it's up to me whether or not it's okay.

I meant, Tommy replied, **it's not okay with me.**

Jonah flinched, instantly hurt, and spilled hot chocolate onto the sheets. Confused, he set the mug on the bedside table and settled back long enough to type: **It's not okay with you that you like me?**

No. God. Jonah.

His breath caught. Reading his own name in Tommy's text twisted something inside him—tight and fluttery, like people holding hands in his stomach, stroking each other's knuckles with their thumbs. He set the phone aside to grab a dishtowel, and when he settled back down, Tommy had sent another text.

It's not okay that I've ruined our friendship over this.

Jonah frowned as a months-old wound started weeping. **But it's okay for you to ruin it by moving overseas and cutting me off without an explanation?**

Fuck.

With a groan, Jonah pressed a hand over his face. He shouldn't have sent that. Not now that he knew why Tommy had done it. Leaving Jonah behind had been Tommy's lumbering attempt to set himself free.

I take that back, Jonah texted, all too easily picturing Tommy's self-disgust. The arrow between his dark brows. The fierce set of his jaw and distant blue stare. **What are you looking at right now?**

God, I'm a prick.

Five things, Tommy.

Jesus. But then he started typing again, and Jonah sipped his chocolate while he waited. **My phone. The city. The moon. It's risen now. The moon's reflection on the lake. And the dark shadow of the mountains.**

You can see all that? Jonah looked up. The bookshelf across the room practically raised a bored eyebrow back at him.

I'm in my study. It's a round room. Panoramic views. In the tallest tower.

Wow. Jonah had wondered what was in that tower. **Do you ever let down your golden hair?**

I did. Tonight. Bad idea. Never again.

Okay, Tommy was still freaking out. **What can you**

smell?

You don't need to do this. I'm not panicking.

Jonah breathed in as he typed. **I can smell onion and spices from the takeaway shop down the street. The timber tang from some of the furniture in here. That damp, almost earthy smell that hair gets from water outdoors. And cocoa, cos I'm drinking hot chocolate.**

You make the best hot chocolate.

Jonah's chest ached. He wanted to pass his mug to Tommy and watch his face soften as he breathed it in.

I'm drinking beer, Tommy wrote next. **All I can taste.**

Hey now. This barmaid is offended.

I meant all I can taste is hops and yeast and barley and bitter melon.

Jonah smiled. **Better.**

Tommy didn't reply immediately. But the silence felt less tense. **I should have told you sooner.**

That's not fair. You can't change the way you felt, and you didn't feel ready until now.

Jonah swore he heard Tommy's quiet huff. **Stop being so understanding.**

Do you mean that?

No, Tommy sent, and the word looked lonely. **Of course not.**

Sighing, Jonah rested the phone on his lap. Maybe Tommy *had* wanted to tell him before now; maybe he'd tried. Had there been moments that Jonah hadn't known were moments? A silence where Tommy had braced himself—only for Jonah to start some meaningless conversation and leave the opening slipping away through Tommy's fingers?

I tried to tell you before I left, Tommy texted. **I was thrown off by Charlie.**

Charlie? *Oh.* Jonah's face heated, though he wasn't sure why. It wasn't embarrassment or regret or guilt. Or maybe it was. Because thinking back on that morning with the knowledge that Tommy liked him . . . it was almost distressing to realize how it must have hurt Tommy and—

Wait. **You tried to tell me?**

Yes.

When? How?

I asked if there was a reason I should stay.

Jonah had replayed that morning's conversation so many times, he knew it word for word. **Even if the reason was small or silly or impossible?**

Three dots appeared and disappeared. Appeared and disappeared. Then: **Yes.**

This doesn't feel like any of those things, Tommy.

Tommy's silence ate a hole through Jonah's breastbone.

Tommy. Jonah shifted, putting down his mug and shuffling until he was lying on his side again. **I know Charlie was there. And that was weird. But you knew that he was just passing through. I didn't feel anything for him.**

After a while, Tommy sent a question mark.

Well. It's just that . . . you asking me if there's a reason you should stay in Sage Haven isn't the same as telling me you like me and wanting to know if I feel the same.

You don't feel the same.

I don't know that, do I?

Tommy's delay seemed startled. **Uh. Yes?**

No. It's like . . . say you want to eat pie, but instead of asking if I also want to eat pie, you ask what I feel like eating. And maybe I'm not craving pie, or maybe I've never considered that pie would ever let me eat it, or would want me to eat it, because I always thought pie was straight, so it's never been an option that would spring to mind. So when I answer that I'm not hungry, you can't assume that means I don't want pie. You'd have to actually ask if I felt like eating pie.

Jonah reread his own text several times after sending it. It was a good point.

Eventually, Tommy wrote: **I've missed you so much.**

Eyes growing hot, Jonah drew the phone closer, running his other hand over his tattoo. **Same.**

But I can't go back. We can't be friends like we used to be. I can't do it.

I know. Can you give me time to figure it out?

Figure what out?

Whether I'm into you, too.

You'd know if you were.

I don't know that I'm not, he countered.

Surely it was possible to develop feelings without a lightning bolt striking him silly. Jonah couldn't assume he'd know if he liked Tommy. Didn't affection come in many forms? Maybe the way he liked people was different to what he'd always imagined. Maybe it was slow and secret, like ageing or his dash of chili powder in brownies. He already knew he could spend every second of every day with Tommy and that would be okay. More than okay. But that was what it meant to be best friends. Jonah wanted to share things with him, like jokes and hard times and breakfast. But again—best friends. He frowned at the small photo at the top of the screen as suspicion nudged him in the side. Tommy was looking at the camera, unsmiling, but soft around the eyes. *Don't be a grump,* Jonah remembered saying with a laugh as he'd taken the photo. *I'll have to look at this every time you call.* How Jonah had lasted four months without him, he had no idea, because even now, just hours after being with him, Jonah felt achy with the need to see his face and—

"Oh," he said.

This was starting to taste a lot like chili powder.

You've had time to figure it out, he texted. **Why can't I?**

Jonah. Tommy seemed frustrated.

I've never let myself consider you that way. The possibility was a doorway he'd never noticed let alone approached. He could see it now; the edges glowed. It wouldn't lead far, not when Tommy was a prince, but Jonah had always tried to be true to himself no matter the hard road. And the question right now was whether Jonah could like Tommy. Not where they could go from there. **You were my straight best friend. You were off-limits. That part of me didn't let itself look at you. It's never even seen you before.**

What are you suggesting?

Jonah knew that tone—knew the way Tommy's top lip curled with sarcasm.

You're going to check me out?

Yes, Jonah replied before he lost his nerve. **Would that be okay?**

It was torture.

Tommy took over an hour to respond.

Jonah typed and deleted a dozen texts. Prompts. Questions. Requests for Tommy to tell him three things he could hear, but he left him alone. Tommy hadn't expected this. He'd prepared for rejection—not the possibility of Jonah checking him out. Unabashedly eyeing Tommy over to discover how his own body reacted. Taking in his lean-hipped stride, the tight flex and release of his ass. The unrelenting breadth of his torso; the wide shoulders that had instinctively thrilled Jonah as Tommy had stood so close in the water . . .

Jonah's pulse stuttered as he grazed a palm over his own chest, right where Tommy had pressed their joined hands. His mouth felt hotter by the second.

He was on his third hot chocolate when his phone finally pinged.

One little word that took a hard left away from friendship and raced them toward something else entirely.

Yes.

7

Tommy woke to the quiet chime of his message tone.

His room was still dark, the sheets sleep-warmed around him. He moved before he could overthink it, reaching for his phone beneath the pillow even as his stomach bottomed out. This was it. The fallout. Jonah probably hadn't slept, instead checking Tommy out in old photos and videos on his phone, straightening out this emotional tangle one strand at a time, crafting the gentlest letdown in the history of rejections, something sweet and thoughtful and heart-wrenching that started with—

A photo of waffles.

That's pesto! The text read. **This place is hidden down a little laneway opposite my apartment and they do savory waffles!** It ended with a head explosion emoji.

Not a rejection.

Exhaling hard, Tommy sat up against the cushioned bedhead. The promise of light hinted at the cracks in his curtains, but sunrise looked a while away. With a knot in his chest, he switched on the bedside lamp and scrolled through last night's message thread. If he'd thought about it, he could have guessed that Jonah's generous heart would offer Tommy comfort before he'd even come to terms with the confession himself. But in literally no universe would Tommy have expected Jonah to ask for time to work out whether he could like Tommy back.

It was a terrible plan.

It would hurt Tommy to feel Jonah's eyes on him—and humiliate him when he fell short.

Jonah's pie analogy had been endearing, but attraction didn't work like that. Not when they'd spent almost every day of their lives together. Tommy wasn't pie that had never been on the menu—he was the breakfast granola that had always been overlooked for one, simple, conclusive reason.

Jonah wasn't interested.

And it would hurt them both less if Jonah would just accept that.

The sun isn't even up, Tommy wrote back, a response with exactly zero emotional risk.

As if I could sleep. Blushing emoji. **Thankfully no one around here sleeps either.**

An uncomfortable heat pushed Tommy out of bed. His confession had kept Jonah up all night. **No sleep? Feeling okay?**

Not even a little sulky. I'm going to keep exploring the city today, Jonah sent. **Will share photos.**

Photos. Great. That was exactly what Tommy wanted from him. He made a noise of frustration but couldn't bring himself to ask Jonah to just rip off the Band-Aid.

What are your plans, Tommy?

Aside from waiting for Jonah to admit they had no future?

Meetings. Rubbing his gritty eyes, Tommy tried to recall his schedule. A private seminar on persuasive technology after breakfast. Discussions on transferable skills in manual labor before lunch. Preliminary talks on new international industry partnerships in the afternoon.

Cool. Then a photo of an empty plate. **Off to explore! Will message again soon!**

And he did.

Every time Tommy checked his phone in breaks and between meetings, there was a new photo from Jonah. A grinning selfie from a lakeside café, yachts and bikinis and bright blue sky in the background. A steep, curving laneway where each door was painted a different color and flowering bougainvillea spilled from low rooftop gardens. A bowl of fruit salad that looked worthy of a royal banquet, with berries and peaches and mangoes all coated in passionfruit pulp and fresh mint. Another selfie with a young, silver-haired woman in front of a bakery.

Each time, Tommy returned the phone to his pocket with an ache in his throat. He had nothing to reply. Last night, he'd taken Jonah's hand and opened his heart, and today, Jonah was sending a stream of chirpy tourist photos. Tommy couldn't find the manners to pretend they were relevant.

It was midafternoon when Jonah sent him another shot. Tommy was leaving the stables after a brief visit and was setting off across the grounds with his old ranch border collies, Buck and Bull, in his wake. It was a photo of the Bearded Bunting, the pale stone exterior with an iron logo mounted above the door. A string of green bunting hung from it like a wayward kite caught in a tree, and Tommy couldn't tell whether it was quirky branding or whether an enthusiastic local had tossed it up there, but either way, it was the kind of playful flourish this city had down to an art.

Kiraly is officially somewhere over the rainbow, Jonah wrote with the full suite of colorful love heart emojis.

Tommy's steps petered out at the cold reality of those words. Jonah was enamored with Kira City in a way Tommy wished he was himself but never could be—not with the crowds and relentless energy that stymied his capacity to marvel. It was cruel, really, how much of a godsend that passion would be in the partner of a socially reclusive king.

Jonah. Tommy couldn't have thoughts like that. Not without a pained flutter in his chest, like a dream trapped in a jar, pounding against the sides. **You're acting like nothing's changed.**

Not quite, came Jonah's quick reply. **Things have changed and this is how I'm acting.**

Tommy huffed out a breath. That was a Jonah kind of distinction. **It feels like you're clinging to our friendship even though I've told you that hurts me.**

End this properly, he wanted to write. *Just do it.*

He stared at his screen, insides bundled in nerves, fingers tapping as he waited.

I'm not clinging, Tommy. This is me trying to put you at ease. That jolted a little. **I don't want you to get awkward when we next see each other. Or turn away from me before I've even started looking at you.**

Tommy tightened his grip on the phone.

Jonah still intended to play this out.

"Damn it," he muttered, because even though he knew Jonah was only dragging out the inevitable—even though Tommy *felt* the hard grip of that truth inside him—he also knew that sometimes his body lied. Knew his anxiety and his body were a team; that this symbiosis could scramble his survival instincts on a fundamental level. Both had taught him self-preservation—that avoidance meant safety. And right now, the dread-clench in his gut was telling him he wouldn't suffer true rejection if he didn't actually offer Jonah his heart.

But if he took the risk . . .

The payoff could be Jonah.

Tommy covered his face with his hand, fingertips digging in around the edges.

No part of him could know what Jonah didn't even know himself.

Also, Jonah texted, drawing Tommy from his thoughts. **These photos could give us something to talk about in case we both go blank. Maybe you should send me something too?**

Distracted, Tommy lifted his phone, took a photo of the palace from his viewpoint near the stables, and sent it.

Jonah's response came fast. **Is that where you are right now??**

Yes, he replied, and almost passed out when Jonah sent back a photo of the main entrance hall of the palace accompanied by three exclamation marks.

But. Tommy sent the word by accident, sudden alarm making his fingers clumsy. **But you're at the bar.**

I took that photo earlier! Didn't want you to feel pressure to see me now if you were in a meeting. I've just finished visiting Kris. Are you free?

"Jesus Christ," Tommy said as his insides locked tight.

Unless you don't want to see me? Which is fine too.

Tommy pinched the bridge of his nose. **I always want to see you, Jonah.**

I'll come meet you!

Shit. **Okay.**

Dazed and bordering on distressed, Tommy spun to his guards a short distance away.

"Your Highness?" Nyaring asked, her voice low as they approached.

"Jonah's here." Had the horses ruffled his hair? Dislodged his shirt? This was the first time Jonah was going to look at him *like that*, and despite believing it wouldn't end well, Tommy still wanted to look good. Still wanted Jonah to appreciate him, even if he didn't desire him. Face hot, Tommy asked, "Am I a mess?"

They blinked as if the question didn't make sense.

"Ah, no," Zoltan said with a small shake of his head. "Quite the opposite, Your Highness."

Tommy pushed his shirtsleeves over his elbows, looking between them.

"Perhaps we'd better go meet him?" Nyaring suggested.

His insides lurched. Right. "Yes."

Pivoting, he set off toward the palace, the dogs trotting at his heels. Hedges as tall as his chest lined the garden paths, and gardeners moved about quietly. He'd walked this route dozens of times, but the glare of the sun felt harsher than usual, the crunch of pebbles louder underfoot.

He had a clear view of the large doors to the west atrium when Jonah strode out in conversation with the head butler. Tommy's pulse burst brightly at the sight of Jonah's easy smile, his lean strength, his dark hair raked distractedly off to one side. As always, he wore his glasses—the same frames that had sent Tommy sprawling face-first into adoration four years ago. Jonah paused at the lip of the steps to the garden, looking out and seeming to reel at the sheer size of the grounds.

Jonah's question carried faintly. "Where do you think he is?"

The butler murmured in response, and Jonah's gaze locked on Tommy.

"Oh my God." Jonah's eyes blew wide, and his voice rose to a shout. "Buck! Bull!"

The dogs jerked beside Tommy, heads snapping up. With startled barks, they raced toward Jonah in a blur as he took the steps two at a time to meet them. The collies pulled up rapidly as Jonah reached flat ground, circling his legs, yipping and whining, tails moving so fast they were quivering more than wagging.

"Hey, you two!" Laughing, Jonah dropped to his knees, and a moment later he was on his back, saying, "You guys, I can't believe it," and "I've missed you so much," as they climbed over him, still whining and licking every part of him they could reach.

God. Tommy would never see anything as wholly good in his life as Jonah's unchecked wholesomeness.

Reaching them, Tommy crouched with one knee on the path and watched.

"Just a sec, Tommy," Jonah said, then made a sound of mock disgust as Buck licked his mouth—which only encouraged the dog to keep doing it. Laughing again, Jonah pushed his hands deep into their coats and rubbed hard. "You guys are the best thing I've seen today."

Tommy's heart flinched.

Jonah wasn't wearing his usual denim jeans and shirt. His top was a blue scoop neck, short-sleeved in jersey cotton, and currently being dragged off one shoulder under Bull's paw. It was a cut that tended to drive Tommy out of his mind—something about Jonah's exposed collarbones and the handspan of bare chest beneath. Who'd have thought Tommy would be into male décolletage, but there was so much he wanted to do to that flat, smooth skin, and looking didn't even make the list. Then there were those jeans. Those. Jeans. Black, fitted, and tight as paint. Tommy lost a breath wondering how long they'd take to peel off—then lost blood flow to his brain imagining what he'd do after that.

"Alright, off!" Jonah said, and the dogs shuffled back with excited, low barks, giving him space to sit up—until he lifted his arms wide in invitation and they moved back in to lean against him, tongues hanging out and tails whooshing. "Oh my God," Jonah said again, pressing his face into Bull's neck. "Sorry, Tommy."

Sorry for his blatant affection for Tommy's dogs? "Take your time."

Buck was licking Jonah's ear as he said, "I have a feeling this isn't how people normally greet princes."

"I'd say you're right."

Dodging the dog's tongue, Jonah lifted his head to grin at him. "Hi."

Tommy smiled back, keeping his gaze steady. "Hey."

Jonah gave a small laugh and looked down with a blush.

Tommy stared. At that soft laugh; the color on his friend's cheeks. "Did I just make you uncomfortable?"

"No." Jonah flicked a dark-eyed glance up at him, then down again. "It just feels real all of a sudden."

Real. This was not the *real* Tommy had imagined. Pinched expressions and apologetic glances, yes—not blushes and lowered lashes.

"Okay, off! I mean it this time." Grinning, Jonah extricated himself and stood, straightening his shirt and brushing the dog hair off his clothes. Tommy rose to his feet and forced himself not to watch the firm slide of Jonah's hands over his body. "I'm all yours."

With no safe answer to that, Tommy nodded.

"Tommy." Jonah's attention shifted distractedly to Nyaring and Zoltan positioned nearby. Then he moved in and lowered his voice. "Is this still okay with you?"

Tommy's blood warmed at just how close Jonah stood. He smelled faintly of lemons—he and Kris had shared the same tartlets that Tommy had been served in his afternoon meeting. "Is it okay that you check me out?"

Wordless, Jonah nodded up at him.

No. "Yes."

"Good. And I'd like to flirt with you, too."

Tommy's pulse kicked. *Sure, let's make this even harder.* "To see whether it fits?"

"That's right," Jonah said, and bit his bottom lip in a way Tommy felt low in his abdomen.

Holy God. "Just don't—tease me."

Jonah's eyes widened and he gave a small shake of his head. "I won't."

Maybe not on purpose. Tommy took a step back and gestured the way Jonah had come. "My next meeting doesn't start for over an hour." He'd intended to use the time to prepare, but he already knew exactly what to cover. "Can I show you around?"

With a smile, Jonah said, "Sure."

An impromptu tour. Tommy could do that.

"Hey." Jonah pointed to where tall panels blocked off an exterior section of the palace's west wing. "What's happening there?"

"That's where the balcony collapsed." Unease stitched along Tommy's spine at the reminder that the man responsible was still missing. "Construction has stopped. We're deciding how to continue respectfully." One of his many priorities. Recently, he'd sat out here with a copy of the old project plans, needing to face the impact of the tragedy to sense how to best proceed. He still wasn't sure.

"Oh." Jonah was staring at it. "I'm so sorry."

"Thank you," Tommy said. "Buck. Bull. Stay outside." He set off, and Jonah silently fell into step beside him.

As they entered the west atrium, Tommy became hyperaware of his inherited wealth. He was always aware of it on some level, a severe discomfort or a distracted curiosity depending on his mental state, but now he saw it afresh through Jonah's eyes. The exquisitely carved plasterwork decorating the walls, elaborate and edged in gold, the classic half-naked statues posing in the three-tiered indoor fountain, and the stained-glass skylights high above. If the palace view alone had cowed Jonah last night, his confidence wouldn't stand a chance at the interior's extravagance.

It wasn't until Tommy was leading him along the wide, brightly lit principal corridor—royal blue carpet on marble indicating it was one of the main arteries of the palace that all eventually led to the central grand staircase—that he realized Jonah was too preoccupied to notice much of their surroundings at all.

Jonah was looking at *him*. Without subtlety, the angle of his head curious, exploratory, and just like that, Tommy didn't know what to do with his own face. He felt stiff and flushed and couldn't get the hinge of his jaw to relax. *Really sexy. This is great.*

They were approaching the grand staircase when Tommy finally met Jonah's eyes. "Don't miss a step," he murmured, arching a brow.

With a shameless smile, Jonah spared a glance for the path ahead. "I don't know how you've liked me without me noticing."

Tommy halted.

Surprised, Jonah did the same a step later, turning back to face him.

"This is how," Tommy said.

Confused, Jonah smiled again. "You—you're just looking at me."

At his full lips, the dark shade of his hair, the sleek line of his jaw. The sweet warmth of his eyes; the minor hollow beneath his cheekbones where Tommy longed to slide his nose. "I'm just looking at you," he agreed, after a long pause. "That's all I've ever needed to do for you to take my breath away."

Awe slid like filtered light over Jonah's features.

"This way," Tommy said, and veered toward the staircase.

"Wait." Jonah was frowning after him. "Why are we going there? Isn't the tower at the eastern end?"

"Tower?" Tommy intended to show Jonah a few of his favored spaces. The sunroom on the first floor. The second-story balcony overlooking the autumn courtyard. The library. Short of the throne room, the royal study was probably the most imposing room in the palace. "I'm not sure—"

"It's just—" Jonah said, holding his stare. "I'd prefer somewhere we can be properly alone. I don't want anyone to overhear us."

Tommy's heart gave a sudden pound. Jonah wanted to be alone and entirely out of earshot while he worked out if he could like Tommy back?

Jonah frowned. "Why do you look like I just suggested we jump from the tower window?"

Holding tight to his composure, Tommy said, "Maybe that's how it feels."

Before Jonah could give voice to his deepening frown, Tommy set off again on a changed course toward the east wing.

His skin prickled as Jonah's attention returned to him.

"You know, it doesn't feel wrong," Jonah said, "for you to be here."

That landed oddly in Tommy's chest. It shouldn't have. Those were words he'd longed to hear—acknowledgement that this role seemed tailor-made for the stable part of his mind. But they were the right words coming from the wrong person. The sincerity in Jonah's voice only made Tommy intently aware of the social void between them. "No," he agreed quietly. "It doesn't."

Jonah resumed his silent assessment until they were almost on the fourth floor. "So, Tommy." He eyed the polished bannister beside him but didn't touch it. "You know your way around the whole palace?"

"Yes." On the landing, Tommy struck right. He'd calculated the simplest route to the tower that would avoid the most ostentatious architecture and design.

"You've memorized it all?"

"Yes." Every room, secret passage, and storage space. It had taken weeks of floorplan revision and late-night explorations when he'd first arrived, but he'd hated the thought of becoming turned around in his own home.

"Do you know where all seventy-five bathrooms are?" Jonah asked.

Startled, Tommy looked at him, slowing their pace along a connecting gallery. "I'd have to count," he said. "Do you need one?"

Jonah grinned. "Buck did get a winning shot at my mouth."

Tommy breathed out a laugh. "He's fast. There's a bathroom up ahead."

"Okay." Jonah's smile faded into an expression that almost looked shy. "And do you know where all one-hundred-and . . . thirty-eight staff bedrooms are?"

Technically, it was one-hundred-and-*forty*-eight, but Tommy would deliver another speech before he'd correct him. "They're in the servants wing past the lower courtyard," he answered. "But more importantly, Jonah Wood, have you been studying palace facts?"

Jonah's cheeks darkened as he smiled. "Only from the brochure."

The image of Jonah poring over a palace brochure, his dark brow creased in concentration as he recited facts under his breath, was a vision so helpless in its perfection that Tommy turned his head the other way.

After a brief stop at the bathroom, Tommy led him to a corridor where the high windows spilled afternoon sunlight on their feet. Their boots echoed off the polished floor, the twin sound decisive yet familiar in the otherwise quiet halls. His chest ached. If only their footsteps could couple and entwine their paths forever.

They came to a halt at a large carved archway marking the entrance to a spiral staircase that wound like a snail shell out of sight.

Tommy stood back and said, "After you."

"No, you first." Somehow, Jonah managed to hook a thumb in that painted waistband. "I'd hate to get lost on the way up."

Tommy arched a brow. "It's one staircase leading to a single room at the top."

"Well." With a laugh, Jonah glanced to where Tommy's guards had moved forward to bracket the archway. "You know me."

Yes, he did. And Jonah's sense of direction was faultless. Then, with a zip of shock down his spine, Tommy realized his intention. "*Jonah.*"

Unrepentant, his friend's dark eyes gleamed. "You did say yes. Twice."

Dear God. "I assumed you'd be subtle."

"I *was* being subtle until you stopped and made us talk about it."

Tommy's skin burned. "I didn't—"

Suddenly Jonah's hand was on his forearm and his mouth over Tommy's ear. "I know you haven't done this before, and it feels uncomfortable, but it's just me, Tommy. And I'm asking you to let me look at your ass, because I'm pretty sure I want to and you must have looked at mine before, so really, it's only fair." He withdrew, and Tommy's ear was still hot, so hot from Jonah's breath and the intimacy of his demand that Tommy raised a hand to trap it.

He said, as levelly as he could manage, "Follow me."

Never, in his entire life, had he been more aware of his own ass. The stairs seemed to stretch on forever, a never-ending call for his feet to rise and fall, urging his body upward and tightening his jean-clad rear in the process. Real or imagined, Jonah's fixed attention spread like an electric hum from his hamstrings right up to the base of his neck.

At the top, he half-expected Jonah to crest the final step with sparkling eyes and a grin—like this was all a big joke—but instead he followed a few steps behind, adjusting his glasses with flushed cheeks, avoiding Tommy's waiting gaze.

"My study," Tommy said, watching him.

There was no hiding his status up here. No pretending he wasn't royalty. The wide, round room was furnished for a king, meticulously procured and arranged—leather couches, wingback chairs, bookshelves of old volumes with gold-printed spines, and the stately desk that presided over it all.

Jonah didn't physically step back, but his posture drew in on itself. "One desk?" His hand slipped around his opposite bicep. "You said this was the tallest tower, right? Shouldn't Mark work here?"

That question thudded against Tommy's conscience. He'd told Frankie to keep his possible ascension quiet, so that he could tell Jonah himself. But the people of Kiraly might ultimately decide they wanted to abolish the monarchy. Why give Jonah another reason to feel inadequate unless Tommy's rise to kingship was certain? Their differences were already difficult enough.

"We share," he answered. It wasn't a lie.

Jonah nodded. Then he said, "Wow," and made a beeline for the nearest city-view window.

Cautious, Tommy closed the door.

It was an unapologetic view of sovereign country. Mountains, the entirety of Kira City, verdant farmland beyond—Jonah stared in silence, his posture stunned. Eventually, he angled his face down at his shoulder, including Tommy without looking at him. "I'm trying to find my apartment, but I can't get my bearings. I think it's hidden behind that crest." His pointing hand was slightly unsteady.

"I think," Tommy said, and moved to stand near him with a raised finger, "it's there."

He *knew* it was there. He'd already stood in this exact spot, angst-twisted and aching as he'd mapped the drive to Jonah's front door.

"Where?" Jonah moved in to share Tommy's line of sight. It was a familiar approach—Jonah seeking comfort because the outside world mattered less the closer that he got to Tommy. The problem had always been that needing Tommy when he felt weak meant nothing if he didn't want Tommy when he felt strong.

"Oh, yeah," Jonah said, adjusting his glasses as he craned his neck. "There's the yellow roof."

Tommy focused on keeping his breath steady as Jonah shifted closer still, sending a shiver down his entire right side.

Then Jonah said, "Tom," and turned around, bending his elbows and resting his forearms on the deep windowsill. A casual pose with his back to the world and his eyes on Tommy. "Are you okay today?"

Uh-huh. Tommy was going to answer *that* honestly. "Sure."

"Good." Jonah lifted a boot and pressed the sole against the wall. Then, with a smile tucked cutely beneath those thick lashes, he said, "Because I'm a bit upset with you."

Careful. Tommy's brain almost short-circuited at that look. *He's flirting.*

"Are you?" Pressing a palm to the sill, Tommy slowly angled his shoulders to face him. They were a body-width apart—if the body measurement in question was closer to Jonah's lean build than Tommy's breadth. He let his voice drop. "I'm sorry to hear it."

"You told me last night when I didn't have my glasses on." Jonah sounded slightly breathless. "I couldn't see your face properly."

Oh. Tommy stilled. "That wasn't deliberate."

"Maybe not. But it would be deliberate for you not to tell me again now."

Yes, it would.

"Jonah." His name came out as deep as dark water. "I like you so much, I'm never not aware of it."

Their eyes met, close and uncensored. As Jonah's mouth parted, Tommy bottled the urge to reach out and slide his thumb over his full bottom lip. The urge was stronger now that Jonah might allow it, just to see how it felt, and Tommy's fingers twitched—then balled. *No.* Jonah might allow it, but it didn't mean he wanted it.

"It's felt so obvious," Tommy said. "Sometimes I've been sure you must know."

"You thought—oh, Tommy." Jonah laughed, all pink cheeks and smile lines, and for a moment, Tommy didn't care about anything but the mouth and breath and happiness between those brackets. "Nothing about you is obvious. I have *no idea* what you're thinking. Ever."

Guilt crept beneath Tommy's skin. Jonah freely admitted that he couldn't guess at the thoughts in Tommy's head—yet Tommy had spent years firmly believing he knew exactly what Jonah thought of him.

Tommy braced. "Do you want to know what I'm thinking right now?"

"Yes." Jonah's throat moved on a swallow; his focus was unwavering. "Yes."

"I'm thinking," Tommy said, and almost stopped at the hammering in his heart. "That I've never been more nervous in my entire life to stand this close to you."

With a speculative hum, Jonah narrowed his eyes. "You don't seem that nervous."

"More evidence you have no idea what I'm thinking."

Jonah smiled.

Not sure what else to say, Tommy returned his gaze out the window.

"Standing close together," Jonah said. "That's what you're nervous about now?"

"Yes."

"Not my pants?"

"Not"—Tommy blinked, then finished with a slow sidelong glance at him—"your pants."

Jonah feigned scandal as he said, "They're *so* tight."

"I hadn't noticed," he said as steadily as he could.

For that, he received a grin like quicksand. "Do you like them?"

"Yes." Tommy looked down at Jonah's legs, and up again, blood hot. "But I don't think they'd fit me."

Jonah's eyes sparkled. "The way my green shirt doesn't fit you?"

Tommy cashed in every credit he had in restraint to not look again. "I suspect they would fit me even worse than the shirt."

"Hm." And then Jonah followed through on his promise from the night before.

He checked Tommy out.

He started low, seeming to assess how the skinny-leg cut

MADELINE ASH

would cope with the bulge of Tommy's calves, then up, over his knees to the muscle of his thighs. Tommy's breathing changed, stumbling as his friend's gaze collided with his body in a way it never had before: intimate, intentional. Color rising, Jonah murmured, "I'd say you're right," as his stare at last inched to the weight at Tommy's crotch. He seemed to get stuck there, his attention pressing down like an experienced palm, and helpless beneath that phantom pressure, Tommy was horrified to feel himself start to react.

"That's enough." His command startled them both. Jonah looked up then quickly away, and Tommy pressed both hands against the windowsill and stared blindly at the city. "I asked you not to tease me."

"I wasn't teasing you," Jonah said, but added, "I'm sorry."

The surface was warm under Tommy's palms. How much hotter would Jonah's mouth would be against his? "I appreciate that you're trying this."

But it's not going to work.

"I'm not having to try very hard," Jonah said softly.

Tommy curled his fingers into fists. Without turning, he said, "Do you mean that?"

"Do I mean what? Tommy. Are you trying to ask whether I'm toying with you?" Jonah sounded upset as he straightened, forearms lifting off the windowsill. "No. And you know that I'm not. I really want to know how it feels to be liked by you. I'm getting an idea. You keep saying incredible things. But the second you say them, you pull away like you don't *want* me to feel how true they are."

God.

Jonah saw straight to the heart of everything.

He was right. Tommy did keep pulling away—but he had to move *in.* Even though it was terrifying. Even though Jonah might conclude he didn't like it and reject Tommy the second he fully

140

let down his guard. Even though it was something his body was clenching and churning against, Tommy had to do it.

In case Jonah *didn't* reject him.

In case he liked it.

Alarmed exhilaration spiked in the pit of Tommy's stomach. It swelled up and across his torso, surged like a current through his bones and muscles and cartilage. Like a fool, he'd been throwing away this chance, too used to experiencing desire as a secret instead of an action. Too used to playing it safe. He knew how he *wanted* to act—he'd fantasized about taking Jonah enough times to know that if he let his guard down, his desire would be decisive, his inexperience irrelevant.

And that was what Jonah wanted.

Not to be told how Tommy felt—but to *feel* it.

"Jonah." His voice was low. Purpose thrummed in his veins, drowning out the whisper of fear. "I'm going to try something."

Jonah's breath caught as Tommy faced him.

"I'm going to come on to you."

Jonah hoped his memory was getting all of this.

He didn't want to forget a second.

Not the way Tommy had just spoken like a promise Jonah hadn't known he'd waited all his life to hear. Not the way his pulse was fluttering, fast and focused, as if it had finally found someone worthy of making it race. And not the growing suspicion that their friendship had always held them on the outside of their true bond, looking in; a bond that burned and swelled and declared that if they'd been inseparable before, Jonah had better get ready to learn the true meaning of the word.

He was ready to learn a lot of things about Tommy.

It was like school all over again. He used to get distracted by details and forget to focus on the actual subject. Right now, he should be trying to comprehend the fact that Tommy liked him; that Tommy was a legitimately powerful prince who liked him. But instead, all Jonah could think about was everything he wanted to learn about Tommy.

Physical, intimate things.

Like where did he wish Jonah would touch him? How would he like to be kissed? What parts of his body would shiver under Jonah's hands? His spine? Behind his ears? Hipbones? What would he say as Jonah touched him? And what sound would he make if he wanted Jonah to touch him lower? When he got hard from Jonah's hand around him?

When he came?

Jonah swallowed at the dark, determined look in Tommy's gaze. *I could find out.* He could slide his hands beneath the soft denim waistband at the back of Tommy's jeans and grasp the taut muscle that had turned his insides molten on the climb up here.

He could stay distracted by details forever.

"Jonah." Tommy's eyes looked extra blue in the summer light, enhanced by the rich teal of his shirt. "Tell me if it makes you uncomfortable."

If what *makes me uncomfortable?* Jonah nodded. *What are you going to do to me and why aren't you already doing it?*

"Or if you don't like it." Tommy watched him carefully. "Or if you want me to stop."

"I will," Jonah said quickly, *but I won't.*

"Don't let me overstep," Tommy warned.

"I think I'm more likely to push you." Many, many steps over.

Tommy's expression dried. "I know you're flirting, but you don't know what I—"

"Please, Tommy." His breath thin with anticipation. "Don't tease me either."

And then Tommy was standing directly in front of him, the low vibration of his presence pulling something taut behind Jonah's belly button. They'd stood this close a thousand times. In line at school, always each other's pair. Hanging over opposite sides of the wire fence between their properties, high school goodbyes stretching on for hours.

Yet this was like standing in front of Tommy for the first time, his intensity lighting up Jonah's insides like an electrical storm, the flashes allowing Jonah to navigate Tommy's quietly raging dark.

"Jonah," Tommy started in a new, throaty voice.

Jonah's stomach scooped so far back he swore it fell straight out the window behind him. "Wow. Yes? Hello."

Lips ghosting upward, Tommy's eye contact didn't waver. "I lied before. I'd already noticed your pants."

Heat flooded Jonah's entire body. "You had?"

"Mm." The hum came from low in Tommy's chest, a base note of appreciation as his gaze moved slowly over Jonah's face. "They look good on you."

Jonah swallowed hard. "Oh."

Tommy's attention reached Jonah's mouth, fixed with a force he'd contained all this time. "But you always look good to me."

"I do?"

"I can hardly look away. And when I do, you're all I see."

Jonah's heart seemed to melt into his bloodstream, coursing through every part of him, as if trying to find an answer to how he felt about that.

Good, he realized. *So good.*

"Would it be okay if I moved closer to you?" Tommy sounded like he wasn't quite breathing, like getting air into his lungs wasn't as important as getting closer to Jonah. At Jonah's nod, Tommy's lashes dipped, a contrast of delicate lines against his razor-cut features, and he shifted until they were toe-to-toe. It

—oh, God, there was that fresh, grassy scent again. Then Tommy looked back up and said quietly, "You feel good near me."

Jonah's head spun. He leaned more firmly against the windowsill. "Yeah," he managed. "I do."

"Do you want to know something?"

The question flared with possibility. "I want to know *everything*."

Smiling a little, Tommy murmured, "You made my favorite word."

"I what?" Jonah was distracted by Tommy's mouth. That smile was new. Small, secret, and so very soft. And all for him. "What do you mean?"

"You asked me what my favorite words were once. Do you remember?"

Jonah looked up as the memory cleared the haze in his head.

Left him cold.

It was a few years ago now, soon after Tommy had come home from college. Jonah had felt bad that he couldn't offer Tommy the clever conversation he must have had with other students, so he'd spent hours researching long and interesting words, repeating them over and over, preparing to list them as his own favorites when Tommy asked his in return.

Stupid. He'd memorized them temporarily but hadn't actually *learned* any of them.

"Yes," he answered.

"Do you remember my answer?" Tommy asked.

Tommy had taken so long to respond, Jonah remembered his own stomach sinking, sure Tommy was scrolling through his list of words, further and further down, the growing silence betraying just how far he had to go to find one he thought Jonah would know.

Embarrassed all over again, Jonah nodded.

"Will you say it for me?" Tommy's gaze had dropped to Jonah's mouth.

Not understanding, Jonah whispered, "Blue."

Are you serious? Jonah had asked, humiliation hot in his throat. *That's your favorite?*

"Pardon?" Tommy asked now, leaning in a fraction closer, his attention still on Jonah's lips.

"Blue," Jonah said again.

Tommy's torso filled on a breath. "I wanted you to ask me why, that day."

"I already knew why." Jonah's voice was small.

What he didn't know was why Tommy had brought this up. To make it clear that their minds would never match? That he liked Jonah despite them not being on the same level? Jonah snuck a glance over his shoulder at the heart-stopping drop to the world where he belonged. *As if I could forget.*

Tommy was frowning at him when he looked back around.

"Because." Jonah pushed himself up to sit on the wide sill. There. They could share eye level, at least. "You knew I wouldn't understand any of your favorite words."

"What?" For a few seconds, Tommy looked too appalled to speak. "No. God, no, that's not why. It's because—" He ran a hand over the base of his throat as if something was trapped there. "It's because of your mouth. I'd noticed the way your lips moved when you said the word *blue,* bunching into this kind of micro pout." His gaze slid to Jonah's suddenly dry mouth. "It's so fleeting, yet so kissable. I . . . sometimes I would orchestrate entire conversations just to get you to say it."

Oh. Wow.

"Like this one?" Jonah asked as *kissable* echoed right to his toes.

"Like this one." A tiny crease formed between his brows.

"Jonah. I would ask you the color of the sky every day just to watch your mouth move."

Jonah's breath caught as realization opened in him like a latch released. *Oh my God.* Tommy didn't just *like* him. All these incredible things he kept saying. Bright stars and lost breath and Jonah being all he could see. That wasn't what people said when they had a crush. That was—it was—

You don't feel the same, Tommy had texted him.

A tremble passed through Jonah's heart. No. It would seem that he didn't, because this, right now, wasn't about whether he might be able to like Tommy.

It was way, way bigger than that.

"Fuck." Tommy's expression stuttered and he pulled back. "That was too much."

"No." Jonah grabbed his wrists before he could step away, but then hesitated, not sure what to do next as he reeled.

Tommy was in love with him.

Tommy's gaze flicked, uncertain, from Jonah's face down to where Jonah held him.

Jonah swallowed, shifting, *wishing* he knew what to do, what to say, but his entire chest felt like it was beating too fast and his thoughts were one big *oh my God.*

"It was too much," Tommy murmured, and tried to tug out of his hold.

"It doesn't matter what it was." Tightening his grip despite his shock, Jonah drew Tommy back to him. Maybe not the smartest move, but his head felt inside out and he didn't want to lose this moment. It was like a whispered conversation after dark —no way was he going to fall asleep when things had finally turned vulnerable. He widened his knees. "Come here."

The column of Tommy's throat moved on a swallow as he allowed himself to be drawn between Jonah's legs, allowed Jonah to place Tommy's hands on the windowsill either side of his hips.

"This is really okay?" Tommy's question was thick with suppressed emotion. His head was angled off to one side, a small effort to keep his distance.

"Yes," Jonah said firmly.

Tommy was his best friend—and the line between them was burning like fire. Crossing it was a shock; having Tommy stand this close licked heat all the way up between Jonah's thighs. But it didn't feel wrong. It felt . . . amazing. "Yes," he said again. "It's okay."

"I understand if it's too fast."

It wasn't fast—it was thrilling, because Jonah was pretty sure Tommy hadn't stood like this with anyone else. And now he was doing it with Jonah. *With me. He's giving this to me.* The thought alone had Jonah squeezing his wrists a little tighter. "It's not too fast. I just got overwhelmed." He gave his best coy smile. "I didn't know any of that favorite word stuff was . . . true."

A strange, sweet little sound came from Tommy as he watched Jonah's lips form the last sound.

"I mean." Reaction twisted Jonah's insides like sweaty sheets. "You could have given me a clue." He paused, his bottom lip holding the shape. "That you liked the view."

Tommy smiled, disbelieving as he murmured, "What are you even saying?"

"Does it matter," Jonah asked, "to you?"

Tommy's laugh was a precious puff of air as he shook his head—and surrendered his weight to his palms. It brought him as close as they could get without touching and he stared at Jonah's mouth like he wanted to pour himself into it. "You're fucking gorgeous, you know that?"

That shot through Jonah like a burning arrow. A hot, unstoppable arc downward. "And you're smiling a lot." *Because of me. Because we're flirting and it makes you feel good.* "I like it."

"Yeah?" Tommy's breath touched his face. The blue of his

eyes was dark, growing darker still as his smile faded. He radiated an intensity that Jonah soaked up like a sponge.

I want it. Every raging storm and unlit room, every urge that made Tommy fear he'd overstep. Jonah wanted it all. When Tommy tugged questioningly against his hold, Jonah hesitated before letting him go—then gasped when Tommy cuffed his wrists in return.

The insistent grip shuddered through him. Jonah had always preferred being held than holding, and Tommy's *I've got you* grasp pressed right on his sweet spot. "This is good, Tommy," he murmured, eyes closing. "Don't let go."

With a rough sound of agreement, Tommy lowered his face, his hot breath curling over Jonah's shoulder. *Oh, God, please kiss me.* Trembling, tingling, Jonah barely resisted the impulse to press his heels into the wall and lever his hips forward. Instead, he tucked his chin down and turned his face the other way in his version of surrender. He hadn't been able to tilt his head back for a man in years, but he wanted Tommy's mouth on his bare shoulder more than the sun in the sky.

It didn't come.

"Tommy?" he whispered, opening his eyes. Tommy had gone still. The only movement was his torso expanding with each breath. "You okay?"

"I'm not doing this today." His words were strained, his posture rigid.

"You can." Jonah kept his face turned aside as he arched his back. They were so close now, and the promise of bigger contact felt like a ripcord in Tommy's hand that he—just. Wouldn't. Pull. "Just a little."

"No," Tommy said, more firmly. "I don't want to rush this."

Because he'd never been with someone before.

Jonah winced. Big oops for forgetting *that* so fast.

"Okay, of course, yeah," Jonah said, straightening. "Let's not rush."

Tommy kept hold of Jonah's wrists as he pulled back to look at him. His pupils were wide, his breath quick. "For next time, is there anywhere off-limits?"

Ah. So Tommy had noticed.

But *oh my God,* he'd said *next time*.

"Not really." Jonah strove for casual. "Just my throat."

Pain flashed in Tommy's eyes. There and gone. "Okay."

"No hands. No teeth." *No lips,* Jonah usually added. "Maybe lips. But not right away."

"Okay."

"Back of my neck is fine," he added, because hands so often ended up there and he'd found it easier to just deal with it.

But Tommy didn't move. "It doesn't have to be fine."

Jonah hesitated. It was just . . . the medics had applied such awful pressure to his throat wound when he'd been airlifted. Although consciousness had been slippery that night, he'd never forget the suffocating sense of that compression. He shrugged helplessly. "I guess it's not fine. What about you? Is there anywhere—"

They both jolted at a delicate knock on the door.

"Damn it." Tommy closed his eyes briefly. "My meeting." Then he released Jonah's arms and called out, "One minute, please."

"Oh," a young woman answered, sounding confused. "Alright."

Something tight balled up beneath Jonah's rib cage, and mildly panicked, he slid from the sill to his feet. "I'll go."

Tommy's expression switched off as he stepped back. His jaw set and his square stance gave nothing away, unreadable once again. "Thank you for coming."

Jonah laughed and poked him in the arm. "Don't get weird."

"I—" With a huff of breath, Tommy ran a hand over his mouth. "I don't know what to do now."

One thing was pretty obvious. "We can safely say I'm into this."

"Jonah." Avoiding his eye, Tommy lowered his hand to tug on his rolled-up shirt cuff. "I'm worried I'll be too intense for you."

"I'm familiar with your intensity." Jonah poked him again. "I've known you for most of my life, you goose."

Tommy's attention locked on where Jonah's finger touched him. Something about his focus prickled all the way up Jonah's arm and landed with a hot thud in the pit of his stomach. It made Jonah want to pull his hand away—and then offer it up to Tommy to direct at his will.

"This will be different," Tommy said quietly.

Oh. Anticipation shuddered low in Jonah's abdomen. "I can handle it."

"I don't want to be something you have to handle. It's about you deserving it. Liking it. Wanting it."

Jonah felt breathless with each phrase that came out of Tommy's mouth. "I want it."

Unimpressed, Tommy pinned him with a sharp blue gaze. "You're just saying that because it sounds sexy."

"Yes, Tommy, the words coming out of your mouth are sounding sexy to me. Isn't that what we were trying to figure out?"

A dart formed between Tommy's brows.

"I meant the part where I begged you not to let me go," Jonah said, face flushing.

Soft disbelief flickered like a question in Tommy's eyes. Then he swept his arm wide to gesture to the tower room. "Even though . . ."

"Um." Well. Frowning, he shifted his weight back and

glanced around. Obviously, the palace wasn't somewhere Jonah would ever belong. This room alone made him uneasy, with the fancy books and the serious chairs and the desk designed for someone powerful. He would *never* want to sit at a desk like that. Or any desk. Jonah liked working outside of his head, not inside it, and the last thing he'd—

There he went again, focusing on odd details instead of the actual subject.

Was he okay pursuing this when Tommy was royalty?

"I can't really get my head around it," he answered, cheeks heating. *But I want my arms around you.* "I can try harder, if you want? And let you know. Or maybe—because we're just seeing how we go, right? So maybe it doesn't matter right now?"

"No." After a moment, Tommy shook his head. "Of course not. If you're okay with it for now, then it doesn't matter."

"Okay." Jonah slid an arm over the growing tightness in his middle. "It's just a lot to take in at once."

"I know."

"Should I come back, Tomas?" the woman asked through the door.

"Sorry, Ava, just a second," Tommy called, holding Jonah's gaze. Then he lowered his voice and said coarsely, "I don't want you to leave."

Oh. *That* explained this tension—Jonah didn't want to leave either. His body was protesting, curling up around the moment he'd have to walk away. "Neither do I," he said, and did his best attempt at doe-eyed. "Promise you'll respond to my messages from now on?"

He'd nailed the look, judging by how quickly Tommy's hand went to the phone in his pocket. "I will."

"And that you won't start doubting that I actually want this. Because I do."

Mouth curving wryly, Tommy nodded.

"And—" Jonah stepped into him, placing a hand on the distinct muscle of his forearm and rising to speak against his ear. He'd done this on impulse downstairs. This time, he did it out of sheer desperation to be close again. "Promise you'll kiss me the next time I see you."

It was an effort to pull back, but he was rewarded with Tommy covering his ear again, like he was trying to trap Jonah's voice inside him. His blue gaze was electric when it landed on Jonah's mouth. "If that's what you want."

"It is," Jonah said.

Tommy cleared his throat and gestured toward the door.

"I miss you already," Jonah murmured as they crossed the room, that truth now a ferocious tangle beneath his breastbone. And it had only been one day. How must it feel to part after years of aching for someone and finally having them within reach?

Gripping the door handle, Tommy said under his breath, "Promise you'll message me before you reach the bottom of the stairs."

That was answer enough.

8

Ava was looking primly disgruntled by the time Tommy opened the door. She might have run away from royal life in the spring, but she'd returned for Mark by the start of summer, and Tommy noted that her absence hadn't softened her regal temperament as much as she liked to believe. Her dark eyes were narrowed at him, the angle of her head cocked with subtle pique.

"Ava," he said, stepping back with the absurd fear she'd be able to tell what had just happened between him and Jonah. The way they'd pressed into each other's space, eyes closed, hips inches apart. His heart hammering, desperate to draw Jonah's top off his shoulder and put his mouth, teeth, and tongue to that smooth skin. "Thank you for your patience."

Ava arched a brow as she entered the study. "I can't be flattered into behaving, Tomas, but you're welcome."

He hid a smile. Ava was smart, well-intentioned, and had a tendency toward sarcasm. He really liked her.

"Jonah." Tommy turned. Jonah was hesitating behind him, looking nervous, and Tommy fought the urge to take his hand. Their new intimacy felt too private to share. "This is Ava. Ava, meet Jonah."

Jonah said, "Your Highness," and bowed.

Which—of course, he did. Ava was a princess. But since Tommy had excused Jonah of the formality, as Mark and Kris had surely done, it was a shock to watch him submit to someone else. Jonah had spent years deferring to the prejudiced majority in Sage Haven, determined to be true to himself while not making waves. It wasn't something he should have to do ever again. Outrage flexed in Tommy's jaw. *If he were my husband, he would take my rank and bow to no one in my presence.*

No one.

"Jonah?" Ava brightened, her eyes widening. "I've been dying to meet you!"

"Hello, Ava." Jonah's wholehearted smile was like a reassuring palm over Tommy's tension. Jonah didn't resent bowing. He knew his role in this world of Tommy's—a world he could hardly comprehend but was doing his best, and Tommy had to be okay with that.

He *wasn't,* obviously. But he had to act like it.

"Mark's told me so much about you," Jonah said. "And Darius, too. And look! Your hands!"

"It's henna." Delighted, Ava extended her arms to show off the intricately patterned ink that ran from her fingertips to her forearms. "From my bridal shower last week."

"It's beautiful." Jonah moved closer for a better look, stopping at Tommy's side. "Mark sent me photos. It seemed like a special night."

"It was." Ava's look at Tommy was casual, conversationally inclusive, but he sensed her question. *How much has he been told?*

"That was the night Kris was attacked," Tommy said quietly.

Jonah inhaled sharply. "Right. Sorry."

"The wedding is in two weeks." Ava's smile was both warm and grateful—an acknowledgement of Jonah's sympathy even as she changed the subject. "Will you still be in Kiraly? Mark and I would love you to come."

A shockwave hit Tommy as Jonah's fingertips grazed his palm. The touch was both soft and electric as Jonah said, "I'll still be here." Tommy struggled to keep his breathing even as Jonah's touch ran lightly up to his wrist. "And I'd love to come."

"Wonderful." Ava smiled and somehow didn't notice the sparks leaping from Tommy's skin. Then, at the sound of footsteps at the base of the staircase, she said, "Will you be joining us today, Jonah?"

"What?" Jonah's touch vanished as his brow buckled uncomfortably. "No. I was just here with Tommy. I'll leave. I need to get some sleep before work tonight. I'm on the late shift."

The late shift. That meant he'd be working until dawn—sleeping all morning and into early afternoon tomorrow. Tommy's schedule was booked out until late evening, and if Jonah worked again tomorrow night—and being a Friday, it was likely—then they couldn't see each other again until Saturday at the earliest. And Tommy didn't exactly get weekends off.

Promise you'll kiss me the next time I see you.

Tommy's stomach twisted. When the hell would that be?

"That's right. You're a bartender." Ava was still smiling. "Where are you working?"

Jonah ran a hand along the back of his neck. "The Bearded Bunting."

"Really?" Ava blinked at him. "How fortuitous."

Jonah cast Tommy a quick frown.

"Lucky," Tommy murmured.

"Would it be too much to ask you to look out for a friend of mine?" Ava moved farther into the study as the footsteps grew louder. "She's had a . . . shock recently. I've been checking in on her most days, but I think she's numbing it with alcohol at night. Your bar is one of her favorites."

"Of course." Jonah nodded earnestly. "What's her name?"

"Zara," Tommy said.

Ava flashed him an anguished glance as she pulled out her phone. After a few swipes, she held up the screen.

"Oh, I recognize her." Jonah winced. "She's, um, not having an easy time."

"No." Pain weakened Ava's voice. "I'm very worried."

"You leave her with me," he said with a nod. "She'll be okay."

Relieved, Ava smiled. "Thank you."

Then Philip crested the top step and stopped short when he saw Jonah, blinking in surprise. Jonah shifted so close to Tommy that their arms brushed, and a moment later, Mark appeared beside Philip.

"Jonah!" Mark grinned and pressed forward to shake his hand. "Hey, man."

"Hi, Mark." Jonah gave a laugh as his gaze slid warily to Philip. "Hello, sir. I'm Jonah. I'm just leaving."

Philip offered a curious smile. "Hello, Jonah."

"Philip is our adviser," Tommy said. "And our uncle."

"That's not exactly—" The older man spluttered and explained, "Their uncle, Noel, was my partner. I'm not *actually* uncle to the royal family."

"Well, they think you are." Jonah glanced between Tommy and Mark. "So, I think that means you are."

Mark clasped Philip's shoulder with a grin. "Jonah knows how it works."

"Let's sit down, shall we?" Ava suggested and led the others to the couches.

Tommy gave Jonah's hand a light tug and stepped onto the small landing at the top of the stairs. Following, Jonah drew the door mostly closed behind him and tilted his face up to look at Tommy. It was quiet out here, with nothing but the subdued conversation inside and hollow silence of the empty stairwell below. Jonah stood so close, it almost felt like they were hiding, tucked away with a secret no one else was allowed to find.

Tommy's pulse was uneven. "I hope you can sleep."

"I don't know." Jonah eyed him over in a sweep of thick lashes, and something about his hooded eyes and the strong, appraising angle of his jaw looked irrefutably turned on. "I don't like my chances."

That blazed in Tommy's chest. Just the thought of Jonah lying in bed, body hot and agitated over *him,* twisting in the sheets, getting more and more worked up until finally he'd surrender, reaching down and—

Stop, for God's sake.

Tommy cleared his throat. "Is there anything I can do to help?"

Jonah didn't break eye contact. "You know the answer to that."

Jesus. "You've felt this way for less than a day. I don't want to rush." That was a huge fucking lie. Tommy wanted to move against Jonah until their pleasure surged and spilled together. But Jonah was used to moving fast and this was bigger than a hookup. He needed Jonah to be sure, because even though he'd made Tommy promise not to doubt his interest, Tommy would never recover if Jonah regretted him. "And I don't want to fuck it up."

"You could never—"

"I want to take you out first," he cut in.

"Where?" Jonah swayed into him, and their chests brushed. They both pulled in a sharp breath. "Where will you take me?"

"I don't know." He had no chance of figuring that out with Jonah's mouth so close. "I'll think about it."

"Okay." With a soft groan-laugh of frustration, Jonah moved down a step. And another. He raised a hand to his forehead and mimed tipping his hat. "Have a good meeting."

Tommy pressed a palm to the wall and watched him go.

He'd scarcely reentered the study when his phone hummed. He swiped to view the message, and for the first time in over three years, he suffered a rush of adrenaline that didn't make him feel like running.

I want to be your first.

Heartbeat sweet in his mouth, Tommy replied: **You already are.**

U

"Thanks for coming." After a glass of ice water and a short stint on the balcony in the blistering summer sun, Tommy had regained enough focus to proceed. Picking up his research folder from his desk, he said, "I've asked you here because I intend to shut down the mines."

The others were gaping at him when he glanced up.

He was getting that reaction a lot lately.

"I'm starting to think I need a hearing test," Philip said weakly.

Mark was frowning. "He leads with the punchline, then goes back. You'll get used to it."

Ava's features were neutral, but her fingers had curled into the folds of her dress.

"We hit peak palladium years ago." Tommy crossed to sit in an armchair facing them. The mines were owned by the crown, which put this decision in the hands of the king. Currently Mark, and hopefully soon to be Tommy. "It's profitable now, but it won't be forever. We need to accept that. We also need to accept that it's environmentally damaging and a high risk for the workers." Tommy's sense of culpability had grown since reading the incident report on Adam's brother, Rudy—for good reason.

"There have been three fatal accidents in the past five years. That's unacceptable."

"I agree completely," Philip said, placing a hand over his heart.

Tommy leaned back in his chair and waited.

"However, that palladium fulfils the entire auto-catalyst demand in Kelehar." Philip gestured to Ava—Princess of Kelehar —as if she somehow proved a point. "Their automotive industry relies on it, and cars are their primary export. Ceasing mining would cripple their economy, Your Highness. You can't make a decision of this magnitude without considering the political and economic consequences."

Tommy held his adviser's gaze. "You believe that's what I'm doing?"

Mark rolled his lips together.

"I—" Philip flushed and said swiftly, "Obviously not. My apologies. I'm still getting past my time with Kristof."

Tommy gave a small smile. "I understand that this will be a major undertaking. We need a strategy. Replacement jobs for those workers. An alternative for Kelehar's car industry. I'm not planning on shutting the mines next week, Philip, but palladium's use in catalytic converters occupies more than eighty percent of demand worldwide—and electric cars don't have catalytic converters. The cars of the future *don't need palladium*." He lifted his folder. "Experts predict we have about ten years until that becomes a problem for demand. I intend for Kiraly to avoid that downturn entirely."

Philip said, "I stand corrected," and looked at Mark.

"I'd like to hear more." Mark nodded at Tommy.

"Tomas." Ava was watching him cautiously. "Why did you invite me to this meeting?"

"Ava." On this, Tommy wouldn't lead with the punchline. He

leaned forward into a gentler posture. "I won't ask you to do anything that you find painful. I understand you never want to see your parents again—and that cutting yourself off from Kelehar is the safest way to ensure it. But I've heard you speak about Kelehar. You miss it. Your country, your people, your culture." He paused, then added carefully, "Your brother—you could see Cyrus more often. Mark could travel with you, and Darius."

Ava's wide stare accused him of pulling out all the stops, knowing those trips would connect her three-year-old son with his heritage, but Tommy wanted this—and he sensed she would ultimately want it too. An opportunity to remake herself, to return to Kelehar on her own terms.

"I'd like you to consider being a representative for international trade on this matter."

Mark's frown had turned protective. His hand covered Ava's on the couch between them. "Tommy, you can't—"

"On what matter, exactly?" Ava's spine was straight, her chin perfectly level with the floor.

"Convincing Kelehar to future-proof their automotive industry by going electric—with Kiraly assisting in the manufacturing of parts."

"God above," Philip murmured.

Mark ran a hand over his face. "This is monumental, Tommy."

Silent, Ava moved her attention to the folder on Tommy's lap.

"You're right, Mark, so I can't do it alone." Tommy placed his research and planning on the table between them and flipped it open. It contained everything from the automakers currently leading global electric car sales, to notes from his meeting with Kiraly's minister for natural resources, mines and energy, to a proposed job-training scheme to reskill miners in manufacturing.

He sat back, looked each of them in the eye, and said, "Let's discuss."

In all his life, Jonah had never felt like this.

He'd had crushes before. His first was in elementary school—a cute, freckled kid who'd been Tommy's partner in a paired project. In high school, he'd gone heart-eyed over a new boy every other month. Mostly the ones who were nice to him, sometimes the pretty ones who ignored him, and rarely, the unfairly gorgeous bullies. Jonah hadn't been out in high school, but he hadn't been one of the boys. No one had messed with him directly, not as a friend of the triplets—not if they didn't want the collective peer power of all three hitting back —but he'd known which guys would have targeted him if they could.

Those school crushes had been zaps of awareness. Quick fixes. Bread rolls while he waited for the main meal. Just someone to think about as he tried to figure himself out. Later, he'd used dating apps to match with interested men traveling in the region (a depressingly rare occurrence). If they were nice enough, he'd taken them home and hardly thought about them again.

But this.

Tommy.

Was *everywhere*. Loud in Jonah's heart, wild in his stomach, burrowed deep in his thoughts. Tommy was at the other side of every message tone, every male voice, every opening door. Jonah's awareness felt stretched tight, achy, a non-stop pull toward Tommy that tried to tug him up the mountain.

And really, he might have better luck reaching Tommy that way. They hadn't been on their phones at the same time since Jonah had left the palace two days ago. He considered calculating the exact number of hours since they'd communicated in real-time so he could be dramatic about it but knew that wouldn't change anything. Tommy had busy things to be doing, and Jonah had to be okay with that.

Besides, Jonah was busy too.

Thinking about Tommy.

Texting Tommy.

Waiting for Tommy to call him back.

Ngh. Okay. He was busy sightseeing and looking up more palace facts and feeding himself often enough that he didn't faint in the heat and roll from the top of Kira City to the bottom. He'd worked Thursday night, given up trying to sleep on Friday, so had gone swimming and picnicking with Nora, and then had worked again Friday night.

Amongst it all, he'd tried calling when he thought Tommy might be free—breakfast, midmorning, and early afternoon, because surely even royalty had snack breaks. Jonah had followed up with texts. Hours passed in between responses. Which wasn't unusual for Tommy, but seriously—*hours*. Sometimes, all he'd send back was a photo. An under-the-table shot of several pairs of trousers and polished shoes. A group-sized sandwich platter. Philip sitting across from the study's desk, frowning at the lens in bewilderment. Photos that included Jonah in Tommy's day but also showed that he didn't have time to send more than that. Once, he'd added: **I'm sorry. Soon, I swear.**

In Sage Haven, if Jonah hadn't been able to reach Tommy on his phone, he'd just walked next door. Problem solved. Now Tommy's home was surrounded by a fence he couldn't jump over and royal guards at the gate. There was no popping around to the palace.

By midafternoon on Saturday, Jonah's frustration hurt so badly, he balled up on the couch and sent a gif of himself saying "blue" over and over, hoping it would drive Tommy wild enough to call. He regretted it instantly. Manipulation must sit in the same boat as teasing, and he'd promised Tommy he wouldn't do that. The gif was all pout, and he'd seen Tommy's hunger for it the other day.

Twenty minutes later, his regret vanished when there was a knock on his apartment door.

He flew across the room—and crashed at the sight of Frankie.

"What?" he said, slumping with disappointment. "No."

"My favorite greeting." She arched a brow. "Hoping for someone else?"

"No. I—I love seeing you, Frankie. Come in."

As he padded back to the couch, she crossed to stand near the window opposite him, hands clasped behind her and black boots shoulder-width apart. Which was a weirdly serious pose.

Unease twisted his legs up onto the couch beside him. "What's going on?"

"Tommy asked me to come by," she said, and Jonah's stomach spun away from him at Tommy's name. "He wants me to tell you a few things before he next sees you."

"Oh." Jonah frowned. "Okay."

Except—

No, that didn't feel okay.

Frankie wasn't here as his friend. She was here to carry out Tommy's orders.

With that, and an awful tearing sensation, Jonah finally *got* that Tommy was royalty. He'd known it in a moon and teacup kind of way, but now his brain ripped the truth from the back of his mind like paper from a notebook and shoved it at him, shouting, *Will you just read it properly!*

Tommy was a prince. A human so important, so above the social rules of regular people, he had sent someone else to have a conversation with his oldest friend on his behalf.

And *that,* more than the view from the tower, or the royal wine vaults he'd just read about valued in the millions, finally horrified him into understanding. The reality of Tommy's status wasn't in the things around them.

It was in the things *between* them.

Unanswered calls. Palace gates. Unmet desires.

And right now—Frankie.

"Actually," he said, and it came out both confused and stubborn. "Why doesn't he tell me himself?"

"He wanted to." Frankie was still standing like a guard. It prickled that Jonah had invited her in as a friend—and she'd entered as Tommy's go-between. "But it's confidential. Not a conversation for a phone call and he needs it to be done before you're next together in person."

Way to make Jonah feel like an item on a checklist. Even knowing that wasn't how Tommy saw him, it stung.

"I don't understand," he said.

Her features were grim. "You will."

And then she told him secrets that made his blood run cold.

She said that Tommy's uncles and cousin hadn't died in an accident. They'd been murdered. She told him that last week, she'd discovered that the mastermind behind the plot had been working as Mark's manservant this whole time. A man named Adam. He was the leader of an anarchist group with members who'd worked in construction and had built structural faults into the balcony that had collapsed.

"Can you slow down a second?" Tension pressed Jonah's knees together, his hands wedged between them. His day had gone from pouting for attention to processing royal murder, and he wasn't finding the transition easy. "Did you say antichrist?"

She paused. "Anarchist."

"What does that mean?"

"Anarchism can go a few ways, but this group rejects

164

hierarchy. They value a society that rules itself. Which means they don't want a royal family."

"But." That didn't make sense. "The boys were always in Montana. What was the point in killing their relatives when they'd just take over?"

"We—" Her features pinched as she looked away. "We don't think they knew about the boys. Most of Kiraly didn't know they existed."

"What? Why not?" he said, and then shook his head to stay on track. The real issue was that group. "Why would Adam work for Mark if he rejects the royal family?"

"To get close. Learn their plans to know how best to strike, maybe? And he got close in more ways than one." Scowling, Frankie explained that Adam had been Zara's boyfriend—the same Zara who was friends with Ava and getting drunk at the bar most nights. "She didn't know what he was," Frankie said, "but she unknowingly gave him the heads up that I was onto him last week. He vanished."

And, she said, the men from the anarchist group?

They were the ones who'd beaten up Kris.

"What?" Dread dropped an anchor Jonah's gut. "These people want to hurt the boys?"

"We don't know what they want." Frankie's jaw tightened and she scuffed her boot on the floor. "It's pissing me off. We caught the assholes who hurt Kris, and they say Adam didn't actually instruct the attack. They did that on their own. And they have no idea where he's gone."

Jonah's thoughts had dropped with the anchor, sinking under the weight of this news. "So he could be anywhere?"

Frankie pressed her knuckles to her forehead and nodded.

"Tommy." Jonah inched forward in alarm. "Is he safe?"

"Yeah." At that, Frankie crossed to sit next to him, grabbing his hand and squeezing. "He's safe. You don't need to worry about that. But this means that once you're seen with Tommy in public, you'll need your own guards. They'll accompany you everywhere outside this building. Until we find Adam, we have to assume he'll try to use anyone close to the boys against them."

"Right." His head felt waterlogged. "Okay."

"I'm making it impossible for anyone to cause trouble. The only reason they got to Kris was because he was being a hotheaded idiot and went off on his own. Can you promise me you won't do that? That you'll stay with your guards?"

"Sure, Frankie." He had no reason to ditch them. "I'll stay."

She hadn't let go of his hand. "Tommy wanted you to have time to adjust to the idea."

"Yeah." Jonah stared at the floorboards. So Frankie *wasn't* a barrier between him and Tommy—she was keeping them safe so they could be together. "Can I think for a minute?"

"Go for it." She put her chin in her hand and seemed to join him.

Okay. So. From the top.

Tommy's family ruled the brightest country in the world. But this guy called Adam didn't like that and had killed the old royal family, and maybe he wanted to kill Tommy and his brothers, too. And that was particularly scary because they didn't know where Adam had gone, but not as scary as it could have been because if Jonah couldn't even get to Tommy, he didn't see how Adam could.

"At least this will be over once you find—wait." He glanced up at Frankie as something connected. "What about the survey? People were talking in the bar last night. They've been asked whether to keep the monarchy? If this group want society to rule itself . . . and society rules to keep the boys . . . then won't they have to go with that?"

"That's Tommy's plan." Frankie smiled wryly. "The survey

was his idea. Let the people decide and, no matter the outcome, the anarchists theoretically can't resent it."

"He's so smart," Jonah said on an amazed breath out.

"Yeah." Her casual tone gave nothing away when she said, "It's good you two are friends again."

"Frankie." Jonah's awareness gave a hard pull toward the palace, reminded of Tommy all over again. "We're *not* friends."

"No? Then why the hell is he going out of his mind trying to see you again?"

Jonah's insides flipped. "He is?"

"Yeah." She rolled her eyes. "And he's bloody rude when he's stressed."

"Oh, he's awful." But Jonah smiled. "And when I said we're not friends, I meant we're something else. He likes me."

She smiled back, but he caught the amused twitch of her eyebrow. "Does he now?"

His jaw actually dropped. "You already *knew*?"

"Jones. We all knew." She clasped his knee in congratulations before standing with a firm, "Don't ditch your guards."

She left Jonah's insides tangled tighter than ever.

Frankie just visited, Jonah typed a minute later, leaning against the front door. His rib cage threatened to give way under the need to be with Tommy. **When can I see you? I need to see you.**

No reply. Because royalty.

An hour later, he almost screamed when he came out of the bathroom, showered and ready to head to his next shift, and found a missed call and text saying: **I'm sorry, Jonah. I'm due in another engagement. Will try again later. x**

By the time Jonah got to work, he was a wreck. An edgy, exhausted, wrung-out wreck. His smile was forced. He nodded when people asked if he was okay—which was almost everyone—and pretended not to notice that they didn't believe him. The other bartenders circled him throughout the night, concerned, patting him on the back more than usual, but not pushing him for an explanation.

It was after ten, as he was working through a line four-people deep, when his phone buzzed with an incoming call in his pocket. His adrenaline spiked so sharply he leaned a hip against the counter for balance.

Not now, not now, he thought, but also, *please, finally now.*

Pouring tonic water with one hand, he slid his phone out with the other, keeping it below the counter and glancing down at the screen.

Tommy's unsmiling photo stared back at him.

"You've got to be kidding me." Urgency fluttered in his chest. He *had* to take this. Desperate, he looked up at the sea of people waiting for a drink and wanted to drop to the floor in distress. There was no way he could take this.

"Hey." Nora appeared, swiping the gin and tonic from him and jerking her head toward the back. Her expression played it cool, but her eyes were bright with curiosity. "Go answer."

Jonah didn't need to be told twice. He ran for it.

"Tommy?" he said as he burst through the staff door behind the bar and jogged toward the rear exit. "Tommy, are you there?"

"I'm here."

Only two days since they'd seen each other, but the sound of Tommy's quiet, controlled voice made Jonah want to cry. What was this feeling *doing* to him?

"Tommy." Outside, he collapsed against the alley wall and slid until he was sitting on the cobblestones with his knees drawn up. "I can't do this anymore. The last two days have been torture. I keep remembering your breath on my shoulder, but you didn't kiss me that day, and I *wish you'd kissed me,* so I'm stuck here feeling twitchy and alone and waiting for something really important that just won't happen." He paused and added woefully, "And it's awful."

Tommy was silent for a few beats too long. "Was there anything else?"

"*Tommy.*" It came out as a pitiful groan.

A soft chuckle. "I didn't want to interrupt you while you were sulking."

"Stop it." He almost smiled. "You know what I'm like."

"Well, I'm here now." Tommy spoke with the tenderness of a cupped cheek, and Jonah yearned to lean into it. "And I'm sorry my schedule was back-to-back all today and yesterday."

"It's not fair. You're finally free and I'm in the middle of a shift." Jonah's voice actually cracked. "You'll be in bed by the time I finish. And I won't be able to sleep because I miss you so much, I think my heart's eaten my stomach and I didn't even know that was a thing, and you'll be busy all day tomorrow and forever and I'll never see you again."

Another quiet laugh. "That is absolutely not true."

"I feel like it is." Thankfully Jonah was alone. He sounded pathetic. "And you don't know that it's not."

"I know that it's not." A firm tone.

Jonah tilted his head back against the stone wall, opening himself to Tommy's reassurance. "Really?"

"Yes. Are you on a break right now?"

"No." The dulled beat of music came from inside. Voices carried from the open rear courtyard. "Nora let me sneak out to answer. But it's so packed in there, I have to get back."

"When do you finish?"

"I'm on early tonight, so around twelve-thirty."

"I'll talk to you then," Tommy said. "I won't be asleep."

Jonah pulled in a disbelieving breath. "Really?"

"Stop saying really like that." It was the sweetest telling off Jonah had ever heard. "It makes me ache."

Jonah's smile was slow. "Really?"

"Yes. Really. Now don't let me be the reason you get told off. Talk later, okay?"

Wishing he could fly to Tommy on a single word, he said, "Okay."

Jonah took his smile back inside. As he pushed through his final few hours, chatting with patrons about their day and the summer heat and their memories of the late royal family, his stomach stayed tangled but in a new type of knot. The balled mass of distress was now the hard tug of anticipation, and only talking with Tommy again would release it for him.

It was almost the end of his shift when Nora leaned around him to get a better look at the main entrance, saying, "That's bizarre. What's he up to?" Then she started tapping Jonah's shoulder and didn't stop. "Um. Act cool, but I think he's looking at you."

With a distracted frown, Jonah glanced to where the crowd had made space around the front door. There, standing just inside the venue, two steps up from the main floor, was Tommy.

He was staring at Jonah.

"Oh my God." Jonah barely stopped himself from vaulting the counter to get to him.

Royal guards ringed him, positioned at arm's length in a formation with a clear message: no one approached this prince. And he *did* look like a prince, even dressed all cowboy in his blue and grey plaid shirt, jeans, boots, and Kris's hat tipped back from his face. He wasn't hiding behind the brim tonight. He'd nailed his brother's cocky stance with his weight pushed onto one hip, his thumb tucked in his waistband, and chin angled up for full jawbone exposure. Tommy's expression was the only real giveaway—his mask of calm confidence was starting to strain a little around the edges.

No wonder. He was on display for the whole crowd to see, but he didn't so much as scan the room as he stared at Jonah over their heads.

It hit Jonah with a jolt—Tommy was waiting.

"Oh, God, I told him twelve-thirty," he said, and covered his mouth with his hand.

"You told—*what*? The fuck!" Nora's eyes bulged as she gripped his elbow. "Jonah! That's *Prince Kristof* you're talking about!"

"I—" Okay, that felt weird. "I know."

She looked dumbstruck. "Well, shit, man. You know how to pull."

Stricken, Jonah looked back at Tommy a second before Frankie's visit made sense. Tommy was attracting attention on purpose. He didn't intend to keep Jonah tucked out of sight. He wanted to be seen picking Jonah up from work, because that way, word would spread across Kiraly. By morning, the nation would know they were a couple.

Or that Jonah and Kris were?

Woah, no. Jonah would have to talk to Tommy about that.

The room was falling quiet as more people noticed the prince in their midst. They were turning, craning their necks to get a good look. Concern edged around Jonah's middle. It might be part of Tommy's plan, but surely it was too much attention. Even protected by his guards, Jonah could see Tommy's chest was moving too quickly.

His gaze was still fixed on Jonah.

"I have to go." Jonah flipped the dishtowel off his shoulder as he lifted the bar flap and plunged into the crush. He'd expected to have to shoulder his way through, but a path cleared for him as he moved toward the entrance. He felt hands on his back and arms, heard people say, "Nice work, man," and "Lucky prince," as he passed. Then two guards were stepping aside, and Jonah was standing in front of Tommy, saying, "Your Highness," and pressing his hand to Tommy's chest because he couldn't *not* touch him now that they were finally together.

"Jonah," Tommy practically whispered. His pupils were wide.

"You're really not asleep."

"No." Tommy covered his hand with his own, pressing it over his racing heart. His *really* racing heart. God. They had to get out of here.

"After you," Jonah said.

With a nod, Tommy used their linked hands to draw Jonah outside. He hit the sidewalk with a sure stride and kept moving, tightening his hold when the venue practically erupted in their wake with excited squeals and disbelieving shouts. Jonah was still grinning when the street crowd thinned several blocks to the north and Tommy finally felt safe enough to stop, facing him in the afterhours glow of a closed teahouse.

Jonah made sure to stop so close, he was practically standing on Tommy's feet.

"How dare you send that gif." Tommy's hand was unsteady as it ran down Jonah's arm, but his voice was even. "I've been out of my mind."

Jonah shivered at the touch. "That was the plan." Then he said, "Hey. You just stood in front of a crowded room. That's incredible."

Tommy grimaced. "It didn't feel incredible."

"I'm still proud of you."

A smile ghosted over Tommy's lips. "Can I walk you home?"

"Yes, please."

"Can I take you for ice cream on the way?"

Jonah heard: would he like to spend longer by Tommy's side? He beamed. "Yes."

It became clear that Tommy had planned the route back to Jonah's apartment. Only two guards escorted them the entire way. The rest just happened to be on street corners or down laneways as they passed. One had gone ahead to the ice creamery, ensuring the small shopfront was empty for Tommy's arrival.

It was as bright as a lightbulb inside. White counters, floors, and walls that made the ice cream display pop with color. Even the serving lady was wearing white, her grey hair back in a bun and her smile nervous.

"Good evening," Jonah said with a smile. "Your shop is beautiful." *And so bright, my eyes are watering.* Then he squeezed Tommy's hand.

"It is," Tommy said, squinting slightly as he looked at her. "Beautiful."

"Thank you." She gave a full wattage smile back and Jonah imagined that a week from now the shop windows would read: *Royally approved "beautiful" ice cream!*

"Jonah." Tommy angled his face toward him. "What would you like?"

With a hum, Jonah scanned the flavors. It was classy. No smashed chocolate bars or jellies or cookies here but serious homemade stuff. The white chocolate and raspberry looked pretty good, but so did the rosewater swirl and the lime and coconut. Wait, the lemon myrtle would be sweet and zingy, so maybe that one would . . . *oh.*

The obvious choice. "Peanut butter."

Tommy frowned. "But you don't really like peanut butter ice cream."

"No." He could take it or leave it. "But you love it."

Pleasure moved softly over Tommy's features. "You want to share?"

"No, no." Jonah swiped his bottom lip with his teeth, wildly overplaying coy and not caring one bit. "I won't be sharing."

Tommy's steady gaze became the eye contact equivalent of clearing a table for sex in a single arm swipe. Voice low, he said, "I see," and turned to order a double scoop of peanut butter and single of chocolate orange. Jonah's all-time favorite.

Back on the street, their silence was charged.

"Thank you," Jonah said, and popped the loaded spoon in his mouth. "I feel better."

"Ply a boy with dessert and he stops sulking."

Jonah laughed, blushing at the affectionate way Tommy had said boy. *That's me,* he thought. *I'm his boy.*

Then he said, "I'm going to sulk a lot more often if it's always this hard to get your attention."

"It's not."

"You sound very sure."

"I am," Tommy said, and nodded politely at a couple who passed them on the sidewalk, expressions bulging with disbelief. "I might have put plans in motion earlier this week in anticipation of you not being interested in me. I knew that I'd need distracting and a ridiculous workload seemed like a good way to do it. Only now, you *are* interested and I'm being overworked by my failure to predict the future."

Jonah took a thoughtful bite of ice cream. "So, you're saying when your workload goes back to normal, I can be the one to distract you?"

"Yes."

Well, then.

They turned left at the next break between buildings and headed up a flight of stone steps that would eventually connect them to Jonah's street. A long string of twinkle lights hung between the upper story windows, and with Tommy close beside him, Jonah felt the glow of every one of those pinpricks dancing on his skin like fireflies.

"When you saw the gif," Jonah said, in a too-casual-to-be-casual-at-all kind of tone. "What did you think about?"

Tommy's glance was dark with heat. "Getting you alone."

They emerged from the stairway, crossed the street, and started up another flight bracketed by town houses, and was it just Jonah or were they walking faster now?

"Please," Jonah said, "tell me you're coming inside." His lungs swelled at the thought.

Tommy tugged the brim of his hat lower over his face. "I'm coming inside."

That hat tilt—he was nervous. But his voice held steady, so he wasn't anxious.

"This is the street," Jonah said as they emerged several buildings away from his apartment. He gestured, and they moved toward it. "How was your dessert?"

Tommy frowned at him. "I didn't think I'd had it yet."

Oh, God, this is happening.

Breath hitching, Jonah scooped the last of the peanut butter ice cream into his mouth. "It's ready when you are."

"Trust me," Tommy murmured, taking his hand. "I'm ready."

9

It was dark inside Jonah's apartment. The blinds were drawn, likely from blocking out the afternoon sun before Jonah had left for work. Tommy closed the door in the same moment he reached out for Jonah's hand, taking the keys from him and tossing them off to one side. He hoped there wasn't something fragile in that direction, because he couldn't see a damn thing.

Jonah yelped as they clattered against the hard floor.

"Sorry." Tommy tossed Kris's hat aside next.

"That scared me," Jonah laughed from in front of him. "Hold on. I'll switch on a lamp."

But Tommy grabbed his hand again, muttering, "Wait," and drawing him back. Jonah came easily, his breath of surrender spilling over the underside of Tommy's jaw, revealing exactly where and how he stood in some kind of heat-puffed imprint, like condensation on the smooth surface of Tommy's skin. He was close, incredibly close, his lips parted and face tipped back.

Waiting, just as Tommy had asked.

Pulse shuddering, Tommy slid a palm along Jonah's cheek and tried not to think about what it meant that he was doing this in the dark. He was the future King of Kiraly—and he couldn't kiss the man he loved with the light on. But being that exposed for his first kiss was as terrifying as having half the city watch on, and he just couldn't do it.

Jonah didn't seem to mind.

He leaned into Tommy's hand with a soft murmur. The sound reverberated across Tommy's wrist, slipping inward at his pulse point and coursing through his entire body with an electric echo.

Heart powering, Tommy shifted, and their noses brushed.

"Tommy." No voice, just the tongue-tap to start his name and the muffled exhale of the rest. "Please. I'm dying here."

Even though he couldn't see, Tommy refused to close his eyes. "Try waiting four years."

Jonah's gasp was helpless. "You've liked me for *four—*"

Tommy kissed him.

It wasn't a demand. It wasn't even a question. The light touch of his lips was more, *can I ask you something?* And Jonah leaned into him, one hand settling on Tommy's chest and the other clenching the shirt at the small of his back in an unmistakable, *yes.*

Unsteady, Tommy pushed a little more and was startled at the softness of Jonah's lips. He'd expected resistance—Jonah's bottom lip holding firm as Tommy explored the full shape of it with his own—but it yielded like a pillow beneath his head and his blood thrilled at the discovery. *I've been imagining this all wrong.* Then Jonah slanted his face, lips parting, and Tommy was grateful for the invitation as much as the guidance on which way to tilt his head—until he did exactly that and fell into the hot flood of Jonah's mouth.

Holy fucking hell.

Jonah *tasted.*

Beneath the sticky-sweet of cream and peanut butter, beneath the mingling traces of chocolate orange, Jonah tasted like

Jonah. Like lying in the grass and quicksand grins and blood-hot hunger. He tasted like home and longing and the need to ensure that no one else ever came here again.

No one but Tommy.

Except, right now, Tommy didn't know how to be here, not properly. He wanted more, ached to take control, but didn't want to end up doing something awkward or gross and ruining the whole thing. Torn between desire and dignity, he kept it slow even as his body screamed for more, until Jonah pulled back, said quietly, "Here, do this," and rose onto his toes to press completely against him.

Tommy almost burst into flames as Jonah hooked one arm around his neck and slid the other deep in the back pocket of Tommy's jeans, bunching hard. Paired with his open-mouthed kiss, Jonah's bold touch set off a surge of reaction in Tommy, and he swallowed a groan. Jonah wriggled farther against him at the sound, an armful of lean man and urgency, and then he was kissing harder, a slick push and pull that Tommy received with less abandon than his hormones were urging. He'd lose himself in this kiss if it was the last thing he did, but first, he focused on every slide of Jonah's tongue and shift of his jaw, learning when to move and when to slow, when to delve and when to draw back, until Tommy was responding in kind and Jonah was lowering to his heels and letting him lead.

"You can touch me," Jonah murmured into his mouth, "if you want."

If I want? What kind of question was that to—

Oh. Tommy's hands were by his sides. They felt heavy, offline. Kissing was demanding so much of his concentration that he'd forgotten about the rest of him. How was Jonah multitasking like this? His hands were all over Tommy, in his hair, rubbing firmly down his arms, and doing something at the base of his back. *Untucking my shirt. Jesus, he's untucking my—*

Tommy lost clear thought at the hot press of Jonah's palm on his bare skin. The slide felt like a glowing heat trail in the dark, arcing across his spine like a comet flare. It was dizzying, a touch like neon on black—and that was before Jonah's other hand skimmed under his shirt to join in. Tommy gasped as his spine stretched and Jonah's palms chased the movement, pushing harder, pressing Tommy more firmly against him, gliding around his rib cage until suddenly, blindingly, Jonah's fingers were edging the sensitive skin of his stomach.

Desperate to return the touch, Tommy broke the kiss just long enough for Jonah's lips to move on to the corner of his mouth, his chin, his jaw, and down his neck. As Tommy tugged Jonah's shirt free at his hips, Jonah dragged his tongue up one side of Tommy's throat in a hot streak of white behind his eyelids. Tilting his head, Tommy's flush of pleasure was cut short when he realized he couldn't do the same to Jonah.

Those bastard men had stolen this thrill from them both.

On a shuddering breath, Tommy abandoned Jonah's waist for the top buttons of his shirt. After undoing them, he pulled the fabric off one shoulder—to the heady encouragement, "Oh, Tommy, please, yes,"—and lowered his mouth to the exposed skin he'd denied himself in the tower. He took it with an open mouth and light scraping of teeth, and, *God*, was it good. Smooth and solid, the skin was slightly salty from working in an over-heated bar all night. As Tommy scraped his teeth a little harder, finding himself sucking more than kissing, Jonah put his hands in Tommy's hair and made sounds Tommy had only ever dreamed about. It was potent; Tommy felt powerful, capable. Vaguely, he hoped Jonah wouldn't mind if he left a mark, because focusing on this one place meant he wouldn't surrender to the urge to strip Jonah bare and kiss his entire body.

Then Jonah was pulling on him, sinking down, urging Tommy to the floor. Tommy went. The dark confused things for a minute, knees bumping, hands grasping, and then Jonah was laughing, saying, "Which way are you even facing?" before Tommy used the sound to find him. Hands curving over Jonah's shoulders, Tommy nudged him onto his back and a second later, settled over his chest with his hips angled away to one side.

"Say something to me," he requested, not wanting to accidentally brush Jonah's neck on his quest to find his mouth.

"I'm so happy right—"

Got him.

Jonah moaned to support his half-finished sentiment, winding his arms around Tommy's neck, drawing him close in a kiss that went on forever.

And ever.

And ever.

"Teach me," Tommy murmured against Jonah's mouth, wondering how long it had been. His lips felt puffy; his arms were burning from propping himself up.

Jonah's voice was husky as he said, "Anything."

Tommy slid his nose across Jonah's cheek and kissed behind his ear. "Teach me how to stop kissing you."

Jonah's laugh was all breath. "Nope. Next."

Then he put a hand on Tommy's cheek and guided his mouth back to where he wanted it.

Resistance grew harder. The dark amplified every touch, gasp, and pulse. Arousal raged inside him, building in force, and he suspected that years of suppressing desire meant nothing when Jonah was literally giving himself over beneath him.

We should stop. Tommy ran a palm inside the collar of Jonah's shirt and over the long-sought sweep of his décolletage. *Any minute now.*

Their groans were getting deeper, their movements more intense. It was everything Tommy could do not to slide his leg over Jonah's hips. He didn't need experience to know that would be the end of them.

Jonah's hands started at Tommy's shirt buttons, his breath fast and body moving restlessly, trying to shift out from under the wall of Tommy's chest so their hips could meet. He succeeded, too, for a wild few seconds, colliding into Tommy with the entire length of his body—and the hard length of his erection.

Tommy cursed into Jonah's mouth as his focus narrowed to one very naked outcome.

"Do you want to?" Jonah asked, withdrawing slightly, breath hot.

"I—" *Yes. God, yes, but—*

On a rough exhale, Tommy hauled himself onto his back, splaying a hand across Jonah's chest to stop him from following.

They both lay panting, lust aching in every breath.

"Not tonight," Tommy made himself say.

It took a few seconds for Jonah to answer, gentle, cautious. "I could show you."

"I know you could. I mean, I hope . . . that you will. It's not that." He was determined to give Jonah their first kiss and first orgasm on different days, even if it tore his desire to shreds. "I don't want to rush into this."

"Of course." Jonah's breath was starting to level out. Curling his fingers around Tommy's hand on his chest, he asked, "What we just did—was that okay? Not too fast?"

"It was amazing."

"Yeah. It was." He didn't need light to know Jonah was grinning. "I guess you probably have to get back to the palace."

"About that." Tommy turned his face toward him in the darkness. "I'd like to stay."

"Stay," Jonah echoed, fingers tightening around Tommy's hand.

"If you don't mind. We both need to sleep properly, and

we're not managing that apart." They were going to become dangers to themselves if they didn't get proper rest. Jonah was miserable, and Tommy's fatigue was feeding his stress.

"I knew it." Jonah's tone joked as he sat up, taking Tommy's hand with him. "You're just here to get me into bed."

Tommy sat up beside him. "You can say no."

"No, I—oh, this is ridiculous, I'm turning a light on." Chuckling, Jonah stood and slipped out of Tommy's reach. His footsteps moved carefully across the kitchen and then a faint amber light filled the apartment from his bedside.

Tommy rose to his feet, watching Jonah run a hand through his disheveled hair, adjust the waistband of his jeans, and straighten his shirt. Tommy had done that—pulled Jonah's hair in every direction trying to get deeper into his mouth, made him hard with arousal, half-exposed his chest in his need to devour him. Jonah drew the shirt away from his shoulder, curious, running his fingers over the red mark.

"I'm sorry if it bruises," Tommy said.

Jonah whirled around to face him with a startled, "Tommy?" Retreating a step, the backs of his legs hit the bed and he sat down abruptly. "Was that you this whole time?"

Face heating, Tommy crossed the room. "I was nervous. The dark helped."

"It sure did." Jonah's smile threw a stone into Tommy's pulse, skipping right through him. "You were good."

Suddenly Tommy was nervous all over again. "I was?"

"Yes." Jonah didn't stand when Tommy reached him. Instead, he leaned on his palms and tipped his face up, lips swollen and cheeks flushed. God, he had exceptional bedroom eyes. "You really want to stay the night and . . . not do anything?"

Tommy swallowed. "That's right."

"Okay." Jonah nodded slowly. "Just to be sure, though, do you really mean that or are you playing with denial so we both end up struggling to keep our hands off each other in bed, and then we accidentally touch, and things get extra hot and achy, and then our restraint breaks and all of a sudden we're on top of each other and—"

"Stop talking, Jesus *Christ*." Tommy planted a hand over Jonah's mouth as the imagery almost undid him. "I mean sleep. And only sleep."

Jonah was nodding again before Tommy let go. "Sure, I just wanted to double check."

"I don't want to make things difficult." They'd promised not to tease. "I can leave if it would be easier."

"No. I can do it. I'd love it, actually. I just got carried away with the failed denial thing."

Tommy unpicked the gleaming thread of those words. "Is that something you've wanted to do?"

"I don't know. Maybe?" Jonah blushed but didn't look away. "There's never been a real chance for it. With hookups, we're there for a reason, you know?"

Tommy stilled. "We won't be hooking up."

"No." Jonah's fingers curled slowly into the bedspread. "We won't."

Heat rose in him anew. "We can try it some time."

Jonah sat up straighter, features gleaming. "Really?"

"I thought I told you not to say really like that." All hopeful and open, like Tommy could never let him down. Tommy didn't deserve that trust after what he'd done.

"Alright, alright." Jonah reached out to take Tommy's hand. "Let's go to bed."

Four years.

Jonah's head spun. Tommy had liked him for *four years*.

That was so . . . sad.

Lying in the dark with Tommy at his back, Jonah couldn't help but wonder whether Tommy would have told him sooner if they'd never been beaten. If Tommy hadn't learned in the worst possible way that it could be safer to stay in the closet. The thought stuck, hot and wretched in Jonah's eyes. After the attack, hiding would have felt less stressful than being open about who he was—and Jonah couldn't judge him for that. Jonah had chosen that safety for a long time before coming out to Tommy, but in the end, he'd wanted to be true to himself.

And there—no matter how tightly he balled up on the mattress to escape it—was the niggle in the back of his mind.

Would royal life be true to me?

Mark and Kris had chosen the right kind of partners. Ava was a princess. She stood straight and spoke smart and attended meetings. Frankie was the head of the Royal Guard, capable of juggling a million balls at once. Even Philip, the partner of the boys' late uncle, was a royal advisor. They all belonged.

Not like a bartender.

Jonah would only fit by pretending to be someone he wasn't. And if he was supposed to understand parliament and policies and crowns, then he'd be pretending every day of his life. He owed the teen he'd once been, brave and terrified as word of his sexuality spread around town, to remain true to himself. He'd fought too hard to give it up now.

"Hey." Tommy's breath warmed his upper back.

Pulled from his thoughts, Jonah shivered to his toes.

"You're supposed to be sleeping."

Jonah turned his head to speak quietly over his shoulder. "How did you know I wasn't?"

"Your eyes are open."

Which would be a totally fair argument if Tommy wasn't *behind* him.

"I can hear your eyelashes scraping against the pillow every time you blink," Tommy added, shifting his hand on Jonah's waist.

They were both dressed in Jonah's sweats and cotton T-shirts, but the movement still shot heat across Jonah's skin. He'd never been in bed with a man he hadn't slept with—never been wrapped in arms that wanted him for him.

"Are you okay?"

Was he? Jonah feared it was impossible to be himself in a future with Tommy. "It's . . . silly," he said, backing out.

Tommy lifted his head. "I'm sure it's not."

"I can't help but think," Jonah started, and unsure how to say it, turned it into a joke. "Princes don't date barmaids."

Tommy was motionless for a few long moments. "Maybe not." His words came from low in his chest, rough and hard, as far from princely as a rope-calloused palm. His wide grip shifted, tightening across Jonah's hip. "But cowboys do."

"Oh." Jonah's skin heated beneath that solid grasp, and he settled his head back down. Of course. Tommy wasn't *only* a prince. And while that didn't ease the niggle, it helped him push it aside. They were only one kiss into their relationship, after all. Why worry about what might come next until it did? "That's true."

"I miscalculated." Tommy slid his nose along Jonah's shoulder blade and murmured against his shirt, "I don't want to sleep and miss a second of being here with you."

Jonah smiled, pressing his face into the sheet.

"Do you work tomorrow night?" Tommy turned his head, angling his cheek to rest against Jonah's back. Tommy was *cuddling,* and it made Jonah feel like a kitten curled in cotton wool—safe and calm and so very kissable. "We have a family dinner, and I'd like you to come."

That fluttered in Jonah's chest. "As your friend?"

"No." Tommy shifted, the sheets rustling as he circled his arms fully around Jonah's torso, tightening, pulling closer, until Jonah's spine was flush against Tommy's front. "As my boyfriend."

"Boyfriend." The word sparkled in Jonah's mouth. "Yes."

"And stay the night?" Tommy's whisper was heart-meltingly shy.

The sparkle suddenly held the heat of chili powder. He swallowed and it spread right through him. "Yes."

"Yes," Tommy repeated softly, as if he couldn't believe it, and drew Jonah even closer, his arms like leather bands around him, his legs tucking against the backs of Jonah's thighs.

Jonah closed his eyes with a sleepy smile.

So Tommy *could* hug.

10

Sunday was a bad day.

It didn't help that Tommy skipped his morning meditation for an extra half hour in bed while Jonah slept. Jonah's skin and sheets smelled like heaven, and the apartment was amber-tinged from the early morning light brushing against the orange feature wall. It was quiet and sacred, and something about Jonah's peaceful features made Tommy feel suspended outside of time.

The sun had risen when security drove him back to the palace, and there in the backseat, Tommy made the mistake of seeking news outside of the articles curated for him to check whether word had spread about his appearance at the Bearded Bunting. He knew better—knew not to distract himself with matters that would pull his focus away from where it was needed most, but he was too desperate to know.

Word had spread.

He'd assumed it would feel good. He *wanted* to be seen in public with Jonah—he couldn't imagine anything more intoxicating that the world knowing they were together. But that was precisely the problem. *They* weren't together. Yes, Tommy was in the photos with Jonah pressing a hand to his chest and looking as if he wanted to melt into him.

But it was Kris's name in the headlines.

Prince Kristof has a new man! Disproving recent speculation that our rogue royal was in a secret relationship with his bodyguard, his Highness was seen picking up his new cowboyfriend at the stroke of midnight last night.

Literally everything about it made Tommy sick. He was forced to swallow the misunderstanding as his own doing, but the oversight cut right to the pit of his stomach. He'd have to talk to Jonah about it.

I need you to pretend to date my straight brother, so I can learn to cope with the social side of being king. Sure, and Jonah would answer, *Of course, exploit us all for your personal gain, Tommy!*

Alarmed, Tommy withdrew to the tower study. He considered a full retreat into the secret stone passageways lining the palace walls, but he at least had to *try* to face this mess.

Frankie was waiting for him—sitting opposite his desk, arms crossed and wearing a look of betrayal. Without saying a word, her attitude-flecked gaze asked where the hell he got off using her fiancé like this.

"I wasn't thinking." Shame was tight in his fists as he sat across from her, sharp in his heartbeat as he asked, "Does Kris know?"

"No." She sounded pissed about that fact. "You asked me not to tell the guys. I've explained it to Philip, because he reads everything printed about this family. We're keeping it out of the others' daily news, which, to be frank, feels dodgy as hell. What exactly did you think you were doing?"

He *thought* he'd been taking control—voluntarily putting himself in a social space despite knowing he would attract attention. Pushing through the fear lodged in his throat because it was his one chance at getting better.

And it had only made him worse.

Throat dry, he answered, "Being seen with my boyfriend."

At her curse, the true depth of his selfishness struck him. What if Frankie wanted to do the same thing once Kris had healed? Not only had Tommy pretended to be someone he wasn't in order to go out in public—he'd been romantic with Jonah while pretending to be the man engaged to Frankie. Kris and Frankie's relationship might not be common knowledge, but that didn't make Tommy's behavior any less appalling.

"I'm sorry." He couldn't move. Couldn't do this. How had he ever believed he was fit for this role? "You've been trying to support me, but we both know you're just humoring a mad prince."

"Hey." Her severe tone startled him into looking up. "I heard your speech last week. Don't use words like that. You're resourceful. Sure, most people can't tap into their brother's identity as a resource, but if they could, I'd bet this strategy wouldn't seem nearly as eccentric. I just think—" She paused, then finished in the careful tone of someone trying not to sound obvious. "You should tell Kris what you're doing."

"I can't." Tommy had nothing to show for it.

He was no closer to being able to look his people in the eye than he'd been a week ago. And while a week was nothing when attempting to overcome a debilitating disorder that had derailed his life for over three years, he could have been at it all year with the same result—because he'd been cheating. He'd taken his brother's name but continued to act like himself, hiding behind his guards and ignoring strangers. And even then, he could still scarcely handle being there. The attention of a crowd held the weight of every person present—and piled it on his chest.

He wasn't even attending meetings as himself. Most of his

guests believed he was Mark. At this rate, he might eventually become capable of small-scale appointments and speeches without photos or questions—but a king needed to be better than that.

Tommy needed to be *so much* better.

And with one month until the coronation, that seemed pretty fucking impossible.

"I can't," he said again, his breath coming faster. "It's not working. None of this is working."

He could set all the plans he wanted in motion, but coping as future king hinged on his mental health. And that had yet to shift toward stability.

"Tommy." Frankie leaned forward in concern. "You don't have to do this. Kris can still ascend."

"No." The burden might break Kris. And while it was threatening to do the same to Tommy, his anxiety hadn't lessened the enduring pull he felt toward the role. He was no more capable of stepping aside and letting Kris take the throne than he was capable of taking it himself. "I should be able to do this. I *want* to do this."

She scanned his face. "Have you spoken to your psych this week?"

"Yesterday." Tommy's fingernails dug into his palms. "She said to keep trying. But it's not working fast enough."

"It was never going to work fast. This is long-term." Frankie ran a hand over her mouth with a frown. "Here's what we'll do. You keep trying the exposure therapy thing, and we won't tell anyone. We'll give it more time. Okay?"

More time.

It wouldn't be enough.

But he couldn't fail this fast. Not already.

"Okay," he said.

He stayed in the tower all day. Thought himself in

downward spirals—pressed his temples so hard he got a headache. Avoided Adam's file, because learning more about a missing murderer who likely wanted him dead wouldn't help his anxiety. Hated himself when he took a diazepam an hour before dinner, because he'd never taken medication to spend time with his family before. But he'd never failed at being a king before, and he didn't want them to sense something was wrong.

Somewhat calmer, he entered the summer dining room in the east wing. The table was set for eight, the natural linen tablecloth and white dinner set doing its best to pass as informal for this family of cowboys who didn't want a fuss. The large room was airy and light, with caramel wood floors, plaster embellishment on the high ceiling, and bifold glass doors that currently exposed his brothers on the balcony, kicking back on outdoor chairs in the fading light. Kris's posture looked a little stiff as he favored one side, while Mark had his boots up on the railing, crossed at the ankle.

"Hey, stranger." Kris glanced at him over his shoulder. Tommy's heavy workload this past week hadn't only prevented him from seeing Jonah. "Get over here."

Tommy moved out to join them, wiping the sweat off his palms by pushing up his sleeves. He pulled up a chair beside Kris.

"Working hard?" Kris raised a brow at him. His bruises had paled to yellow since their poker night, but Tommy wasn't in the right headspace to look at him properly. "Mark's told me about your plans with the mines. I never would have thought of that."

"*Our* plans." Jesus, why had Tommy charged into this like it would all work out? The initial thrill of putting his ideas into action had stopped him from being realistic. "If Mark didn't like them, we wouldn't be—"

"Tommy." Mark set his feet on the tiled balcony floor and

leaned around Kris with a frown. "Don't you think we can stop pretending that I'm the king?"

Christ. Tommy cut his attention between his brothers. *But I'm the one pretending.*

Kris smiled, seeming to misinterpret Tommy's look as positive disbelief. "Seriously, man. You're it."

He was it.

Despite his desire to lead Kiraly as a progressive, peaceful nation, Tommy wanted to bolt. He couldn't be healed by resourcefulness—not in four weeks, and probably not ever. His hands were clammy. He kept his palms against his thighs and prayed the drug in his veins would keep him from fidgeting. "We should give it more time."

"If you'd prefer," Mark said. "But between us, you don't have to ask for my permission or approval anymore. You lead."

The hinge of Tommy's jaw started prickling. He fought the urge to clench it hard enough to wear his teeth down. "I'd still like your opinion."

"I'll give you mine." Kris slapped Tommy's back casually.

"The issue is how *not* to get yours," Mark said, and grunted out a laugh as Kris elbowed him in the side. "Seriously, though, this is good, Tommy. I don't have to worry anymore."

Tommy's brain fired sarcasm and despair simultaneously. *Great, more worry for me,* and *Please don't say that.*

"What were you worried about?" Kris asked.

Mark eyed them both as he rubbed the back of his neck. "This'll sound bad. But since Ava came back and you suggested taking over, Kris, I've worried about that plan not working. That I'd still end up as king and . . . lose Ava." He leaned forward, brow lowered, his gaze on the gardens below. "I know she'd choose Darius—as she should," he rushed to add. "She doesn't want this life for him. And even though she returned for me, she only agreed to stay when the plan was for me to abdicate, which means if that failed and she was suddenly expected to be queen, then she wouldn't—"

They all turned at a soft scuff behind them.

Ava stood inside with a hand resting on the top of a dining chair. She was staring out at Mark with a look of stunned sadness on her face.

"Ava—" Mark shot to his feet so fast his chair jolted back.

"Markus." She took a step toward the balcony doors, hand falling to her side. "Do you really believe that? I thought you knew—there is no choice. It's both of you now. If you have to be king, then we'll figure it out. We're getting *married*." The word came out stricken. "And you believe I would leave you?"

Mark's face was red. "I want what's best for you and Darius. If you had to—"

"No." She shook her head, dismissing the rest of his sentence. "We're here now. Together. And that's where we're staying."

Mark pushed his chair aside to get to her, and Tommy turned toward the gardens as they embraced. *Thank God.* If Tommy failed and nothing went to plan with Kris, at least Mark ascending wouldn't mean an end to his happiness.

Kris shifted back around a moment later.

"How are things with Frankie?" Tommy asked to give the others privacy.

"Strained." Kris scratched the underside of his jaw. "We're not supposed to have sex for another few weeks because of this stab wound."

Tommy snorted. "You ever gone this long?"

"Hey." Kris punched him lightly in the arm. "Be nice."

"I was being nice." Kris hadn't exactly settled for just one woman before Frankie. "How's your recovery going?"

"On track." Frustration edged his voice. "Just stir crazy."

"And," Tommy said before hesitating at the drop in his stomach. "Mentally?"

Kris shot him a quick glance of surprise. "Okay, I think. Chatting with Jonah has helped. I feel better, can sleep better." He gingerly changed position and ended up leaning into Tommy. "It's a bit odd, though. Whenever he talks about the attack, he never mentions you."

Tommy's skin chilled.

He had no idea what to make of that.

"He's talked about the entire thing in detail—but it's like you weren't there."

The anti-anxiety drug suppressed the peak of Tommy's reaction, but it couldn't keep his panic from prodding him right beneath the surface. *Why didn't I take two tablets?*

"Hey, crew." Frankie's voice interrupted from across the room, instantly securing Kris's attention. "Look who wanted to wear his engagement party outfit to family dinner."

Muscles locked, Tommy twisted around. Darius was sitting on her shoulders, wearing little trousers and a collared shirt, grinning from ear to ear. Ava and Mark exclaimed in amazement, closing in as Frankie set him down at the table.

"Goddamn it, that's so cute." Kris started to get to his feet, using Tommy's shoulder for leverage. "Just when I think I couldn't love her any more, she puts a child on her shoulders. I give up. I'll just get more stitches."

Tommy arched a doubtful brow.

"Oh, and Tom." Kris kept his hand on Tommy as he lowered his voice. "I know we haven't spoken about it, because it's . . . you know. Awkward. But she wants kids. So that'll happen at some stage. Just—because you're good at thinking ahead—I thought maybe you'd wondered about . . ."

"Heirs?" Tommy offered, aiming for wry.

Kris cringed. "Yes."

He wasn't wrong. Tommy *had* thought about it. How it could work if Ava and Mark had children together. Ava didn't want her children to endure the pressures of the crown, and with Mark's intended abdication, the line of succession shifted to Tommy.

A line one person long.

Until very recently, his future had looked single and childless, and now, it hardly mattered what happened between him and Jonah. Same-sex relationships had no place in hereditary monarchy.

Hiding his bitterness, he said, "Thanks for letting me know."

It would work. As the third-born triplet, Kris would become the heir presumptive if Tommy ascended, and his and Frankie's children would fill the line of succession.

"Sure." Kris straightened, looked inside, and grinned. "Hey! Uncle Phil's here!"

Still on edge and in no state to be shouted over, Tommy ducked off to one side to lean against the railing and look in through the open balcony doors.

Philip was eyeing Kris levelly. "I recall you saying you wouldn't be a jerk."

"Damn you, past Kris." Still grinning, Kris made his slow way to the table. "Welcome to family dinner. Come sit next to me. You won't regret it."

Philip gave a long-suffering sigh but obliged without protest.

Standing alone, Tommy watched from the balcony as the others moved closer to Kris. No one would sit at the head of the table. Mark and Ava would sit beside Philip and Kris, with Darius always keen to sit next to Frankie on the other side. That would leave a place for Jonah on Darius's left, with Tommy beside him.

Jonah. Where was he? Tommy jumped as Darius dropped a fork, the clang bruising his nerves. Maybe Jonah wasn't coming. Maybe he'd realized that last night had been a mistake. The hard rub of their bodies in the dark, chests and hips and thighs, and clothes, far too many clothes. Except in the cold light of day, maybe Jonah had been thankful for those layers, because kissing his best friend had been weird and uncomfortable and complicated. Jonah should never have done it—and coming to family dinner was not only too soon, it was too *wrong*—

The door opened.

Jonah walked in, expression easy, already smiling.

Tommy's breath turned shaky at the sight of his overnight bag. *He said he'd stay.* Yet that didn't stop a frantic part of Tommy interpreting the bag as Jonah leaving Kiraly. *He's here to say goodbye.* It was like being two people at once. The rational part of him despaired that his anxiety could be so foolish—but his anxiety knew better. It always knew better.

Not noticing him, Jonah moved to the others with a wave. "Hey, everyone!"

Grinning, Kris reached out for a handshake, while Mark stepped forward for a hug. Ava and Philip smiled their hellos, while Frankie said, "Hey, Jones."

"Ma'am," Jonah replied, tipping his head.

Her eyes flared. "Why you—"

"This is Darius," Ava said over the top of her. "Darius, this is Jonah. He's very nice."

"Hi, Darius." Smiling at the boy, Jonah reached into his bag. "I hoped you'd be here. I've got something for you."

Darius turned excited, disbelieving eyes on his mother before snapping his attention back to Jonah.

"I heard you like reading," Jonah said, and presented him with a picture book. Tommy caught a glimpse of a horse and child in watercolor on the cover, and the knot inside him stopped tightening. "I hope you like it."

"I love it!" Darius immediately passed the book to Frankie, who sat and opened the cover. "Thank you."

Smile fading, Jonah asked, "Where's Tommy? He's coming, right?"

Mark nodded toward the balcony. "He's out there."

"Oh." Jonah glanced outside, his gaze locking with Tommy's. "Excuse me."

Tommy pressed back against the railing as Jonah crossed to him, feeling too many things at once. Discomfort that he hadn't come inside at Jonah's arrival. Alarm that the bag might still mean he was leaving. Embarrassment that he could even think that. And dizzying, heart-swallowing adoration that this man had bought a cowboy picture book for Darius.

Then Jonah was standing in front of him, gorgeous and grounded and smelling fresh out of the shower. He cocked his head curiously. "Hello."

Tommy swallowed and looked away. "Hey."

"You didn't think I was coming." Jonah's tone was light as he slipped his palm over where Tommy's hand clutched the railing. His touch was warm; secure and without judgement, and Tommy relaxed his grip a little. "Did you?"

"Most of me knew you were."

"Silly boy." Jonah pressed his other hand to Tommy's chest and rose to kiss his cheek. Tommy closed his eyes at the heat of Jonah's lips, the slight rasp of their cheeks sliding together as Jonah moved his mouth to Tommy's ear. "I'd have been here this morning if I could get in."

"God. Sorry." Tommy was *so* bad at this. "I'll get Frankie to make sure the guards admit you at the gate without question," he said a moment before his gut sank. The guards would assume Jonah was arriving for Kris.

"Tommy." Jonah was still at his ear, breath curling hot into Tommy's hair. "I think you should hug me."

His tone didn't tease or make light of how Tommy should have figured this out for himself. It was just a statement. Tommy wound his arms tightly around him, his face buried in the slope of Jonah's shoulder. It felt like his first proper breath all day. He was safe here—seen and understood. An involuntary noise of need escaped him, and he held Jonah harder.

"Shh." One of Jonah's hands settled at the back of his neck. "What's going on?"

"I'm having a bad day," he murmured, eyes closed beneath a scrunched brow. "And you're making it better."

He heard Jonah smile, and for a truly innocent moment, the gentle stroke of Jonah's fingers removed Tommy's tension like an adult taking a harmful object from a child. *Here now, this is safer with me.* With Jonah's cheek pressed against his hair, this felt like the only thing going right. Not his inability to be social, or the way he'd screwed up going public, or kissing Jonah in the dark, but *this* sense of acceptance right here between them.

Maybe it wasn't too late?

In a matter of days, Jonah had slid from best friend to boyfriend with the ease of shifting sunlight. And he was so incredibly warm—seeping through Tommy's tension with the bright radiance of a stained-glass saint. With Jonah at his side, maybe Tommy could turn this mess around—accept Jonah's support as a chance to self-correct and keep trying to pull this off.

In Jonah's arms, that didn't feel so hard.

"Okay." Tommy pulled back, collecting Jonah's hand. In an effort to change the tone, he asked, "So you really want to stay over?"

"Yes. I realized that I haven't been in your bedroom since high school." Even in the gloaming, Jonah's cheeks darkened noticeably. "And I really, really want to be in your bedroom."

That admission glittered like a sparkler waved too close to Tommy's skin. "So you don't regret—" He blinked when Jonah's fingers pressed over his lips.

"No." Jonah stood so close that his toes were on top of Tommy's. "I don't regret last night. And I'd know if I did, because I've replayed literally everything you said and did and didn't say and didn't do all day. All it's done is make me hot and antsy."

Suddenly the sparkler was inside Tommy, powder-full and flaring. He spoke quietly against Jonah's fingers. "What didn't I do that made you hot?"

Jonah's laugh came from further back in his throat than usual. "How long have you got?"

"All night."

A dart formed between Jonah's brows a moment before he withdrew his hand. "You mean to talk?"

Tommy's gaze dragged to Jonah's mouth. "Perhaps."

"But." Those beautiful lips frowned. "You don't want to rush."

"I didn't want to." And he hadn't. Now it felt like the only thing he *did* want to do.

"Okay," Jonah said slowly. "But it's kind of a big deal to just change your mind. I know I'm not good at hiding what I want, but I'm not trying to pressure you into anything." Then he shook his head and started to move away. "We can talk about it later."

Tommy hooked a finger through one of Jonah's belt loops, keeping him close. "One thing," he said, voice low between them. "Tell me one thing I didn't do last night that's made you hot wanting it."

"Tommy . . ." Jonah rolled his lips as he tucked a glance over his shoulder at the others. His gaze was hazy when he looked back and murmured, "I wanted you to grab my ass. Not rough or anything. Just like you wanted me."

Tommy curled his itching fingers into fists. The movement pressed the knuckles of one hand into the soft space directly beneath Jonah's belt. "What else?"

"I wanted you to . . ." Jonah glanced down, all lashes and lust. "Take off your shirt."

Easy. "What else?"

"Let me undo your belt. And jeans." His breath shook as he placed his palm over Tommy's hand, fingers firm and sure, as if to say, *here, I've been hot thinking about you down here.* "And strip you naked."

Tommy's blood pounded. "What else?"

"Greedy." Desire was black in Jonah's eyes. "No more. We're here to eat, you know."

Right.

Dinner.

With other people.

Tommy dragged in a breath, but the air smelled like Jonah and only blurred his concentration. "Ready to meet my family?"

"I don't know." Jonah feigned nervousness. "I've never met a man's family before."

"Just watch out for Kris." Tommy raised his voice slightly, meeting his brother's curious glance as he gestured Jonah inside. The others moved to take their seats. "He's protective of me, so be prepared for a hard time."

"Oh *no*." Jonah gave Kris a wide berth as Kris pointed two fingers at his eyes and then turned them on Jonah. "He looks very scary and not at all ticklish."

Kris's eyes bulged as he sucked in a horrified breath.

"Wait, what?" Frankie's attention snapped to Kris across the table. "You're ticklish?"

"Nah," he said, far too casually, then rounded on Jonah with an outraged, "*No*."

Tommy drew out Jonah's chair and was rewarded with a secret smile as he pushed it in.

Frankie was gaping at Kris as Tommy took his seat. "How did I not know this?"

"I guess it was easy to miss when you spent our friendship actively avoiding touching me." Kris leaned back to make room for the serving staff who had materialized with their meals and murmured, "Looks amazing, thank you."

"All the boys are ticklish," Jonah said, causing Ava to turn to Mark with delighted interest and Tommy's skin to heat at the thought of Jonah confirming this truth. As if on cue, Jonah reached out to brush his fingertips from the back of Tommy's hand all the way up to his elbow. "Right, Tommy?"

Tommy jolted, flushed, and shoved his arm under the table. *Jesus.* The touch had skimmed the dark hairs on his arm, yet somehow stoked the heat at his groin. It turned out being tickled while aroused caused a paired reaction that he wanted to explore very thoroughly—just absolutely not over family dinner.

Opposite him, Kris was snickering.

"What about you, Darius?" Jonah asked, with all the innocence of apple pie.

With a small squeal, Darius covered his tummy with his arms. "No!"

"Okay." Jonah laughed. "I believe you." Then, once everyone had been served, he said in sudden concern, "Do you guys ever get to eat leftovers anymore?"

Kris grinned. "I still raid the fridge. Fridges. All the fridges."

"Fridge just stopped sounding like a real word," Mark said, picking up his cutlery. "And the chefs are happy to serve leftovers if you ask them, Kris."

Kris snorted. "Then what would I eat when I get snacky overnight?"

Jonah smiled, looking between them. "It's so good to eat with you guys again."

Tommy froze, guilty, before Jonah placed a comforting hand on his leg under the tablecloth and leaned close. "Don't," he said quietly. "It was because you liked me. You can't feel bad about that."

Twisting his fingers around Jonah's, Tommy let himself believe that.

"It's good to have you here, Jonah." Mark held his eye with obvious sincerity. Then he angled his head and added, "It would be nicer still if Mom and Dad were here. Like old times."

"Sure would," Kris said, and Tommy nodded—then frowned as he realized he couldn't eat while holding Jonah's hand.

Okay, then. He sat back in his chair.

"They're doing well." Jonah looked to all three brothers, his brows raised in conviction. "I visited them every week. We'd talk about the neighbors and work and you guys. They miss you a lot, but they're doing okay."

God. Tommy had abandoned him—and Jonah had made an effort to check in on his parents.

"I've been meaning to ask, though," Jonah continued. "Why did they leave Kiraly in the first place? I tried to ask subtlety, you know, but they never mentioned."

Philip shifted uncomfortably as he cut his potatoes but didn't speak.

Kris raised a shoulder. "Dad left in a stand against our Uncle Vinci's ruling style. He was selfish and indulgent and used the nation's money for his own pleasure. Mom was newly pregnant, and Dad didn't want any child of his being raised thinking that behavior was okay."

Philip turned to stare at Kris in equal parts shock and affront.

"Philip," Tommy said. "What do you know that we don't?"

"I'm sorry." Philip gave a disbelieving shake of his head. "But that's not what happened at all."

Jonah's hand pressed into Tommy's thigh.

"I assume you know King Vinci's marriage to the queen was strategic? They hadn't met prior to their engagement, and there was no love between them on their wedding day." Philip gestured briefly to Tommy and his brothers. "But your father was

202

the youngest of three princes. He didn't have the same pressure to make an advantageous match, so had the freedom to pursue your mother. It—" Philip paused, apology all over his face. "Your father was young. Tactless. Obnoxiously in love, I'm afraid to say, to the point that he was critical of the relationship between the king and queen. What Erik didn't realize was that the queen's illness changed something in Vinci, and by the time she passed away, Vinci was devoted to her. He'd lost a woman he could have spent the rest of his life loving—and the irony of not knowing that until it was too late was almost too much for him to bear."

There was an unsettled silence as they waited.

"This isn't public knowledge," Philip said. "Noel told me years later. But apparently, on the day of the queen's funeral, your father attempted to reassure Vinci by saying at least he hadn't loved her, because Erik couldn't imagine the torture of losing his own wife. He said that Vinci was lucky it had only been a strategic marriage after all."

"What the hell?" Kris reeled back in his chair.

"Dad said that?" Mark was pale.

With an awful crawling sensation in his chest, Tommy remembered phone calls with their father when they'd first arrived in Kiraly. He'd demanded that Tommy not let Mark ruin his life by agreeing to the strategic marriage to Ava. His father had almost hung up on him when Tommy had claimed it was Mark's decision.

"Vinci ordered Erik and your mother to leave Kiraly immediately." Regret lined Philip's thin features. "He cut off their access to the royal accounts and refused them staff and security. Since they were so happy together, he claimed they shouldn't need anything but each other."

Kris was shaking his head in shock.

Mark looked ashen.

And Tommy was . . . okay. He breathed slowly, his focus

split between the conversation and the increasing heat of Jonah's touch. This had all happened twenty-five years ago. It didn't change the father Tommy knew, humbled by small-town life and hard work. It didn't change the wonder of Jonah sitting beside him, halfway across the world from where they'd met, a thousand dreams ahead of where Tommy thought they'd ever be.

It didn't change the fact that Jonah would spend the night in his suite.

And that Tommy had waited for him long enough.

They just had to get through dinner first.

"That's why Kiraly didn't know about us," he guessed, in an effort to stay present.

"That's right, Tomas." Philip sounded as if he wasn't sure whether he should continue. "Vinci banned the media from mentioning Erik after that. He didn't want the reminders—didn't want anyone tracking Erik down and putting him back in the headlines. Not that it helped. The queen's death changed him. Vinci shut out the world, and like Kristof said, he became indolent and selfish in his depression. He wasn't the great king he'd once been—but it wasn't why your father left, and it's unfair on Vinci for you three to believe it was."

The silence that followed was heavy with dismay.

But surprisingly short-lived.

"Well," Jonah said, looking from Tommy to Kris to Mark. "I'm glad your dad used to be a jerk. Because if he hadn't done any of that, he'd never have moved as far away from here as possible, and I never would have met you. My life would be . . ." His hand slackened on Tommy's thigh as he finished, "Much worse."

"Same." Tommy never wanted to consider a life without Jonah.

And right now, he dared to hope he'd never have to.

"If it helps," Jonah continued, brightening. "You could figure out what you want Erik to be remembered for in Kiraly."

"What do you mean?" Tommy moved his thumb over the back of Jonah's hand. Neither of them had picked up their cutlery. "Most people have forgotten him."

"I know." Jonah looked unsure as he turned to him. "After you mentioned that you don't know how to continue with the construction work on the west wing, I started asking people at the bar what they liked most about your uncles and other family. I thought it might give you some ideas? You said you wanted it to be thoughtful. I've written down some good answers for Vinci and Noel, and your cousin, and some of the older patrons mentioned the queen, too, but no one's said anything about Erik. It would be nice if you guys decided. Then you can make sure the renovation tips its hat to them all somehow."

Everyone stared at him.

"Jonah." Tommy fought the urge to drag him away and love him until that kind heart was well and truly racing.

Philip said, "You would—that could be Noel's legacy?"

"I think so." Jonah nodded in earnest.

Blinking a little too fast, Philip said, "Ah," and looked out to the balcony.

"So, Jonah," Ava said, smoothly shifting the focus from the adviser. "How long did you originally plan to holiday in Europe?"

Tommy stiffened at the implication that Jonah's plans had changed. They hadn't spoken about it. It was too early for Tommy to ask about their future without coming across as expectant or desperate, and—he had to keep reminding himself—it wasn't as if this new intimacy between them trumped Jonah's travel plans.

"Oh, uh." Jonah seemed as uncomfortable as Tommy. "It's not exactly a holiday."

"I apologize." Ava picked up her wine glass. "I didn't intend to trivialize your work at the bar. Of course, it's not a holiday. I should have said travel."

"No, it's not that. It's just—" His expression was strange as he looked at Tommy. Hesitant, almost guarded. "I'm not going back to Sage Haven at all."

He wasn't?

Hope swelled in Tommy like an ocean. *Is he committing to this?* Three days ago, Jonah had admitted to not having his head around Tommy's royal status—he'd just wanted to see where this exploration took them. Tommy had no idea it had taken them so far already.

Tommy couldn't help it—he smiled. "You're staying?"

Jonah made a sound that was either *I'm* or *um,* and shifted, fiddling with the hem of the tablecloth with his free hand. "Actually, I was going to tell you later."

"You guys need to let each other go and start eating," Kris muttered, mouth full.

Tommy ignored him. "You're not going back at all?" Despite the swelling in his chest, he tried to be practical. Jonah couldn't live to regret packing up his entire life. He had to be sure about this. "What about the house?"

"Tommy." Suddenly, Jonah withdrew his palm. The absence dissolved something in Tommy's chest that he hadn't noticed was there. "I've already sold it."

Sold it? How he could he possibly have—

Oh. Jesus.

Properties didn't go to market and sell within a week—Jonah must have sold before he'd come to Kiraly. Must have already decided not to go back. *Because of me.* Dismayed, Tommy stared at him, at the way Jonah gripped the edges of his chair, shoulders tight, gaze fixed on his lap. His discomfort was palpable, the low-key anguish of someone who hated making others feel bad.

Except Tommy *should* feel bad. Jonah had loved that property—until Tommy had abandoned him and clearly nothing about Sage Haven had been the same. "I'm so sorry," he said, scarcely aware that the others had started their own conversation at an elevated volume.

"No, Tommy it's not because—" Jonah's face flushed. He shook his head and the stiff movement held distress. "I . . . I was going to sell anyway. I was planning on selling it before you left."

Tommy felt like he'd slipped over.

Moving forward one moment, losing all sense of balance the next.

Before you left. He almost asked what Jonah meant—but he already knew.

God, he knew.

Jonah's inhale was uneven as he shot Tommy a stricken look. "I was planning on moving away by Christmas."

Everything around Tommy crystalized, as if the lights and smells and voices were all suddenly coated in shards of glass.

"Tommy?" Jonah spoke quietly, but the word seemed to cut into Tommy's senses. "Can we go somewhere else?"

Tommy stood and inclined his head in a stilted imitation of *follow me*. And, after Jonah said a heartfelt, "I'm so sorry, everyone, please keep eating without us," they strode from the room.

In the corridor, the air held static electricity—crackling against his skin, sparking painfully in his lungs.

At his suite, Tommy stood back to hold the door open. Jonah's glance was cautious, but it didn't stop him passing unnecessarily close, elbow grazing Tommy's stomach as he entered. He took one look at the large sitting room, shook his head, and strode on to the bedroom.

Perfect. Because *this* was the first memory Tommy wanted them to share in there.

Pulse tight, he followed, closing the door behind them and watching as Jonah tossed his bag at the foot of the bed. *Still planning on staying.* The lights in the wall sconces were dimmed, emitting a glow that turned Jonah's dark hair into toffee and his skin to bronze as he took in the room. The simple furnishings—nightstand, dressing table, armchair—couldn't disguise the ornamentation on the walls and ceiling, the blue-sheeted bed the size of a small lake, or the chandelier that Tommy had requested be left during the refurbishment.

The room belonged to royalty.

"I was going to tell you." Jonah's tone held apology as he faced Tommy.

"You were going to *leave*." It came out too accusing, too raw. "Before any of this."

"Yes." Jonah's stance widened, a movement of skin-hugging jeans and strong thighs and sleek calves, and for a moment, his vicinity to the bed derailed the hell out of Tommy's focus. "And before you compare us, I would never tell you the same day I left. I was going to give you more than six months to get used to the idea. I was going to make it *work* for us. Being apart. We would have stayed friends. I'd have kept in touch. Every day, you know I would have. And I'd have visited as often as I could, so it's not the same."

It wasn't the same.

Tommy would have had to live in Sage Haven without Jonah.

It was stupid that it hurt this badly. It hadn't even happened. Yet Jonah had *intended* to leave, and discovering that was like Tommy putting his foot through a floor he hadn't known was damaged. It stopped him—brought him abruptly to his knees.

And all he could see down here was guilt.

Jonah was watching him carefully. "You know why, don't you, Tommy?"

Fighting the truth, Tommy said the first thing that came into his head. "Because I wasn't enough."

"What?" Jonah pulled back. Irritation flashed across his face. "How could you say that? You were everything I needed in a friend. More. But friendship by itself can't make me feel whole. You were like . . . like all the water I could drink—but the town was empty, and I could never get enough to eat. Humans can go for longer without food than water, you know, so I think that's what I'd done. You kept me alive, but I'd never had enough to eat. And I was hungry, Tommy. So hungry to belong."

Something hot and sickly was churning in Tommy's heart.

Jonah stepped toward him. "Because I *never* belonged there."

It was rising higher in his chest. A foul flush at his collarbones.

"Tell me you know that."

Tommy's throat grew thick at the atrocity of this man being allowed to starve; at Tommy's own culpability.

Jonah peered at him with a frown, eyes narrowed, stepping closer. "You need to talk to me, Tommy. We're having this conversation."

"You didn't belong."

An old truth. It had swum in the dark depths of his awareness, a cold silhouette, so far down he'd let himself forget for months at a time. Now it lurched around, churning deep, tail thumping, unable to be ignored.

"You stayed because of me," Tommy said. "And I was selfish. I never asked if you'd thought about moving away. I refused to give life to that conversation, because I didn't want to hear your answer. I didn't want you to do it, I—" Shame made him hesitate. "I didn't want you to leave me."

Jonah was nodding. "I didn't want to either. It would have broken me. But I can't stay somewhere I'm not accepted for who

I am. Not anymore. Because that was breaking me every single day."

There it was—the steel at Jonah's core. Easy to miss, hidden beneath his ever-present smile and desire to get along, but underneath his general acquiescence was a self-respect that no one could touch.

Jonah knew what he deserved—even if he'd rarely received it.

It hurt to ask, "Where were you going to go?"

"I don't know. My only plan was to open my own bar." His brow dipped, and he continued almost warily. "I still want that. Do you remember? It's all I've ever wanted. A place where I can build my own community and make everyone feel safe and welcome."

An honest dream.

Incompatible with a future together.

If Jonah stayed with Tommy, he'd be expected to commit to royal life.

Alarmed, Tommy realized that he'd underestimated the threat Jonah posed to their relationship. The greatest risk had been Jonah ultimately not wanting to be with him, but that had lessened with every text and flirtation and touch. Now Tommy had to accept that no matter how well their relationship progressed, Jonah could choose to put his yearning to belong above a life with Tommy.

In a surge of panicky need, he crossed the floor and grabbed Jonah's hand.

"I guess we're even," Jonah said softly, sliding his palm more securely into Tommy's and bringing his body closer. The proximity sucked like a vacuum seal in Tommy's torso, locking their energy together. Jonah's eyes half-closed as he swayed into him. "You left me because you were finally putting your heart first, and I was going to leave you to do the same."

Silent, Tommy clenched his teeth.

Stay with me, he wanted to beg. *Let me be your heart to put first.*

"Tommy?" Jonah lifted Tommy's hand to his chest, setting it exactly where Tommy had touched him in the lake. Despite the innocence of it, Jonah's breath was getting quicker, his eyes darker. They were alone in Tommy's room. Strain knotted Tommy's stomach as Jonah tipped his face up to him, the promise of an invitation that hadn't yet been extended. "If you hadn't moved to Kiraly, and I'd gone ahead with my plans, you wouldn't have told me how you felt before I left, would you?"

Tommy wished he could lie. The air around them ached. "No."

As he shook his head, Jonah's other hand found Tommy's waistband, several fingers slipping beneath the denim. His body heat traveled through the tucked cotton shirt, jolting across Tommy's middle. *Touch me.* Leaning harder into the contact, Tommy lost a breath when Jonah angled his wrist and slid right down to his knuckles, the backs of his fingers pressing into the sensitive edge of his hipbone. *God, I want him to touch me.*

"It's given me a scare," Jonah said. "Discovering you feel this way. Knowing I was going to leave and never find out. I came so close to missing the most intense feeling of my life."

The close call was hitting them both.

Tommy couldn't understand how he'd walked away that day —honest to God couldn't comprehend it. It shouldn't have been physically possible to leave this man, but he had, and he could hardly breathe remembering it.

He truly had pulled out his own heart.

Surrendering that pain, he said, "I can't not be with you, Jonah."

Jonah took a step backward, pulling on Tommy's jeans, more insistent than suggestive. There was no trace of his coy smile or flirtatious lashes. His desire was serious, determined, and it turned Tommy on faster than anything he'd done before.

"Talking about being apart makes me sad." Jonah took another step back. Blood roaring, Tommy allowed himself to be led. "And even more desperate to be close to you."

"Jonah . . ." This mood between them was new. Heavy, hot, and stinging. Tommy's entire body felt like a storm about to break. "I haven't done this before."

"We don't have to." Jonah's voice was getting hazy. "We can hug. I just need to be against you."

"No." Adrenaline was throwing Tommy's heartbeat out of rhythm. His thoughts were stuttering, coming in stops and starts at the possibility of Jonah's naked body under his. This wasn't about their future. This was about right now. "Not just hugging."

"Are you sure?" Jonah kept backing up.

"Yes."

"You can stop being sure at any point, alright?"

Then the back of Jonah's legs hit the bed, and Tommy closed in—hands on either side of Jonah's face, fingertips sinking into his hairline, kissing him without warning or grace. It was messy, insistent in a way he hadn't allowed himself to be last night, and Jonah reacted with a full-body shudder and hard-fingered scrabble at the base of Tommy's spine. Then his shirt was untucked, and it was bare palms against skin, and mother of God, this was really happening.

Kissing harder for how close he'd come to never telling Jonah how he felt, Tommy slid one hand fully into Jonah's hair and dropped the other to grasp the heart-stopping curve of his ass.

It was—*Christ*—firm and curved and shaped as if molded by Tommy's own palm.

Jonah whimpered, arching until their sternums met, aligned like pulsing lifelines, and Tommy reveled in instinctive satisfaction. *That, more of that.* More taking hold of Jonah's pleasure, causing it, drawing it out of him in a helpless burst. The responsive weakening of his limbs betrayed there was so much more to find, an abundance of pleasure right beneath the surface.

Tommy tightened his grip, and the push-back of Jonah's kiss hinted at a deeper delight that wouldn't give itself up quite so readily.

It was up to Tommy to draw it out.

God, yes. Hot greed rippled across his abdomen. He wanted to be the driving force, the weight pressing down, the commander and caregiver. Every time he'd imagined this—and fuck, he'd imagined being with Jonah more times than his hand remembered—he'd *always* been the one in control. Kissing him against the stable door, swallowing him in the cabin of his truck, pressing into him by the campfire. Erotic, confident fantasies—

That had never, ever involved a power dynamic skewed so appallingly in his favor.

Oh. Jesus.

"You okay?" Jonah drew back, looking a little dizzy. "What's wrong?"

Wrong. Tommy was a would-be king in his own palace wanting to dominate the friend he'd deliberately abandoned. Their disparity made his gut churn.

Jonah's sexual experience was the only card he held over Tommy, and it wasn't even an enduring power. He deserved to use it tonight.

"I just . . ." With a flush, Tommy yielded this domain. "Need you to tell me what to do."

"How about," Jonah said, and glanced over his shoulder, "we head down there?"

Approving, Tommy put a palm to Jonah's chest and nudged him onto the mattress.

Jonah went easily, kicking off his boots and sliding back to lie in the center of the bed. He paused briefly in a pose of heady seduction, one knee bent outward and an arm outflung over his head, before murmuring, "Actually, I'll just—" and stripped his shirt over his head. Like it was nothing. Like after a few days of courting and candor, Tommy should have somehow been prepared for it.

He wasn't. The sight of Jonah laid out half-naked in his bed, waiting for him, *wanting* him, was nothing Tommy had ever . . . It wasn't a reality he'd ever expected to . . . Jonah's hair was in disarray, his gaze sex-softened like the supplicant angle of his limbs. A present with the ribbon artfully undone.

How did lungs work again?

The shirt had tousled Jonah's hair, knocked his glasses a little to one side. As he went to set them straight, Tommy found himself saying, "Don't move."

Jonah froze. His hand hovered inches from his face. Only his lips broke the order, parting on a shaky breath.

"Just—let me." Breath shallow, Tommy toed off his boots and went down onto the bed, starting at the shallow crescents of Jonah's calves and stroking a hard line up the underside of his knees—Jonah shivered—then over the lean strength of his thighs. "Jesus," he muttered, half aware that he'd become lost in the feel of Jonah's legs, the hamstrings, the insides of his knees, the raised muscle of his quads, before advancing higher—Jonah gasped, hips canting, fighting against Tommy's request not to move—to grab his belt and work him free. "Lift," he said, permitting Jonah to raise just enough to peel the jeans over his hips, his ass, all the way over his feet.

Then Jonah was naked but for his underwear, rib cage swelling on each breath, stomach scars white in the low light, coal-black eyelashes practically resting on his cheeks as he kept his eyes on Tommy.

Overcome, Tommy said, "You're so . . ." but let the sentence go.

He'd never be able to decide on an ending.

With his heartbeat harsh in his chest, Tommy resumed his exploration. Skin and muscle reacted beneath his hands and his lips, jolting, locking, driving him crazy, until his palms were passing over the fabric either side of Jonah's erection. Need sparked at Tommy's groin at Jonah's quiet moan, so he swept his thumbs inward over the cotton, tips grazing the sides of his shaft, and said, "Louder."

Jonah obliged as Tommy swept back the other way.

God. Jonah's blood-filled heat was flame against Tommy's nerve endings. *I'm touching him.* He could do more. Give more. Right now. Pull Jonah's underwear down and curl a hand around him, stroking until his desire spilled from the inside out.

"Not yet." The uneven sound of Jonah's voice startled him. "Tom? Come here."

Tommy stretched out over him, mindful of his belt buckle and Jonah's bare skin as he positioned himself between his thighs. Even dressed, Jonah's nakedness burned him. He was naked, *right here*, and felt so fucking good that Tommy didn't understand how anyone got anything done when they could have sex. They could do this whenever they wanted. In the mornings before breakfast. After breakfast. Morning tea. And lunch, he'd start taking lunch breaks, and who the hell needed dinner? They could just come to bed and do this, over and over, and that would be—

Jonah's laugh was soft, endeared. "Good?"

"Yeah." Bracing one arm in the sheets, Tommy reached out and resettled Jonah's glasses on his nose. "You?"

Jonah nodded, heavy-lidded. "You feel amazing on me."

With a low hum, Tommy ran a hand along Jonah's side— the tender skin under his arm, the dip beneath his ribs, and back up to the curve of his shoulder. It was smooth and sturdy and, right in the center, red with tiny broken blood vessels.

Pressing his lips to the mark, Tommy murmured, "You can move again."

That was giving over control, right?

"Oh, wow, thanks." Jonah's voice was a rich blend of amusement and lust before his arms came around Tommy and he shifted his hips, pressing their cocks together.

A surge of sensation had Tommy gasping and curving at the waist, seeking harder friction as his mind frayed. *This.* This was sex with another person. With Jonah. The pressure of their bodies. The torture of Jonah's endless skin. And the heat, God above, the heat.

Tommy had to get his clothes off.

"I haven't told you." Jonah spoke from beneath him. "I said your name once."

Breath in tatters, Tommy pulled back.

"With Charlie." A blush was dark on his cheekbones. "He was—busy with me, and you came into my head, and for a second I thought it was you. So I called out your name instead."

"Say it," Tommy demanded, reeling.

Surprise lifted Jonah's features. "What?"

"My name." The urge was physical. A pounding in the base of his being. "Will you say my name like that?"

Jonah scraped his bottom lip with his teeth, feigning confusion as he pushed Tommy's hair back from his face. "Like what?"

Growling faintly, Tommy kissed him on the corner of his luscious mouth. The underside of his chin. The soft skin at his temple, above and then below the arm of his glasses. Then he rocked his hips at the exact moment he murmured in Jonah's ear, "Like a promise."

Gasping a mindless, "I promise," Jonah rolled beneath him, a wriggling wave, and Tommy marveled that he could unravel Jonah's entire body with just a few words.

"Jonah." Tommy outlined the shell of his ear with his nose. "You don't even know what you're promising."

"Anything." Though it sounded more like *aaahhyeahanything,* because Tommy's teeth had started tugging on his earlobe.

"Say my name like a promise." Tommy was not in control of himself, blood thickening, need rumbling like thunder across the plane of his chest. *I have no right to ask this.* But something primal inside him wanted it, a base note of demand, so he said, "That you'll never say anyone's name like mine, ever again."

His heart stopped as Jonah stilled to stare at him.

Then a helplessly whispered, "Oh, Tommy," set it beating again.

Swallowing, Tommy said, more firmly this time, "Tell me what to do."

"I told you." Jonah hadn't moved. With a heavy blink, his eyes turned from awe to arousal. "I told you earlier."

Yes. Earlier. He'd told him.

Rolling off to one side, Tommy then rose to his knees in the sheets and peeled his shirt over his head before tossing it behind him. Then he waited, suddenly unsure how Jonah wanted to undress the rest of him.

"Oh my God." Jonah actually sighed as he pushed onto his elbows, nudging his glasses back up his nose and gaping. "You're a lot to look at, aren't you?"

Tommy had no answer to that.

Sitting up, Jonah twisted to rest on his shins, staying low, and Tommy's next breath was ragged, a swift staccato of inhaled *oh-oh-ohs,* like he'd been running his whole life to reach this moment and couldn't catch his breath now that it was here. Flicking a distracted smile at him, Jonah grasped his waist and laced a string of open-mouthed kisses low across Tommy's middle. Which was, *fuck,* too close to his erection and too pushy with tongue for

Tommy to contain a sudden rush of pleasure. It was too heavy for so early, too thick to push back, and alarm shot through him as Jonah's hands slid to Tommy's belt.

Think of something else. Anything else.

But there *wasn't* anything else as his buckle came undone and Jonah's hands set to work on his button and zipper. The illicit sensation of someone else's hands—*Jonah's* hands—moving against his junk tore a groan from the back of his throat and he closed his eyes, gripping Jonah's shoulder as if that could hold him back from the edge. "Do you really need to push that—"

Tommy pitched forward on a strangled groan as Jonah's knuckles stroked him firmly through the denim.

"—hard?"

"Tommy." Jonah's voice was deep and doughy as he slid both hands inside the elastic of Tommy's underwear and lowered everything in a single sweep. There was a moment of utter stillness, a hitched breath, before he said, "Would this be okay?"

Tommy barely refrained from covering his eyes with his hand.

Jonah sat on his heels in front of him, hands cupping the backs of Tommy's thighs right beneath his ass, looking up, his pupil-black eyes unwavering. His pulse fluttered in his neck; his lips sat open, heavy with his meaning.

"Uh." Tommy tensed. *I'll come in seconds.*

"You know," Jonah said easily, drawing back and rising to his knees. The air grew heavier in Tommy's lungs. "I've wanted to have you since you climbed the tower in front of me."

Tommy almost sank into Jonah in confession. "And I've wanted you for—" *ever.*

"You have." Jonah leaned in slowly to kiss his neck, and *goddamn it,* it happened again—the solid heat of Jonah's mouth seemed to have a direct line to Tommy's impending orgasm, because just one kiss had his pleasure gathering with mortifying insistence. Jonah moved along the entire column of his throat, nibbling gently, dragging Tommy closer and closer to the edge. "Do you want this?"

"Yes. I want it." It came out coarse, almost broken. Then he mentally bit down on his pride and added in a red-faced whisper, "But I won't last."

Jonah pulled back so they were eye-to-eye. "Oh, you definitely won't," he said, and the boldness of those words neatly switched the implication from Tommy's failure to be a virgin marathon lover to Jonah's undeniable ability to please him. He placed a hand on Tommy's solar plexus. "Don't let it bother you. We'll just do it again later, if you want?"

The world went silent in Tommy's ears.

He must have nodded, because moments later he was staring at the ceiling, breath labored and body trembling as Jonah broke him apart with the firm slide of his hands—over his stomach, the juncture where leg met hip, the untouched insides of his thighs. And finally, his cock, the barrel of Jonah's hand gifting perfectly pressured strokes before palm gave way to mouth.

And Tommy

lost him

self

Spilling like a heatwave over the edges of his body, burning like the stars on the backs of his eyelids, the brightest of all in this bed with him, lighting him up with every pull and slide and suck —every shared sound of pleasure from low in his chest, every glorious second that reduced the entire fucking cosmos to one man's wet, hot ecstasy.

In the mindlessness of his final thrusts, he hoped it felt good for Jonah, too.

Then he was coming down, reforming, relearning to breathe. He heard his panting before he felt it—heard himself groan as Jonah carefully released him. He sank into the mattress, a satisfied glow in his muscles. Somehow, he'd ended up clasping one of Jonah's hands over his chest, their fingers laced and squeezing. The other was buried deep in Jonah's hair, which he withdrew slowly, tugging lightly on the tips of the strands and receiving something close to a purr in response.

Jonah raised his head, eyes hungry.

The look pushed Tommy up onto his elbows. "My turn."

"I need to hold you," Jonah said, sounding miles away yet right between Tommy's ribs as he slid up and over him. His underwear was gone; there was nothing but skin as their bodies locked together. His breath seared Tommy's neck; his grip was eager on Tommy's biceps.

Let him. Tommy clamped down on the instinct to roll, to cover him, to feel Jonah writhe beneath him. He'd failed to give Jonah control earlier. *If this is what he wants, let him do it.*

"Tommy," Jonah breathed against his ear, hot and fragile and desperate. "Hold me." Not an order, but a plea.

Tommy banded his arms around him.

"Tommy," he said again, head moving almost helplessly, nose brushing Tommy's lips, forehead grazing his brow, mouth passing over his chin. "Please. I need you. Please."

"Hey." Tommy angled his head to capture his mouth, stilling Jonah's agitation. Jonah weakened at the kiss, settling over him, his cock a slick weight between them. He was trembling. They both were. They'd been friends for twenty years and never been this exposed, never asked this much of each other. Desperate to give him everything he needed, to not disappoint him, Tommy slid a hand to the base of Jonah's spine, applying pressure as he rocked his own hips upward. "Is like this okay?"

Jonah mirrored the movement, mouth slipping away with a groan.

Tommy took that as a yes.

Their bodies found a rhythm as Jonah gave Tommy

everything he needed—his name in Jonah's mouth, voiced over and over like Tommy was his clearest thought, his purest fantasy, the only man Jonah would ever want to please him.

It was enough to go to Tommy's head.

More than enough to fill his heart.

The sheets were damp when Jonah's movements grew restless, like a tangle of twine with no end that Tommy would eagerly spend the rest of his life chasing. *Please let there be no end.* But there was, and it was building in the quickening rubs Jonah made against him, his deepening gasps and groans, his pleasure-drenched babble. "Tommy, oh, God. I love this, please, hold me, Tommy, please." Until finally Jonah said, *"Oh,"* in a completely different way and clamped both hands with startling fierceness over Tommy's shoulders.

And Tommy turned to ice.

He was pinned.

Men were jamming him into the ground. Three of them, maybe four, no—

One—just one—it's Jonah—fuck—not this—not now

They were victorious and vicious and not going to stop. They had Jonah and a knife, and they were not going to stop—

no, fight it—it's not real

Panic clamped him as the knife slid to Jonah's throat—

stop, no

The blade met skin, and Tommy wanted to fight, wanted to kill, wanted to die, but he couldn't move beneath the weight of the men, couldn't reach Jonah or scream or stop them, stop them—

"Stop," he croaked.

The pressure stilled—then released him abruptly.

oh, God—breathe—just breathe

He opened his eyes, half-expecting a violent-struck country

road, but couldn't see at all. Oh Christ, why couldn't he see? Why couldn't he—

"Tommy?"

Something touched the side of his face, and he sprang back in dread, scrambling, trying to get to his feet, but the ground was too soft. Disoriented, he fell back, slamming against a hard surface. Pain flashed across his shoulders. His pulse was racing, fear tight in his larynx. He still couldn't see.

He blinked rapidly, breath shredded, waiting and holding down panic.

Gradually, his palace suite came into focus. Safe; guarded. A world he controlled.

And Jonah—

oh, God

He was crouched on the tumbled sheets halfway down the bed—naked, shaking visibly, watching Tommy. He held one hand over his mouth, the other between his legs. Tears pooled in his eyes.

"Fuck." Tommy swallowed a sudden acid reflux. It kicked back in his gut and rose again as he found himself pressed against the bedhead like a frightened animal. "What—did I—oh, Jesus, I didn't mean—"

Jonah lowered his hand and began saying, "Shhh," on a soft breath.

Tommy stared, silenced, distress ripping away his half-formed thoughts.

Jonah gazed back, tears on his cheeks.

The sound stretched on, steady and guiding like the hum of traffic when lost in the woods, until Jonah finished with a gentle, "Share."

Tommy covered his eyes. His palm was instantly wet. *I can't.*

"Tommy, please."

He forced himself to say, "I'm too ashamed."

"You have no reason to be ashamed." Jonah was whispering. He didn't move any closer. "It's okay."

Okay? Nothing was okay. How the fuck could this be okay?

"Tommy?" Jonah's voice wavered. "I want to come to you. Do you need me to stay over here?"

He didn't know. He didn't know. How the hell was he supposed to know?

"It's okay. I'll stay here."

Humiliation burned on Tommy's tongue, but the ache in his chest had him lowering a hand to the pillow beside him, palm up.

The bedcovers rustled, and then Jonah was taking his hand with agonizing wariness.

"I'm sorry." Rattled, Tommy wanted to cry, would have settled for a scream, but didn't want to scare Jonah more than he already had. "It was our first time, and I ruined it. I fucking ruined it."

"You didn't." Jonah's thumb brushed over his knuckles. "It was amazing."

"You—" Tommy lowered the hand from his eyes. Jonah rested on his shins, knees tucked under a pillow. "Did you make it before I . . ."

"Oh. No." A strange expression shadowed Jonah's face—confusion tinged with a queasy dismay. "I mean—I was about to, but then you said stop. And I tried to—I really did—but my body was already there, you know, so it ended up on the sheets." He looked as if he wanted to lower his face but refused to be disgraced.

Mortification burned at Tommy's core. Jonah had been calling his name like a fantasy come to life, and Tommy had frozen—he'd told Jonah to *stop* on the precipice of climax, for Christ's sake. That had to make him the worst lover of Jonah's life. Self-disgust flooded him, so hot that his diaphragm lurched, threatening to purge it out because it sure as hell couldn't stay inside him.

"Everything else was amazing," Jonah added.

Tommy closed his eyes, debilitated by his failure.

"Hey." Jonah's hold on him tightened. "You know what would have ruined it? If you'd felt like that and *didn't* say stop. I'd never have forgiven myself."

So it was just Tommy who'd never forgive himself. "I hate that I've disappointed you."

"You haven't. Tommy. Sex is more than orgasms." As Tommy started shaking his head, Jonah said, "I'm sorry I didn't realize you were anxious. I should have noticed."

Oh, the irony. "I wasn't anxious."

Jonah's pause seemed confused. "Will you tell me what happened?"

Don't tell him. Not about the position; the trigger of Jonah's grip pushing him down. *He might not forgive himself for that either.*

That left Tommy with a truth he'd battled in some way or another for over three years.

He opened his eyes. "I couldn't reach you."

Jonah frowned at their joined hands.

"It was an intrusive memory of the attack." Tommy's voice came out thin, as if it had lost a lot of blood—just like the sudden pallor of Jonah's face. "That's twice since it happened to Kris. It's triggered these memories, and I can't—"

Forget.

Couldn't shake the trauma of thinking Jonah had died. The powerlessness of being held down, unable to help him. The indignity and terror and outrage, and the single fear that continued to bleat in his heart: *I can't get to Jonah.*

"I can't reach you." His voice cracked. "I can never reach you."

Jonah shifted, his thigh resting against Tommy's knee, as if to say, *I'm right here.* He didn't speak. Probably because he wasn't comfortable offering words that might not hold into the future. Or, Tommy realized with a thud, because they hadn't spoken about that night in years. An open conversation, just the two of them. They always talked around it. Tommy, because he hated remembering, and Jonah, because he was sensitive to Tommy's needs.

Well. Maybe freaking the fuck out while losing his virginity was a sign that he might have missed this step in his recovery.

"Kris said you don't talk about me."

"Oh." Jonah drew back, looking caught out. "Did he? Huh. I guess not."

In the silence, Tommy grabbed the bedspread and dragged it over their laps, lifting their joined hands to rest on top. Then he said, possibly for the first time in their entire friendship, "You need to tell me more than that."

Jonah ducked his head. "I just—I've dealt with it? I know it was about those men and their issues, not about me. Your brothers rescued us, so I know I was worth saving. And you all supported me after, helped me recover, and never told me it was my fault." He flashed a pained glance at Tommy. "I believed that for a while, but you caught me, remember?"

Yes. Months after the attack, he'd glimpsed Jonah's tattoo under the sleeve of his shirt—the *h* added in ballpoint between the first two letters. Tommy had scooped him up and carried him into the bathroom without hesitation. *"They don't get to win,"* he'd said, scrubbing at the pen mark, scared to the point of fury at Jonah's silent tears. *"They don't get to do this to you. You're the best person in this town. I won't lose you to shame, you hear me?"*

"I've processed it." Jonah shifted, uncomfortable. "But you haven't, Tommy. I've walked away with a horrific memory, but you have to deal with this every day. It's the one thing I can't get over. That you're like this because of—"

Tommy's hand covered Jonah's mouth.

"No." It came out like a curse.

With a soft sound at the back of his throat, Jonah's shoulders sagged. His spine slumped as he pressed his weight forward into Tommy's hand. His dark eyes pooled again as he nodded.

"Jonah"—and in his mind, Tommy added, *my love*—"I would walk down that road again, one hundred times, right beside you." A tear landed on his hand. "I *want* to be beside you—whatever that entails. I wanted it then, and I want it now. I'm not like this because of you." He paused as his stomach roiled. "If anything, it's because of me."

Jonah jerked his head away from Tommy's palm, but before he could argue, Tommy said, "I'm the reason you left work early that night. The reason we were even on that road."

Jonah frowned. "You'd wanted to tell me something."

"Yes."

Too intrigued to wait until the end of his shift, Jonah had got off early.

"I was going to tell you how much I liked you."

Jonah's brow dipped a second before he flinched.

"Don't," Tommy said roughly. "It's not like that."

Dark eyes darted to his. "How do you—"

"You think that because it was a hate crime, it made me too scared to come out. That it was the reason I didn't tell you until now."

Swallowing, Jonah nodded.

"I waited because I wanted to get better first. For you. Get my head straight. Go back to how I used to be." The longer he'd left it, the more convinced he became Jonah would never return his affection. But in those early days . . . "I was a mess, and I wanted to be strong for you."

The absurdity of that admission choked him. With a sound of strangled bitterness, he knocked his head against the headboard.

"Hey." Jonah wrapped a hand around Tommy's neck, drawing him away from the hard surface. "You *are* strong."

Stung by the falsity, Tommy looked down. "I can't even have sex."

"So? What's sex got to do with strength? But also, you're wrong, because you were doing very good sex before that happened."

Tommy shook his head.

"And even though it didn't ruin anything, and I'm not disappointed," Jonah said, voice steady, "it hurt you, and because of that, we need to make sure it doesn't happen again. Because if you still want to, Tommy, we're going to keep getting naked together, and it's going to be incredible."

God, Tommy wanted that so badly. He forced out, "I can't be underneath."

Surprise broke Jonah's lips apart. "Okay."

"Ever."

"Then you never will be."

"It reminded me of being held down. And I—" Should he admit this much? "I didn't like it. Before then. I liked being against you, but I wanted to be on top—covering you, protecting you." He hesitated, not wanting to sound messed up, but that ship had well and truly sailed, so he added, "Controlling you."

"Oh," Jonah said, a new note in his voice. His eyes were wide. "Okay."

"It's *not* okay."

"Why not?"

Tommy held his stare. "Because I control a lot of things in this country, and you shouldn't be one of them."

Jonah blushed. "Maybe I want to be."

What? Incredulity twisted in Tommy. "Surely not every time. What if you want to change—"

"I'll never want to be somewhere you don't want me," Jonah cut him off. "Ever."

Tommy stared, speechless at Jonah's certainty.

"So." Jonah gave a cautious smile. "You still want to? Not tonight, but . . . sometime?"

Humiliation lingered in Tommy's bloodstream, the cold shame of poor performance. His pulse was unsteady with residual panic from the triggered memory, and somehow, Jonah was still here, willing to try again.

"Yes," he said, unsure whether he believed it.

"Yes." Jonah's attention dipped to Tommy's mouth, and a moment later, he'd reached out to run the pad of his thumb over the chip in Tommy's front tooth. On instinct, Tommy closed his lips around him, sucking lightly and tasting salt.

"Tommy," Jonah said, with the tremor of someone trying to disguise a serious question with a light tone and failing. "Why didn't you get this fixed?"

His tongue pushed Jonah's thumb aside, swiping the broken edge.

Because I was bitter and broken and thought it would be symbolic to never smile again without the taint of what those men had done.

And, because he was an asshole, he'd never considered that it would hurt Jonah to see it—an inescapable reminder of the attack every time Tommy smiled.

Softly, he asked, "Do you think I should?"

Jonah didn't answer as he withdrew his thumb. Then he nodded.

"Okay," Tommy said, and it felt a little like healing.

They sat in silence, still naked and troubled and painfully

raw. Vulnerability stuck to Tommy like cooled wax, and he had no idea how to get it off.

"Hm." Jonah glanced over his shoulder. "We need to leave this room and come back."

"I could eat," Tommy offered.

Jonah smiled at him. "Same," he said, and his brows flew up. "Oh my God! I've got three words for you. Picnic. Champagne. Strawberry patch." Then he pulled a face and added, "No counting."

Heart swelling and stinging equally, Tommy nodded and raised Jonah's hand to his mouth.

He kissed down three words of his own.

11

Maybe Jonah should have expected it.

He just hadn't had the time. After Tommy had kissed him in the dark and stayed over, Jonah had spent Sunday in a daze with reality spun like sweet cotton candy around him. Sure, he'd been online and seen that everyone believed he was dating Kris, but he hadn't boarded that train of thought to consider the people of Kira City would treat him differently because of it. Why would they? He was just Jonah.

Yet by the time he left the palace Monday morning, it turned out that he wasn't himself anymore.

He was the boyfriend of a prince.

It started with the unsettling feeling that he was being watched. No one actually *stared* at him, but he got the sense they were aware of him as he strode down the steep streets. He caught little glances in the corner of his eye, overheard animated whispers. It was weird, and at one point as he waited to cross the road, he was pretty sure the youth next to him held their phone up for a selfie that included him over their shoulder.

Then there was Nora. He met her for brunch at a lakeside café, astonished that she'd reserved the exclusive table on the shaded rooftop. It looked out over the lake dotted with rowboats, had fancy table settings (he'd have claimed they were fit for a king if he hadn't sat at an actual royal table the night before), and came with an entire waiter all to themselves.

"How did you manage this?" he asked excitedly, tucking his chair in. "Isn't the roof for important people?"

Her brows hung high as she stared at him. "Yeah."

"Oh my God." He leaned forward, lowering his voice. "Who are you really?"

"Jonah!" Laughing, she smacked him on the arm with a menu. "You're dating Prince Kristof."

"Oh." He leaned back quickly, and it felt like falling. "So?"

"You have influence now, man." Her silver hair was bright, her nose ring glinting. "We don't lose our heads over royalty here, but we treat them right. You're not going to blend in with us commoners anymore."

"But I am a commoner." He held the term possessively. "I want to blend in."

"Babe," she said, shaking her head. "You're directly involved with the royal family. The way we treat you is reflective of the way we view them. Giving you the good table is, by extension, giving them the good table. And they'll never dine with the plebs."

But the boys didn't want the good table either. "He sat in a regular booth at the bar."

"Because he specifically requested it. Same way he asked for everyone to pretend he's not a prince when he comes in. That's not the way we actually view him." Nora's frown was confused. "Haven't you two talked about this?"

Dismay settled over him. "Not yet."

"Okay." She sounded unsure. "Maybe you should? Things are going to change for you. Effective immediately, because your face is literally clogging up all my social feeds." She provided proof by showing him her phone and scrolling until he couldn't bear another post claiming he was Prince Kristof's cowboy lover.

"Were you friends in Montana?" Nora asked, sliding her phone away. "When he picked you up the other night, you looked so familiar with each other, I figured you've either known him your entire life or you're soul mates."

Both, Jonah yearned to confide, because he'd been struggling to process the realization on his own. *I think it's both.*

He smiled, and said, "Yeah, we were friends," which was weird and wrong and painful, because Nora was also his friend and he wanted to be able to tell her the truth. That he wasn't with Kris—he was with *Tommy.* That Jonah was falling for him so fast, his eyes should be watering. That they'd had sex for the first time last night, and it had started out intense and ended in a nightmare, and even though Tommy had gone out with him to the garden, eating the picnic Jonah had assembled in the palace kitchen, he'd been distant—unfocused and quiet, retreating into a haunted kind of silence, which had made it really hard for Jonah to pretend to be okay, because drinking Champagne between the rows of sweet-smelling fruit should have been cute and romantic, and it had just made him want to cry.

Tommy had slept with his back turned, and this morning, he'd kissed Jonah goodbye on the cheek.

Yeah. Jonah still kind of wanted to cry.

"I probably shouldn't ask about him, sorry." Nora grimaced. "Hey, do you want to go to the pride parade with me on Sunday? It's huge here."

Grateful, he nodded, and the conversation moved to a protest in the eighties that had led to Kiraly's Pride.

But she was right about things changing.

At a street market that afternoon, the stall owner refused to accept Jonah's payment for a bag of spiced nuts. "It's my treat," she kept saying, hands behind her back. "It's my treat."

Smiling uncomfortably, Jonah put his money on a jar of candied almonds and walked away without change.

At the corner supermarket near his apartment, the cashier gave him a look of surprise as he put down his groceries. "I didn't think I'd see you again," the man said. "Surely you have people who'll do your shopping?"

Jonah smiled. "I can do it myself."

"It's less about *can* and more about *should,* if you know what I mean."

Jonah nodded, pretending he did.

His biggest mistake was detouring to the boutique fashion district for outfit ideas for Mark's wedding. It was just that he'd never been able to dress up how he wanted before and didn't want to waste the opportunity. He was standing in front of a glamorous shopfront, mannequins posing beneath chandeliers, when a woman rushed out to convince him to be her client. "Let me dress you," she said, waving her hands dramatically in front of his body. "No more of this—only style and class to prove you belong next to our prince, yes?"

"That's so kind," he said, backing away with her card in his hand. "I'll think about it, thank you."

Shaken, he wanted to get an iced coffee and sit in the shade to think, but he turned to his guards first. "Are people going to be like this everywhere?"

They both nodded, murmuring apologetic agreement.

Straight home, then.

"Oh, God," he said twenty minutes later, upset as he pulled every piece of clothing from his travel bags. Aside from his new black pants and shirts, he only owned jeans and shirts without style and class. Did he have to dress differently now? Did Tommy expect it?

Like in that royal movie. He'd watched a whole bunch once the boys had left Sage Haven, trying to learn what life would be like for them. Not the one with the stuttering king. The other one, with the schoolgirl who hadn't known she was a princess and had a makeover so her appearance matched her true status. Would he have to start wearing contacts too? He got all squeamish touching his own eyes, but everyone had been so proud of the way she'd changed, and Jonah wanted to make Tommy proud.

The boys got away with wearing their old ranch clothes because they were royalty. But Jonah—an everyday cowboy without a sparkle to his name—had to *prove* he belonged by their side.

Confused, he sat on the bed, head between his hands. Surely changing himself to prove he belonged would just prove that he didn't?

Except I do belong with Tommy.

He knew that as surely as his own name. Nothing else could explain the ache in his chest that hauled his awareness toward Tommy every second of the day. The hum of a sunny beehive in his heart when they were together. The exhilarated clench in his stomach every time he remembered the way Tommy had looked at him or touched him or confessed his love in every possible way except for the phrase itself.

"I always want to see you."

"I would ask you the color of the sky every day just to watch your mouth move."

"I can't not be with you, Jonah."

So why was Jonah upset? It was getting hard to sort it out in his head.

It became horribly clear once he started his work shift that night.

At first, it was just the looks—sideways glances from the patrons and too bright smiles from the staff, and all-round strange moments of eye contact that made him feel like he'd swallowed something he hadn't chewed properly. He couldn't break it down, make it fit comfortably inside him—until he realized that he *knew* this feeling.

He was on the outside, looking in.

This was how life had been in Sage Haven, minus the hostility and judgement. He was among these people, but he wasn't one of them. Not anymore, not now that he was the partner to one of their beloved royals.

The joking-yet-serious comments he received as he served drinks drove it home.

"If you play your cards right, you'll never have to work again."

"And here I'd thought you were like us—when are you moving into the palace?"

"Macy and I reckon you'll become a gay icon!"

And the utterly serious, "Two beers, if it's no trouble, thank you, sir."

Jonah's dread was a cold stone in his stomach.

He'd been edged out of the most inclusive community in the world.

What did this mean for opening his own bar? Would anyone be relaxed enough around him to feel comfortable or would people only visit out of obligation? His head spun. How could he create a welcoming community when he couldn't be part of it?

He texted Tommy when he next ducked out the back to change kegs. **Do gay icons have to wear contact lenses?**

Elton John, Tommy texted back, and then sent a question mark.

I'm not royalty if I'm only your boyfriend, right?

Tommy replied as Jonah left the cool room. **No. You'd be royalty in name if we married.**

Jonah had no time to process *that* before Tommy's face filled his screen. He glanced at the barroom door. Would he even get scolded for taking too long now that he was the prince's boyfriend? After setting the keg down, Jonah leaned against the corridor wall and answered, "Hey, Tommy!"

"Are you alright?" That cool, level voice had Jonah pressing the phone harder against his ear, hoping Tommy's calm would ground his scattered thoughts. "That didn't seem like a real question."

"It wasn't." Jonah looked down, cheeks warming. "I just— everyone is being weird now. It's like I'm not me anymore."

There was the sound of a mug clunking on a hard surface. A soft sigh. "I know what you mean."

"I think you know half of what I mean." Jonah rested his boot against the base of the keg. "You're treated completely differently to how you were back home, but it's because of who you really are. But I'm being treated differently because of who *you* are, too, yet I'm still just me, working behind the bar, not making policies or talking to presidents or anything."

"I'm sorry." Tommy had an odd tone that Jonah couldn't place. "I should have asked before picking you up from work."

"No. I want to be seen with you." Then he cringed, because the last word sounded like an accusation. *You—not Kris.* But Jonah couldn't ask Tommy to come clean about that, not after last night. Tommy was actively trying to stop his anxiety from hampering his life. How could Jonah protest about a little discomfort at being publicly paired with Kris, when Tommy was trying to beat something a thousand times more serious? If posing as his brother would help him, then so be it. "It would be worse if you'd kept me a secret," he added.

"Would you like to talk it through?"

Jonah should get back—and Tommy sounded preoccupied. But today had been upsetting, and there was something he needed to get straight. Tipping his face to the ceiling, he asked quietly, "If I'm your partner in the future, can I run my own bar here in the city?"

He wanted Tommy *and* his dreams. If being with a prince meant he was treated differently and his bar didn't have the relaxed atmosphere he'd always imagined, well, that would be a small price to pay, right?

"No," Tommy said.

"What?" Jonah couldn't stop the distressed hitch in his throat. "You mean, actually no?"

"I mean actually no."

"But . . ." Tommy's words choked him. "I'd hoped I could have both."

Tommy's heavy silence didn't give an inch.

"Because," Jonah went on, "you're not just a prince—you're a cowboy. And you said cowboys date barmaids, remember?"

A surprised breath carried down the line. "I—didn't realize this was what you'd meant by that. I thought you felt inadequate about leaving the bar with me that night."

"No, I . . ." *I was already thinking about our future.* "It's just," Jonah said in a wave of confusion, because this wasn't right, couldn't be right. "Frankie still does her job."

"That's different."

Jonah would have taken a step back if he hadn't already been against the wall. "Because it's an important job to the royal family, not serving the common people like me?"

He'd expected Tommy to disagree or at least reword it to be kinder to Jonah.

But Tommy just said, "Yes."

Oh. *My God.* Ouch.

"It's royal expectation," Tommy said. "Not my opinion. It would threaten the status of our family and weaken the institution of the monarchy in the eyes of our people. I'm sorry. As royalty, our roles cannot be comparable to those of regular citizens. This is the same for our partners. In this . . . future, where we're together, hierarchy would prevent you from working as you are now. And," he paused briefly, "from running your own bar."

I'll never own a bar? Lightheaded, Jonah laid his head against the wall. So royal life really *wouldn't* be true to him. He'd have to give up the future he'd always wanted for himself.

His dreams might be small, but they were big to him.

"I'll have to decide." The realization winded him.

"You have to be happy." Tommy sounded distant, distracted. "I want that for you."

What? Jonah pulled the phone away to stare at the screen. What was going on with Tommy? Phone back against his ear, Jonah said, "I'm happy when I'm with you."

Tommy didn't answer. There was the sound of a pen scratching across paper.

"Tommy? I am. But—" God, how could he express this? "This is the first time I've ever been completely myself in public. Without worrying what people are thinking or what they might say. I don't have to be careful about accidentally making them uncomfortable, and it's . . . I don't know." *Beyond my wildest dreams.* "Like if I'd found a genie in a bottle in Sage Haven, I wouldn't have even *known* to wish for a place like this. And maybe it's not about opening my own bar anymore." Except that it definitely was. "It's about being an outsider again. I'll be an outsider if I'm with you. So, even though I adore you, that doesn't make this easy."

There was a long silence. Jonah chewed the inside of his cheeks and waited.

Finally, Tommy said, "You'll get more pleasure from building your own community. It's what you've always wanted."

Jonah froze, breath taken and mouth open at Tommy's use of the word *pleasure.*

So that was what was going on here.

"If we leave things here," Tommy continued, and Jonah was sure he'd tilted the mouthpiece away from his face, the over-the-phone equivalent to looking out the window mid-conversation. "Kiraly won't take long to lose interest in you. Not once Kris and Frankie announce their relationship. You'll be one of them again. You can belong. Be yourself. Open a bar and foster a community."

And Jonah thought, *He's giving up on me.*

"How dare you say that like it's simple." Jonah kicked at the keg. "And would you please stop pretending to be distracted, because I know I've got your full attention right now. What would you do, when being a prince makes so much sense for you? Would you sacrifice it for me?"

Tommy took so long to answer, Jonah almost thought he'd put the phone down. He sounded frustrated by pain when he said, "I want to say yes."

"But you can't. Can you? Because we're both more than each other."

Tommy's swallow carried down the line. Had he thought more about Jonah's plan to leave Sage Haven before any of this royalty stuff had happened? Had Tommy, because of that, already decided that Jonah would get too hungry in the palace and wouldn't choose him?

It was true Jonah wouldn't belong there.

But he *did* belong with Tommy.

Whatever his decision, he'd be half of who he wanted to be.

"Do you need me to decide right now?" Jonah made himself ask, squeezing his eyes shut. *How am I supposed to choose?* "It hasn't even been a week since I found out how you feel, but if you can't do this without certainty, you have to tell me, Tommy—not make the decision for me by pushing me away."

"I—" A sharp breath out, followed by a slap that sounded

suspiciously like a hand landing on a forehead. "No. I don't need you to decide now."

"You said that in the tower last week, but I'm worried you don't mean it."

"I mean it." He didn't sound like he meant it.

"You took me to bed last night without us having a set future. Do you regret it?"

A pause of utter silence. "Not that part."

"I have to get back to work." Jonah hoisted the keg under his arm. "But we're not done here. If I call you when my shift ends, probably around breakfast, will you answer?"

"Yeah." Tommy didn't sound distracted anymore—he sounded resigned. "I'll answer."

"Good," Jonah said.

He was pretty sure he knew how to fix this.

Jonah made good on his promise to Ava that night.

As sunrise approached, the crowd thinned, leaving Jonah to collect the glassware and usher out the stragglers. Zara was his last stop, curled up on a booth table in the back corner.

She was a wreck. Her nights seemed to follow the same pattern. Arrive looking like cornered prey. Drink a lot and drink fast. Dance until she couldn't stay upright. Continue drinking in a booth, any booth, until the bar staff had no choice but to stop serving her.

Jonah figured he'd act the same if he found out he'd been intimate with a murderer.

"Hey, Zara?" He waited for her to grunt before saying, "Zara, I'm going to take you home, okay?"

It was an ordeal getting her on her feet, but eventually she was leaning fully against his side. "I'm Jonah." He held a large glass of water in front of her. "Drink up."

"I know whoyar," she slurred, eyes glazed. "Erryone knows whoyar."

He tried to ignore that. "Then you know I'm trying to help."

Grunting again, she drained the water, and then he was steering her half-functioning feet out the door and into the predawn darkness. Her apartment was uphill, and as they walked, several extra royal guards fell into step behind them.

Zara had been given her own security.

"Are you okay?" he asked as they slowly climbed a sidewalk made of steps. "Can I do anything to help?"

She gave a hollow laugh. "How's Tomas?"

"What?" Jonah pretended not to understand.

"Ava has Mark. Frankie's is Kris," she said, keeping her voice hushed even as she waved a hand around. "Your one's Tom."

"Uh. Yeah. He's okay, I guess."

"Hm." She stumbled, surprisingly heavy for her slight build. "Not good 'round people."

"No." *Not good around himself either, sometimes.*

"I shugive you advice. S'my thing."

God, she was getting heavier. Jonah looked over his shoulder, pulling a face at one of her guards in a silent plea for help. "Giving advice is your thing?"

"Uh-huh," she said, as the guard jogged to catch up. Once he was positioned at her other side, they increased the pace. "He loves you, sweetcakes. Go forrit."

Jonah's heart twisted. "He can't have told you that."

"No. But iss what aways happens."

Not following, but also not particularly needing to, Jonah let it drop. As they were heading up the apartment block stairs, he asked, "Are you sure there's nothing I can do?"

"I juswant my mum," she said, and the sudden sorrow in her voice tightened his throat.

"Is she around?" he asked gently.

She shook her head—then stopped abruptly, face going slightly green, hands landing on her stomach. After a few seconds, she made a sound of disgust and kept climbing. "Died."

Oh. "I'm sorry."

"Me too." Her foot missed the next step. Jonah and the guard caught her fall before hoisting her up and carrying her the rest of the way. "But I can't pickum. I shouldave picked him, you know? So stupid. Stupid, stupid, stupid."

Jonah and the guard exchanged a helpless glance.

At her door, he took her keys and unlocked it, and she stumbled over the threshold, drunk and in no shape for whatever her Tuesday had in store. It wasn't until she looked back at him, hand swiping at the door and repeatedly missing, that he caught the torment and desolation in her gaze.

"I'm so stupid," she said, and managed to smack the door closed.

Tommy let Mark persuade him out on an early ride. "No talking —just the rush," his brother had promised, so Tommy surrendered to the mountain bridle paths—anything to stop him dwelling on how badly he'd screwed things up with Jonah. He opened himself to the freedom of the route—the sunlight filtering through the silver firs and pines, and the dry, warm tang in the forest air.

Riding always steadied him. It had to. Horses were too receptive to negative emotions, so Tommy had no choice but to keep calm in the stable and saddle. *For the horse's sake,* he used to tell himself, because he hated the thought of unsettling his mount, or worse, the alternative of having to avoid horses entirely. His regulated breaths held his stress in check as he rode hard on Mark's tail.

Nice while it lasted.

His tension returned at breakfast. Expecting to eat in solitude, as he had for the past few weeks, he faltered at the sight of Kris sitting in the blue parlor with Frankie. His brother must have finally conquered the stairs. And while that was heartening, Tommy wished he'd climbed in a different direction so Tommy could keep avoiding him. He wasn't in the right frame of mind to sidestep Kris's tactless approach to conversation—and the last thing he wanted was his brother prying into his and Jonah's dinnertime departure the other night.

"Morning, Tom." Kris shifted around with a smile, preparing to include him in their chat.

"You're here," Tommy answered, sitting on the opposite side of the table, several seats up from them. "Good to see." Then he opened the book Zoltan had passed him in the doorway—his guard always carried one for him—to signal he didn't want to talk.

"Thanks," Kris said. "Good book?"

"Yes." Tommy didn't look up.

"Cool." Kris tapped his fingers against the table a few times before taking the hint. Resuming his chat with Frankie, Kris only addressed him again when Tommy stood to leave. "Hey, man, when can I get my hat back?"

Tommy stilled, his chair half-pushed in. "Already sold it at auction."

Kris grinned. "Seriously, though."

Shit. "Soon."

Frankie frowned at Kris. "Why the hell do you think you need your hat?"

"No reason." Kris tousled his hair. "I just miss it."

243

"Too bad," she said. "This is what you get for running off without security."

"I assumed *this* was what I got." He gestured wryly to his various injuries.

"And no hat. You scared the shit out of us. Deal with it." Her green gaze locked on Tommy. "Security briefing is on your desk. Need me to swing by?"

"No." He had nothing to discuss. Then he hesitated because he still hadn't finished reading the information she'd gathered on Adam. "Unless there's news?"

"None," she said, and muttered, *"the fucker,"* under her breath.

By the time Tommy reached his study, the calm from his morning ride was long gone. He had a headache and couldn't shake the pervasive uncertainty of the past few days. How did people make decisions when they were the meeting point of opposing forces? His life had become that slipping sensation between magnets of the same polarity. His anxiety and predisposition to isolation pushed against his desire to be king—just as the humiliation of failing Jonah in bed pushed hard against his ache to be with him. It felt impossible to move in any direction.

He'd barely sat down when Jonah called.

Tommy flushed from the cloying layer of shame and denial beneath his skin. *This is it.* Over the phone last night, Jonah's sudden focus on the problems with their relationship had betrayed he was looking for an out. It didn't take a genius to know why.

"Hey," he answered, his stomach knotting as he switched to speaker and set the phone on his desk. He opened his laptop and entered his password, trying to fool himself that he was in control. "That was a late close."

"No one ever leaves." Jonah's voice was warm and weary-soft. "And then I walked Zara home."

Of course, he did. Because Jonah was perfect, like weather that made people smile and breathe in deep to taste the day. Tommy held his breath and said nothing as the knots in his stomach worked their way to his throat.

"I stopped for breakfast too, but I'm home now." Water ran in the background, then turned off. "About to head to bed."

Tommy shot a sharp glance out the window, straight into the sun. *Don't picture it.* Jonah casually stripping to nothing, taking the final few lazy steps to the bed, collapsing bare and beautiful onto the sheets.

"Okay," Tommy said, picturing it in glorious detail.

Jonah's sigh of contentment drove home that he was happy to curl up alone. Gone were his sulky claims he missed Tommy so much he couldn't sleep. Something twanged sharply in his chest at the knowledge this call was to conclude their discussion from last night.

Jonah had decided.

"Tommy?" There was the softest rustle as he shifted to get comfortable. "Are you alone?"

Christ, I ruined it. Pain clamped around his chest. *I ruined everything.*

Taking the phone off speaker, Tommy crossed the study to lock the door. He wasn't expecting Mark or Philip until after lunch, but he wouldn't risk being walked in on with his heart in pieces. Bracing, he fought to keep his voice level. "Yes."

"I'm in bed now."

Good? So he had a pillow on hand for his tears of regret? Tommy moved toward an armchair. If he didn't keep the memory of this conversation away from his desk, he'd never work again.

"Tommy? It's hard to sleep without you."

Tommy's pulse stuttered. *He thinks that's what I want to hear.* Just like in bed the other night. Jonah had reassured him, saying it was okay, it was amazing, he wasn't disappointed, but what else could he have said given the situation? Jonah had slept with experienced men; was an experienced lover himself. The only reason he'd been angling to get Tommy naked the past few days was the thrill of the unknown.

And now he knew.

Tommy spoke through his shame as he sat. "You don't have to say that."

There was a pause. "Say what?"

"About still wanting to be with me."

"But"—a pause in which Tommy was absolutely certain he heard the jingle of a belt buckle and the scrape of a zipper—"I do. Will you help me fall asleep?"

Elbow on the armrest, Tommy set his forehead in the spread between his forefinger and thumb. Sidestepping must be common when someone as nice as Jonah had to instigate a breakup. "I don't sing lullabies."

Jonah startled him by chuckling. It came from low in his throat, a sexy tumble that landed in the base of Tommy's abdomen. "Good to know, but not exactly what I want right now."

And that was when Tommy heard it.

The catch in Jonah's voice; the same hint of breathlessness as when he'd tugged Tommy toward the bed the other night.

Slowly, Tommy lowered his hand. "What *do* you want?"

"Well, I can't sleep while needing you this badly." It was unmistakable now. The rough edge to his words that conjured images of parted lips and dipped lashes. "So a little help with that, maybe?"

"With—"

Comprehension hit him like a fastball.

His body throbbed with a strange, scandalized heat. "Are you—"

"No, but I want to." Jonah's breath was coming a little faster. "Like this, with you. I can't wait until we're together again. Will you help me?"

"Help you." Tommy's heart hammered. *Is he serious?*

"Talk to me. That's all. Listening to you makes me hot."

Jonah wanted to touch himself with Tommy on the line? But —*Jesus.* Tommy shoved an unsteady hand through his hair. "Aren't you going to break up with me?"

"I—" Jonah gave a small, helpless sound of disbelief. "Are you for real?"

"Yes."

"No. I'm not." Certainty cleared the haze from Jonah's voice. "I know the other night has thrown you off your game, and I get that. It was pretty full on, but it hasn't made me want you any less, and I hate the thought of you avoiding sex forever because of one bad experience, so I thought this might feel safer for you. There's no risk of physical triggers or anything, but it would also feel good for me, because yeah, while I obviously want your body and your hands and your mouth and—you know, your *everything* —your voice is part of you too. And that's something I could have right now, if you wanted. So I'm just wondering if you'll give it to me?" A beat of questioning silence. "Sex, I mean, with your voice."

Staggered, Tommy said, "Sex with my voice."

"Yeah? Because, whether you believe it or not, I want you. And the way I feel isn't just about your body. It's all of you. The way I want you, it . . . what's the word? Like goes beyond something?"

Tommy's head spun. "Transcends?"

"That's it! It transcends your touch. All I need is you, Tommy, in whatever way you can give."

Well, fuck.

"Okay." Tommy's hands were shaking. "Yes."

"Okay, yes." Jonah's echo came out on a satisfied sigh, and Tommy imagined him settling back onto the sheets, bottom lip tucked between his teeth.

Then there was silence.

Jesus, how does this work?

His attention caught on the windowsill Jonah had perched on last week, thighs spread, head angled in invitation, murmuring for Tommy not to let him go. That it felt good, being in Tommy's grasp.

But letting go was exactly what Tommy kept doing. The second he got spooked, he spiraled headlong into the conviction that Jonah didn't want him, wouldn't choose him, instead of acknowledging the wildly fucking obvious fact that ever since he'd sat on that windowsill and liked it, Jonah had been facing an epic, life-altering choice.

Tommy—or his identity as he knew it.

That Jonah was even hesitating proved how serious he was about Tommy. He was legitimately considering giving up his dreams, the man he'd always wanted to be, so they could be together.

And what choice am I facing?

Whether to answer Jonah's calls? Whether to believe him when he said Tommy made him happy? *Jesus Christ.* Tommy had made Jonah's struggle all about him. *Not anymore.*

A wave of full-body pins and needles flooded him, as if all the physical places that manifested his doubt and anxiety had been warned. Not. Any. More. Tommy would believe every word that came out of that gorgeous, guileless mouth and support Jonah through this decision.

And give him transcendent phone sex.

Gripping the edge of the armrest with his free hand, a thrill zapped along Tommy's spine as he closed his eyes. "What should I say?"

"Tell me how much you want me. What you'd do to me if we were together. But you can't pretend. I'll be able to tell if you don't believe it."

God. That stipulation. Jonah knew so much more than he gave himself credit for.

"I'll believe it. First," Tommy said, because his mind was demanding a solid picture before this went any further, "are you still dressed?"

"Mostly."

"Take your clothes off." A quiet command.

There was rustling, a few light *flops* of clothes being tossed onto the floor, then breathing and silence.

Way too hot already, Tommy counted back from five. "Are you naked?"

"Yes."

"Good." He pitched his voice low and appreciative, and was rewarded with Jonah's shaky exhale. "Are you on your back?"

"My side," Jonah said, then understanding what Tommy wanted, he added, "Facing away from the room, so you'd see my back if you walked in now. The blinds are closed, but there's a strip of light on the pillow next to me. It's lighting up how hard I am for you."

Tommy swallowed. Need prickled through him, harsh and restless, and he felt himself start to strain against his jeans. "I wish I could see. I'd lie right behind you, right up against you, up on one elbow so I could kiss you as I touched your face. Your shoulder. The unbelievably soft skin of your side." Tommy imagined that silky path from underarm to hip beneath his palm, smooth and ribbed and muscled. *God,* he wanted to be touching it right now. "And you. You would . . ."

There was a taut, aching silence.

Jonah whispered, "Please, Tommy."

"You'd beg me to touch you properly." His skin was tingling, his muscles locking in sensual expectation. Not that he had any intention of releasing alone in a room that didn't belong to him exclusively. "I'd wrap my hand around you and give you exactly what you wanted."

Jonah made a series of conflicted sounds—a sigh, a whimper, a helpless *"please"*—that betrayed the start of his relief was nowhere near the end.

Tommy held still, face hot and blood coursing. "I'd start easy, not too slow, but not rushing either. Firm enough you couldn't feel anything but the slide of my hand, but not tight, not yet. Can you feel me?"

"Yes." Spoken like an arm flung overhead, a bent leg falling outward.

"I'd kiss you while I stroked, hungry for you, not able to get enough, and you'd arch into me, pressing our bodies together." The vision tangled around him, a phantom touch of desperate desire. "Then you'd get restless, needy, and start moving your hips to make me speed up. Is that what you're doing?"

"Yes." The increased rhythm of Jonah's movements carried down the line. "Yes."

Fuck, Tommy wanted that to be his hand so severely, he dug his fingers into the chair until the fabric squeaked. Air stretched thin in his lungs as he said, "I'd go a little faster. How does it feel? Tell me."

"Good." The word trembled. Tommy didn't need to see him to believe his pleasure was real. "Hot. Slick. Incredible."

Tommy struggled down a groan. The intimacy of this shared fantasy where Jonah was vulnerable to his every word . . . where Tommy was equally defenseless against his moans and pleasure-soft utterances . . . it rocked him. They were apart, yet together in their minds so intently that their imagined pleasure took physical form. Tommy *felt* Jonah's body as a pressure against his front. Felt his breath as heat on his neck, and the force of his desire as a tight ball of sensation at his groin. He could practically feel himself lying against Jonah, stroking him, kissing him—and it wasn't enough.

He needed to give Jonah everything.

Overcome by need, by the truth that Jonah really did still want him, he said, "Then I wouldn't be able to handle it." Because he *couldn't* handle it. "I'd want all of you. Underneath me. Around me. I'd get you ready, and then you'd be on your back, and I'd be over you, our fingers laced, our hearts raging together."

Tommy battled to keep his breathing in check—his gathering urges from getting the better of him. Then Jonah groaned and the eroticism of it nearly destroyed him.

"I need you." Jonah's words were muffled, and Tommy pictured his face turned into the pillow, eyes scrunched, the tendons in his neck straining. "Oh my God, Tommy, I need you so badly it hurts."

"But it feels good right now," Tommy told him.

"*Yes,* oh my God, so good, so good."

"Then I'd push inside you." Tommy was getting light-headed. He hadn't moved, hadn't so much as looked at himself, yet the scene he'd built with Jonah had arousal shuddering through him, overheating at his core. "Do you want it faster?"

A barely audible, "Yes."

"Faster, then."

He heard the pace quicken, Jonah's helpless, early cries.

Then Jonah gasped around a demand. "Tell me how you feel about me."

Cock aching, Tommy clenched his teeth and said, "I want every part of you."

"Not want," Jonah said, breath ragged. "Feel."

"I—" *What?* "Christ. Uh. I feel . . . mad for your body. Your mouth. Your laugh. I—I adore your kindness. Your strength. And I love that your glasses make you look nerd-hot and hot-hot, even though no one should be both. That's too unfair, but you're both. You're *more*. You're just every fucking kind of hot."

Jonah choked out a laugh that quickly rolled into a moan. "More."

"I love the way you like being close to me."

Hitching breath. Rapid rhythm.

"I love that you get sulky when you're tired and settle when I reassure you."

Dazedly, Tommy realized he was using *love* a lot. That it might get him in trouble. But he was flush against his own edge, and despite not having laid a finger on himself, he knew so much as shifting his hips could push him over.

"More," Jonah said.

"I love your hands. Your heart."

Oh, God. Smaller sentences. Getting too close. He had to stop.

"And I—I—" *Don't say it.*

"Yes." Jonah's voice was all rasp. "Tell me, please, please."

"I . . ." *No,* he thought, and instantly argued back: *Why the hell not?* He'd already endured the excruciating regret of hiding this truth. He couldn't live through that again.

"*Tommy.*" Jonah was there, tipping over.

"I love you."

And Jonah gave a heavy groan of release.

Jesus Christ.

Tommy opened his eyes, pulse ramming inside his chest, fingers clamped around the armrest and phone. He listened as Jonah sighed and settled in contentment—then started laughing. "Oh my God, it's everywhere. What am I, fourteen?"

Tommy was too hot for the image to be anything but wildly

debauched, but Jonah's laugh coaxed out his smile. "It sounded good."

"It was, so good, oh, Tommy." The words rushed out, warm and glowing, and Tommy wished he could draw Jonah against him in the afterglow. "Did you make it, too?"

"No." Tommy glanced at where he filled his jeans. "But it's . . . still possible."

Jonah's hum was silky smooth. "Want me to come over?"

Yes. "That would defeat the purpose of this call. Do you think you'll be able to sleep?"

"Mm, yes. So tired. Could you stay? Then hang up when I start snoring."

"Okay," Tommy said, and added without thinking, "I bet your snores are adorable."

"Aw." Jonah sounded pleased, blissed out. "I don't."

Tommy smiled again.

"I'll call you when I wake up."

"Please do. Sweet dreams." Tommy got a snuggly little murmur in response, so he sat in silence, blood too hot, nerve endings straining, and listened to his best friend's lengthening breaths. Just as he started thinking Jonah had dozed off, his voice drifted down the line.

"I heard you, Tommy." Jonah's words stumbled with sleep. "And I love that you love me. I already knew, but it's good that you know that I know. That it doesn't scare me or overwhelm me."

He already knew.

Unsure how to respond, Tommy murmured, "Thank you, Jonah."

Within half a minute, Jonah was asleep, and Tommy won their bet.

His snores were *so* adorable.

12

When Jonah had first walked the palace halls ten days ago, he hadn't been able to comprehend how it could all belong to Tommy and the boys. The architecture; the wealth. The status that had everyday people working for them, admiring them, literally *bowing* to them. He was used to that now—or at least, he'd accepted it like a thing he didn't understand but was just the way it was.

It was harder to accept the people of Kiraly treating *him* like an outsider—and the palace staff acknowledging him as a royal family insider. The staff had hardly noticed him on his visits to Kris last week, but today, as he strode toward the east wing, every single person paused their duties to incline their heads and murmur a greeting.

Jonah said hello every time, smiling, knowing he made zero sense as their superior but not letting that get in the way of good manners.

He was in a corridor with crimson carpet when his phone rang. "Hey, Frankie!"

"Where are you going, Jones?" She sounded curious. "I can see you from the surveillance room."

"I'm trying to visit Tom—friend," he corrected with a mortified jolt. His guards knew he was involved with Tommy, but the attendant hurrying past him with a smile would believe Jonah was there for Kris. "To visit my boyfriend," he repeated quickly. "But this doesn't look right."

"You could ask your guards."

"Yes, but I wanted to find him on my own. I thought I knew the way." He stopped, glancing around. None of it looked familiar. "Where am I?"

"You've almost reached the throne room," she said. "The antechamber is on your left."

"Oh." He didn't exactly know what an antechamber was, but the giant double doors on his left stood open, revealing a vast space that seemed made for guests in glittering gowns and hand-stitched suits, fine wine and a string quartet. If a string quartet was as posh as it sounded. "Could I look? Or is Mark busy in there?"

"Mark?" Frankie was silent for a beat. "Uh, no, a king doesn't just sit in the throne room all day. It's for ceremonies. It'll be used for the coronation next month. You can look."

He did.

He shouldn't have.

It was . . . overwhelming. The sheer size of the room made the gold and blue-cushioned throne at the far end look laughably small. But he didn't laugh. Not at the royal blue curtains that rose behind the throne, not at the walls that soared high, dressed in the same blue velvet and bordered by intricate creamy-gold trims, not at the extraordinary ceiling design with figures carved straight into the plaster, all facing the center of the room and the biggest tiered chandelier he'd ever seen. It was like a gold fountain flowing heavy with diamonds, hundreds of them, probably thousands, but he didn't want to get close enough to tell. Other thrones were displayed along the outer edge, thrones that must have belonged to Tommy's ancestors, kings and queens with sharp minds and the blood of rulers in their hearts.

Warily, he poked his head over the threshold—and yanked it back. This place had a *presence*. It rippled down his spine, gripped low in his stomach, as if the essence of royalty was bound to the room's greatness. The silence felt commanding, a growl so deep it didn't register in his ears but thrummed across the back of his neck, prickling his baby hairs and making him shiver. It felt like—

It *felt* like—

Tommy.

"Oh my God," he said, confused, because how many times would he have this realization before it sunk all the way down? Tommy was a prince who *belonged* here. Not just because of his family line, but because of who he'd always been. All these months, Jonah had had it back to front.

Tommy wasn't a prince.

Prince Tomas was a cowboy.

Head spinning like a yoyo at the end of its string, Jonah swiftly stepped back.

"It's intense, hey?" Frankie said quietly.

"Yeah," he breathed. Prince Tomas had fallen in love with him—had loved him for years. *I'm worried I'll be too intense for you,* Tommy had said that day in the tower, and Jonah had laughed him off, not thinking beyond Tommy's physical presence. "Intense."

"Head back to the stairs near the portrait of the busty noblewoman," Frankie said. "The painting is eighty percent tits —you can't miss it. Go up to the next floor and you'll know where you are."

"Okay." His breath caught. "Thanks."

"Jones. Are you the reason I couldn't get a straight word out of Tommy this afternoon?"

Jonah flushed, striding out of the antechamber. "I sure hope so."

"I'm happy for you, but I want zero details and need you to fix it. Ideally now." She ended the call.

Laughing a little at her abrupt hang-up, Jonah retraced his steps. Sure enough, he recognized the corridor on the second floor, so followed it in the direction of Kris's chambers before climbing the narrow stairs Frankie had used that first day to show Tommy reading in the garden. He continued along that corridor, because it was the same one Tommy had taken to reach the tower study.

He arrived at the base of the spiral staircase in both pride and apprehension, and after asking Tommy's guards if he was allowed to pass—"You're allowed everywhere here, Mr. Wood"— he headed on up.

At the top, Jonah hesitated, knocked, and opened the door.

Tommy raised his head from where he sat behind the desk, features harsh, startled.

Then he blinked and frowned. "Jonah?"

"Sorry to interrupt." He stepped inside but didn't close the door behind him. Was it okay to turn up on a prince's doorstep uninvited? Judging by Tommy's expression when he'd walked in, absolutely not. "You look busy. I thought I'd pop around because I had an hour to fill before work, but I should have texted first, shouldn't I? God, what a goose. I can't believe I just—"

Tommy stood.

Without a word, he left his desk and strode across the study, the severity of his expression flipping a switch at the base of Jonah's spine and turning him on with a sweet, steady hum. Tommy didn't slow, but raised a hand at the last second, his palm colliding with the door over Jonah's shoulder and slamming it shut. He stopped *just* short of making contact, broad and bold and so very powerful.

Silent, his attention fell like an ember over Jonah's body, the slight shake in his breath flaring it into flame.

Dazed, Jonah put a hand on Tommy's chest, right over his heart, feeling the source of his influence beat against his palm. It was there—cruelly tangled in anxiety and trauma—but *there,* the strength and authority of a man who would walk into that throne room like he'd arrived home.

Jonah reeled. "You're a prince."

Tommy's brow lowered, and he scanned Jonah's face with darkened eyes. "I am."

"You love me."

"I do." Something shifted in Tommy's expression—a softening. "I love you."

"You believe I want you," Jonah said, palm lowering on Tommy's chest. It was clearly the cause of Tommy's distraction—his acceptance that desire really did still burn between them—and Frankie *had* asked Jonah to fix it now . . . He arched a playful brow. "This morning was good, but in person would be better."

"I—" was all Tommy said, voice bare, before he moved in.

Jonah surrendered—mouth opening and tongue sliding and fingers clutching Tommy's shoulders. *I came from the sound of his voice.* Inflamed at the reality of what their friendship had become, Jonah pressed fully against him, and Tommy surged back until Jonah's spine was hard against the door. They made out, solid and sure, the urgency growing between them until Jonah felt a tugging at his belt—and the release of his zipper. His eyes flew open a second before Tommy went to his knees.

"Tommy!" His senses spiked in a dizzying mix of shock and arousal. He'd expected Tommy to take him to his suite. "Is here okay?"

"Yes." Firmly. With a jerk of his hands, Tommy opened the front of Jonah's jeans. Then he paused. "Is it okay with you?"

"Yeah, it's just—" This tower. It was important. For important people. "Is it disrespectful?"

"Who does it disrespect for me to adore you?" Tommy slid down Jonah's briefs.

Jonah's focus went wobbly at the hot gust of breath against him. "Um." Jonah's hands crabbed outward against the door behind him until he'd grasped the doorframe. *Certainly not me.*

Tommy kissed the skin beneath Jonah's belly button and said, "There is nowhere on this earth that I wouldn't kneel for you."

"That's—" A nice thing to say. Not as nice as Tommy's hand curling around his base, dragging an instinctive flex from Jonah's hips and a soft sound from the back of his throat.

"No matter where I am, *who* I am, I'll always belong to you before anyone else." Tommy pressed a palm to Jonah's hip, restraining him against the door. Then his eyes lifted to Jonah's, serious, almost pleading. "Do you understand what I'm telling you?"

"I—you—" *Telling me. Something.* Then his lungs emptied. His heart fell over itself. *Yes.* He put it into the language Tommy had chosen, back when they'd both been cowboys but Tommy had known he was a prince. "We're the same."

And nothing could come between them.

"Yes. We're the same. I acted like a prick last night, and I'm sorry. I love you. I won't doubt you again. And I desperately, *desperately* want to please you without it going wrong, as in right now, because it's literally all I've been able to think about all day."

"Oh, wow. Yes. Okay, thank you."

Tommy's eyes crinkled a second before he moved in. It was greedy and new and as quiet as Jonah could manage, and when both sound and seed were swallowed, Jonah dropped to the floor, pressed a shaking palm over Tommy's mouth, and returned the pleasure.

After, they fixed their clothes and slumped shoulder to shoulder against the door, breathing hard. Jonah felt dazed and delirious as Tommy grabbed his hand, holding tight, as if he finally had Jonah where he wanted him.

Jonah said, "Smile at me."

Tommy ducked his head. He hadn't caught his breath, but clamped his mouth shut anyway, running his tongue along his front teeth. Self-consciousness lurked deep in his gaze when he lifted his face. "I can't on command." An edge in his words added, *I can hardly smile at all.*

"Oh. Okay. That's fine." Casually, Jonah turned into him. "I'll just tickle you, then."

Tommy yelped as Jonah's hands found his underarms—avoiding his middle so he wouldn't feel stuck—and for a few glorious seconds, Tommy let him do it. A second after that, Jonah found himself flat on his back, pinned, staring up at Tommy's grin.

Oh. Wow.

"Tommy." Breath catching, Jonah tugged a hand free and carefully thumbed the even line of Tommy's front teeth. So his kiss *had* felt different. Tommy didn't move, his gaze unwavering as Jonah touched the smooth edge. Curious, Jonah raised his head, sliding his tongue along the repair, and resettled. Tommy smiled at that, and Jonah's stomach bundled up beneath his ribs.

It was Tommy's old smile.

A little less rare, perfectly even, and entirely unharmed.

Jonah's eyes blurred. "You fixed it."

Gently, Tommy curled a hand around Jonah's wrist and pulled him up to sitting. "I'm sorry I didn't do it sooner. And I'm sorry I keep pushing you away. This morning, I . . . you knew. What I needed. You always know, even when I don't." His grip slid to Jonah's hand, lacing their fingers so carefully it made Jonah shiver. "You always know."

"I'm good at guessing."

Tommy shook his head. "I'm not. I keep guessing wrong and it hurts us both. I've been too busy guessing that you're about to leave, and it's made me thoughtless. Insensitive to the position you're in. I don't want to do that anymore. *Be* that. I want to support you. If you need to talk about us—about anything— please come to me. I won't shut down on you."

"Oh." Relief slid across Jonah's shoulders, and he shifted to kneel on his shins, facing Tommy. "Thank God. I've been so confused. What do people do when the one person they always talk to about hard stuff is the person the hard stuff is *about?*"

Tommy's jaw slid, but his expression was sheepish. "Talk to them anyway."

Jonah smiled. "Now?"

"No, I'm busy now." But Tommy swept an amused gaze over their spent sprawl.

"Right." Jonah's stomach curled. "Well. I have been thinking about the survey."

Tommy frowned. "Okay."

"And that I might wait until the result to decide about—" *You. Us. Everything.* "—if that's okay?"

Swallowing, Tommy nodded.

"Which, uh." Jonah's fingers twisted in Tommy's palm. "When will that be again?"

"The end of next week. Ten days."

"Ten days, okay." Jonah hoped he sounded brave because he didn't feel it. "I've also been wondering about what would happen if everyone decided they don't want you guys?"

Tension flickered across Tommy's face. "We'll take public opinion seriously and host a referendum for Kiraly to officially become a republic. And we'll no longer be royalty."

So . . . if Kiraly didn't want the monarchy anymore, Jonah wouldn't have to make a choice at all between Tommy and his dreams to open a bar? Hope rose in him so fast, it rushed straight out of his mouth. "Would you stay here, do you think, if that happened? In Kiraly?"

"Jonah." Tommy looked down at their joined hands. "I want to stay—right here. I want them to want us. I've avoided thinking about what I'd do if they don't, so I honestly don't know. But— the city is very busy."

"Oh." Distress thickened Jonah's throat. *Oh my God.* What if Tommy stopped being royalty—but went back to Sage Haven because he couldn't handle the people and energy here? Jonah would stay in Kiraly. He knew that already. *No, that's too unfair.* The universe couldn't be that mean. Couldn't always put Tommy in a place Jonah didn't belong.

Pushing the thought away, he said, "You know, people call you guys the lost princes. But they also call you the last princes. As in the last of the line. Is that really true? The actual last? No extended family, or second or third cousins or anyone who'd be annoyed if they had to stop being royalty? The survey made me wonder because I thought noble families always had heaps of distant relatives."

"No, we really are the—" Tommy cut off with a sharp inhale, stiffening, and Jonah's heart leapt into his throat in fear of another flashback. But no, while Tommy's face was pale, his attention was focused intently on a bookshelf across the study.

Confused, Jonah asked, "What is it?"

"Oh my fucking God." Suddenly Tommy was on his feet, extending a hand that Jonah took with a frown. "You're a genius."

"Uh." Standing, Jonah raised a shoulder. "No, I'm not."

"You are. I have to call Frankie. Immediately." Then Tommy said, "Listen," and Jonah tilted his chin up, swaying into him.

262

"I'm about to be very distracted, but I want to see you. Will you sleep in my bed? After your shift? Even if it's morning. Will you come here and sleep in my bed? I want you there."

Oh. Jonah had no idea what was happening, but this felt like a *moment*. A moment in fast-forward, hurried along by whatever Tommy had just realized, but no less significant. His whole life, Jonah had been free to come and go in Tommy's home. Now, not only was he welcome in this palace—but in the bed of Prince Tomas. It was like being given his own key *and* his own drawer.

He grinned. "Alright."

Tommy's blue gaze sank to Jonah's mouth. "The guards can direct you to my suite."

"It's okay." Certainty echoed in Jonah's heartbeat as he stepped back. "I'll find it."

"Adam's not an anarchist."

Tommy sat behind his desk, facing Frankie and Philip, cursing himself for not piecing it together sooner. At the pair's baffled frowns, he added, "He wants the throne."

"Ah." Philip gave a faint smile. "You really do lead with the punchline. What a fun trait."

Frankie scowled and sat on the arm of Philip's chair. "I'm lost."

"I've read all volumes of the Jaroka family history." Frustrated, Tommy held up an old leather-bound book. "In this one, there's mention of a succession dispute."

Frankie crossed her arms, features intent. "I remember you talking about that."

He nodded once. "Six generations back, there were four brothers. Jaroka princes. The older two died from ill health, with no male heirs, while the third prince—childless—was believed to have died at war. The crown passed to the fourth brother. Two decades later, a youth arrived at court claiming to be the son of the third prince, who hadn't died at war after all. This young man is referred to as 'the claimant' in the text."

Frankie slowly stood, muttering, "No way."

Philip's frown was disturbed. "This couldn't possibly . . ."

"The royal family didn't acknowledge his claim but placated him by offering him a place at court and an annual allowance, which he accepted. In return, they stipulated that he go by his mother's maiden name, not Jaroka." Tommy gestured to the files on Adam and his brother Rudy. *This* was what had eluded him when he'd read the first few pages. The name had been too familiar. "You can guess."

"Boller," Frankie spat.

"The claimant is only referred to once more after that." Not that it was an excuse—Tommy should have made the connection immediately. "As time wore on, his place at court became less secure, until he ended up in a position serving the royal family."

"Adam's dad worked here." Frankie eyed Philip. "So did his grandfather. I didn't search further back, but have the Bollers always worked in the palace?"

"I believe so." Philip held a hand to his cheek in affront. "They're a well-respected family in Kiraly. There is great prestige in serving our royals."

"Yeah, well." Frankie kicked the leg of the desk. "Guess who got sick of serving."

"If this is true," Philip said, face pale as he looked between them. "What makes you sure Adam wants the throne? And Rudy, before he died? They involved anarchists. Doesn't that strike you as counter-productive?"

"Are you kidding?" Frankie shoved a hand in her hair. "It's brilliant. Hide behind a movement notorious for dismantling power structures. Incite rebellion, get the anarchists to do all the hard, murderous work, then throw them under the bus and appear as a savior to the royal line." She arched an eyebrow at Tommy as if to say, *right?*

"Exactly," he said.

"Oh." Philip's nod was dazed. "Of course."

"Philip, could you tell Ava and the boys?" Frankie held out a hand to Tommy, and he passed her the leather volume. "I'll update the authorities and—" Her lips pinched. "Zara."

Tommy hid a grimace. That wouldn't be easy.

"Thank you both for handling this." He leaned forward, elbows on the desk. "Is there anything I can do to help?"

"Only if those books of yours tell us where he's hiding," Frankie said wryly, then paused as she angled a piercing stare at him. "How the hell did you figure this out?"

He straightened as pride rose inside him. Adam had been missing for two and a half weeks. His disappearance had prompted a nationwide manhunt, the authorities and the royal guard both assigning their best to the task. And no progress had been made until today.

Until someone had finally asked the right question.

"Jonah."

13

The hardest part about dating Tommy was not dating Tommy.

Jonah kept slipping up in public. Which was so silly because their mismatched schedules and Tommy's anxiety meant they could only go out for short bursts, and surely he should have been able to keep it in his head to say Kris for an hour at a time. But he was a big name user, and after twenty years of *Tommy* being his every tenth word, second nature wouldn't budge.

On Wednesday, he woke in Tommy's bed alone—after being absolutely *not alone* hours before—and spent time with Buck, Bull, and the horses until Tommy took him for an early dinner of savory waffles. It was almost perfect. Sharing this place with Tommy; doing something normal together. And what a sight they must have made. Two grown cowboys, dressed in jeans and checked shirts and hats, eating waffles in a cute, cobbled laneway. Their long legs stretched out on either side of each other's chairs, wearing leather boots made for stirrups and pastures and dusty roads. Jonah secretly hoped one of the other diners took a photo of them that he could find online later—until he accidentally said

Tommy's name three times in conversation and prayed to God no one had recorded a video.

He tried to cover it up, but judging by the extra strain around Tommy's mouth, it sounded pretty weird that he kept asking his tummy questions.

"I'm sorry," he said that night, face in a soft palace pillow. "I'm an idiot."

"You're not an idiot, and it's my fault." Tommy drew him close, lips pressing against his forehead. "Don't be sorry."

But Jonah *was* sorry, because the next morning he took Tommy to his favorite coffee stand by the lake, and Jonah slipped up in the first five seconds, literally to the barista's face.

"A caramel latte for me, please, and Tommy will have a long black."

Too mortified to know how to reform *that* into something not suspicious, Jonah watched helplessly as the young man flicked a confused glance at Tommy and stepped behind the espresso machine.

"A joke." Tommy slid an arm around Jonah's shoulders. It was a casual, lounging movement that embodied Kris—except Jonah could hear the quiet speed of his breath. "I've recently changed my coffee preference to the same as my brother's, and do you think I can live it down?"

"Ah!" The man laughed. "Very good, Your Highness."

Face hot, Jonah turned and burrowed into Tommy, whispering, "I'm sorry, I'm sorry," against his chest.

Tommy stroked his back but didn't answer.

Jonah was so scared of messing up when Nora unexpectedly dropped by his apartment that afternoon, he panicked and rushed to put on loud music. She gave him a strange look, held up several large bags, and shouted that they were going to make pride outfits.

"Yay!" he shouted back with a grin.

Laughing and rolling her eyes, she emptied half a craft store onto his lounge floor: brightly colored fabric, accessories, and costume pieces, all bold and full of potential and . . . actually, almost overwhelming. Throat tight, he knelt and picked up a pair of colorful suspenders. He'd never attended pride before—never felt accepted enough in Sage Haven to wear tight jeans let alone a rainbow. He hadn't even gone to prom, because it would have meant pretending to be someone he wasn't.

In a perfect world, I'd have worn something like this.

Nora knelt beside him, sliding a hand down his back. Smiling softly, she handed him a magazine and pointed at one of the pictures.

Oh. Excitement sparked in his chest. He met her eyes and nodded. *That.*

They got to work.

Nora's good manners put Jonah's to shame—she tolerated the crazy-loud music for several hours without saying a thing. They cut and stitched and tried things on, singing and giving encouragement through gestures and grins. It was fun, having a new friend, even if it was safer without conversation.

Finally, after returning from the kitchen with two cups of tea, she switched the speakers off entirely and sat on the couch with a sigh.

"So, you don't have to answer this," she said, and Jonah's stomach balled up. "But is your man bi? We could do him something in those colors."

Tensing, Jonah squeezed out way too much glue. *It's okay—just think first.* Nora meant Kris. And people had made comments about Kris seeming close with his bodyguard before Jonah had arrived in Kiraly. So if Nora had noticed Kris and Frankie's chemistry when they'd been at the Bearded Bunting together, and then seen how intense Tommy was with Jonah—

thinking he was Kris—it made sense she'd wonder whether he was bi.

"Um." Jonah pretended to concentrate as he glued down a line of purple feathers. "He's, um."

Ahh, how was he supposed to answer? He couldn't lie. It would just make this tangle worse. But he couldn't tell the truth, because Kris was straight and that wouldn't make any sense, and Tommy was—

Well, Tommy was . . .

Oh my God. Jonah reached for his phone in disbelief and sent a quick, confused text.

Are you gay??

Three dots instantly appeared on the screen. Disappeared. Then Tommy replied: **I think I'm demi. Not sure about anything else.**

Okay, cool!

Then he looked helplessly at Nora. "What's demi?"

"Demisexual." She was replacing the band on Jonah's cowboy hat with a rainbow ribbon. "That means he only experiences sexual attraction to someone he has an emotional connection with. He isn't drawn to someone based on physical appearance or sex appeal. Romantic attraction will always come first."

That didn't sound quite right. "But he told me I'm hot."

"Okay, he feels that way now. But even though you have a ridiculously hot body, and your mouth looks like a portal to heaven, and basically everyone at the bar wants to bang you, your love affair with the prince all started because he wanted you for you."

Jonah's pulse went weird and fluttery as he blushed to the roots of his hair. "Oh."

She laughed. "Your face right now."

My heart right now.

"So—" He tried to focus, because this was important, and he didn't have it yet. "Does that mean he could be gay?"

She eyed him, frowning. "From what I've seen, he's not gay." Because *obviously* they were still talking about Kris. *Why can't I keep this straight in my head?* "But people can be demi and gay, sure. Or bi or pan or straight. But he might not know or want a label."

"I think he's not sure." *Tommy has only ever liked me.* So how *could* he know?

"That's okay, too." Nora stitched the ends of the ribbon together. "He'll be at pride, right?"

"Um." Jonah opened a bag of green feathers, keeping his head down. *No, Tommy won't be there,* he wanted to say. *He doesn't like crowds.* "I don't think so." Kris wasn't in any state to attend either. "He hasn't said anything."

"Really?" She tossed his hat onto the floor beside him. "I just thought he might. Prince Noel always came."

Jonah glanced up. "With Philip?"

She frowned. "Who's Philip?"

Oh, God. *How many names aren't I allowed to say?* Too confused, he held up his design. "More feathers, do you think?"

Stress had made thick knots of his shoulders by the time Nora left. Guarding his tongue was hard—and upsetting and sad because all he wanted was to talk about Tommy, and he wasn't smart enough to do it using Kris's name as code.

How long would he have to pretend? He couldn't ask—wouldn't put that pressure on Tommy. With Kris still too bruised and sore to leave the palace, Tommy could keep up the act for another week or two. *Until the end of next week,* Jonah realized with a flinch. It was like walking into a low branch. Tommy's coping strategy meant that if Jonah made the heartbreaking decision not to continue their relationship once the survey results were announced, no one would ever know he'd been with Tommy at all.

Jonah still had his face in his hands when Philip called.

"Wonderful news!" the man said. "You've been cordially invited to be a guest of honor at the annual luncheon of the Kiralian Equine Veterinary Association tomorrow."

The phone almost slipped out of Jonah's suddenly damp hands. "I have?"

"It's nothing too formal." As if that alone would reassure him. "The Royal Family is a patron, and with Mark previously engaged, Kristof indisposed, and Tomas unable to attend, the association hoped you might like to join them instead."

"Oh." A *luncheon?* How was that different from regular lunch? "Really?"

"Yes." It sounded like Philip was smiling. "It's only small. A couple dozen members at the most. Equine vets, veterinary students and graduates, and volunteers. It could be a good way to cut your teeth for future royal duties."

"Future—" Jonah sat heavily on the couch. "Duties?"

"You're partner to a prince, Jonah. I understand that it's daunting, but this is an honor. It's a sign of acceptance." There was a pause before Philip continued more quietly, "Kiraly knows your name, knows you stand beside their prince. Participating in official duties such as public engagements means that you're a welcome part of the family."

Something tightened beneath Jonah's breastbone. He'd known he wouldn't be able to open his own bar if he stayed with Tommy, but he hadn't considered what he *would* have to do. Apparently, whatever he was told.

"I, um," he said, and rubbed his face. "What do I have to do?"

"Attend. Shake hands. Dine. Talk and be personable." As if

reading Jonah's mind, Philip added, "I'll remind them that it would be inappropriate to ask about your relationship. Discussion will be kept strictly to horses—a comfortable topic for you."

Jonah hesitated. He didn't like the way Philip had neatly removed all ground Jonah could have stood on to say no. *But Tommy must know about this and believe I can do it.*

At that, his apprehension retreated. "Okay."

He'd do it for Tommy.

All in all, it didn't go terribly.

There was no mention of the boys. It was an easy-to-identify three-course meal. And the attendees happily discussed horse health practices from start to finish. The only gut-twisting moment was when one of the extra-smart-sounding vets asked Jonah a question he didn't understand—and Tommy wasn't there to help him answer it.

Embarrassed as all eyes turned to him, Jonah did the only thing he could: smiled, shook his head a little, and said, "I have no idea what most of those words mean. Could you ask me in a different way? I'd really love to answer."

There was a startled silence, during which Jonah wrote the headline *Stupid Childhood Friend Shames Royal Family*. Then the man smiled back, the rest started teasing him for his "verbosity", while a woman farther down the table looked at Jonah with a hand over her heart and *bless* in her eyes.

Jonah answered the man's rephrased question and hoped he did Tommy proud.

On the ride home, he slumped as his tension drained away and texted Tommy about four million times. He wouldn't hear back until later—Tommy had an important meeting about sustainable cars most of the day—but that didn't stop Jonah sending a stream of consciousness in short messages about what he'd eaten and how he'd felt and what he'd said and basically anything else that crossed his mind.

It was weird

I don't think I liked it

But now that it's over I'm remembering it like I liked it

Do you ever get that?

They were nice

They seemed to like me

Asked lots of questions

I felt included

Special, you know

Important

But terrified

Omg Tommy, it was really scary

There were two forks

And because we didn't actually eat anything at your place the other night, I didn't know what to do

But the woman next to me explained it

She was friendly

I told her she could come and see the quarter horses at the palace

And then I kind of invited everyone

But that wasn't right

Was it?

I shouldn't have done that

Omg, sorry

They'll probably come over tomorrow

As in they definitely will

At ten in the morning

I said they could

Omg, so sorry

Then there was this moment where I was pretty sure they wanted me to do a speech

And I got all hot and cold

Because Philip said it wouldn't be expected

But I stood and tapped my glass with my spoon because that's what they do in the movies

Even though no one was talking

And I said

May you be committed to supporting equine veterinary professionals in everything you do

And they all laughed like it was a joke

And then I remembered reading that on their website on the car ride to the lunch

Eon

Luncheon

So I laughed like it was on purpose, and we started eating dessert

It was a chocolate brownie with sauce

THE SAUCE, OMG

And on it went until it occurred to him that he was nervous texting. He hadn't known that was a thing, but he stopped quick smart because he *was* nervous.

He was starting to think nervous was his new state of being.

By the time he got behind the bar that night, he was ready for the crowd to work its magic. He wanted to be in that zone, absorbed by their energy. But even with the buoyant music and staff in-jokes and super friendly patrons, he just couldn't *get* there. Too much was happening in his life, and it was getting harder and harder to let it go.

"You okay?" It was nearing ten when Nora cornered him by the glass washer. "You seem off. Again."

"It's just," he said, and leaned in, "they keep asking about Kris."

Her eyes flared slightly. "So he goes by Kris? I *knew* he was too laid back and sexy to be Kristof all the—oh, I mean, that must be really annoying. People should shut up about it."

He forced a smile. "It's just overwhelming."

If he opened a bar here, would people be asking what it had been like dating Prince Kristof for the rest of his life? Would Tommy ever correct the misunderstanding, or would the resulting media interest be too much for him? And if Jonah stayed with Tommy, he'd have to attend events like the luncheon today (that should have been called a lunch, it was just lunch) without grounding himself in bar work afterward.

His throat grew tight; a miserable weight dragged him down.

This is too hard. He just wanted a simple life with Tommy. *I don't know what to do.*

"Hey." Nora ran a comforting hand over his back. "I've spoken to Jess upstairs, and she's happy to swap with you. She said to warn you that the function up there tonight is really boring, and they're hardly ordering drinks because they're talking so much, but at least no one will ask you things they shouldn't. You want to head on up?"

Touched, Jonah brightened a little. "Now?"

"Well, like," Nora said with a smile, "finish your order first."

Upstairs, he cut through the bar storeroom and emerged behind the counter. One of his guards stayed in the corridor outside, while the other positioned herself in the shadow beyond the storeroom doorway. Jess flashed him a smile, mouthed, "*So boring,*" and headed downstairs.

Taking a breath, Jonah pressed his palms to the counter and scanned his guests. About fifteen of them, with the tables arranged in a horseshoe so they all sat facing inward. No one had noticed his arrival; no one seemed to need a drink. After checking the bar was in order, he tugged out his phone and held it low.

Tommy had texted him back.

I thought my phone was glitching when it said I had 345 unopened messages. I adore you. You have a midnight finish, right? I can come and get you.

Jonah glanced up. The guests were in deep discussion.

Midnight, yeah, I'd love that, he replied. **Nora moved me to the upstairs bar, but it's really quiet so we can text a bit.**

You feeling okay?

Just confused. Which made it sound way less difficult than it was. It was like his heart and dreams had said their goodbyes and were heading off in opposite directions, leaving Jonah frantically looking from one to the other, both still close enough to touch. But another few steps and he'd have to decide which one to follow. **Really confused.**

I'm here if you'd like to talk.

Jonah knew that. And he'd tried to talk about it the past few nights, but his eyes had filled before he'd even opened his mouth, so he hadn't said anything at all. The last thing Tommy needed to deal with was Jonah crying over whether or not to choose their relationship.

What's the function? Tommy asked.

Not sure. Let me figure it out. Jonah looked up again, tuning in to the conversation. The group was serious, talking with aggressive passion. He didn't understand much of what they were saying, but it sounded pretty intelligent, and they really cared about it. Maybe this was philosophy? Frowning, he sent a few phrases to Tommy.

Does 'civil disobedience' and 'social enslavement' mean anything to you?

Tommy's response was instant. **What??**

Jonah flushed. **I didn't come up with that. It's what they're talking about. I think. Now a guy is saying something about revolutionary socialism?**

Jonah. Are you sure that's what they're saying?

Pretty sure.

Stay there, Tommy texted, and as Jonah frowned at the screen, he added, **I'm coming with Frankie. It sounds like an anarchist meeting. Act normal.**

A chill shot down Jonah's spine a second before he sensed both of his guards move to the front of the storeroom. *Oh man.* Frankie didn't muck around. *Obviously.* These people might be a part of the group that had organized the murder of Tommy's relatives and the attack on Kris. And they would recognize Jonah if they looked over—everyone in Kira City knew his face by now.

Dizzy with alarm, he gripped the counter to stop himself hiding behind it. *Do they want to kill me, too?*

He clung to Tommy's instruction to act normal by a thread, because what he really wanted was to dart into the storeroom, down the rear stairs, and not come back. He swallowed through the racing pulse in his neck—the fear that this group could easily overpower him and his two guards—and started slicing limes.

He had no idea how much time passed, but one second he was gripping the knife in a white-knuckled hand, and the next Frankie was barging into the function room, and Tommy was beside him, hatless and disheveled, whispering that it was okay now and gently prying the knife from his fingers.

Guards streamed in behind Frankie—a dozen, two dozen, or

was it ten thousand? *She marched them up to the top of the hill and she marched them down again.* He giggle-snorted, because it was either that or start crying, and received a baffled glare from Frankie as her guards ringed the startled group.

Tommy locked an arm around him. Beneath the counter, he kept hold of Jonah's knife.

"What is this?" One of the men was on his feet, seeming confused and concerned.

Frankie stood inside the circle of guards. She didn't move, didn't raise her voice. "I'm head of personal security to the royal family of Kiraly, and you have precious little time to explain the nature of this meeting before the authorities arrive and start making arrests for the murders of the late royal family."

The man sat abruptly, face white. A wave of alarm drenched the group before he said in a helpless tone, "But that was an accident."

Frankie levelled a stare at him. "That's not what I asked."

Swaying on his chair, he said, "We're just discussing politics."

"Be more specific." Tommy's quiet command cut across the room.

The group's attention snapped to the bar. After taking a second to process this next shock, they leapt to their feet, exclaiming, "Your Highness!" and "Prince Kristof!" and bowing deeply. From his safe place tucked under Tommy's arm, Jonah frowned, because none of them looked worried in the way a criminal might when surrounded by guards and one of the most powerful men in the country. They just seemed bewildered and uncomfortable.

No one sat back down.

"Anarchy, Your Highness," the man finally answered weakly. "But it's theoretical. A purely academic debate. We would never"—the remaining blood faded from his face—"*kill* the royal family."

Frankie's flat expression was unsympathetic. "Do you know Adam and Rudy Boller?"

Surprised, an older woman said, "They used to come to our meetings. Back when we met at the Bull's Quest. But we haven't seen them in over three years."

"Why not?"

"Well," the woman answered, inclining her head. "To be honest, ma'am, we didn't like those brothers. Or Rudy, anyway, and Adam did everything he said. Rudy was obsessive and angry, and kept recruiting new members like him. Angry. Hungry. Wanting to take action. That wasn't the point of our group, so about half of us split to get back to discussion and debate."

"Huh." Frankie's jaw flexed. "You formed a new group and didn't tell the police about the others? Because I assume by *action* you mean violence."

Frowning, the woman's gaze flitted to the other man who'd spoken. "Jorge and I did mention it to the police at the time, ma'am, but there was nothing for them to pursue. The others were getting worked up about trimming the royal line, but there was no way they could ever—"

Silence hit like the room like ice water.

Most of the group looked ill as they seemed to remember Frankie's initial accusation. Hands pressed over mouths or stomachs or gripped chair backs for balance. *They didn't do it.* Jonah was convinced of it as he looked between them. *Not these people.*

"Did you know about us?" Tommy asked. Instead of relaxing in the face of their innocence, his fingers were digging harder into Jonah's upper arm. "Me and my brothers?"

"We didn't know there were three of you, Your Highness."

Jorge was sweating, his skin glossy. "No one knew. After your parents left Kiraly, rumor was that they had one son."

Tommy suddenly went rigid beside Jonah.

"Perhaps that's all Rudy was talking about?" the man continued. "Not that he'd have been able to find you. No one knew where you were."

"We'll need you all to give a statement to the police," Frankie said. "Tell them every—"

"You found us, Frankie."

Tommy had spoken softly, but everyone stilled. The odd blend of accusation and realization in his words sent a streak of unease through Jonah. *I'm missing something.* The dread that flickered like a failing bulb across Frankie's face as she turned to Tommy confirmed it.

"I did," she said, too carefully.

"If you found us," Tommy said, "others could have."

Her featured blanked. "That's why I stayed."

Body still stiff, Tommy looked at Jorge. "Your group split just over three years ago?"

Frowning, the man nodded.

Tommy started trembling so hard, it was like he'd been grabbed by the shoulders and physically shaken.

Jonah exclaimed, "Tommy!" as concern reared inside him. And Frankie said, "Your Highness," very loudly, reminding Jonah that he'd just said the wrong prince's name *again*.

Jonah clamped a hand over his mouth, but Tommy didn't seem to notice.

His focus was on Frankie. "Rudy and Adam had plans to trim the royal line about three years ago," he said to her. "They thought there was only one of us. They could have come to Sage Haven hunting for *one* man of our age to trim."

Frankie stared back, pale and wide-eyed.

"But they didn't," Jonah murmured, confused. Tommy had

280

enough to worry about without getting worked up over *what ifs*. "It's okay. It didn't happen."

Still shaking, Tommy faced him, lips pale, tendons jutting from his neck from the force of his clenched jaw. He fixed his spooked stare on the scar across Jonah's throat and murmured, "Maybe it did."

With an alarmed jolt, Jonah shot a hand over it.

What? He felt faint, sick and disordered as the possibility tried to rewrite his most traumatic memory. *No. Stop.* It hurt. Made his head feel tight, toxic, like little firecrackers were exploding inside his skull and there was nowhere for the acrid smoke to go—except maybe down the back of his throat because he was pretty sure he could taste it.

"Don't," he said, wrapping his other arm around himself. *That's not what happened.* He wasn't aware that he'd left Tommy's side until he felt the liquor shelf against his spine. "They hated me."

"Don't do this here," Frankie said, striding toward the bar.

"Did they?" Tommy's eyes were pupil-black and agonized, like *he* was the one who'd been sliced across the throat and stabbed in the stomach.

"They hated who I was. Who I am." Jonah's tongue was numb—his memory of that night sharp yet blurring as if someone had shattered a water pitcher right over the top of it. "That's why."

Tommy rubbed his face. His eyes were wet. Anguish pushed at his brow.

"They hated me." That was what everyone had believed. The sheriff, the town, him.

Not once during the unprovoked violence had the men actually used slurs, but their hatred had been in every mark they'd made, every break and rupture and organ-deep wound.

"They hated me," Jonah repeated, shaking his head

because even that part, the harshest, darkest, most damaging part of that night was starting to wash away, and he couldn't make it out.

Frankie hoisted herself over the counter in a single jump and muttered urgently about getting the hell out of public earshot.

"Unless," Tommy said, "they hated *me*."

Tommy had lost feeling in his hands and feet. All sensation had converged in his chest, choking his heartbeat. *I can't handle this.* Shock, guilt, dread—and a truth that could snap the rope barely keeping his shit together.

In brittle silence, Frankie led them into a smaller, unoccupied function room across the hall. The lounge had late-night lighting and couches and carpet the color of purple plums. Tommy jerked around, hyperalert when she snapped the door shut, then watched her sit on the very edge of an armchair, hands shoved between her thighs.

He started pacing, jittery, trying to jam his spiraling thoughts as Jonah took the couch opposite her. Jonah's breath was disturbed—he hadn't taken his hand off his throat. It got harder to blink as images of the night Jonah got that scar accosted the back of Tommy's eyelids.

"Let me explain," Frankie said.

I can't be here. His pulse was a gasp in his veins, and he found himself across the room at the window. It overlooked the rear courtyard. Strings of lights crisscrossed at eyelevel, and the pulse of music and people dancing below made him queasy. *Fuck.* He needed to run or ride or swim or scream. The old paint of the window frame curled under his nails, but the timber beneath was solid. *Or slam my head against this so I don't have to think.*

"Tommy," Jonah said, sounding watery, and Tommy turned, because he would always turn toward Jonah. "Sit with me?"

Sit? He could hardly stand still.

"Please?" Jonah looked stricken, shaken up, seeking an anchor.

Tommy was by his side a moment later.

Once he'd taken Jonah's hand, Frankie said, "I'm so sorry."

Tommy tried to focus on stroking Jonah's knuckles with his thumb, raising them to his lips, soothing his distress. On a shuddering breath out, Jonah sank against his side.

Tommy met Frankie's gaze. "Explain."

"You're right." Her confirmation was like a puncture in his lungs. "Your attack was royally motivated. We've only recently found the men responsible. They've admitted that Rudy sent them to Montana. That his plan was to murder an heir. Like everyone else in Kiraly, they believed Erik only had one child, a son." She turned to Jonah, shoulders tight with regret. "That night, they thought it was you."

Tommy tasted metal.

For years, Jonah had shouldered the burden of their attack. It didn't matter how well he'd processed it—trauma could never be left behind. It had shaped him—a jagged edge in the contour of his sexuality, a splinter in his sense of belonging. An echo in his muscles that, just minutes ago, had clutched a knife for protection and shuddered beneath Tommy's arm.

Jonah blamed himself for Tommy's anxiety. *It's the one thing I can't get over,* he'd admitted, thinking Tommy struggled because of him. But no. The truth was infinitely worse.

Jonah had almost *died* because of *Tommy*.

"I didn't know at the time." Frankie looked exhausted. "I had no idea."

"How do you know now?" Tommy could feel it—his temper attempting to relieve his agitation.

"I—" Her lips tightened, and she pitched forward at the waist. A small, tortured movement. Then she groaned and said, "Fuck. I can't do this. It was Kris. Kris knew, okay? He told me a few weeks ago. It's how we found the men. He asked me not to tell you."

Kris? How the hell would Kris know?

Uncomprehending, Tommy circled his brother's behavior from that night. Kris had been the only other person to see those bastards up close—they'd visited the ranch before the attack, asking where they could find Jonah. Kris hadn't told them; he'd pretended he didn't recognize the name. The men had left the ranch only to encounter Tommy and Jonah on the road home. Not knowing this, Kris had called the sheriff—and Mark and Frankie—and they'd gone in search of the men.

And found them with Tommy and Jonah unconscious at their feet.

Kris had hounded the sheriff to keep searching for them throughout Tommy and Jonah's recoveries. Even though none were caught or questioned, Kris had never accepted it as a hate crime.

Tommy had always thought Kris maintained that stance for Jonah's sake.

Now his spine tightened with unease. "Tell me what?"

"He didn't want you to blame him." Frankie sounded weak.

"Why would we blame him?"

She leaned forward, face in her hands. Jonah shifted closer against Tommy's side.

"Okay," she said, seeming to psych herself up. "When Kris answered the door to those men, they didn't ask for Jonah. They asked where they could find Erik Jaroka's son."

Jonah made a soft noise of confusion. His hand wound around Tommy's bicep.

"They looked dangerous," she said. "Kris was alone, and it

scared him to think what would happen if he admitted to being one of Erik's sons—so he told them the man they were after lived next door. Jones was working at the bar—he was supposed to be out late. Kris only sent those guys to his house to buy time. He called Mark and me and the sheriff, and we raced over to confront them. But," she said, and her eyes filled. "Jones finished early that night, and you were both on the road home at exactly the wrong time."

Tommy's mind felt like a sheet of lightning—floodlit, blinded.

"So." Jonah's grip grew tighter. "You're saying it wasn't because I was gay?"

Sniffling, Frankie shook her head—and the lightning went out.

"Why the hell didn't Kris tell us?" Tommy was on his feet, hands fisted around feelings he couldn't name, his temper unravelling from shock, body vibrating with rage or betrayal or something that could have been the blistering end of grief. His voice rose, climbing over the clench of sorrow in his throat. "How could he leave us to think Jonah was the target? Kris was the *reason* they targeted him, and he didn't tell us? It's been *years*. Who the fuck does that? And you—you've known for weeks? And you've kept it from us? How dare you even—"

"Tommy!" The snap of Jonah's rebuke gripped Tommy's uncontrolled emotion—yanked it around to face him. Jonah was on his feet, face pale but dark eyes steady. "Don't talk to Frankie like that. It's not her fault everyone asks her to keep secrets."

Rage was the only thing delaying the panic crawling up Tommy's throat. "She could have said no!"

"That's not fair, and you know it."

Frankie cleared her throat. "Jones, you don't have—"

"You're telling me she's not keeping any of your secrets right now?" Jonah demanded of Tommy, whose stomach plunged to the floor. "Exactly," Jonah said, searching Tommy's face. "Don't take this out on her just because you think she's strong enough to put up with it."

Tommy stared back, trying to get a hold of his breathing. It was out of control, ravaging his lungs like a hailstorm. He wanted to murder Kris—or punch him so fucking hard no one would ever recognize him again.

"Come on, Tom," Jonah said very quietly, then tilted his head toward Frankie.

Jesus. This felt like struggling to cross the choppy waters between two boats. Jonah had dragged him over the side of his temper, but it was a long haul to reach a level head.

Tommy turned and managed a tight-jawed, "Sorry, Frankie."

Still sitting, she didn't meet his eye. "I should have told you."

"No." Tommy had been taking advantage of her backbone recently, and the fact that she'd do anything for him and his brothers—including tolerate his moods. "Kris should have."

I'll kill him. I'll fucking kill him.

"Is there more?" Jonah's question was wary.

"That's the core of it." She stood to leave. "Get the rest from Kris."

Fury must have flashed in Tommy's eyes—she winced as she stepped around him.

"Thank you for explaining," Jonah said, and with an uncomfortable mumble, Frankie left, closing the door behind her.

Within seconds, Tommy's stress erupted. Grasping his head in both hands, he bit back a scream. "I can't do this. Why did I think I could ever do this?"

"Tommy—"

"Fuck." He launched across the room as if speed alone could dislodge the dread riding his spine. Clutching the window frame, he lowered his head, shoulders lurching, lungs burning as he battled the devastation shredding him apart. *I can't do this. I can't do this. I can't do this. I can't—*

"Tommy."

No. He couldn't talk. His pulse points jabbed like gunshots. He wanted to howl, smash the glass with his fist. He'd been trying so hard to pull himself together, and this was going to tear him apart.

"Tommy." Jonah sounded stern, bordering on put out. "Tell me why you're upset."

On a surge of disbelief, Tommy threw himself around to stare at Jonah. He'd followed Tommy most of the way across the lounge but kept a cautious distance. "Because Kris lied to us! Because he kept this a secret! Because the truth we believed wasn't the truth. Because you've lived with shame and fear and scars, and all this time, you've thought it was your fault that—"

"But it's *your* fault?" Jonah cut him off, brows rising. "Right?"

Tommy jerked back. Not because Jonah meant that, but because he didn't. Guilt was pulling Tommy apart, and Jonah didn't understand. All this time Jonah had blamed himself—dealt with the atrocious conviction that those men had believed their hate was worth more than his life.

But they hadn't believed that.

They hadn't cared about Jonah at all.

"It *is* my fault." Tommy's words came out harsh. It was really sinking in now. None of it would have happened if he'd been honest about his lineage. If Sage Haven had known he and his brothers were Jaroka royals, then the world would have known. Their family would have had proper security, and no one could've breezed into town to take them out. The attack would never have happened, let alone included Jonah. But Jonah had suffered because of *him,* felt hated because of *him,* feared for his life and almost lost it *because of him.*

It was too much. It wrenched his rib cage tight; constricted every beat within. *Good.* If it would just squeeze tighter, his heart might—

"Was it my fault?" Jonah's question came from nearby—he'd moved closer. "Back when we thought they'd targeted me? Did you blame me?"

Tommy shook his head, helpless, furious. "You know I didn't."

"Well, this is no different." Jonah closed in until they were a step apart. His face was gold and brown in the lamplight, and Tommy could smell him, feel the familiar pull of his body. "Do you remember what you said to me? When I was ashamed and blamed myself?"

"They don't get to win." Fighting the lump in his throat, Tommy reached out, pushing Jonah's shirtsleeve up and over his tattoo. Tommy had scrubbed at the penned *h* that day, desperate to remove Jonah's shame, scrubbed until Jonah's skin was pink and hot. Now he swiped his thumb over the word that bound them and felt Jonah's reactive shiver. "They don't get to do this to you."

Jonah said, "So don't let them do this to *you*."

Do what? Eyes stinging, Tommy curled his fingers around the muscle of Jonah's arm. What had they done exactly? Infested him with thoughts that bypassed logic? Condemned him to anxiety-induced reactions he couldn't always predict or identify? If those men hadn't attacked them, Tommy wouldn't be like this.

They made me this way. Robbed him of calm and confidence; crippled him of the ability to stand before his people—to simply be *among* them.

Maybe they'd won after all.

They hadn't even needed to kill him.

"Sometimes I think I'm losing my mind," he said, blinking hard.

"You're not." Jonah wrapped a hand around the back of Tommy's head. Fingertips massaging, he drew Tommy closer until their foreheads touched. It settled Tommy a little, the world

288

shrinking to this manageable moment; being skin-to-skin with an angel. He swore the room blurred over Jonah's shoulders, a shimmering disturbance where his wings should be. "You've just got too much on it."

Letting out a breath, Tommy closed his eyes. "Why aren't you upset about this?"

Jonah hummed, the deep sound stirring low in Tommy's belly. His fingers kept moving like he was firming soil around a seedling. Steady, sure presses to keep Tommy from toppling.

"It can take me a while to figure out what I think about things, you know," Jonah said. "I have to process. I feel like all I've been doing recently is processing. But I usually know how I feel right away—and aside from shock, it doesn't feel bad to know that it wasn't about me. They didn't hate me. Tommy, they didn't hate the way I loved. Why would I be upset about that?"

Because you had to believe it for so long. Tommy snapped his eyes open and glared at Jonah's mouth. *Because the world is so fucked that no one questioned it.* "And Kris?"

Jonah was silent.

"I'll never forgive him," Tommy swore, and a part of him died at the thought, an entire chamber of his heart falling still.

"He loves us." Jonah's hand dropped to Tommy's chest. "Remember that when we talk to him, because I'd like to hear what he has to say."

Tommy turned away with a harsh laugh. Emotion tremored in his nerves. He fisted his hands—found himself pounding them against the windowsill.

Who was he these days? *Where* was he, the part of him that made sense? The part that thought the way he used to, clear and succinct and sensible?

He didn't know anymore.

"I have lost it." His mind; his self. Distress shoved him to his knees, his face in his hands. He couldn't cope with this. Those bastards had turned him into someone who couldn't cope. "I can't find me anymore."

Maybe he didn't exist.

Maybe he was nothing but a head full of trauma and chaos and impulse.

"Tommy, sweet," Jonah murmured, crouching before him. His warm palm pressed onto Tommy's thigh. "You're here. I see you. But you're hiding. You've been hiding for a long time, and I don't think it's good for you."

Hiding. Tommy couldn't remember a time when he hadn't hidden a part of himself.

He'd hidden the prince he'd always been behind a small-town cowboy.

Hidden his ache for royal duties behind a passion for his ranch.

Hidden his love for Jonah behind lifelong friendship.

Hidden his sexuality.

His desires.

His body—from his family in secret palace passageways; from the Kiralian people since he'd arrived. He'd finally emerged —only to hide his identity behind his brother's hat and swagger.

Tommy lowered his hands, too ashamed to speak.

"Hey." Jonah tipped his head, regarding him with a soft smile. "I think you'd be easier to find if you accepted who you are."

"I have," he said, then thought, *bullshit.*

"To be honest," Jonah said, as if Tommy hadn't just lied to him. "I don't want to keep hiding you. I don't like it. I can't seem to call you Kris, and even if I could, I wouldn't want to. He's your brother. I'm with *you.* I only want to be with you."

Heart aching, Tommy wanted to kiss the word *you* right off Jonah's slightly pouting lips. It would transform this defenseless kneel to a position much more deliberate—except even if Jonah hadn't just told him no, it would be another form of hiding, ducking behind intimacy to avoid change.

And I do have to change.

Steeling his pride, he met Jonah's earnest gaze—and did something he'd never done.

He whispered, "Help me."

Jonah actually swayed in surprise. "Okay," he said, and took Tommy's hands. "First, we're going to go to the lake, and you're going to swim until your body stops buzzing and your head feels clearer. Then you'll swim back to me, and we'll eat leftovers from your fancy fridges, and you'll spoon me to sleep."

Clinging to every word, Tommy nodded. He could do that. "And the rest?"

"We'll talk to Kris together. We'll tell Kiraly the truth together."

And then will you choose me? Tommy wanted to ask, but he said, "Okay."

"Okay." Jonah stood and, with a firm grip, helped Tommy up beside him. His features looked worn, but his skin flushed as he lowered his lashes and shifted closer. "Was it okay that I called you sweet?"

"Yes." The endearment glowed inside him, all the more precious for its incongruity. "Would you like me to call you . . ." *My love. My heart. Soul mate.* "Something?"

"If you'd like. But I like it most when you say my name." Jonah's dark eyes did an almost shy sweep of Tommy's mouth. "Gives me butterflies."

Tommy pressed a hand to his middle. "Same."

Smiling, Jonah nudged against him, a fond brush of his body. "Really, Tommy?"

Belly rolling like an impassioned embrace, he said, "Yes, Jonah."

And Jonah laughed, cheeks growing even darker as he took

Tommy's hand. At a light tug, Tommy let himself be led across the lounge by the only person who could truly calm him; who both understood and stood up to him; whom he loved with every unpredictable, discordant part of his being.

He'd never ask Jonah to call him by his brother's name again.

14

"Tommy?" Jonah's hand was running along his arm. "Hey, wake up."

Sucking in a sharp breath, Tommy lifted his head and blinked to pull his bedroom into focus. There was a pressure against his hip; Jonah had a knee on the summer-weight sheet beside him, pulling it taut as he leaned in close. His dark hair was mussed and his cheek held the imprint of bunched fabric, but he was up and dressed.

"Hey," Tommy mumbled. It was barely morning, and he was already drained.

"Kris is here." Apprehension flickered in Jonah's eyes. "He's asked if he can explain."

Tommy dropped his head back onto the pillow, swearing under his breath. He didn't want an explanation—he wanted his brother to never have lied in the first place. Rising to sitting, Tommy ended up practically nose-to-nose with Jonah.

"Don't react on my behalf out there," Jonah said, holding his gaze. "Okay?"

Tommy almost scoffed. How could he not? Jonah's pain was as good as his own. "I'll try," he said, then ran a hand through his hair. His arm felt like lead, and he dropped it to his side. "I'll be a minute."

Jonah nodded, said, "When you're ready," and retreated to the sitting room.

Chest tight, Tommy showered and attempted to rein in his sense of betrayal. His brothers were the earth beneath his feet, the axis of his world. Their three lives were fused together, a whorl of wood grains, and Kris's destructive lie felt like a crack in the foundation of Tommy's existence.

How could he do this to us? Tommy slammed the base of his fist against the bedpost as he sat and shoved his feet into his boots. Obviously, he wasn't going to punch his brother. Tommy might be furious, his trust in Kris dismantled and flung wide— but he'd be damned if it showed on his face.

In the sitting room, Jonah had let Kris in—but Kris had only entered far enough to close the door behind him. Head snapping up, features haggard with remorse, Kris watched Tommy sit beside Jonah on the couch.

Wordless, Tommy crossed his arms, hooked one ankle over the other, and stared at him.

"I wanted to come last night, but Frankie told me to leave you alone." Kris's stance held none of his usual idle lounging. He was here without pretense, unprotected by ego and confidence, standing unsure with arms slack by his sides. "Christ, you two. I'd be begging for forgiveness at your feet right now if it wouldn't make this apology about me."

Tommy didn't react—just stared at his brother, until Jonah said, "You can sit, Kris," and gestured to the couch across from them.

Kris moved like a scolded dog and sat with a pained hiss of breath.

Then he said, "I'm sorry. I'm so sorry that I almost got you both killed." On a fast exhale, he ducked his head, pressing the heels of his hands into his eyes, and Tommy's throat thickened. "It's my fault. The whole thing. They came to the ranch, and I panicked. I thought you were working that night, Jonah. I shouldn't have assumed, but I did, and I sent them right down the road to your place. I told them your name. I don't know why the fuck I did that, but I'm shit at lying so it just came out. I didn't think it would matter when we caught them, but Jesus, they caught you first."

Jonah sniffled but didn't lean against Tommy.

"I sent them straight to you." Kris lifted his head, eyes red and burning with self-loathing. "I've never forgiven myself. I don't expect you to ever forgive me either."

I won't, Tommy thought fiercely, even though his heart knew better.

"Why didn't you tell us this before?" Jonah's voice wavered.

Frowning, Kris's attention darted from Tommy to Jonah and back again. "At first, it was because Tommy was traumatized. For a while there, we had to pretend it hadn't happened or he'd fall apart. Remember? I wasn't going to bring it up until things settled. And the longer I left it, the more impossible it felt. I hated myself for what I'd done. Then I hated myself even more for not wanting *you* to hate me. It's selfish, but that's why. I couldn't lose you. I love you both, and I was terrified you'd cut me out if you knew."

Tommy fought to keep his features unresponsive as Kris turned his full attention on him.

"I knew you loved him, Tom," Kris said, and Jonah shifted suddenly beside Tommy. "And I knew you'd never forgive me. How the hell could I have told you?" He paused, derision curling his mouth as he adopted a mock-casual tone. "Hey, so I know you're in love with Jonah, but I gave those men his name, sent them to his house, and they slit his fucking throat right in front of you. We still good?"

Tommy jerked, closing his eyes then hurling them open when he saw the knife settling against Jonah's throat.

Instantly, Jonah moved in, circling his hands around Tommy's upper arm and pressing his face into his neck. "I'm right here, Tommy."

Pulse racing, Tommy latched onto his touch, turning his face into Jonah's hair.

"Christ." Kris sounded faint, mortified. "I shouldn't have said —sorry, I'm so sorry."

"Kris," Jonah said, breath hot and alive on Tommy's skin. "If I'd been in your position that night, and it had occurred to me to send those guys to the empty house next door so they wouldn't hurt me, I'd have done the same thing."

Kris's eyes bulged in disbelief. "You *what?*"

"It was good thinking." Jonah adjusted his head to see Kris better, his hair brushing against Tommy's face. "That's not the part we're upset about."

"How the hell is almost killing you both *not* the part to get upset about?" Kris's voice fractured with such desperate incomprehension that Tommy suddenly understood how this had happened.

Years on, Kris was still trapped in the decision he'd made that night—in the horrific consequences of his actions. Ravaged by guilt, it seemed that he hadn't stepped back from the attack to see the damage his silence had caused since. Yes, it should have been goddamn obvious, and yes, he should have told the truth regardless, but as Tommy well knew, extreme emotion could be blinding.

"What else is there?" Kris pushed, lost.

"Not *telling* us," Tommy answered, and it came out exhausted.

Kris stared back at him. Confused distress widened his eyes. "What?"

For the love of God. Sometimes Kris made Tommy want to pull out his own hair. "You let us believe Jonah was the target all this time."

"I—" Kris turned helplessly to Jonah, face pale. "Jonah. I'm sorry. Jesus Christ."

Jonah shifted closer to Tommy, vulnerable and seeking comfort, and as Tommy slid an arm around his shoulders, Jonah resettled with a leg hooked over Tommy's knee.

"This explains why you've always tried to convince me it was a mugging," Jonah said. "A mugging where they knew my name and the road I lived on."

Shamefaced, Kris mumbled, "I told you I'm bad at lying."

"And I'm bad at being upset at people I care about," Jonah said, and thanking God for that, Tommy held him a little tighter. "You know how terrifying that night was for me. I've told you all about it these past few weeks. But you don't know how hard it was believing that it was my fault. That something about me was worthy of hate. I'm going to tell you about that next. Okay?"

Nodding, Kris ran a hand over his face before his eyes skimmed Tommy's in question.

Unforthcoming, Tommy stared back.

Kris ducked his head to stare at the floor, and an uncomfortable silence fell.

Finally, Tommy asked, "You really thought I'd never forgive you for the attack?" The sting from that admission was getting stronger. "You're my brother, and you couldn't have known what was going to happen. How could I hold that against you?"

"But it still happened. And, you know. . ." Trailing off, Kris looked away, jaw sliding uneasily.

"And I know what?"

"I'm the weak link, Tommy." The words were resigned, not bitter, as he met Tommy's gaze. "I'm not sensible like Mark or smart like you. We all tease me about it, and that's fine. I get it. But it's true."

Tommy frowned, waiting for him to talk sense.

"I mess things up," Kris said, raising a shoulder. "It pisses you off. It can take days for you to come around. I just—I couldn't imagine that you'd ever come around from something like that. So, yeah. I wasn't sure you'd ever forgive me."

The base of Tommy's throat tightened. His eyes were hot.

He loves us, Jonah had reminded him, as if Tommy needed reminding. As if he might forget that crucial factor motivating almost everything Kris did. As *if* Tommy was capable of doing exactly what he'd threatened last night and exactly what Kris feared—never forgiving his own brother.

He took in a long, deep breath. And released it just as slowly.

"I forgive you for that night," he said, and Jonah pressed his lips to Tommy's neck. "But lying about it will take a lot more time."

"Yeah." His brother's nods were shallow and quick. "I get it. Thank you."

Not in the mood to tolerate another awkward silence, Tommy stood, said, "Wait here," and went into his bedroom. He returned with his brother's hat, crossing the room and holding it out to him.

Kris hesitated, not taking it. "You sure you're done with it?"

Tommy frowned.

"Tommy." Kris sighed. "I know you've been pretending to be me in the city."

Stomach dropping, Tommy shared a startled look with Jonah. "Frankie told you."

"No one told me. I've been homebound for three weeks, man. I've been so bored, I agreed to play scrabble online with mom, so of course I started reading the news."

Humiliation simmered at the base of Tommy's pride. "How long have you known?"

Kris arched a brow at Jonah. "Since Jones and I hooked up."

That long? Tommy turned away on a hard breath out as Jonah said, "Oh my God," and tucked his feet up on the couch as if Kris's words were flooding the floor. "Please don't say that again."

"But we look so hot together." Kris flashed a grin. "Kiraly loves us. People are writing stories online about us. Did you know? More than Mark and Ava. I've been reading them, too, because boredom, and some don't hold back, if you know what I mean."

Jonah blushed, looking uncomfortable as he curled his bare toes into the couch.

"Kris," Tommy snapped. It wasn't funny.

Kris raised his hands, palms open. "I'm just saying it's okay. With me. If you need to keep doing it until I've recovered. It's nice that you two can go out together. I figured that's why? This takes the focus off you a bit?"

"That was the idea." Disgrace prickling his skin, Tommy tossed the hat in his brother's lap. "It's hardly worked."

Kris picked it up, brow lowering. "It's worked a little. You've been in the *city,* Tommy. There aren't places for you down there, but you've stayed long enough to have dinner and coffee. That's great."

Great? Bitterness forced Tommy to look away. He was a king being congratulated for sitting through a meal. He should be laughed out of the palace.

"You know," Kris said, more quietly. "If you'd told me, I would have supported you."

Tommy thought of a handful of cutting responses about hypocrites and secret-keeping—but then he noticed Jonah waiting earnestly for his response and his gut twisted. Jonah, the sweet soul, had kept this secret for him without even knowing why.

Tommy ran a hand over his face. "I didn't want to disappoint you when it didn't work."

Kris looked appalled. "Never. I would *never* be disappointed in you."

Too tired to argue, Tommy just shook his head. "I shouldn't have done it. And I'm not doing it again."

I'm not hiding anymore. The coping strategy hadn't transformed him. He hadn't started to heal behind the screen of his brother's identity. Maybe he would have in time, but he didn't *have* time, so the act had to stop here.

"I'm going to correct this. I want to be seen with you, Jonah." *I want everyone to know you're mine,* he thought, as Jonah smiled softly up at him. *Even just for now.* "Publicly, so there's no room for doubt. Would that be okay?"

"Yes." Jonah reached for him, nodding like it was the only thing he wanted. "Please."

"Okay." Tommy took his hand, ignoring the way his body shuddered with nerves. "Tomorrow."

He knew exactly how to do it.

15

Jonah's heart soared, buoyed by the rainbow-feathered wings on his back and the roar of a mountain city in celebration. Crowds and color crammed the steep streets, flying flags, dancing, and hollering chants. Jonah and Tommy's approach had a silencing effect, a momentary hush as people caught sight of them, staring, piecing together what they were seeing—and then erupted louder than before.

"We're going to own it," Tommy had told Jonah yesterday. "Every part of who we are."

And the people loved what they saw.

A prince and a cowboy riding on horseback through the city, hands clasped, surrounded on all sides by the Royal Guard.

Jonah wore his old clothes, made proud by the ribbon around his hat and the huge wings fanning out behind him. Today his celebration of who he'd always been; his protest to the censored life he'd had to lead because of it.

For Tommy, it was coming out and coming clean. He was in the traditional suit for a Kiralian prince, tailor-perfected in a fabric the color of bluebells, piped and fringed with gold. To his chest, he'd pinned a small grey ribbon. He took Jonah's breath away, riding tall and reserved and regal beside him, unfolding before his eyes, expanding into the man Jonah had always known was inside him. Royalty was Tommy's true space. Sage Haven had always been too small, too confined, and for years, Tommy had lived folded too many times over. Only now, given a tower in the sky, did he have enough space to fill his true form.

Prince Tomas.

There was no mistaking him as Kris.

The news spread like a fed flame—*it was Prince Tomas all along*—and Jonah's ever-swelling emotion became too big to hold inside. He grinned so hard his face ached, even as his eyes blurred with tears. For not having to pretend anymore; for the intensity of feeling accepted by thousands of people all at once. He was a small-town cowboy, lover to their prince, to Tommy, and everyone was cheering.

There were feather boas and drag queens, water bottles and every color of ice cream. People sat on each other's shoulders behind the barricades, held hands and made out as they marched with the floats. Jonah got so swept up in a performance to his left that he forgot to check in on Tommy until his fingers started tingling.

Tommy was squeezing his hand in a death grip.

"Tommy?" Jonah swiftly nudged his horse closer, his awareness of the parade dissolving at the sight of Tommy's bloodless face. "You going okay?"

Tommy kept his eyes fixed ahead. The hinge of his jaw stood out as he clenched and unclenched. "I don't think so."

"Fifteen minutes and we'll be done," he said, because the plan was to do a lap around the top streets closest to the palace. They were currently passing a few blocks from Jonah's apartment. "Too long?"

Tommy had taken his anti-anxiety tablets an hour before their procession had left the gates. He'd meditated for an hour before that and told Jonah over a breakfast Tommy hadn't eaten that he *had* to do this. There'd been something stark in his eyes as he'd said it, something worryingly close to desperation. Now he swallowed, tendons standing out in his neck, looking like a man who'd taken a leap and was falling before he'd managed to grab hold of the other side.

Mute, he mouthed to the road ahead, "Too long."

"Okay, that's okay." Jonah tried to smile as he scanned the packed street. In the event of panic, the plan was for Tommy to rein in his horse, dismount with a wave, and retreat into the security car behind them. But Tommy's grip on Jonah was too tight, his hold on the rein white-knuckled. To get him into the car, Jonah would have to help him in front of the whole of Kiraly, and Tommy's pride would never recover.

The main road was jammed with people, as were the sidewalks, side streets, and intersections. Two men on horseback couldn't just peel off into a crush of pedestrians. They were trapped, right here in the middle of the parade.

That's okay. We can do this.

"Frankie," he said, doing his best to sound calm as he used the security earpiece she'd given him. "We reckon we're done now. Tommy can't dismount, so I'm hoping you can cut us loose."

"Goddamn it," she replied, sounding cranky and concerned, then after a few moments, said, "Next side street on your left."

"Good news, Tommy," Jonah half-shouted over the roar of the crowd. "We're almost out of here."

Tommy didn't respond. His hand was clammy. He flinched as glitter burst above them.

"Pretty, isn't it?" Smiling to mask his concern, Jonah leaned in to lightly blow the glitter off Tommy's face—mainly because Tommy wasn't going to, and that kind of unresponsiveness would look pretty weird to everyone watching. "One minute."

Tommy just shook his head. His posture was stiff; his

shoulders were starting to heave as panic took over. He was too worked up to hide it, but they couldn't go any faster. Distressed, Jonah almost stood in his stirrups to see the road ahead, but the pace of the security car was set by the march. *Oh, God, this is the worst.* They couldn't even speed up into a trot. *Come on, come on.*

"We'll turn off up ahead," he said, pretending not to notice the way some people were frowning at Tommy. His breathing was growing hoarse—Jonah could hear it over the crowd. "Think of five things you wished you could see, and we'll almost be there. You'll make it."

Tommy leaned forward to press his forehead against the neck of his horse.

Helpless, Jonah said again, "You'll make it."

Tommy didn't make it.

He didn't even know where he ended up. There was a hard floor beneath him and a hard surface at his back that made his skin sting. Wherever he was, it wasn't loud anymore. *God*, it had been so loud on the street he couldn't see straight, though that could have been the strain from his raging sympathetic nervous system pushing against the back of his eyeballs. He couldn't remember how he'd escaped the crush. He'd barely remembered how to carry a breath from his mouth to his lungs. He was still struggling with that now, hauling air fast and shallow, squeaking a little on every inhale.

Faintly, he heard Jonah shushing from somewhere nearby.

"Shhhampagne," Jonah finished, then laughed softly and said, "Was that cheating? I'll do another one," and started over again.

By the third word, Tommy let the calm immediacy of the

sound draw him to the surface, though it felt like breaking through an oil spill. Choked by his reality, he opened his eyes.

Jonah was sitting on his heels a few feet away. Concern rushed over his features as their gazes met, but his soft "Shhh," stretched on right to end of his steady breath.

Then they both sat in silence. With a heavy blink, Tommy looked around. Jonah's apartment. No wonder it smelled safe. The blinds were mostly closed, with narrow strips of sunlight slanting through the cracks, and the open space had the comforting stillness of a home at rest. Jonah's hat and wings lay discarded on the floorboards behind him.

"What?" His nonsensical question was scarcely audible.

Jonah frowned as he scanned Tommy's face. "It was faster to bring you here. Our guards are downstairs. I was going to get you settled on the bed, but you dropped here, so . . ."

So Tommy had hyperventilated against Jonah's front door.

Exhausted, he murmured, "I hate that I keep being reduced to this."

Hated that it told a story he didn't want to accept. He'd collapsed to his knees in the function room the other night, cowered against the pillows the first time he'd taken Jonah to bed, and just weeks ago, he'd curled up on his sitting room floor after being triggered by Kris.

"I can't do it."

He'd known better than to put himself in front of so many people with no escape, but desperate to prove himself, he'd taken a shortcut. One lap would have meant he'd improved. That he could handle a short burst of overwhelm. He'd have leaned on that achievement, drawn confidence and reassurance from the fact that if he'd pulled off the parade, he could do any number of smaller-scale interactions. But he couldn't. He couldn't do any of it.

I can't be king.

"I've failed," he breathed, desolate.

"You haven't failed." Jonah scooted closer. "You've *tried*. Failing is not even trying."

Coming from anyone else, Tommy would have sneered at the postcard platitude, but Jonah, born with the rare expression of earnest wisdom, somehow distilled the words to a profound truth.

Tommy had tried. Something he hadn't done in a very long time.

Tried and failed, the cynical prick in him added.

"And besides," Jonah went on as light from the nearest window glinted on his glitter-specked shoulders. "I heard that it's bad for us to stay in the same position for too long. That we're supposed to move around to protect our spine or posture or something, and I can't help but think the same goes for being a good prince. That if you spend all your time behind that desk in the tower, you might not remember what it's like to be on the ground. So if you sometimes sit like this, down here, I don't think it's reducing you. It's keeping you rounded."

Who are you? Tommy would have asked in helpless affection if he weren't numb with failure. *How are you even real?*

Instead, he said, "I can't be who I really am."

Jonah's jaw moved, small and agitated, like he was chewing something tiny between his teeth.

"I could have done it, once." Tommy was hollow. Regret echoed within him. "But not anymore."

"Tommy." Jonah held out a hand and waited pointedly for Tommy to take it. "The other night you said you'd lost yourself, but I think you meant that you're not who you used to be. Is that right? Because we all change. None of us are who we were three years ago or even three days ago, but I'm worried you've got this idea in your head of who you really are —and that it's three years out of date. You think the true you is the man you were before the attack. And all you want is to get back to him."

Jonah's words rapped against Tommy's pressure points. He felt limp with defeat.

"You'll never be him again, Tommy." Jonah spoke with gentle conviction. "Just because he didn't have to deal with anxiety and panic attacks and all these negative thoughts doesn't mean he was the ideal version of you—the version that you should spend your whole life comparing yourself to or trying to get back to. That's not how people work. *I'm* not waiting for you go back to the way you were before. This is who you are right now. This is you."

"But." *I don't want this to be me.* He wanted to beat this and be the man who would have offered to replace Mark as king weeks ago. He wanted to be quiet but calm, reserved but confident. Abruptly, his eyes filled. "But he was better than the way I am now. He could have done this. And you'd have been able to trust him. Be safe with him. Be *seen* with him."

"But," Jonah said, and his breath shook as he brushed a hand down Tommy's chest. "I wouldn't have fallen in love with him."

"You—" Tommy's throat suddenly felt too swollen to speak.

"You were my best friend back then." A tiny smile started at the corners of Jonah's mouth. "I loved you, but not romantically. Now I'm beside myself for you. I do trust you, and I've never felt safer than I do with you. And I don't care if I'm seen with you or not, as long as I can *talk* about you. I want everyone to know I'm with *you*. And now they do."

Eyes blurring, Tommy covered the hand Jonah had settled over his breastbone.

Jonah smiled and leaned in close. "I love you, Tommy."

"Even when I'm like this?"

"No." Jonah shook his head a little. "There's no *even* in loving you. I love you when you're like this. When you're saying super smart things that I don't really understand. When you're with your brothers or hanging back in the shadows or swimming with your shirt off. When you're sleeping or worrying or—"

Tommy kissed him. Softly, because his energy was waning; tenderly, because it was the first time he'd tasted love in the warmth of Jonah's mouth, and he didn't want to rush past it.

When Jonah pulled away, his face was flushed, his lashes lowered.

Tommy curled a hand around the back of his head and kissed him again.

"Tommy," Jonah murmured when they next parted, foreheads pressed together, his breath on Tommy's cheek. "You're my prince."

That jabbed at Tommy's bruised pride.

Just a prince.

"When I said I can't be who I really am," Tommy said, and hesitated as the pain spread to seize both his purpose and identity. "I meant the King of Kiraly."

Jonah's breath stopped warming Tommy's skin for several seconds before he withdrew with a frown. "What?"

Stupid, right?

"When I said I failed, it was about more than the parade. It was about my attempt to replace Mark." And, as Jonah slowly shifted farther from him, frown deepening, Tommy explained that Mark intended to abdicate, that Kris had trained to take his place before he'd been beaten, and that Tommy had finally strived for the position himself. "But I can't do it. I can't deliver speeches, and I can't show my face in public." *Big fucking surprise.* Bitterness eroded his voice as he said, "I'll go back to being an antisocial prince who wastes his life hiding."

Jonah shook his head like Tommy had never had a *chance* of being king.

"I know." Tommy ran a hand over his face. "It was a crazy dream, and it's over."

"No, you . . . didn't tell me."

Tommy's inhale died in his throat. He sat back hard against the door.

"I want to know why," Jonah said, fiddling with the pull strap of one of his boots.

"Why I wanted to be king?" Tommy asked, and Jonah's brows knitted together above the frames of his glasses. "Or why I didn't—"

"Tell me, why didn't you tell me?"

"You were overwhelmed and feeling—" Inadequate, but Tommy was hardly about to point that out. "Dazed. I didn't want to make that worse. And it was never going to work, really, so it would only have intimidated you unnecessarily. The others have been humoring me. That's all."

Jonah tugged on his bottom lip with his teeth, upset, not meeting Tommy's eye. "You knew I was trying to decide whether to be with you." Wounded dark eyes met his in a flick of *how could you?* "What if it *had* worked? I might have decided to be with a king without even knowing it. How is that fair?" He lifted a hand to cover his tattoo. "When you told me what to expect as your partner, were you actually telling me what I'd have to do as the partner to a king?"

Tommy's guilt flared. "Yes."

Jonah shook his head. "You should have told me so I could make an informed decision."

He's right. Cursing, Tommy ached like he'd punched himself in the gut. *He's always right.* "Jonah, I'm—"

"Stop that." Jonah cut him off, pain flashing in his eyes. "Stop feeling bad."

"You—" Bewildered, Tommy hesitated. "Don't want me to feel bad about lying to you?"

"No. Obviously that wouldn't make any sense. But when you feel bad about me feeling bad, I feel bad that I've made you feel bad."

Tommy did his best not to frown as he worked his way through that sentence. "You mean when it hurts me to confront the pain that I've caused you—you feel bad about it?"

Jonah nodded, swallowing. "It makes me want to say that it's okay, so you'll stop feeling hurt. But it's not okay."

"No," Tommy agreed quietly. "I should have told you, even if it overwhelmed you. Even if I didn't believe it would work."

"Yes. Is honesty that hard to understand?" On a huff, Jonah pushed himself to his feet. Glitter rained lightly over his boots. "Am I really the only person who doesn't lie around here?"

"Yes," Tommy said.

Jonah blinked at him.

"You're the best of us, Jonah."

"Well." He crossed his arms, looking more disgruntled than resentful. "Sometimes I wish I wasn't. Then I wouldn't be so bad at being upset at people I care about. It would be more satisfying to not forgive you literally straight away."

Tommy stood carefully, both so he didn't come across as trying to take control and because his muscles were too fatigued for speed. "I could pretend you haven't forgiven me."

The gleam in Jonah's narrowed eyes said, *I'm listening.*

"I don't have to go back to the palace for a while," Tommy started.

"Oh," Jonah interrupted. "I've already told Frankie I'm keeping you here until tomorrow." He winced, then lifted his chin a little. "That was before we were going to pretend that I haven't forgiven you."

Tommy almost smiled. "I could spend that time working for your forgiveness."

This time when Jonah bit his lip, his eyes darkened. "That could work."

For me, too. "You'll have to at least pretend to resist."

"I'm not good at resisting you."

The alpha in Tommy cocked its head at that, gratified, and stepped forward. Instantly, Jonah swayed into him, sighing as he tilted his face back and parted his lips. *So easy,* Tommy marveled, and understood this kind of responsiveness was a gift to treat with care. "I lied to you," he said softly, and Jonah lowered his chin a little. "And I'll try to make that up to you. But I need to sleep first. Weren't you going to meet up with Nora after our lap?"

"Yeah." Jonah nodded, seeming distracted by Tommy's mouth. "But she heard about—I mean." His eyes snapped to Tommy's, suddenly wide. "I've messaged her to cancel. She says it's cool."

Tommy went cold.

But she heard about my breakdown.

People knew. *Of course, they fucking know.* He'd deliberately drawn the attention of thousands as he paraded through the heart of Kiraly—and once everyone was watching, he'd had a panic attack so severe he could hardly remember it.

There would be photos. Footage. Write-ups.

"Oh my God." Shaken, he staggered around Jonah, his palms landing on the kitchen counter to keep himself upright.

Prince Tomas would no longer be enigmatic—the mysterious brother rarely glimpsed.

He'd be unwell—the mad prince the royal family kept out of sight.

"Whatever you're thinking, stop." Worry lowered Jonah's tone as he muscled his way between Tommy's arms and sat on the counter in front of him. "It's not a big deal. It's good, even, because now you don't have to hide it. Here. Answer a question for me." He pressed an index finger against Tommy's chest, a physical anchor, and Tommy's focus narrowed around it. "You've been training to be king the whole time I've been in Kiraly, but if you're not going to do that anymore, what *will* you do?"

Return to a private library on the second floor of the north wing. Modest, for a palace room, with a view of the mountain so the city might well not exist.

"Focus on my portfolio." The rollout of the mental health program, primarily, and a few other projects he had in the works. "Major decision-making and planning will go back to Kris. Closing the mines. Reskilling thousands of workers. Future-proofing an entire industry with sustainable practices. He'll handle those projects from here."

"I'm sure Kris would appreciate your help," Jonah said.

"Yes." But it wouldn't be the same as leading.

"And me?" Jonah asked so quietly it was as if the question itself was scared of the answer. "What would be expected of me if I was your partner?"

If. Tommy closed his eyes. Jonah was in love with him and still couldn't decide whether to choose him.

Except—

Tommy curled a hand around the finger Jonah pressed into his sternum and said, "Less."

Surprised hope flickered in Jonah's eyes.

"You still couldn't run your own bar," he said, fearing that was the true dealbreaker but needing to make it clear. "But you could spend time in the city. I would avoid public appearances, so we'd never be seen together outside of the occasional state event. Locals would know you, of course, but they'd pretend to forget. You might be able to feel normal. Beyond that, you'd be asked to attend events. Launches. Conferences. Celebrations."

A very serious dart had formed between Jonah's brows.

Struck by the mortifying suspicion that Jonah was about to

decide whether or not he could be with Tommy on the spot, he said quickly, "Speaking of celebrations, you should go back to the parade. Those wings deserve more attention."

Jonah scooted a look over Tommy's shoulder. "Really?"

He nodded and excused it on the exhaustion turning leaden in his torso. "I need to sleep. Don't miss out because of me."

After searching Tommy's face for signs of false conviction, Jonah grinned and slid off the bench. "I'll text Nora. It's so amazing out there!"

Tommy wanted to smile, but the memory of the crowd forbade it.

"Jonah," he said, as Jonah slid the wings on. "You can talk about me. To your friends. If you want."

Jonah straightened, facing him, an angel in true form. He looked wary. "You sure?"

"I don't want you to have to lie for me anymore."

Distractedly, Jonah scooped up his hat and flipped it onto his head. "What if they ask about earlier?"

The whole of Kiraly would have seen Tommy's breakdown by now. Journalists would be unpicking months of his hermit-like behavior and analyzing it against his recent deception. Everyone would have an opinion. What damage would the truth do?

"Tell them," he said.

Jonah's eyes shone. "See? You're already different from when you walked in the door."

Tommy managed a small smile.

Yes, he thought. *I'm just a prince.*

16

Jonah returned home to find Tommy sleeping.

Still buzzing from the street party and maybe one too many beers, Jonah grinned as he tiptoed about, removing his wings, then hat, boots, shirt, and socks. It felt incredibly domestic, coming home to Tommy sleeping in his bed, lying with his back turned, silhouetted in the early evening light. Being terribly careful not to wake him, yet unable to resist that beautiful bare shoulder, Jonah nibbled it just a tiny bit before creeping into the kitchen.

Humming the song that had been playing at the street party, Jonah poured a glass of water after a few tries, drank it all, then rummaged in the pantry quiet as a mouse. White dust clouded up over his legs when the bag of flour jumped from his hands, but it hadn't actually spilled, so he picked it up and leaned back in to find the sugar.

He emerged with his hands full to find the man of his dreams leaning against the kitchen counter, shirtless and sexy and very, very shirtless.

"Tommy!" This was the best! "You're up!"

Tommy arched a bleary brow. His dark hair was mussed and

tuggable, his posture soft with sleep. "Would you believe I woke all on my own?"

"Yes! That's great! I'm making pancakes."

Scanning the assembled ingredients, Tommy asked, "Blueberry?"

"What else?" Then he gasped in horror. "Oh my God! I don't have blueberries!"

Tommy smiled a little as he pulled his phone from his back pocket. "I'm on it."

"Amazing!" The perks of dating a prince! After switching on the kitchen light, Jonah pulled a mixing bowl from under the counter and poured in a nice amount of flour. Then he opened the bag of sugar and did the same.

"Shouldn't you measure it?" Tommy asked, and when Jonah's jaw dropped at his super intelligence, he added, "What were you drinking out there?"

"Just beer." His head went a little dizzy as he looked around for something to measure with. "I wasn't being silly about it, I just—need pancakes."

With a doubtful hum, Tommy stepped around him, *smelling scrumptious,* and Jonah turned with him like a hungry shadow, hovering at his shoulder as Tommy refilled Jonah's water glass. Silent, Tommy slanted a glance at him, the smoky blue of his eyes clearly aware of just how close they were standing, his unsteady exhale even more aware of Jonah's hands making their way up the hard slope of his bare back. Swallowing, Tommy passed the glass with a murmured, "Drink it all."

"I'll drink all of you," he said, taking it.

"Jonah." Firmly, yet with a flush.

Blood tingling, Jonah drank the water without taking his eyes off Tommy. He set the glass in the sink with extra care, and said, "Did you have a good nap, Tommy? Tommy. I want to say your name all the time, forever, Tommy. Let's go to bed."

Tommy's expression was strained as he moved away and pulled a measuring cup from the second drawer. "How was the parade?"

"Fine." Pouting, Jonah slinked over to him. "Not much fun without you."

Tommy's lashes snapped to where Jonah had touched him—low on Tommy's naked stomach, right above his waistband. Maybe it was instinct or a teensy bit of intoxication, but Jonah's lust bloomed at the intensity of Tommy's attention—neck tendons straining, chest expanding—and he ached for that power to be held over him. *I told Nora and Milosh and everyone who would listen that Tommy was mine, and now I need to be his.* Tommy's skin was hard, hot in that way the body could get right after waking up, and he smelled good, *so good,* like heat and sheets and the sweet, sinking sensation of two bodies merging. Jonah gave a helpless growl but stayed where he was.

He wanted Tommy to control this.

"I hope that's not true." The direct stare Tommy leveled at him made Jonah's breath come quicker. "It's important to be able to enjoy ourselves when we're apart."

"Oh, yes, absolutely. You mean like phone sex?"

Tommy's jaw flexed as amusement glinted in his eyes. "No, Jonah."

"Okay." Grinning, he raised his palms with the hope Tommy would snatch them up and take over. "That's good, because I actually didn't stop dancing the whole time." His strange halfway status had dissolved among so many people, and their energy had whisked him into fluffy abandon. "Tommy. I might have been celebrating something."

Tommy pressed the measuring cup into his hand. "Pride, surely?"

"You goose." Jonah tossed the cup aside and poked his stomach—then slid that finger downward to tug on his waistband. He growled again, completely without meaning to. "I meant staying with you."

Tommy's abs locked as his features shuttered.

"Tomas." Jonah grew still, serious. "I've decided."

A strange emotion crossed Tommy's face. It left his lips too thin and his eyes too wide.

Jonah frowned. "Tommy?"

"You were going to wait until the result of the survey."

Scanning Tommy's features, he said, "I realized I didn't need to."

"What did you decide?" Tommy's question was an impossible tangle of vulnerability and command.

"I'm going to stay with you." Spoken calm and sure. "For our lives. If you'll have me. If you'll live with me in Kiraly, no matter what, because this is where I want to live, and I want to live here with you."

Tommy made hope look like a ledge that couldn't quite bear his weight. "You're not just deciding this because you're tipsy?"

"I'm tipsy because I decided this."

"When?" The question was mostly breath. "When did you decide?"

"Earlier." When Tommy had said *less* and Jonah had realized that would be enough for him, would have to be enough, keeping one foot on the ground and the other by Tommy's side. If he could still belong in one tiny aspect of his life, spending time with locals in the city, he thought he'd be okay.

"Then," Tommy said, something incredulous shifting in his eyes, "we'll live in Kiraly."

No matter what.

Jonah laughed as relief flooded him, carrying away all the angst and agitation of the past few weeks. Giddy, he leaned toward Tommy to celebrate properly.

"Not yet." On a quick inhale, Tommy started to step back. "Go shower. I'll cook. You said you need pancakes."

Hopelessly hopeful, Jonah curled his index finger through Tommy's belt loop and kept him close. "But I might need a hand in there . . ."

"If you weren't being silly about how much you were drinking," Tommy said, sounding stern but looking flustered, "you won't need a hand."

Jonah tugged the belt loop harder. "Spoilsport."

"No." In warning, Tommy put a hand to Jonah's chest and pressed him back, back, back until Jonah was against the closed bathroom door and Tommy was right there with him. His chest loomed close; his breath was rough with restraint. "I'm sobering you up so I can spoil you beyond all recognition."

Oh. My. God.

Jonah had never showered so fast.

It got harder to remember that Jonah wanted Tommy to control this. After he emerged from the bathroom in light sweatpants low on his hips and dripping wet hair that he *knew* made him look irresistible, Tommy hardly seemed to notice him. Instead, he insisted Jonah eat a stack of pancakes, the bully, coated in extra blueberries he'd simmered in maple syrup on the stove.

"Those berries were so blue," Jonah said, nudging his empty plate away and drawing out the last word shamelessly. "So, so blue."

"I'm not going to look," Tommy murmured from the sink, sounding mildly pained. "I'd prefer your full focus before I give in, and considering your pants are on backward, you're not there yet." Then he turned, doing that unreadable face thing, and switched the plate for a water glass. "Drink."

Tommy made him drink more water, then walked with him up and down the apartment building stairs several times, and then *finally* he invited Jonah to stream a film in bed.

Jonah used the bathroom before settling delightedly in front of where Tommy sat against the headboard, murmuring his contentment and nestling between Tommy's hard horse-riding thighs, arms hooked loosely over his knees. Then he nestled a little more, pretending he couldn't get comfortable, circling his lower back right where Tommy was growing firm. He kept it up as the film began, restless little sighs and movements that were unmistakably turning Tommy on, but every time Jonah tried to twist around to face him, well and truly ready to get started, Tommy clamped his knees so tightly against Jonah's sides that he honest to God couldn't move.

"Tommy!" Jonah complained, stuck for the millionth time. "I don't actually want to watch this."

"Then choose something else."

"Tommy!" he exclaimed again because Tommy was tight and trembling beneath him and it made Jonah feel like bursting out of his skin.

"I'm not trying to be an asshole, Jonah. But I'm not comfortable going further than we already have unless I know for sure that you want it. So unless you want—"

"I want *all of you*, Tommy. I want—"

"That's what I thought." Somehow, his knees got tighter. "I also thought you wanted to play with denial?" It came out battered around the edges, like a note-to-self Tommy had torn from the recent past and kept scrunched in his hand.

"I do." Jonah tipped his head back and sideways in a horribly unattractive way to meet Tommy's gaze, hoping Tommy could read the plea in his upside-down eyes. "But not on the night I've told you that I love you and want to spend my life with you."

Tommy smiled, soft and more beautiful than Jonah could bear.

His knees stayed firmly pressed against Jonah's sides.

"Please, I love you, I love you, I love you," Jonah said, wriggling uselessly to get free so he could show Tommy just how much he adored him. *It hurts.* Hurt so badly, having this love and not being able to give it to him. Was this how Tommy had felt for the past four years, loving Jonah and not being able to express it? *God, that just makes me hurt even more.*

"You're a very needy drunk," Tommy teased gently, and Jonah nodded even though he wasn't—he was just very needy for Tommy. Getting all tangled and twisted when he wasn't with him; wanting to be in contact with Tommy every second of the day, talking to him, touching him, and becoming sulky and hopeless when they were forced to be apart. He'd kind of always been like that for Tommy—it just felt much bigger now.

Tommy said, "Sleep for a bit," and started raking his fingernails over Jonah's scalp.

I will not sleep. Jonah frowned, shaking his head to throw off Tommy's hand, but the light scratching was like fireflies dancing on his scalp, nudging his eyes closed, seeping into his . . .

Sometime later, he stirred.

Streetlight was a dull glow through the window closest to the bed. Tommy must have got up to open the blinds at some point, exposing the night sky, which explained why Jonah was curled on his side instead of still lying nestled between Tommy's thighs. Blinking, he pushed onto his elbows, looking around—and found the vague shape of Tommy sitting against the pillows, an arm stretched out along the top of the headboard.

The shape moved, reaching for the nightstand before passing something to him.

Jonah accepted his glasses with a soft, "Thanks," and slid them on.

It was definitely late. A few hours before dawn, if he had to guess by the crowd-pleasing classic echoing faintly from the bar down the road. Strange. He was often awake at this hour, yet the darkness felt different, fragile and stolen, like he'd awoken outside of time alone in bed with Tommy.

Tommy . . . was staring at him.

Staring like he was done waiting.

Jonah's insides thrilled. The look on his face was almost predatory. There was no trace of the Tommy from earlier—defeated, slumped on the floor, unable to acknowledge his own worth. No sign of the disciplined Tommy that had come after that, and that was the thing, wasn't it? Tommy was like a mixed packet of seeds that had grown all together. This magical mess of variety that meant some parts of him didn't have the strength to stay upright, while other parts grew like nothing could get in his way. And okay, everyone was like that, but Tommy had so much trouble being human—being strong and powerful in one place, and vulnerable and unstable in another. It drove Tommy to distraction that he couldn't just weed out the parts of himself that he didn't like, and Jonah was pretty sure Tommy redirected that frustration into making his strengths even stronger.

Because right now?

Tommy was in his full power.

And it was *intense.*

He radiated an authority that tightened every nerve in Jonah's body—stared with such charged command, it was almost too much, like that look was made to be diluted across an entire country, and here Jonah was taking all of it.

Aching, Jonah wrapped a hand around Tommy's shin and breathed, "Okay."

Tommy's gaze flickered to Jonah's touch. "Do you know what woke me earlier?"

Jonah thought back—then with a flush, covered his face with his free hand. "Oh my God, did I bite you? I'm so sorry."

"You did." Tommy's voice was low and warm. "How are you feeling?"

"Better." Sleep hadn't dulled his desire. It was right there, on the tip of his being, like something he'd been meaning to say for a very long time. He tightened his hold on Tommy's leg. "And like I'll literally die if I can't have you."

The full force of Tommy's attention dropped to Jonah's mouth. "So melodramatic."

Jonah sat slowly, the pulse his in neck fluttering. "Is it melodramatic if it feels true?"

"I—" A shudder ran through Tommy as his gaze swept over Jonah's body. The intensity of the look alone tightened Jonah's skin and the space between them, and Jonah leaned toward him on instinct. It was physical, the sway Tommy held over him. "You really want me that badly?"

"Yes." Impatient, Jonah moved onto his knees, wishing he knew where Tommy wanted him so he could already be there, surrendering to him, pleasing him, without being asked.

Tommy still hadn't moved. "You want me for the rest of your life?"

"Yes, yes," he said, because Tommy was his best friend, his lover, and they belonged together, had *always* belonged together. "My whole life."

Tommy sucked in a sharp breath. Silent, he spent a few moments with that truth.

Then—

"What exactly do you want?"

"You." Jonah took in the power pose of Tommy's broad frame, one arm still draped along the headboard, fingers gripping the timber. Taking up space with his legs extended. Getting his scent all over Jonah's sheets. Wearing a borrowed pair of sweats, several sizes too small for those rock-like thighs. Jonah swallowed. "I want you where we both know you want to be."

Covering you, Tommy had said. *Protecting you. Controlling you.*

Tommy was ready for it. He'd lain over Jonah the past few nights, energy taut and gathering like a wave desperate to break, his eyes near black with desire, and each time, Jonah had slid a hand between them instead of letting Tommy inside him. Denying Tommy at such a peak had taken resistance Jonah hadn't known he had, but the last thing he wanted was to risk it being too soon. Jonah had needed to trust that if something went wrong, Tommy would speak up without fear of ruining it.

"If that's okay," he added, arousal a sweet weight in his blood.

Tommy was clenching the sheet by his hip in one hand, holding himself back, vibrating with an energy Jonah wanted to drown in, would drown in, maybe had already drowned in for how completely it filled him.

"Tommy?"

"Undress," he said, and Jonah might have whimpered his gratitude.

His anticipation glinted like the secret glitter in Tommy's hair, a bright flare of light in the dark room as he lay on his back to strip. *This is happening.* Pulse surging, he slid off his pants and briefs together, and before he had the chance to return to his knees, Tommy was on him.

Naked, powerful, solid as a wolf pinning Jonah to the bed. His shoulders seemed huge overhead, broad and kind of staggering, and Jonah swooned, clinging to them like the world was about to open up beneath him but he'd be okay if he never let Tommy go.

If Tommy never let *him* go.

"Thank you for choosing me." Tommy feathered a hand down Jonah's side, a delicious lightness to contrast the weight of his body until everything was weighted—Tommy's mouth on his, and the breadth of his body, and the palm he slid with firm possession all the way back up. Sinking into the sensation, Jonah kissed him back, long and heated and wide open, his heartbeat a quickening *yes, oh, yes* between his ribs.

Yes to Tommy's hips purposefully shifting Jonah's thighs apart, *yes* to the growl that was riding on the back of Tommy's deepening kiss, and *yes* to tasting and taking and loving. It felt right, the two of them, like sunlight meeting cool water and creating the most dazzling sparkle. That Jonah hadn't considered doing this years ago seemed absurd. He just—hadn't known pie was on the menu.

Now he knew.

And he wanted all the pie.

For a while, they were nothing but skin and heat and mindless grasping in the dim city glow. Jonah dissolved at the scrape of Tommy's fingernails on the inside of his elbow and reformed at the imprint of Tommy's teeth on his shoulder. He gasped when Tommy rubbed his washboard stomach over Jonah's cock and actually purred when Tommy drove his palm between Jonah and the bed to grab his ass. It was a little rough, the way Tommy handled him, like he'd learned just enough in the nights they'd spent together to disguise inexperience with primal greed, and it was working—seriously, *no arguments here* —but Jonah felt the tummy-twisting shyness of a first time, too, and did nothing to hide it.

He let himself hesitate before rubbing Tommy's erection with the groove of his hip; allowed a rush of bashfulness to tuck his face to one side when Tommy swooped down to kiss him. It didn't matter that they'd done this part before, and it definitely didn't matter that Jonah had done the rest before, physically, because he'd never done it with Tommy.

Never with the intention of doing it forever.

They were both trembling—on the verge of something endless.

Then Tommy whispered, "You're the only one," against Jonah's ear and it sounded raw from all the years he'd waited to say it. Shivering at the hot breath, a peculiar thickening filled Jonah's chest, a feeling made of other feelings that shouldn't go together. Joy that what Tommy said was true and fear that it wasn't; regret that he hadn't figured it out long ago and awe at knowing now; surprise at how absolutely he felt the same and panic that one day one of them might not. *This is love.* All these emotions gravitating to it like moons paling in comparison.

Still, it was a lot at once. His whole torso ached.

"Will you hold me?" Jonah bent his spine, pressing against Tommy. "Like I can't break."

With a quiet groan, Tommy banded his arms tightly around him, yet it was just *not* enough to relieve the straining ache inside Jonah, because it was both everywhere and nowhere at once, because it was love and nothing Tommy did could ever take it away.

He gasped when Tommy released him, falling back onto the bed and breathing hard.

"Too much?" Tommy's fingertips rushed gently around Jonah's hairline.

"No." Jonah kissed Tommy's throat. His best friend's pulse butterflied under his lips. "That's how I want it, soon, okay?"

Tommy's fingers slid to tangle in Jonah's hair. "You sure? It doesn't make you feel—"

"Safe," Jonah said, not wanting Tommy to trigger how the position made *him* feel. "It makes me feel safe, like no one else can touch me."

Amazement lifted Tommy's features.

"I mean it. Just with you." *And only with you.* "That's how I feel."

Then he ground his hips, and when Tommy's mouth dropped on a shocked gasp, Jonah caught it with his own. Jonah kissed like he was struggling to find an answer that he *knew* Tommy knew, his whole body demanding it. Wound tight in response, Tommy flung a hand onto the rumpled sheets beside them.

Vaguely confused that Tommy was about to pull the covers on as they worked up a sweat, Jonah wrapped his hand around Tommy's bicep and tugged, saying, "No," into his mouth.

"No?" Tommy paused, holding up a small tube and packet.

Oh. Jonah's confusion turned into sudden delight. "Tommy, you went through my drawer!" *And hid what you found in preparation.*

"I did." Propped up on one elbow, Tommy's lips quirked as he flicked open the tube with his thumb. "It was either that or request a guard to drop off lube and condoms."

"Oh my God, please never do that." Laughing, Jonah buried his face into the crook of Tommy's elbow. Then, face still flushed, he drew back and said almost shyly, "Also, we don't need the condom. If you don't want." His hookups had always been protected, and he'd been checked to be sure. "I'm okay. But we can. If you'd prefer."

Tommy stared at him for a second before the condom sailed across the room.

Jonah laughed again.

Smiling, Tommy rolled off to one side and gestured down Jonah's body. "Do I just . . ."

"Yeah." Jonah nodded, trying to keep himself from panting before Tommy had even touched him. "Unless you want me to?"

"No." He kissed Jonah's shoulder, and speaking against his skin said, "Just tell me if I hurt you."

Always. And when Tommy pleased him and scared him and misunderstood him. Jonah would tell him everything, always.

Tommy's fingers found their way carefully, slightly more cautiously than Jonah liked, but gaining confidence when Jonah melted into the bed, hips moving, gasping guidance like *there* and *a little more* and *good, that's so good.* And then, after a time, when Tommy's preparations moved deep and slick, *okay,* whispered in chest-heaving approval as Jonah pressed their damp foreheads together.

Beyond ready, Jonah took his turn with labored breath, holding Tommy's dark stare as he tossed the tube aside and glided slippery fingers over his friend's hard length.

Tommy seemed broader than ever when he slid on top of him, braced on his forearms, until Jonah realized that no, *he* just felt smaller, snugger, more settled.

He was in place, beneath Tommy.

Their breaths merged, hot and pushy as Tommy focused on positioning himself. Trying to be patient despite his aching body, Jonah ran his nose along Tommy's jaw and down the column of his neck, loving him, loving that he got to share Tommy's first time, all of his first times, now and forever. When Jonah nibbled the smooth skin on the side of his neck, Tommy made a faint strangled sound and collapsed over him.

"Jesus," Tommy muttered, and something about his embarrassed frustration and desire-thick vulnerability was hot as hell. "Sorry. I can't concentrate when you do that."

Jonah rested his head back on the sheet, biting his bottom lip with a smile.

"I'm taking too long," Tommy said, strained.

"You're not," Jonah said, and hurried to join Tommy in his vulnerability. "Besides, I want you to do something first."

Tommy's expression accused Jonah of humoring him.

Jonah's heart knocked against his sternum as he said, "This."

And he tilted his head back to bare his throat.

A moment of utter stillness. Then Tommy took in a quick breath. "Jonah . . ."

"Please." Jonah swallowed but kept his chin tipped.

"You want—"

"Just lips." He'd wanted it before, when Tommy had done that sucking thing on his shoulder and it had shot tingles right up his neck. "I want to know why it drives you crazy."

"I . . . okay."

Carefully, so carefully, Tommy cupped a hand against the side of Jonah's face, his thumb resting gently along his jawline. Then he dipped his head and Jonah closed his eyes, lungs shuddering, his throat already trying to trick him into feeling crushed.

Several layers of breath touched him first. One so light, it was mostly imagination, and the next, a warm spring breeze from across the hayfields. Then he felt the unmistakable heat and vapor of Tommy's breath right above his skin, tracing the line of his scar.

Hot and soft and only good.

"I'm okay," he whispered when Tommy didn't descend.

So Tommy touched Jonah's throat with his lips, softer than down, lighter than a soap bubble, and the sensation blew right through him like a ripple on water, tingling and trembling right to his edges.

"Again," he said, and stopped breathing when Tommy pressed a gentle kiss in the hollow at the base of his throat. Jonah's nerves seemed to cluster in velvet-thick anticipation that grew with each kiss as fine as the curl of an eyelash. A kiss above his collarbone, on the end points of his scar, against the sensitive skin that stretched beneath his ear. The strongest cluster throbbed between his legs, winding him up, building in force with each kiss until he realized too late that he'd been rubbing himself against Tommy.

"Oh, God," he said urgently, wrapping his legs around Tommy's hips. "Please, like this."

The position had Tommy breathing hard and cursing in a good way, and Jonah shifted, helping, until Tommy was pressing into him, and Jonah was pushing back. His chest tightened, because this had never happened before yet had already happened more times than he could remember. It was a marvel, how he could go through life never doing a certain thing, like kissing or traveling, and then do it, and a part of him that somehow felt older than he was said, *can't you feel it? We've always done this.*

He'd always made love with Tommy.

It awed him—Tommy above him, against him, inside him. Their fingers linked, their mouths not daring to be more than a breath apart as their bodies surged together. After a few stuttering strokes, Tommy sank into a rhythm, glides becoming long and bliss-deep, and Jonah wanted to curl up tight around him and fall apart beneath him at the same time.

It was just that he hadn't known—had never known sex could—

Build, *oh my God, yes,* like the weight of a river against a dam—

Pull tight as wet silk stretched so hard it tore—

Burn and glitter and pound, like a forge or a parade or a galaxy, *yes,* a galaxy. They were making actual stars. Jonah was making sounds he had no control over, a never-ending reaction to everything he could feel, everything Tommy was doing to him, harder, higher, hotter, and he loved it—loved it so much he almost swore, almost let it slip into the air crackling around them, a demand that Tommy do exactly what he was already doing.

Vaguely, he heard Tommy's gasps turn into groans, and his groans turn into a stream of soft words, beautiful words, and those words gradually turn into something else entirely.

"Jonah," he said, voice hollowing out, and "I can't," and, "Jonah, please."

"I'm here." Jonah clasped a hand around the back of Tommy's neck. *I've always been here.* "You've got me."

"I—" Tommy opened his eyes, looking dazed, stunned. "I've got you."

"Yes, see? Now hold me tight," Jonah said, and Tommy circled his arms around him, covering him like Jonah had asked, all the while moving deeper, heavier, touching every part of him inside and out, his body trembling with the strain of his mounting climax. And that was how they came, wrapped together as tightly as a label hugs a bottle—Jonah first in a spill of heat between their bellies, and Tommy seconds later, emptying inside him with a muffled cry.

It was—Jonah had never known it could be like this.

Satisfying and sacred and just *everything.*

His heart swelled at the sweetly self-conscious look Tommy gave him when he pushed onto his elbows; at the kiss Tommy brushed over Jonah's mouth before easing out of him. Too wrecked to do more than wipe the sheet half-heartedly over his sticky front, Jonah rolled onto his side with a happy groan as Tommy settled beside him.

"Was that—" Tommy's skin was flushed, the roots of his hair damp. "Okay?"

Jonah wanted to reassure Tommy with amazing words, the kind of fancy and praisy words Tommy would give to him, but Jonah's body was sinking, and his eyes were drooping and all he could manage was, "Yes, okay, very . . . yes. You?"

"Very yes for me, too." Tommy dragged a pillow beneath his head and regarded Jonah with a curious smile. "Near the end there . . . did you ask me to fuck you?"

"I—" That yanked Jonah back into alertness. "Hope not!"

Amusement gleamed in Tommy's eyes as he swept Jonah's hair off his forehead. "I think you did."

Mortified, Jonah half-buried his face into the sheet. "Oh my God, I didn't mean to."

Tommy's low chuckle traveled through the mattress. "Swearing a little is okay, you know? Just to me. You can be apple pie to everyone else."

Face hot, Jonah peeked at Tommy despairingly. "I'll honestly die if you say anything about cream right now."

Tommy's grin was wicked. "Christ, you're too wholesome to handle sometimes."

"Handle me anyway," he said quickly, and smiled when Tommy laughed.

"Come here." Gently, Tommy rolled Jonah over onto his other side and tucked his strong, worn-out body against Jonah's back. "You're an angel and I love you."

Jonah glowed, lit up by the tender kisses Tommy was pressing between his shoulder blades, and when he slept, his heart burned like the brightest star in Kiraly.

No. The *world*.

17

Jonah wasn't as happy as he should have been—and he *should* have been delirious.

It was Tommy. Something was wrong.

The day started out well—sleeping in and making love and eating pancakes. Jonah even plucked up the courage to ask whether he was allowed to keep the apartment, since he could spend time in the city and all. He wanted a normal space to come back to sometimes when the palace got too much. Because it would definitely get too much, spending most of his life somewhere he didn't belong and having to call it home—not that he said that last part to Tommy.

Tommy said yes. Of course. "Come here whenever you want. It's yours."

So that was good. Jonah felt better about that.

He felt less good about the discussion Tommy had with his family back at the palace.

The others were waiting for them in Kris's suite. Kris and Mark, Frankie and Ava, and Philip. Afternoon tea was laid out on the coffee table, uneaten, and they all fell quiet when Jonah and Tommy arrived hand-in-hand.

"Hey, everyone," Jonah said with a smile. *Tommy and I are going to be together forever.*

They smiled and said, "Hey, Jonah." No one spoke to Tommy.

Tommy's thumb slid over Jonah's knuckles a moment before he pulled away to stand in the space between armchairs. It was only family—the kind of situation where everyone just made themselves comfortable anywhere. But not Tommy. He stood at the head of the gathering, turning himself into the one person that everyone faced.

"I have something to say," Tommy said.

"I think I might just . . ." and Philip sat, gripping the arm of the couch.

Already knowing what Tommy planned to tell them, Jonah leaned against the side of the armchair Ava sat on, arms crossed loosely, and scanned their faces. A prickle ran down his spine. *They're looking at him differently.* Tommy's presence had always demanded attention, but this seemed like more than that. They looked at him like they were . . . waiting. For instructions—for him to tell them what came next.

Into that expectant silence, Tommy said, "I can't be king."

His words hung in the air—then shattered like the expressions of his family. And Jonah realized with a jolt *that* was how they'd been looking at him.

Like he was their king.

Shock had Jonah sliding lower to sit on the arm of the chair.

"Obviously I can't," Tommy snapped, as if there had been a room-wide protest instead of stunned silence. Jonah's head spun, because yes, it had seemed obvious when Tommy told him he couldn't do it last night, but now, something was tilting rapidly inside him, throwing the world into a different view, and he didn't know what it meant.

Tommy had explained it wrong on the car ride here. No one

in this room had been humoring him. They hadn't assumed it wouldn't work—hadn't been expecting this announcement all along. Tommy had made it sound like a trial, a temporary arrangement, like he was a boy who'd run away from home, and everyone had let him go, indulging him, waiting for him to realize his mistake and turn back for comfort and safety.

But that wasn't what was happening. They looked like they didn't want him to turn back—and Tommy was behaving as if he didn't want to either.

Frankie stood. "If this is because of yesterday—"

"It's because of every day." Tommy cut her off without raising his voice. "I've been anxious *every fucking day* knowing I'll have to be around people. That I'll have to deliver speeches and attend events and have my face on camera. I can't even stomach the thought of sitting at the head of a state banquet, looking and talking to no one, let alone duties that require me to engage. I can't live like this. It's not sustainable. I can't do it."

Frankie stayed on her feet, hands in fists, body tense. She looked like she'd argue with his logic if she could figure out how.

"Besides." Tommy lifted his attention to the large window behind his family, as if he was talking about something that hardly mattered. "The whole of Kiraly saw what happened yesterday. If they decide to keep the monarchy, it won't be because of me."

"What?" Jonah frowned. "It was just a panic attack. People have them."

In a flash of blue, Tommy looked to him. "Not people in charge of a country. Not *in front* of their country." Then he addressed Philip. "I assume it's made the news."

The advisor inclined his head with a grimace. "Yes, Your Highness."

"Right." The word was as tight as a full stop. For several

seconds, Tommy didn't move, gaze distant out the window that overlooked the city. "That's it for me, then."

Wait. Distress burbled at the base of Jonah's throat as he looked at the others. They were sad, so sad that Mark and Kris were struggling to even look at Tommy. Ava's lips were pressed too tightly together, Philip had his face in his hands, and Frankie was shaking her head like she wanted to punch up the universe.

Jonah didn't . . . he hadn't taken the time to think about this properly. Tommy had confessed that he'd intended to be king—but couldn't do it. And that was the problem with only being let in on a secret right at the end, wasn't it? Because Jonah hadn't thought backward. He'd heard *I'll go back to being an antisocial prince* and moved on from there.

But no one else was moving on because King Tomas had been their plan all along.

I didn't know. Jonah's breath caught with a cutting little jab. *I should have known.* How significant it was when Tommy confessed this truth, crumpled there on the apartment floor, needing the support and reassurance of his boyfriend. But instead, Jonah had gone all selfish and accused him of lying, when he should have paid more attention to what Tommy had told him.

When I said I can't be who I really am, Tommy had said, *I meant the King of Kiraly.*

Jonah should have been there for him. He should have—
Wait.

That was who Tommy really was?

Was that—was that why the throne room held his energy? Why he'd persisted in torturing himself just to be in public? It wasn't about easing his social anxiety enough to do everyday things like eat waffles or order a coffee.

I could have done it, once, Tommy had said, and Jonah had assumed he'd meant tolerate crowds enough to join the parade.

But no, *oh my God,* he'd meant that his anxiety stopped him from doing something that Jonah couldn't even comprehend.

It stopped him from being king.

"I'm sorry, Kris." Tommy kept his gaze out the window, standing still, so very still. No tremoring hands or jiggling knees. Just the awful calm of defeat. "You'll have to do it."

"But." Kris threw a pleading look to Mark before turning back to Tommy. "You're the best fit. This isn't right."

"There are two facets to the position—behind the scenes and in public view—and I'm only fit for one of them." Somehow, Tommy kept his expression blank despite the way his voice twisted bitterly around the word *fit.* "You can do both, Kris. Policies and planning might not come naturally, but you were doing a good job before your injuries. Mark and I will support you."

"I—" Mark looked between them. The movement was heavy with guilt. "I'll support either of you."

Tommy's jaw locked as he seemed to stare at something in his own head. Then he shifted his gaze to Mark and Kris, and his expression fractured into regret and pain. "I'm sorry," he said. "I wish I could do this for you. I tried. But I can't."

Jonah's throat stung. It was killing Tommy that he couldn't do this for his brothers.

"Nah," Kris said, his brow puckering in an effort to look breezy. "It's okay. I'll do it. Frankie's been pretty pissed about not getting to be queen, just quietly, so this is good."

Frankie's distracted frown flattened as she glanced at Kris. Then she paled and sat abruptly with a muttered, "Oh shit."

"Frankie." Tommy waited until she turned her mortified gaze to him. "You'll make an exceptional queen."

She started shaking her head. "I don't think I—"

"I'll help you," Ava said, and her voice held the same guilt that was still written on Mark's face.

Jonah blinked fast, because a number of things were occurring to him quite quickly—the biggest being why he'd finally been able to decide to spend his life with Tommy. At the time, he'd based it on Tommy saying he'd be an antisocial prince, and that without being seen in public with Tommy anymore, Jonah could slip under the radar a little and back into the general community. A life like that offered a shred of normality, and after weeks of believing it had to be all or nothing, Jonah had pounced.

He'd thought he could be with Tommy *and* stay true to an important part of himself. The part that belonged with ordinary people, talking to them, befriending them; the part that had spent most of his life yearning to be accepted as a valued member of a community; the part that didn't want to have to continuously prove his worth in a place he didn't belong.

He'd been so happy that he'd danced and drank and felt like he was made of bubbles.

Now, he felt like an asshole, because apparently, he'd based his decision on a future where Tommy was less than the man *he* wanted to be. And that was horrifying.

Except it was also occurring to him that Tommy had been in love with him for four years (*four years*) yet hadn't offered to retreat from public view for them to be together. From the very start, it had been up to Jonah to decide whether he was willing to give up his own sense of belonging to be with Tommy—never that Tommy would pull back on his position for Jonah. And that was okay. It wasn't a fair comparison because Tommy was royalty and Jonah was obviously the one with less to lose. So. Yeah, that was okay.

Kind of.

Or—no. No, it wasn't.

My dreams matter, too.

If he was being honest, Jonah had assumed all this time that Tommy was doing the least public-facing princely stuff that he could. That he'd wanted to be with Jonah so badly, he'd done everything he could on his end to allow Jonah to say yes.

But he hadn't.

He hadn't offered to give up being king for Jonah.

He hadn't done that.

The only reason Tommy had stepped back from the position now was because his anxiety had strong-armed him into it—and that realization blurred Jonah's eyes faster than anything else.

"We'll need to issue a statement," Philip was saying apologetically. "Regarding the parade."

"I know. I'll write it. In my own words." Tommy's cool mask was back in place. "I'll have it to you by this evening."

Ava shifted. "You don't owe them anything you don't want to share, Tomas."

Jonah glanced at her through watery eyes. Mark had given up being king for Ava.

But Tommy hadn't even *told* Jonah that he was trying to be king.

"Yeah, it's none of their business," Kris said viciously.

"But it is," Tommy said. "We're their royal family. Their lives are, quite literally, our business. And that makes our lives their business."

Heart lodged in his throat, Jonah accidentally sniffled way too loudly.

Tommy snapped his attention to him with a startled, "Jonah?" He cut across the room to kneel at Jonah's feet. It wasn't fair, the way Jonah's insides twisted at his sudden closeness—the way those intense blue eyes could make him feel like the very soul of the world. "Do you want to leave?"

Jonah's nod felt heavy, because apparently, souls weren't as important as kings.

He didn't feel so bright anymore.

Concern roughened Tommy's heartbeat as he led Jonah to their suite next door and sat him at the table. It wasn't like Jonah to avoid eye contact, but with their chairs facing each other and knees folded together, those big dark lashes remained resolutely lowered even when Tommy angled his head to try to get Jonah to look at him.

"Why are you upset?" Tommy reached for him—and froze to find Jonah's hands behind his back. Worry spiked in the pit of his stomach. "Could you tell me?"

"I didn't know how much it meant to you." Jonah sounded small. "I didn't understand."

Tommy tensed.

"I feel bad." A scrunch on Jonah's brow betrayed he was working to put his thoughts into words. "I only decided to stay with you after you gave up being who you want to be."

That timing had stung, but Tommy couldn't resent Jonah for basing their future on his failure. "It's okay."

"No," Jonah said, and looked up at him. "I feel bad for *me*."

Tommy's gut dropped.

"Trying to be king was incredibly important to you," Jonah said. "But I wasn't important enough to know."

Alarmed, Tommy leaned forward. "That's not—"

"You keep lying to me, Tommy. You said you felt bad about not telling me you were royalty, but how bad could you have felt when you've done it again?"

"I—" Tommy's tongue failed him as he fumbled for an explanation. "It wasn't like that. I thought if I told you, you'd get scared and say no without giving us a try. And I knew I probably wouldn't be able to handle it anyway, so telling you would've complicated things for no reason."

"No reason? To tell me about the thing you want above

anything else?" Jonah's frown was wounded. "I'm starting to think you expect me to understand every time you do something like this, because you know I love you. You expect that I'll always find a way not to feel hurt because I don't *want* to be hurt by you. But I shouldn't have to do that work. You should work harder not to hurt me in the first place, because if you haven't noticed, Tommy, the things that hurt me keep getting bigger, and it's almost too much to—"

Bear?

Jonah shook his head, face lowered.

"You're right," Tommy whispered, struggling not to panic at the hole expanding in his chest. "I'm sorry."

"Well, I don't forgive you."

Tommy went cold. Never in their lives had Tommy had to wait for Jonah's forgiveness—and only now did the sheer significance of that strike him. Jonah had always been willing to react to intention, rather than execution. A rare quality that had likely held their friendship together all these years.

And broke it apart now.

Jonah didn't consider Tommy's intentions on this to be any better than his actions—and that twisted Tommy's body into something lumbering and terrified.

"It's up to me whether we're together or not," Jonah said in an odd tone. "Isn't it?"

Jesus. If it was up to Tommy, there'd be no question. Together forever. But he could hardly decide that level of commitment on Jonah's behalf, so of course it had to come from him. "Yes."

It was small, but Tommy could have sworn Jonah flinched.

And then Tommy flinched right to his core as his blood ran cold. "Are you ending us?"

Jonah's sudden stare was wide. "What would be the point in that?"

"I—" Tommy cut off as Jonah's response slid uneasily down his sternum. "There doesn't have to be a point, if you feel hurt."

"Of course, there does." Jonah gave an incredulous sniffle. "I'm not about to give you up for nothing. I just . . . I can't support you if you don't tell me what's important to you. And I want to support you—that's important to *me*."

"Okay." Tommy blinked back lightheadedness. *He's not ending us.* "Thank you. God, thank you for not giving up on me."

"Giving you up," Jonah corrected warily.

Tommy frowned at him.

"I'll never give up on you, Tommy." Jonah eyed him before saying quietly, "I still want to spend the day with you."

Pulling in an unsteady breath, Tommy said, "I want that, too."

Jonah nodded. "But you have to write that statement."

"I do." Carefully, Tommy placed his hand on Jonah's knee. "I'd like you to help me write it."

"What?" Alarm flung itself across Jonah's features. "No! I'll just try not to bother you while you do it. You know I'm not good with words."

"I'm not good at talking rationally about my anxiety. And you said you wanted to support me. This is important."

"I didn't mean support you with royal stuff! I can't do that." Discomfort settled between Jonah's brows as he shifted on the chair. "I meant emotionally."

Exactly. Tommy flipped his hand palm up. "Please will you help?"

"Oh, I don't . . ." Reluctant, Jonah slowly pulled his hands out from behind his back, and after hesitating for several long moments, he finally placed a palm in Tommy's. "On one condition," he said, and fixed Tommy with a chastising gaze. "No more lies."

"To put an end to speculation, I'd like to confirm that my abrupt departure from the parade on Sunday was due to a panic attack, an experience that was both terrifying and debilitating. This was not how I intended my first public appearance in Kiraly to end, and I sincerely regret that I was unable to properly celebrate this occasion with the people of Kira City.

The panic attack was not an isolated incident. I suffer from severe social anxiety and find unfamiliar social situations unendurable. This mental illness predates my arrival in Kiraly and, I must reassure you, is not the result of any assumed stresses, pressures, or expectations in my role as Prince of Kiraly.

My role as prince, however, does present obvious challenges to one operating within my limitations. Many of the responsibilities and duties that come with a life of public service are outside of my ability at present. My avoidance of public engagements since my arrival in Kiraly has been well-observed and understandably questioned. You now have my explanation.

Also well-observed are my recent visits to the city. These were an attempt to reduce my anxiety in public settings via exposure, but despite my desperation to progress into a more visible state figure for my citizens, this approach has ultimately proven unsuccessful. Public situations remain a matter of fight-or-flight for me, an expression of acute anxiety.

. . .

Due to this, I will be withdrawing once more from public appearances. I deeply regret this decision. However, I see no other way forward. I will remain an active member of the family in a governmental capacity, dedicating my life to strengthening national unity, equality, and stability.

Sincerely,
His Royal Highness Prince Tomas Jaroka

18

In the days that followed the issued statement, Tommy's chest split open. He was utterly exposed; the damage inside him irreversibly observed. He didn't want to know just how wide he was being pulled apart or how deep the media's hands were digging. He focused on moving his workspace back to the private library in the north wing, but even then, he found it impossible to walk through the palace with dignity. His staff had known he was withdrawn, but now they knew why. Their judgement pressed in on him with every murmured greeting and bow.

Zoltan and Nyaring were quiet as they accompanied him. In fact, his entire family seemed to struggle to find words around him. Everyone but Jonah.

He hadn't forgiven Tommy, but that didn't stop him wanting to understand what Tommy's days had been like before he'd tried to be king.

Simpler, Tommy told him. He'd mostly kept to himself—buried deep in learning all he could about Kiraly, from history to laws, culture to causes for concern—only scheduling the occasional meeting with a minister or specialist when he sought additional information. He'd managed the development of several new programs, though leadership of the initiatives he'd proposed while king-in-training would now pass to Kris.

"Kris would let you keep control of those," Jonah said with a helpful nod over breakfast. "Even if it's behind closed doors. Surely."

"Kris isn't a puppet," Tommy answered. "I won't turn him into one."

Jonah gave him a strange look over his toast but didn't answer.

Tommy's return to the private library came with an insidious familiarity that undermined everything he'd tried to achieve. If it weren't for the loss amassing between his ribs, it would feel as if he'd never attempted to possess the royal study at all. Cream-painted bookshelves edged with embellishments were in-laid in the high walls, stretching around a wide central space that branched off into alcoves and reading corners. Several spiral staircases led to the upper levels. It was as quiet as a heartbeat and late every afternoon, golden sunlight drenched the bottom shelves, thickening the air with the rich scent of aging paper and warmed leather covers.

A space that used to feel like a refuge now reduced him to his shortcomings.

Midweek, Tommy was sitting at his old desk near a mountain-view window researching mine closure processes when a gentle little knock came from the entrance.

"Come in," he called, distracted, and continued reading until the end of the paragraph.

When he leaned back in his chair, Ava and Darius were standing in front of his desk.

"Ava," Tommy said, and suffered a rush of shame that she had to visit him here instead of the tower. "And Darius, good to see you."

Darius gave a nervous smile and shuffled behind Ava's legs.

"We've just finished playing with Dolce, haven't we?" Ava glanced at her son before sending Tommy a warm smile. Dolce was one of Tommy's late uncle's dogs. "And weeding our veggie patch to get ready for planting autumn vegetables next month."

The boy peered around her legs at Tommy, eyes bright.

"Oh?" Tommy tried to look outwardly curious despite the hollow incompetence he felt on the inside. "What will you plant?"

"Um." Darius glanced quickly up at Ava. "Peas. Beans. Potatoes."

"Wow," Tommy said, and immediately ached for Jonah's bar shift to be over. "That's very exciting."

Darius nodded. Ava smiled and gestured further into the library. "Why don't you try to find as many green books as you can? I'd like to talk with Uncle Tomas for a minute."

Tommy closed his laptop as his soon-to-be nephew set off on his task.

"I've thought about your offer," Ava said, her posture somehow becoming even more faultless as she tucked her shoulder blades together. "I've also discussed it at length with Markus and Cyrus—and I'd like to be the representative for international trade to Kelehar regarding the future of the automotive industry."

Tommy almost smiled, but the bitter bruise inside him blossomed at the thought of passing control of the project over to Kris. "I'm relieved to hear that."

With a soft hum, her gaze drifted in her son's direction. "I'd like to visit home again, for him. For Markus. For me." She lifted her chin and returned her attention to Tommy. "But I also want to do this for Kiraly."

This time, he did smile. "Thank you."

Within seconds, her smile turned speculative, and his insides lurched at all the possible observations he didn't have the skin to hear right now.

"How are the wedding plans?" he asked.

Her brows shot up. "Good, thank you. Everything is arranged, and our honeymoon will be the day after the coronation. My only worry is Zara. I had hoped she'd be able to show Cy around Kira City this week. He landed yesterday. But she's refused, saying she's the last person he should be near—or that anyone should be near." Concern pinched Ava's features. "She's not herself."

"No," he murmured, having heard from Jonah that she was still a heart-wrenching mess.

"Anyway. Tomas." Ava seemed to haul her focus back on track. "There is something else."

His whole midsection tightened as he arched a brow.

"I've been thinking," she said, "about the Succession to the Crown Act."

Disgust wrenched through him, but he schooled his features into calm neutrality.

"And how it's in need of revision."

He frowned. "After Mark abdicates, the line—" Reality cut deep into his lungs. "I mean," he said, unable to hold her gaze. "After Mark and I both abdicate, the line of succession will move to Kris and Frankie's children. Your children will be free of that expectation. Nothing needs amending."

"On the contrary." She moved a hand to the back pocket of her burgundy jeans. "While I approve of certain modern sentiments, primarily that brothers do not precede sisters in the line of succession and that no one in the royal family requires consent from the monarch to marry, the act still contains some rather glaring prejudices, does it not?"

On an unsteady breath, Tommy met her dark stare.

"I imagine if Prince Noel had been firstborn, the act would

already have been updated to allow for any children he might have had to be considered heirs." Ava withdrew a piece of paper and unfolded it carefully. "I've taken the liberty of arranging a draft of new legislation. I know it won't be applied to you, Tomas, following your abdication, but we should still right this wrong. Oh, and I've done away with gendered language entirely. Heirs are heirs."

"You—" A lump formed in his throat. "Ava . . ."

"I'm proud to be part of this country." Passing the draft to him, Tommy's future sister-in-law added, "But I'll be prouder still when the monarchy practices the equality it preaches."

Jonah still hadn't forgiven him.

Tommy didn't know how to navigate it. Jonah's lack of forgiveness wasn't obvious in the way he spoke or behaved, but every now and then, Jonah would look at him with a wary kind of sadness that left Tommy floundering. Jonah might not be able to stay upset at people he cared about, but he could stay hurt. It didn't help that time together had been scarce while Jonah finished the last of his rostered shifts—meaning for the most part, they'd spent the week sleeping while the other was awake.

Tommy had shown him more of the palace, including the hidden passageways. One secret couldn't make up for another, but Jonah had asked what his days used to entail and disappearing from sight had been a key feature. He'd spent way too much time inside the stone walls—and had tried to hide the sense of peace and safety that overcame him as they'd walked the large tunnel connecting the palace to a cabin in the mountains.

By Friday morning, Jonah's sad looks had turned into dull detachment as he sat with Tommy in the library study. His dark gaze was lost out the window, his features unusually grave.

Torn by the distance, Tommy slid his work aside. "Will you tell everyone it's your last shift tonight?" Guilt weighted his soft question. He wanted to beg Jonah for forgiveness, kneel in repentance for lying about trying to be king; for the classist discrimination of the monarchy that demanded Jonah quit the work he loved.

"Um." Jonah blinked, brows creasing as his focus moved to the shelves. "I guess?"

"They'll miss you."

"I guess," he said again, running a hand over the back of his neck.

God, it was torture, the way Jonah avoided his gaze. "We can have pancakes for breakfast when you get back."

"Tommy." Humor flicked up the corners of Jonah's mouth as he finally looked at him. "Are you fussing?"

"If you'll let me."

"I . . ." Sighing, Jonah shook his head. "I'm okay. And you have work to do. I've noticed those folders are still on your desk. What are they?"

Tommy eyed the small stack. "Adam's files."

He hadn't wanted to burden himself with the extra stress while striving to be king, so had avoided reading them. Now it hardly mattered how he reacted. What difference would it make if his anxiety climbed another tier?

In a bitter kind of trepidation, he drew the stack closer. "Will you stay while I read?"

"Of course."

Bracing himself, Tommy started by rereading Rudy's folder. Vocal about his anti-establishment views, aggressive personality, died in a mining accident—a summary that fit the way Rudy had been described at the Bearded Bunting the other night. He'd been the leader of the group, the man who recruited vulnerable minds and incited radical action.

"Adam's brother planned the balcony collapse," Tommy told Jonah without looking up.

Then Tommy moved on to Adam.

It started with background information on his family, childhood, working history, as well as character depictions from both palace staff and the anarchists who'd attacked Kris. And from Zara. *God help her.* Those were grueling pages to read, but a picture emerged of a much less forceful personality than Rudy. Considered, sophisticated, and without the decisive fire of his younger brother. When Rudy died, the anarchists claimed that Adam's grief fueled him to carry out the plan, but in the weeks after the royal family's death—when Tommy and his brothers had appeared and stunned them all—the wheels had started falling off. Adam had promised a new plan, assured them he was making progress, but failed to deliver.

"Does it say that the brothers think they're royalty?" Jonah asked, curious.

"No." Tommy sent him a faint smile. "You helped us figure that out for ourselves."

So he overlaid everything he read with the fact that Adam and Rudy's end goal had not been to dismantle the monarchy, as they'd led the anarchists to believe, but to take the throne.

If the original plan had worked, Adam would now be king.

Pausing, Tommy turned that over in his mind.

If Erik Jaroka's ill health had prevented him from ascending—

If Erik really only had one son, as Adam and Rudy had believed, a son who'd died in an unprovoked attack on a dirt road in small-town Montana—

If Adam had been able to prove his royal heritage—

Then at this very moment . . .

"He would be king," Tommy murmured, and a chill dug into his scalp.

"But he's not." Jonah leaned forward in reassurance. "And he never will be."

No. And neither will I.

With a dark shock, it hit Tommy that the only person who might understand how it felt to be pulled so inexorably toward the throne but not be able to take it was the same man who might well be plotting to kill him. That Tommy might be the only person who could understand how failing to attain the throne—after coming so close—felt to Adam.

It's ours. The chill speared deep into his gut. *Jesus Christ, we both believe the throne is ours.*

"Tommy?"

As a Jaroka prince, Tommy had always been aware of his royal blood. The powerful resonance of a great destiny biding its time within him.

And as a descendant of the claimant, Adam would have always believed his historical ties to the throne made him the rightful king and that his destiny was one and the same.

"Tommy." Tommy jumped as Jonah's hand circled firmly around his forearm, his thumb sweeping the inside of his elbow. "He can't hurt us. I'm sure Frankie's search has scared him halfway across the world."

Had it really?

Where could he have gone? Tommy sucked in a sharp breath as he rephrased the question. *Where would I have gone?*

He came up blank. Even though he could never be king, Tommy couldn't imagine turning his back and leaving the palace behind. These walls held a precious part of his life force; held the power and unflinching responsibility of his ancestors. He wasn't in a position to fulfil his true role, but he could never give up this physical connection to his history—not when he *knew* he belonged here.

Tommy's insides lurched.

What if Adam feels the same?

Adam's family had worked in the palace for generations, biding their time, believing they belonged here in the most literal sense—believing the palace belonged *to them*.

"Jesus, Jonah." Heartbeat thudding in his ears, Tommy flipped back to the transcript of Zara's interview. *There.* Zara admitted she'd told Adam about Ava and Darius's escape from the palace several months ago. "He knows about the secret passageways."

Jonah's thumb strokes stilled as Tommy sat back in disbelief.

"What if he's still here?"

"Frankie." Tommy's strides devoured the shortest route to the old map room on the third floor. Cresting a flight of stairs, he pressed the phone to his ear and tightened his grip on Jonah's hand. "Are there any blind spots in the passages that aren't fitted with security cameras?"

"Uh." Frankie's bewilderment lasted a beat. "I don't think so. I can pull up the security map to confirm?"

"Do it. We're on our way to the map room now." Tommy charged along a corridor with embellished arches and artfully painted ceilings. "Call me back."

His pulse pounded. *Does this make any sense?* Could Adam have somehow been living in the palace walls? Could he have risked discovery as the most wanted man in the country just to stay close to his home?

Could he have been on the other side of the wall to Jonah all this time?

Fear and fury collided in Tommy's stomach. Queasy, he tugged Jonah closer and used the press of his elbow to trap Jonah's arm flush against his side. "I hope I'm wrong."

"If you're right," Jonah said, "Frankie might be able to find him."

If I'm right, I've had you within his reach.

Bursting through the grand doors of the map room, he ignored the curated collection of maps pasted on the walls and instead strode to the drawer in the corner, unlocked it, and withdrew the large sheet he wanted.

A map of the palace and Kira City.

Tommy had studied it often—a copy hung on the wall of the bunker beneath the cabin he'd shown Jonah earlier in the week. He laid it on the table, hands shaking, and assessed the section that showed a floor plan of the palace, detailed with inset maps of each floor and bold lines that represented the secret passageways.

His phone rang. "Frankie?"

"No," she said. "There aren't any areas that our security cameras don't cover."

Disappointment winded him. He stepped back from the table.

"Why?" Concern sharpened her voice. "What's going on?"

"Tommy." Jonah shot him a confused frown from where he leaned over the map. "Where are the rest of the secret passageways?"

Tommy drew the mouthpiece aside. "What do you mean?"

"These bits are the passages and tunnels?" Jonah gestured to the map, looking uncomfortable that he mightn't be reading it properly. Tommy nodded. "But there's a whole section that doesn't have them. That seems weird. I don't understand why not?"

"Well," Tommy said, and returned to his side. He'd only ever looked with the intention of memorizing the routes of the passages, not to question the pattern of the network as a whole. Jonah was right, of course. An entire section of the palace was disconnected. "It's because that's the servants' wing."

Jonah's frown didn't clear. "And that makes sense?"

"What use would the royal family have for sneaking into the servants' wing when they could march down there whenever they wanted?"

Jonah gave a skeptical hum.

"I want to know what's going on, Tommy," Frankie said in his ear.

"Did your ancestors run out of money while building the palace?" Jonah asked, and Tommy shook his head, barely suppressing a scoff at the enormity of his ancestors' fortune. "Then why wouldn't they put passageways everywhere, just in case? I know servants are considered inferior, but that doesn't mean the royals wouldn't want the option to spy on them like everyone else."

That was—true. Tommy had read the historical accounts of the palace's original construction, but none included details on the secret passages. Obviously, because they were *secret*, but it did mean he was in the dark regarding the architectural decisions behind—

"Wait a minute," he said. Frowning heavily, Tommy studied the lines again.

The secret corridors ran through every part of the palace except the servants' wing.

"This map," he said, staring at the date stamp as suspicion itched inside him, "is not old." The cartographer had signed and dated it just over a century ago. "But it's the only map I've come across that includes the passageways." Presumably, that had been when the royal family first divulged the existence of the hidden network to the Royal Guard. "It was drawn decades after the Boller line had been edged out of court and into serving positions."

Jonah stared, eyes wide behind his glasses, seeming to hang from Tommy's words without really grasping them.

"What?" Frankie demanded as the quick tread of her boots carried down the line. "Put me on speaker."

Palms slick, Tommy obliged and set the phone on the table.

"What if . . ." He didn't generally entertain *what ifs,* but this whole theory was nothing but speculation anyway. "The claimant found out about the passages from a member of the royal family while he was first at court. And that knowledge has stayed in his family as a closely guarded secret ever since."

"You mean," Jonah said, sounding unsure, "Adam knew about them anyway?"

"I mean," Tommy said, trying to keep his voice steady. "Adam and his brother might not be the first in their family to have taken action. Maybe their great-great-great-grandfather, for instance, who lived in the servants' wing, decided to claim a portion of what he believed was lawfully his. A portion of the palace. Jonah, this section of the map might not be without passages at all. Maybe they've been blocked off."

"What the hell?" Frankie cursed as the sound of rapidly decelerating footsteps came from outside the room. The door flew open, and she practically fell inside, her green gaze incredulous as she flung her attention to Tommy. "Come again?"

Tommy faced her. "Block off one section at a time, over time, and it could have gone unnoticed."

Lungs heaving, she asked, "You think Adam's hiding in the fucking walls?"

"Not all of them. Just those that once lined the servants' wing."

"You think," she said again, "he would stay this close?"

Yes. I would stay.

But he answered, "I think we've run out of better ideas."

"Well, shit." She ran a hand through her hair, looking disgruntled, moody, like the possibility had tackled her sideways and her temper was rising fast to fight her way back up. "Give me a second."

"Tommy?" Jonah spoke his name quietly, worriedly, as he leaned close, his hand sliding into Tommy's palm.

"We're okay," Tommy told him, head spinning.

"Yeah, you're okay." Frankie nodded as her gaze refocused. "We can verify this. I'll get a team to scour every tunnel and passage for signs of tampering. It could take a while. If it's true, the closed off sections have had a long time for the dust to settle."

Good. Tommy inclined his head. "Thank you."

"No need to thank me." She crossed her arms as a scowl descended over her features. "That bastard tried to kill you and Jonah, actually killed your relatives, inspired his goons to beat up my fiancé, and put a target on all your backs. If he's been hiding under my nose, he's about to learn a very serious lesson." Her gaze burned as it cut between him and Jonah. "No one threatens my boys."

◡

It was an extensive search. On first inspection, the guards found nothing. On second, they were joined by the authorities and deepened the sweep. The wait was excruciating—none of them could forget that the man who'd murdered, wounded, and traumatized their family might be hiding within arm's reach. Oddly, the thought didn't flood Tommy with anxiety.

It made him *furious*.

The rest of the day passed in an edgy haze. Jonah skipped his final bar shift, and although they were all too distracted to focus, Tommy, his brothers, and Jonah gave it their best shot, playing poker in an effort to celebrate the eve of Mark's wedding.

They were into their third hand when news came.

A section of wall had been identified with irregularities in the stonework—it would be disassembled overnight.

Once Frankie finished sharing the update, Tommy followed her into the corridor. "Don't go in without me," he told her. "I want to be there when you find him."

Her frown was wary. "You know I can't allow that. He's dangerous."

"You will allow it." A memory lodged at the base of his throat, and though he managed to swallow it down, it left his voice hoarse. "I was pinned, Frankie, when they tried to kill Jonah. I couldn't save him. Couldn't fight or scream or tell him I loved him. I did *nothing*."

Pain flooded Frankie's face a second before she schooled it.

"Adam might not have been there, holding the knife, but he planned on wearing the crown left behind." Rage billowed black and beastly within him. "I won't do nothing this time. I won't be held back."

Frankie's level gaze held his. "You know why I couldn't stop Kris from getting hurt."

"Because he was an idiot," Tommy spat.

Her lips slanted upward. Then she raised a questioning brow.

"I won't be an idiot," he said.

Inhaling through her nose, she rolled her head back to stare at the ceiling. "Fine."

Tommy didn't sleep. Jonah lay silent in the sheets beside him, watching, his dark eyes grave.

"If they find him," Tommy said at one point, "I'd like to kill him."

"No, you wouldn't," Jonah whispered, and curled a hand around Tommy's bicep.

No, I wouldn't. "I'd want him to suffer."

"You know." Jonah's foot slid over Tommy's ankle, soft as a brushstroke. "I've heard that a good life is the best revenge."

Tommy turned his head toward him, heart aching. *Then my revenge is you.*

"I want you to do that instead." Jonah's voice caught, and he quickly pressed his face against Tommy's shoulder. All Tommy could see was his scrunched brow as he murmured, "Promise?"

It was the easiest promise he'd ever made.

And it was why, when Nyaring and Zoltan knocked at his suite door in the early hours of the morning, Tommy pushed against the violence that rose like a storm inside him. He allowed himself to be led into the bowels of the palace, surrounded by heavily armed security, and approach the recently exposed passageway lined with what appeared to be the entire Royal Guard.

Frankie waited for him, cheeks flushed, sweat dampening her hairline. "You ready?"

He nodded, blood thundering.

"Let me lead." She actually raised a finger at him.

Arching a brow, he gestured for her to go right ahead.

She turned then shot a sparkling glance back at him. "Can't believe you were right."

"Can't believe you're not used to it," he murmured.

Grinning fiercely, she motioned for her team to get to work.

They poured in. Soft-footed. Silent. Searching.

Tommy stood at the rear with his guard, pulse pounding, skin stinging—inching forward with every passage that was explored, found empty, and left behind.

Flashlights and lanterns lit the cold stone walls. Shadows loomed and darted onward.

Time passed. Frankie had long gone off in front.

The team moved deeper on whisper-quiet feet.

When the muffled sneeze of a guard sent alarm bulleting

down Tommy's spine, he shoved himself into the pit in his mind that bristled with protectiveness, hackles up and claws extended. *Jonah.* Adam wouldn't get near him ever again. *I'll see this through for Jonah.*

Frankie's shout rang out.

The search had ended.

Tommy's anger couldn't stop his cold sweat. His guards snapped into a tight ring around him, weapons drawn, as other guards rushed ahead. Instructions were called, clipped and controlled, and there was the sound of swiftly moving bodies taking formation.

Then silence.

"Your Highness," Nyaring said under her breath, and the ring parted.

Heartbeat jagged against his ribs, Tommy approached. Adrenaline twitched in his muscles, ached in his gums, as he moved past the guards lining the passageway, around a corner, and into a brightly lit room crammed with security. In their midst stood the head of palace security, her red hair bold against her blue uniform as she held the cuffed criminal in a white-knuckled grip.

Adam.

Tommy had expected him to be struggling, mouthing off, shouting that he was the rightful king—his expression wild with conviction, evil finally revealed.

Instead, the man stood with defeat. Shoulders caved in, head hanging, defenseless.

"You," Tommy said with quiet loathing, "killed my family."

The startled jerk of Adam's head revealed a man in good condition considering he'd been hiding in the walls for a month. Blond hair mussed, but not tangled, and his facial hair only a few days old. His shirt was unpressed, but clean, his trousers the same, and though his black shoes had lost their gloss, they were neatly tied. He should have looked sick or half-starved by now.

Ah. These unmarked passages must contain a route down to the city.

I'd like to kill him.

Staring at Tommy, Adam's skin turned ashen, blue eyes flaring wide. Perhaps he feared that down here—with only his loyal guards to witness—Tommy could do exactly that.

"Your men attacked my brother."

Adam's swallow carried across the room. It appeared to be old living quarters for palace staff, sparsely equipped with a single bed, standing robe, and fraying armchair—rare for its entrance into the walls and presumably another part of the palace that the Bollers had long concealed.

"Your men almost killed me." Tommy managed to speak of the trauma, armed with those sharp claws of protectiveness. He let the brutal tips flash in his eyes. "Almost killed the love of my life, though his sweet soul had nothing to do with any of this."

Adam stepped back into Frankie. She hissed and shoved him forward.

"Did you plan to try again?" Tommy asked. "Wipe me and my brothers out together?"

"No." Ducking his head, Adam said, "I—haven't known what to do."

I'd like to kill him.

Tommy's voice dropped as he moved closer. "I don't believe you."

"I—alright, yes, I thought about it." Adam's reluctant confession had the guards shifting their weight, rolling their shoulders back. "It's what my brother would have wanted. He wanted us to change Kiraly."

"Then why haven't you acted?" This from Frankie. "You've been down here for weeks."

"I . . ." Adam tried and failed to look up at Tommy. "I heard what you were doing. And it didn't make sense."

Tommy waited for him to spit it out.

"Rudy and I, we—" Adam's voice wavered at his brother's name. "We resented the entitlement of your family for assuming they were the rightful rulers—then you came along and ordered a nationwide survey that allowed the people to decide whether or not to keep the monarchy."

For a horrifying second, it seemed that Adam meant Tommy specifically. That his traitorous network had wormed deep enough to know Tommy had trialed as king. But no. Adam was doing what most people did—referring to him and his triplets using the one pronoun.

Swallowing again, Adam continued. "We resented your family for living in luxury while your people slaved away for royal gain. My brother worked hard every day in the mines, and all it did was fatten the royal purse. He *died* doing it. Then you —" Blond brows buckling at the floor, Adam shook his head. "You started planning for the mines to close and for safer career alternatives for those workers."

Just because you're capable of murdering my family, Tommy bit back, *doesn't mean I'm capable of endorsing the death of yours.*

"After the queen died," Adam went on, "King Vinci held onto his role for over two decades despite no longer being fit for it. He was numbed by grief, careless with his power, and never valued his people enough to step aside. But you—your statement to the press acknowledged you weren't fit to be a prince with public duties. You stepped down from that role instead of simply not doing what was expected of you. You made it harder to hate you."

A shudder tore through Tommy as he fisted his hands. Did Adam even know why Tommy was unfit for those duties? The role his own ambition had played in pulling Tommy's out of reach?

I should be king.

That truth screwed up tight, stricken and suffering inside him.

I'd like to kill him.

But Jonah curled a phantom hand around his arm. *No, you wouldn't.*

No. Tommy wanted him to suffer. This man who'd deemed himself deserving of the crown—who'd stood in the shadows while his younger brother spilled blood on his behalf.

"You," Tommy said.

Fury set like ice in his veins when Adam met his stare. *You ordered the attack that almost stole Jonah from this world; that forced me to live with trauma and anxiety. You murdered my uncles and cousin, attacked one brother, got too fucking close to the other, and intended to take my throne.*

"You disgrace this kingdom."

Adam shrank away from whatever he saw on Tommy's face, and seconds later, Frankie hauled him into the passages and out of sight.

That was it.

Adam was gone.

And Tommy would never get his throne back.

19

It was an outdoor ceremony. Tucked away on the outskirts of the palace grounds where Ava had first seen Mark, the towering alpine forest casting shade over the gathering, Tommy stood beside his brothers, listening to the exchange of vows and allowing himself to feel lighter than he had in weeks.

They were safe.

Jonah had chosen him.

And his brother was getting *married*.

Apparently, that was all it took for his defenses to drop lower than reason—to admit thoughts he'd otherwise never have entertained—because as the small wedding party cheered for the kissing newlyweds, Tommy turned to smile out at the guests and met the unexpected intensity of Jonah's colt-wide gaze. He was smiling too, as he clapped, but distractedly—mostly staring at Tommy like he ached to fall into his eyes, like he wouldn't want to exist anywhere else but in the sparkle he created; staring with longing and neediness and adoration, staring as if *they* were the newly—

And just like that, it hit Tommy that Jonah wanted to marry him.

The man who put the bright rush of blood in Tommy's veins, the pulse of purpose in his every heartbeat.

Wants to be my husband?

It was so many steps past forgiveness, Tommy struggled to believe it, but the idea gleamed stronger as the evening wore on.

After the ceremony, Jonah took his hand and begged him not to let go for the rest of the night. He clung on as they stood for photos, Champagne, and conversation. When the sun slid lower on the horizon, Philip called for everyone's attention and announced that the survey results were officially in—the people of Kiraly had unquestionably decided in favor of the monarchy.

"You'll do great things." Jonah turned into Tommy, circling his arms around his neck and tilting his chin up in a way that made Tommy's ribs ache. It felt impossible that his best friend would yield to him so completely, right here in front of other people, but he did, features serious and almost desperate as he waited for Tommy's kiss.

So Tommy kissed him, slow and deliberate—a kiss that dared to ask if what he suspected was true. And Jonah pressed so hard against him that it felt like they'd become engaged without needing to exchange a word.

Eventually, the party was escorted to a section of garden set up for the reception. Summer flowers sweetened the air and strings of lights and ribbon draped above a long table set out for the intimate dinner. Seated, Jonah inched his chair so close, their bodies touched from shoulder to boot, and Tommy wanted to curl his hair back with gentle fingers and whisper in his ear.

Will you be my prince?

The question hitched in his chest, an addictive hook that stole his focus as if he'd been forced to put down an unstoppable book. It clenched in his gut, rerouted his thoughts—no matter that it was Mark's reception and the celebration shone with the food and drink and laughter. The question took on a bubbly sense of anticipation, an internal flip and jolt every time he remembered it anew. It fractured his grasp of time, and he marked the night with spikes in his senses. The subtle-sweet taste of the angel food wedding cake, delicate as a dream with vanilla and almond and cream. The explosive glitter of fireworks above the palace, silver and gold and bridal white. The applause as Mark and Ava said their farewells. The heat of Jonah whispering in his ear, "Will you come with me? I want to talk to you."

"Yes," Tommy said, rushing back to the present, thrown by the possibility that Jonah might have been acting so serious because *he* intended to propose to *Tommy*.

Jonah's touch was gold light as he led Tommy down low-lit palace corridors. It glowed on Tommy's skin, the spark of Jonah's palm, the shimmering brush of his elbow, his shoulder, and the iridescent tips of Jonah's fingers pressing into the ridges of Tommy's hand.

Somehow, they were at the base of the royal study.

Frowning, Tommy eyed him. "This isn't my space anymore."

"I know," Jonah said, adjusting his glasses as he regarded the elaborate archway and the spiraling stairs beyond.

Okay. If that was how Jonah wanted to do this. "You first this time."

"Oh." Shaking his head, Jonah stepped back, fingers slipping from Tommy's hand. One arm wrapped around his middle. "No."

He's so nervous. In incredulous anticipation, Tommy led the way, the prickle of Jonah's attention arcing from his shoulders to the backs of his knees. He ignored the cramp of inadequacy that tightened the higher he climbed; ignored the sense that he was returning home as he opened the door at the top and switched on the dimmed lights. His failures couldn't devour him—not with Jonah working himself up to say something Tommy hardly dared to believe.

The study was exactly as Tommy had left it: desk bare, chairs posed dutifully before it. If Tommy breathed deeper than necessary, savoring the soaring tower air, he refused to admit it.

Jonah crossed to the city-facing window where he'd first responded to the truth of Tommy's attraction. Tommy had stood there many nights, the spectacular view of Kiraly magical in miniature, shadowed buildings and amber windows and streets that stretched like glowing lifelines across the palm of the mountain.

Jonah pressed his hands to the wide windowsill, lowering his head.

Not sure where he should stand, Tommy moved to lean against the desk facing him, half a dozen strides away, gripping the edge either side of his thighs—giving him space, granting him the floor.

The silence felt charged, like it was humming on the verge of change.

Jonah was wearing his favorite sage green shirt. The fabric cupped his shoulders, swept down the lean strength of his back, and disappeared like a suggestive wink beneath the line of his belt. It was any wonder Tommy had stolen it away with him to Kiraly.

On a shaky breath, Jonah turned to him. "You're so beautiful, Tommy." His voice was as quiet as a turned page. "I can't understand why I never saw it before."

The blood in Tommy's veins must have doubled for how heavily it swelled in his chest.

"When you're not anxious, you have this . . . presence. This way about you that everyone can see, no matter how you try to hide it. You're the kind of man who can hush a crowd, not because of your status, but because of what you radiate. Power. Inner strength. It takes my breath away. All I want is for it to overwhelm me."

Tommy wanted that, too, so keenly it snapped and crackled across his skin.

"I, um." Jonah looked down at his tangled hands, lashes thick and shadowy. "It's good news that Kiraly wants to keep you guys as royalty. I wanted to know that for sure before doing this."

Tommy's heart almost burst out of his chest. *He waited to know for certain what it would mean to marry me?*

"I know you've avoided the public's reaction to your statement this week," Jonah went on. "And I know the others haven't told you about it. I asked them not to. I asked them to hold off, so that I could tell you now."

Tommy waited, not understanding how this would circle back, but trusting it would.

"Everyone has assumed it's part of your mental health program." Jonah flicked his eyes up then down again. "That your statement fits with the public stigma reduction campaign. They respect that you're practicing what you preach. That you're trying to make change from the top down. Everything I've read—and Philip and the boys, they've been reading it, too —it all supports you. I mean, there have been a few articles that don't, but there always will be, and you should see the comments section. Oh my God. Kiraly is *very* protective of you."

"I . . ." Blindsided, Tommy swayed. "You mean they're not calling me a . . ." When Jonah didn't offer any suggestions, Tommy finished quietly, "Nutcase?"

"No, Tommy." Jonah shook his head toward the floor. "Why would they? They're calling you their anxious prince, their queer prince, their prince who's proving that no one is immune to mental illness. And it's *good.* The way they're saying it—they're so proud. They love that you've opened the floor for others to share their stories."

Tommy's head spun. Never, not even in the most naïve

corner of his mind, had he considered nationwide acceptance a possibility.

It drenched him in new shame.

He hadn't believed his own speech. He'd stigmatized his anxiety. He'd held so tightly to his negative concept of himself that he'd genuinely feared public opinion would decimate him. Yet Kiraly had listened and viewed his condition as a *benefit*.

A catalyst for change.

"Kiraly understands why you can't be with them in person. They like that you told them. They feel like you trust them. And that makes them trust you in return. I'm not guessing this, either. It's what they've been saying to me at the bar. It's been Prince Tomas this and Prince Tomas that all week."

What? Tommy gaped as Jonah's hands clenched into fists by his sides.

"The thing is, Tommy . . ." And now Jonah looked up properly. It put an odd flutter beneath Tommy's breastbone, because he still wasn't smiling. "I don't think you should be their prince at all." Tommy blinked as Jonah raised his chin. "You should be their king."

All the breath left him.

"And you're going to be," Jonah said.

That made no . . . Tommy frowned, shaking his head. "Jonah, what are you—"

"I spoke to your family about it." Voice wavering, Jonah pushed his shirtsleeves over his elbows. "We've figured out a way it can work. Because they agree with me. You should be king. And since Kiraly knows about your anxiety and doesn't expect you to do the public stuff, you don't have to worry about what they'll think. Mark said he'll attend meetings and briefings that have more people than you can handle. And Kris said he'll do everything involving the public. Appearances and speeches and events. Philip seemed nervous about that, but we think it'll be okay."

It was starting to occur to Tommy that Jonah wasn't going to circle back. That this was why they were here.

Jonah was returning Tommy to his rightful place.

Doubt thundered up his rib cage. "I don't think this is—"

"It *is*." Jonah half-turned away, but his voice grew in strength. "You worried me when you showed me the passageways. I could tell you were comfortable there, and I could see it, could see you going backward and retreating there more often. But you *can't*. You don't belong in hiding, Tommy. That man did. He hid down there. But not you, not anymore. You belong right here, and *everyone knows it*."

Tommy swallowed a wave of disorientation.

Was this—could this really happen?

Could he be a catalyst on such a scale?

"That man wanted to kill you," Jonah said, and turned his back completely. Tommy saw his face reflected in the window, and he looked heart-stoppingly, gut-sinkingly sad. "His men almost killed me instead, but his intention was to wipe out your family. He wanted to stop you taking the throne. And earlier this week, he won. Didn't he? What the attack did to you . . . It made you believe you couldn't do it. But anxiety doesn't change who you're meant to be. He doesn't get to win."

It ached—Jonah's faith in him. How long and hard he'd thought about this; how he'd pulled everything together behind the scenes for Tommy.

"I've listened to your speech." Jonah met Tommy's eye in the window, seemingly by accident. He quickly ducked his face. "A lot of times. And I think you need to prove Kiraly right. You told them that being diagnosed with a mental illness doesn't reduce someone's value to society. And your value to this society is being king. Since they believe you're leading by example, you need to follow through on that and lead them *as king*."

Tommy moved before he'd consciously decided to, standing right behind Jonah, arms caging him against the window. A surge was building inside him, affection and pride and sheer amazement that Jonah had marched down pathways that Tommy didn't have access to—mental routes that proved it was possible for a man like him to be king. Jonah had thought it, pursued it, and turned it into a reality.

"Jonah," he said, a growl that spoke of a long night of building need.

"Please, Tommy." Jonah's tone weakened as he angled his head back and down, toward Tommy, but not at him. "I'm almost done."

Jonah had probably been rehearsing this all night in his head. The least Tommy could do was let him finish.

He inched his arms closer against Jonah's sides but suppressed the urge to finish what they'd once started on this very windowsill.

"You—" Jonah dragged in an unsteady breath. "You also said in your speech that some people suffer from thinking they shouldn't need help. But everyone needs help sometimes. And your brothers are offering it to you. They're desperate to support you—they always have been. So I want you to take their help and not think any less of yourself. You can do this together, and that's okay. This will be your good life, Tommy. This is your revenge."

With the lightheadedness of acceptance, Tommy said, "He doesn't get to win."

I can be king. It would be unconventional, unprecedented—but reassigning his public duties wouldn't make him any less invested in serving his people. Allowing for his anxiety wouldn't make him any less of a monarch. *I can do it.*

Jonah was silent.

"Thank you." Tommy waited a beat before closing in, his chest pressing against Jonah's rigid back, his arms wrapping around his waist. His mouth found Jonah's shoulder, pressing hot over the fabric as he said, "I didn't think you'd want this."

And Jonah said, "I don't."

He . . .

Tommy's vision flickered.

The very tower seemed to lose its balance beneath him.

"Tommy." His name was all breath in Jonah's mouth. "Let me go, please."

With a jolt, Tommy found himself against the desk once more. The edge felt harder, sharper, cutting into the backs of his thighs. "Jonah. What?"

"I would never ask you to give this up for me." Turning, Jonah pulled his glasses off to rub his eyes. His skin glistened as he slid them back on. When he met Tommy's gaze, the look was all distress. "But you asked me to give up my sense of belonging for you. It was always up to me to decide whether we have a future. You'd already made up your mind about which was more important to you. Me or your kingdom. And I get it. You're made for this." Blindly, he gestured to the room, the view, the city below. "But I'm not. I'm not."

Tommy felt sick—his heart gushed blood straight into his stomach.

Jonah ran the back of his hand under his nose. "I've spent most of my life in a place I didn't belong because I couldn't bear to leave you, Tommy. And I was finally going to change that before all this. Now I think—I need to do it. Be *me*. I had to fight so hard to be me in Sage Haven. I don't want to fight all over again."

Tommy didn't make a sound. It hurt so badly he thought maybe his body had stopped.

Just—stopped.

"I want a community," Jonah said with a sniffle. "I want to be a part of somewhere I belong. That's my dream, and I'm—" His eyes filled fast, and he hauled in a sharp breath. "I don't want to give it up."

Pain roared in Tommy's ears; lashed in his chest.

"Jonah," he whispered when he wanted to scream. "I love you."

"And I love you." The words sounded too big for his throat. "You know I do. But I don't belong with a king, and you need to be one."

Yes, you do. But Tommy couldn't speak. His throat had closed over, burning and squeezing, his head barely holding on to what was happening. *He's breaking up with me.* Now, when Tommy had finally learned to trust him, finally stopped doubting Jonah really felt the same, *now* Jonah was leaving him.

"We're not the same, Tommy," Jonah said, "and we never have been."

"Don't." Tommy threw himself onto the word like a fallen sword. He could pick it up, fight with it. "Don't."

"I'm sorry, Tommy."

Don't—

Don't do this.

Don't make this real.

But it was because Tommy was already weeping.

Graceless, he reached for Jonah as he made to leave. Jonah made a small sound of anguish as he stepped aside.

"Thank you for loving me, Tommy." It came out watery, sodden, like he was being flooded from the inside out. "You'll always be my best friend."

Then stay with me. Please. Don't leave.

But in the end, Jonah got what he'd wanted.

He was the one to walk away.

20

Tommy would be king.

Jonah had done the right thing.

For them both.

They were more than each other.

And Tommy hadn't said no.

To being king.

Even when Jonah had broken up with him because of it.

Not that Jonah had wanted him to say no.

Tommy had to be king.

But Jonah had noticed.

That Tommy hadn't said no.

It hurt, so badly it felt like he was coming down with death or trapped forever in the moment right before it. It hurt—*God, it hurt*—making him realize how he'd taken good health for granted, unaware that being unaware of his body was probably one of the luckiest feelings in the world—same as not being heartbroken, that was another lucky feeling. But right now, Jonah was both, his heart piercing him like shards on every gulpy, ragged breath, his throat burning on every sob, his stomach twisting on every still-crying heave, and there were these weird shooting pains in his legs that made no sense, but he should probably stay in bed to be safe—

Nora messaged him.

Asking where he was.

He was missing his shift.

Because he'd never actually quit.

He told her he was over.

He didn't know what he meant.

Over life, over love, over hurting so badly it felt like he was made of pain, like his nerves couldn't detect pleasure anymore— just pain, in every swallow and blink and sniffle, every memory and thought-spiral. But he couldn't make it stop because only Tommy knew how to make him feel better, and he'd left Tommy broken in the palace, in the fierce protection of his family, so he would be okay, Tommy would be okay, and then he would be king just like he deserved, and Jonah would be okay someplace else, someplace he belonged, where it felt like home. *Yes, home.* Jonah longed to go home, but he didn't know where that was anymore, because home had always been Tommy, but that was okay, it was okay, it would be okay, because he'd done all this to make a new home for himself, so as soon as his heart stopped trying to die, he would—

Nora was here.

Crawling onto the bed beside him.

Saying she wasn't going anywhere.

Fuck their shifts.

The others would cover them tonight.

They sent him their best.

Because he was one of them.

And they always supported their team.

Their work fam.

He was part of their work fam, didn't he know?

Family, except he could date them.

If he wanted.

They all wanted.

Hey, was that a smile?

He'd be okay. They had him. They'd get him through this.

He'd be okay.

There were footsteps. In his sitting room. Several sets. Awareness flickered through the disorder of Tommy's mind, tiny and fleeting, like a glimpse of headlights through the trees at a great distance.

His brothers.

They'd finally noticed his absence.

He hadn't left his room. At first, because the sheets still smelled like Jonah and he hadn't wanted to miss a breath as it slowly faded to nothing. Then because he couldn't move, not after Jonah's cruel game of catch where Jonah had been in Tommy's arms until he'd tossed Tommy a kingdom. On instinct, Tommy had caught it, unaware that he'd let Jonah go in the process. Then Jonah had backed out of range while Tommy's hands were full with something too precious to drop.

But Jonah had known that.

Jonah had *wanted* that outcome.

The breakup pulled Jonah's behavior at the wedding into ugly focus. He hadn't been desperate for his and Tommy's own marriage—he'd been saying goodbye. All the huge eyes, touching and tasting had been the sensory equivalent to throwing possessions into a cardboard box to remember him by—a final lap of Tommy's body just to be sure he didn't miss anything.

Then Jonah had left.

The shock of it had flashed too brightly in Tommy's mind. It had been hours before he'd had a coherent thought longer than *he's gone* and *this isn't real* and *but he loves me.*

Because Jonah *did* love him—wanted to be with him. Yet that hadn't been enough for him to say: *You should be king, and I'll stand beside you.*

Tommy didn't understand.

He wanted so badly to understand.

"What the hell is going on here?" Kris demanded as he burst into the bedroom, then said in a wildly different tone, "Tommy? Jesus, what's going on?"

"God, Tom, how long have you been in here?" Mark sounded baffled, and a moment later, sunlight flooded the bed.

Silent, Tommy turned his face into his pillow.

"Uh, why does he look like this?" The mattress dipped as Kris sat on the edge of the bed. Concern weighted his words; the hand that came to rest on Tommy's shoulder. "Where's Jonah?"

"Not sure," Mark said from much closer as the mattress slanted dramatically. "Tommy, you can't ignore us."

Pity that was true.

Turning toward them, Tommy said, "Mark, you're a married man."

Or someone said it. The numb, detached voice sounded nothing like him.

"Thanks for remembering," Mark said dryly. "Obviously, it's too much to ask that you also remember to get out of bed or eat or shower or ask for help."

The scolding barely touched him. Blinking and with great effort, Tommy pushed himself up, twisted, and slumped against the bedhead. "Jonah said you'll support me as king. Is that true?"

"Yes," his brothers said together, firmly.

Tommy rubbed the blur from his sandpaper eyes. "It was his idea?"

"It was," Mark said, brows creased in earnest. "He got us all together to suggest it. He couldn't bear the thought of you not being who you're supposed to be."

"Except." Kris was frowning at Tommy. "You appear to be having a bad reaction to the idea. I can still do it. Jonah just thought—"

"Jonah," Tommy said, "left me."

They stared.

"What?" Shocked, Mark gave a small, uncomprehending shake of his head. "Why?"

"Yeah, what the hell?" Kris stood, instantly defensive. He was moving so much easier now. "He can't arrange this and then leave. That's not what we agreed to. This is bullshit."

A vicious snarl of bitterness twisted beneath Tommy's solar plexus. "He doesn't need your permission to break up with me."

"Yes, he does," Kris spat, but at a warning glance from Mark, said, "Fine, I'm in shock, but why would he do that?"

Tommy pressed a hand to his middle, vaguely surprised it was still there. Agony had been eating him alive for two days. He'd almost assumed he'd be empty, a hollow scoop exposing the bare bones of his spine. "He told me that he doesn't belong with a king."

Mark ran a hand over his mouth, frowning.

"And you said . . ." Kris tipped his face down a little, watching Tommy from beneath his brows.

"I—" Tommy swallowed, but pain still reared up his throat. "I said I loved him."

Kris nodded, waiting, while Mark's frown grew.

"I said don't," Tommy added slowly, with the sudden suspicion his brothers could see this situation more clearly than he ever would.

"But after that," Mark said, with a troubled glance at Kris, "I assume you didn't leave him to think the choice was between belonging out there and not belonging up here?"

Tommy stared.

"Yeah," Kris said, nodding. "I assume you tried to convince him that he *does* belong here? Because he does. Right?"

Right. The suggestion felt like a plank of wood whacking Tommy upside the head. *Why didn't I try to convince him of that?* Accepting Jonah's reason not to be together essentially told Jonah that it was valid.

"But," Tommy said, and oh yes, this was why he hadn't. "But he wants to open his own bar. Build a community where he gets on with everyone. Make everyone feel safe and welcome. He never had that in the Haven, and he got hungry. So hungry to belong."

And Tommy couldn't ask him to starve.

Not by his side.

His brothers were frowning at him.

Then Kris sighed, looked at Mark, and jerked his thumb in Tommy's direction. "This guy."

Mark shook his head gravely. "Where did we go so wrong?"

"People say he's smart, but I don't really see it."

Mark snorted. "There are different types of smart."

"Alright," Tommy snapped, but his heart wasn't in it. It was too busy being confused and terrified and incredibly, cautiously hopeful. "You can see something I can't. Are you going to help me or not?"

Kris reached out to grasp his knee. "When will you learn, man?"

Mark smiled. "The answer to that will always be yes."

The trouble was, Jonah wasn't even sure he wanted to open his own bar anymore.

Well, he *did*, but it was just . . . making less sense.

As he poured two white wines, doing his best to function while heavy and heartsick, the woman on the other side of the counter slid a business card across to him and spoke over the music. "Come and relax, love, on me. I run the best day spa on the mountain."

"Oh." After handing her the glasses, Jonah picked up the card. It was aquamarine with words, but he couldn't focus enough to actually read them. "Thank you. That's so kind."

He'd never been good at hiding the way he was feeling. Everyone could tell he was devastated—yet no one beyond the bar staff actually knew he'd broken up with Tommy. It seemed like the kind of thing the royal publicist would want to handle, so Jonah had sworn his work fam to secrecy and sidestepped when strangers asked what was wrong. Not that it stopped him ghosting around behind the bar, trapped on this earth without a tether, numb yet simultaneously teeming with loss and pain and guilt. He got orders wrong, didn't sing and clap along to the latest hit, and kept rubbing the center of his chest while thinking about stars.

Yeah, okay, so everyone must have absolutely figured it out.

Swallowing thickly, he slid the card into his pocket. Maybe he should do it? Maybe he should accept all the offers he'd been given tonight. It was scarcely eight and he'd already received more support and invitations for free comfort than his sad, slow brain could keep up with.

Of course, Nora had been keeping track for him.

"Jonah, he's the best chocolatier in Europe, yet I didn't hear you say yes," she'd commented earlier, leaning in while pouring a neat Scotch. "You'll collect that pamper hamper tomorrow, thank you."

And, "Have you been out on the lake in one of their rowboats yet? It's peaceful AF. You should totally do it."

And, "I *can't believe* she just offered you a free stay. She owns the swankiest hotel in the luxury tourist precinct."

And, "Did you know that guy? Did he just invite you to visit horses with him? Is he a vet or something?"

And, "Ignoring the fact you shouldn't physically be able to consume any more ice cream after the past twenty-four hours, their honeycomb vanilla crunch is off the chain, so you should accept a jumbo tub of that."

Other people offered him hugs and movie nights and road trips, and although no one said it would help take his mind off Tommy, it was obviously what they meant. Somewhere beneath the ache in his chest, somewhere he was only half-convinced existed, because he ached *everywhere*, top to bottom, front to back, inside and out, but somewhere inside him, the outpouring of kindness warmed him. The most inclusive community in the world had ushered him back into its fold.

And that was the trick, wasn't it? In the arms of so much support, how could he leave the Bearded Bunting to open a competing business? And why would he, anyway? The dream had made sense when he'd never been to a place like this. His vision of such a safe, friendly venue had shone in bright contrast to the bar he'd tended in Sage Haven.

Now, well, everything he'd imagined was already here.

It would make more sense to start a bar somewhere else entirely, somewhere lacking the acceptance and enthusiasm of Kiraly. Somewhere that needed him. But . . . he loved this city. He had friends. He didn't want to live anywhere else.

So what was he supposed to do now?

"I'm sorry." Nora interrupted his thoughts as she gestured toward the person Jonah had just served. "But did they seriously just offer you a goat?"

"I think so."

What Jonah really needed was to clear his head on a ride. Set out at sunrise with food in his pack and no destination, just him and nature and his horse. Unwind to the sway of the trees, the call of the birds, and the steady tread of hooves. He'd always found perspective in the saddle. But he'd left that life behind.

He'd left so many things behind.

And it *hurt*. Just because Sage Haven hadn't embraced his sexuality, didn't mean he wasn't the result of a small-town upbringing; didn't mean his veins had stopped pumping with cowboy blood. Those things made him *him*. He'd adored living on the edge of the Rockies, calmed by the wind-swept fields and the endless blue sky. He'd loved the easy pace, the familiar faces, the late summer sunsets. That town had been his home. It was only because *other* people didn't accept him that he'd left it behind.

Same as Tommy.

Jonah swallowed a pained grunt as he turned and pushed through the staff door to the back. He just had to sit for a minute. Slumped against the corridor wall, he put his head between his knees and fought the urge to call Tommy. *I could just ask how he's going—hear his voice and imagine him cupping my cheek and saying it'll be alright.*

But it wouldn't be alright, because Tommy had been Jonah's home his whole life, too, and he couldn't be that anymore. It didn't matter that Tommy loved him. Mark had married a princess, and Kris was engaged to the head of palace security. Smart, powerful, and important life partners. Jonah wasn't any of those things—and a simple man couldn't stand beside a king.

The people would never accept him.

Don't, Tommy had begged, dread streaming down his face. *Don't.*

But Jonah had.

He'd left Tommy behind.

Jonah's arms were wrapped tight over his tucked head,

squeezing his biceps, when the bar door opened and quickly closed again.

"Hey." Nora had slipped out. "You've been a while."

Had he? Misery seemed to play strange games with time. "Sorry."

"It's okay," she said, and he looked up to check whether that was true. She wore a sympathetic grimace as she angled her head. "But you should probably come back out."

"Okay." He stood. Only forever hours of his shift to go. "Maybe I'll get another goat."

She snorted. "We can only hope," she said, and stood back to hold the door open.

Blame it on the fog of sleep deprivation and despair, but it took him a while to notice.

He stepped past Nora, turning to swipe a fresh dishtowel from the stack and flip it limply over his shoulder. *Yeah, nice.* Gold medal for enthusiasm. *Come on.* Bracing his hands either side of the sink, he tried to rustle up some energy from the hollow pit inside him.

"Come on," he said under his breath, and stilled when he realized he'd heard it.

Realized that bar was *really quiet.*

The music was off. No one was singing or talking or laughing. It didn't even sound like anyone was *moving.* And the other bar staff—Jonah glanced sidelong with a frown—had all stopped serving, and instead, were looking overly occupied with tasks that put their backs to the room.

Nora stepped out beside Jonah. Her lips were rolled together to hold back a smile.

Alarmed, Jonah turned.

It was—*oh, God*—it was bad.

At least half the patrons had gone. The rest were motionless, some standing, some sitting, but all with their backs to the center of the room like some tiny attention bomb had gone off and blasted their focus outward. A dozen or so royal guards stood in that center point in a horseshoe formation, also facing outward, their feet apart, hands clasped behind them, their neutral attention set above the heads of the patrons.

At their core stood Tommy.

His gaze was fixed on Jonah.

No. Jonah sucked in a horrified breath as he backed up against the sink—even though he *wanted* to jump the counter and tell Tommy to never let him go.

It was nothing like the last time Tommy had stood here, posing as his brother while he waited for Jonah to finish work. His stance was straight, even and tall, and despite his boots, blue jeans, and his nicest casual shirt, he was royalty, pure and powerful. His black hat was angled just high enough for him to meet Jonah's gaze.

His eyes were crisp blue, sharp as arrows yet soft as tears.

No, no, no. Jonah's heart and stomach merged into one aching, clenching mass. He thought he'd avoided this. That first night and all of yesterday, he'd feared Tommy would come after him. That he would beg Jonah to reconsider—attempt to convince him that they were meant to be together. *Because we are.* After nothing but silence, a part of him had relaxed (while another part cried harder), because he didn't want to say no to Tommy all over again.

Not when it would break them both beyond repair.

Not in front of all these people. Not anywhere.

"Jonah." Tommy's low voice traveled the abnormally silent room. It sounded like the first word he'd spoken in years; the only word that could ever drive him to break his silence.

"Please don't," Jonah managed before covering his mouth with his hand.

Tommy's features tightened. "I'd like to try."

Jonah shook his head, but it was more in distress than denial.

"Jonah," Tommy said again, and *oh, God,* he was going to do it. This man who had hushed a roaring venue with the thrum of his being; this man who didn't belong at ground level, but higher, so much higher than where Jonah would ever be able to breathe. Tommy was about to make messes of them both. "The other night, I should have said more."

No, Jonah would never have made it out of the tower if Tommy had protested properly.

"The problem was that you stayed in Sage Haven because of me," Tommy continued, settling into a steady tone, level and in control—the same he'd used in the speech Jonah had listened to a dozen times. It was a voice that acknowledged he had an audience, even though no one watched him but Jonah. "I made you stay because I was too scared to lose you. The other night . . . I didn't want to do that again. Make you stay with me just because I didn't want to lose you. I want what's best for you. And if you want to work a bar, if that's your life's calling, then I understand. That's what you need to do."

That—kind of sounded like Tommy was agreeing with him. Thrown, Jonah lowered his hand. Was this . . . maybe Tommy was here to reestablish their friendship?

Tommy tracked Jonah's hand, then looked up, brows creased in question.

Unsure, Jonah raised a shoulder. "I think it's my calling."

Tommy stared, stricken, and then seemed to force himself to nod. "You told me that you'd never had enough to eat in Sage Haven. That you drank deep from our friendship, but you were starving to belong. And I think, with the way you've glowed and thrived recently, this city has finally filled you up."

Jonah nodded, vaguely aware that the staff and patrons were starting to cast sneaky glances in his direction.

"But I wonder," Tommy said, and tilted his hat back, lighting the strong lines of his jaw, his nose, the wariness bracketing his mouth. "Whether I've helped with that, too."

Jonah stopped moving.

"I wonder," Tommy said again, chest rising on a swift breath, "whether my love nourishes you."

With a small sound of pain, Jonah *just* stopped himself saying of course it did.

"Because your love has given me a life that I didn't know I could have." Tommy's hands balled by his sides as the column of his throat moved on a hard swallow. "I'm kinder and more patient and forgiving because you teach me to listen and talk and see things from the most wonderous perspective. I'm stronger and braver with your hand in mine. I've stood in my own city. I've ordered coffee and ice cream, and they're not—they're *not* small things. I can stand here, right now, with you looking back at me. You give me life, Jonah, in every way."

"Tommy," he said, brokenly, shaking his head. *Don't keep doing this*.

"I know the reason you—left me," Tommy said, hurt passing whip-quick across his face. "You don't think you belong in royal life. You think it would starve you. Judge you. Refuse to accept you. But I don't believe that's true."

"It is." Jonah was nothing but a teacup that would shatter beneath the full weight of the moon. "Don't humor me, Tommy. We can't base a life on that."

"I never humor you." Frowning, Tommy moved forward to stand between the front two guards. Tommy's personal guards. His shoulders settled slightly being closer to them. "Jonah, on the night I told you I liked you, you could have reacted in so many ways. But because you're the best friend in the entire world, you didn't tell me that you didn't feel the same. You asked for time to think—to see whether you *could* feel the same. And it turns out that you do."

I do, oh, Tommy, I feel everything for you. Tommy was love-heart bubbles popping in Jonah's rib cage, he was the sure swell of safety, he was a sense of great unfolding at his core, growing into the true shape that had hidden inside him. But—

"But I'm worried," Tommy continued, his gaze unwavering, "that you didn't also take the time to see whether you could belong by my side. Being with royalty was never something you'd let yourself consider. And I should have been more mindful of that, because I've learned, way too late, that asking if you want to spend your life with me isn't the same as assuring you that it's where you belong."

Pain spilling over inside him, Jonah said, "I don't."

Tommy arched a brow. "You don't know that, do you?"

Jonah blinked, tripped by the echoes of a previous conversation.

"Maybe it's like . . ." Tommy hesitated, his cheeks growing pink. "It's like two things that have never gone together. Like, um, eclairs and . . ."

"Blueberry pancakes?"

"Blueberry pancakes." Longing and affection pushed and pulled across Tommy's face. "Yes. If you stop and think about it, there's no good reason why they can't go together. There are *reasons,* proclaimed by eclairs throughout history and today across the world, because they've always thought they're too good to be paired with pancakes. That it would undermine and diminish their flavor. But those aren't good reasons. They're fears. And we don't live in any of those fucking backward patisseries anyway. We live here, and the citizens of Kiraly judge people on their hearts, not their class. And I want us to go together, Jonah, because combined, we'd make a sweet that serves everyone."

Oh, God, that didn't quite make sense, but it sure sounded amazing.

No, stop. I knew how I felt about this. Panicking, Jonah stuffed a hand through his hair. *I knew for certain, and now I don't anymore.*

"I don't want to pretend to be someone I'm not." He still knew that much. "I've had to pretend for too long."

Inclining his head, Tommy said, "I understand that. But, Jonah, you haven't pretended since you arrived. You're already the Jonah everyone loves. No one expects you to become someone you're not just because you say yes to me."

"I dressed differently," was all he could think to say.

Tommy angled his head, as if to say *come on, now.* "You love those pants."

"I had to go to the luncheon."

"And from how you described it in your texts, you didn't pretend there either. You were nervous, but you adjusted and interacted with authenticity and meaning. That's what people want. They want you."

"I don't know that." Helpless and overwhelmed, Jonah shook his head. "How can I know that?"

Tommy said, "You could ask."

There was the unmistakable sound of a few hundred ears pricking up.

"Oh my God." With his face burning and an arm circling his middle, Jonah glanced around at staff and strangers. Tommy meant *now.* "Um. Excuse me, everyone. I suppose you've all been listening?"

Answering nods and murmurs of agreement spread through the room.

"I just . . . I know you love your royal family. You voted for them to stay, or whatever it is you do in a survey, and I'm glad, because those boys are better than you can even imagine. They'll do everything in their power to help you. But you know me. I'm just normal, you know? And I like being me. So, if I spent my life with Tommy, I'd just be—

He broke off as Tommy ducked his head, wiping a hand over his face.

Jonah's eyes grew hot.

If I spent my life with Tommy, I'd just be me.

"I can see what you're asking." Nora spoke loudly enough for everyone to hear. "And it sounds like you expect not to belong with Prince Tomas. Not that you've actually experienced any evidence of not belonging. In the time you've worked here, no one has criticized you. And I work behind a bar. People tell me *everything,* and not one person has had a problem with the thought of you and your prince. And speaking for myself, knowing you, knowing the kind and genuine man you are, I would be proud to accept you as part of the royal family."

The other bartenders all nodded. Some people clapped.

"We'd thought you and His Highness were a done deal," a woman said from near the front entrance, sliding a look at Jonah but very deliberately not at Tommy. "When we took the survey, it was with you being part of the royal family in mind. We like our royals. And we like the idea of you with them."

"Oh," he said, and gripped the counter behind him as his world tipped. "Really?"

"You listen to us." This from an older man in a back booth.

"You talk to us." A late-forties woman.

"You laugh with us." A young guy.

"You make sure we're safe."

And Jonah's lungs tightened, because that was Zara.

"We're not classist here," another woman said, and her friend added, "Yeah, you do you, babe."

"Besides, who doesn't want a pancake in power!" called a guy from the rear courtyard.

Jonah gave a wet laugh, and Tommy's features softened as he watched him.

Then Milosh said, "We'll miss you, though," and Jonah's humor fled.

"Then there's your dream." Tommy nodded carefully. "You've always imagined it in the form of a bar because it's perfect for it. You want to make a safe space for people who don't fit elsewhere—but, you know, not everyone fits in a bar." Tommy paused, dropping realization in the pit of Jonah's stomach. *Tommy* didn't fit in a bar. Kiraly was packed with welcoming venues—for everyone except its king and anyone like him. "With me, Jonah, the whole of Kiraly could become your community to build and tend and serve."

Jonah's pulse pounded. Here Tommy stood, in a room he'd had to mute and manipulate just so he could stay long enough to try win Jonah back. *That's not right.* Tommy should have somewhere to go. Everyone should have somewhere they felt safe.

Jonah could make sure Kiraly included *everyone.*

"You could focus on those who slip through the cracks." Tommy sounded as though he was trying very hard to be informative, instead of the verbal equivalent to wafting temptation right under his nose. "You know what it's like to be excluded. If there's anyone with the sensitivity and generosity to support those most in need, it's you."

"Oh my God," Jonah said, because a ball of wonder had started sparkling and spinning in his chest. *Could I do this?* "But I don't know how."

Tommy grew very still. His features flickered in awed disbelief before he said, "You think Mark, Kris, and I knew how to be royalty when we arrived? You'd work with advisors, ministers, project managers, publicists. And me. You'd always have me."

I'll always have you.

Jonah was going to cry.

"The way I love you, Jonah . . ." Finally, Tommy lost control of his voice. It cracked into something vulnerable and whisper-thin. "You told me it wasn't silly or small or impossible. And now I'm telling you that neither is a future where you live by my side."

Jonah's uneven breathing shuddered into the silence.

No one spoke; no one moved.

Tommy made waiting look like torture.

"I'm scared," Jonah whispered.

Tommy's chest heaved on his next breath. "I'll be with you."

"I'm not smart."

"Your heart is smart," Tommy said, and his voice wasn't weak anymore.

"I'll miss this place."

A dart creased Tommy's brow. "You can come back. Kris visits all the time. You can come as a patron whenever you want."

"Oh." Jonah's smart heart hadn't thought of that. "Right."

"So," Tommy said, with a gut-wrenching tangle of hope and fear in his eyes.

"So." Those heart-shaped bubbles were bursting inside him—so many, so rapidly, it felt like his entire torso was fluttering. He tilted his head down a little, biting his bottom lip and making the most of his thick lashes. "What will people call me?"

Tommy closed his eyes. Turning to one side, he pressed his forearm along Zoltan's back and rested his forehead on top. His back rose and fell on several deep breaths. Steadied, Tommy turned back to Jonah and said, "That depends."

And he went down on one knee.

"Yes!" Jonah exclaimed and covered his mouth with both hands as his eyes blurred.

"I haven't asked yet." Tommy's voice was warm, rich with

sudden certainty. "Jonah Wood—"

"Wait, stop, stop!" Jonah removed his glasses and rubbed his eyes with a laugh. "You've already said one amazing thing when I couldn't see you. I want to see this."

In the time it took him to mop up his tears and slide his glasses back on—not helped in any way by Nora's sobs and sniffles—Tommy had appeared in front of him.

"Oh, Tommy." Jonah's sigh came right out of his soul as he swayed into the pull of Tommy's body, pulsing strong and safe and true. "Yes."

Smiling gently, Tommy brushed Jonah's hair back from his forehead. "Please, can I ask?"

Jonah nodded, wiping his wet cheeks.

"Jonah, sweet." Tommy took his hand and knelt on the sticky bar floor, because there was nowhere Tommy wouldn't kneel for him. Jonah felt the attention of every person in the room swing to him, sensed hundreds of breaths held alongside his. But Tommy was all he saw—his serious features bright with warmth and love, his sky-blue eyes softening to the sweetest dusk. "My best friend. My backbone. My soul mate. I love you. Will you marry me and be my prince?"

As Jonah nodded, and Tommy swept to his feet to kiss him as hot as a naked flame, he wondered how his heart was supposed to keep hold of it all. This king, who needed Jonah as intensely as Jonah needed him. Royal life with family and guards and one-hundred-and-thirty-eight staff bedrooms. And a vibrant rainbow of a country that accepted him and trusted him with its care.

Maybe if Tommy thought his heart was smart, then it was big, too.

Big enough for everything.

Pulling back with a laugh, Jonah pressed their foreheads together and said, "Yes."

Yes to it all.

AFTER

To say that the coronation of King Tomas of Kiraly was celebrated by his people would be putting it mildly.

Kira City went absolutely wild.

The streets couldn't be seen for people. The crowd stretched like one cheering, dancing mass from the palace gates right down to the lakeside. Food flowed from storefronts and market stalls, streamers and bunting and confetti billowed overhead, and music came from every corner, the beat echoing like an applause into the summer sky. Reveling in their exuberance, the people flooded the steep streets with flags and banners and colorful cowboy hats.

"They look like sprinkles from up here." Jonah stood on the tower balcony beside Tommy, his suit the shade of budding bluebells, piped in gold. "Hundreds and thousands of them."

On a deep and unsteady breath, Tommy faced him. Just days ago, they'd promised their lives to each other on this very balcony, the marriage witnessed by their family at the tiniest of ceremonies. And today, Tommy would make his vows to Kiraly. He would swear an oath, receive the sovereign's regalia, and be crowned.

As Tommy's husband and consort, so would Jonah.

Crowned as Prince Jonah of Kiraly.

"Remember," Tommy said, and lost a heartbeat when Jonah turned to him like a bloom chasing the sun. "You bow to no one in my presence."

"I take your rank," Jonah recited with a nod, eyes wide, because he'd bowed to Ava just yesterday to her stuttering embarrassment. "And you remember, Tommy, I won't be out of reach, not for a second."

Nervousness twisted at Tommy's navel.

Attendance would be widespread, Philip had informed them. National media and international press, visiting royalty, nobility, dignitaries, and political figures from across the world. Hundreds of guests of significance who had traveled to Tommy's small nation expressly to watch his formal inauguration. Sweat had plastered Tommy's shirt to his back before Philip had concluded with a critical detail.

None of them would be permitted in the throne room.

"This is why I lead with the punchline," he'd told his uncle dryly before putting his head between his knees.

The ceremony would instead be livestreamed to viewing parties throughout the palace and city. In the palace, guests could attend the grand ballroom, the banquet hall, and the gardens to watch the ceremony and afterward indulge with cocktails and canapés, live music and dancing, and an official appearance by the three Jaroka brothers and their partners later in the evening. In the city, it would stream in every corner pub and venue with a screen, in the homes of citizens, and according to Jonah, the Bearded Bunting would host the biggest party the mountain had ever known.

The throne room would be limited to family and government officials.

That the event itself would be broadly unattended was unorthodox and bordered on scandalous—but so was a queer king whose children would be born as heirs to the throne. So was the ascension of triplet cowboy brothers and the closure of a profitable mine for the sake of human and environmental life. So was fucking everything until someone decided the future looked better different.

It looked better to Tommy.

Stronger. Brighter. Safer.

Safer still, for Adam and his family line no longer posed a threat. Regardless of his guilt, he had insisted he was the rightful heir in the days following his capture.

"Put an end to speculation," Tommy had ordered. "If he consents to a genetic test, do it."

Adam consented.

The test found no markers to tie his ancestry to the royal line.

Finally, it was certain.

Kiraly wanted a monarchy—and Tommy's birthright was assured.

A knock came from the royal study door.

"God above," he muttered as his insides mangled. *This is it.* Sweat dampened his skin and his pulse kicked hard, yet somehow, he remained in control. He owed it to the changes in the ceremony and his medication, a two-part strategy that eased his anxiety to a level where the pulse of prophecy inside him could strengthen into an inevitable beat. *I'm ready.*

"Hey," Jonah said, and Tommy met the warmth of his dark gaze. "I'm so proud of you."

With a soft tumble in his chest, Tommy held his husband's gaze and called, "Come in."

He didn't have to look to know that Mark and Kris entered, followed by Philip and Frankie and Ava. Jonah squeezed Tommy's hand and tugged him inside.

"It's time, Your Majesty," Philip announced, his words tremulous.

Tommy inclined his head. "Thank you for getting us here, Philip."

Kris slung an arm around Philip's shoulders. "This was always meant to be you, Tom."

"The crown will suit you," Ava said, as Mark nodded and said, "We've got your back."

Tommy looked between his brothers. "King or not, I'll always look up to you both."

"Isn't that sweet." Frankie arched a brow as she gestured to the staircase, but her smile was warm. "The Royal Guard awaits."

"Thank you, Frankie." Settling his shoulders, he held her stare. "For everything."

She brushed that off with color on her cheeks and stepped back with the others, facing inward to form a path out the door. It was time for Tommy to take the lead—with his family right behind him.

"You know, Tommy." Jonah leaned into him, an angel in human form, a man who saw the world in hearts and truths, a cowboy whose steady footsteps would entwine with Tommy's forever. "I've got a good feeling about today."

Tommy smiled at him. "Same."

COWBOY PRINCES

Her Cowboy King #1

Her Cowboy Prince #2

The King's Cowboy #3

Her Royal Christmas #4

Her Royal Christmas (novella)

A bonus Cowboy Princes story, called Her Royal Christmas, will be out in 2022. This novella will give Zara her own happily ever after and revisit Kiraly and our beloved Jaroka royals at Christmas.

ACKNOWLEDGMENTS

There's no denying it—writing this book got me through 2020. It was a shockwave of a year for all of us, and I'll be forever grateful that Tommy and Jonah wove me into their spell of love and lust, letting me ride out back-to-back lockdowns in the escapist wonder of Kiraly.

Dom, you got me through the year in every other way. Thank you for being my remote working buddy, my brainstorming partner, my safe space.

Grace, you went heart-eyed over this story before I'd even started writing it. Thank you for your melty texts, abundance of exclamation marks, and feedback along the way. These are your boys too.

Anna Cowan, your feedback completely turned this book around. You knew exactly where I needed to dig to deepen these characters as individuals and as a couple, and challenged me to push my writing to a higher standard. Thank you.

Thanks also to Mark O'Brien for your time and wisdom. Lauren Clarke and Anna Bishop for your edits. Indie Royalty for sharing your self-publishing prowess. Kristin Silk for knowing what matters most in romance. And Mum for handing back manuscripts filled with red pen and smiley faces that always look a bit wicked.

My gratitude goes to my advance readers for giving these cowboy princes your precious reading time and wonderful reviews.

I would also like to respectfully acknowledge the Boon Wurrung people of the Kulin Nation, who have traditional connections to the land where I wrote this book.

And to all my readers, thank you for coming on this journey with me. I love having you here.

Xx

ALSO BY MADELINE ASH

Rags to Riches series

The Playboy (#1)

Alexia needs to become sexually confident for an upcoming acting role and playboy Parker agrees to teach her. Now all they have to do is let each other go.

Her Secret Prince (#2)

2016 RITA Award finalist

As a teenager, Dee had her heart broken by Jed. Years later, he's back in her life—but will a surprising royal discovery ruin their second chance together?

You For Christmas (#3)

2016 RUBY Award finalist

Black sheep Regan arrives on Felix's doorstep to take up the debt he owes her. Will they act on their feelings this Christmas or are their pasts too painful to bear?

Breaking Good (#4)

2017 RITA Award finalist

2017 RUBY Award winner

Years after spending a night with bad boy Ethan, Stevie runs into him again. She's shocked to discover that he's alive—and she has to tell him he has a son...

Morgan Sisters series

The Wedding Obsession (#1)

2019 RUBY Award finalist

After life-changing surgery, Emmie is overwhelmed by the urge to marry. Despite his love for her, her best friend Brandon struggles to believe her proposals—until a shocking revelation changes everything.

His Billionaire Bride (#2)

Business investor Carrie is guarded for good reason, while artist Edwin —rejected by his family—will only settle for commitment. Their intense chemistry builds them so high she's blinded to the fall. And the only way out is to break both their hearts.

ABOUT THE AUTHOR

Madeline Ash is an Australian contemporary romance author and two-time RITA Award finalist. She has won Australia's Romantic Book of the Year award (RUBY). She delves deep into the hearts and minds of her characters, creating flawed and compassionate leads—who are always rewarded with a happy ending.

madelineash.net

instagram.com/madelineashauthor
facebook.com/MadelineAshAuthor
bookbub.com/profile/madeline-ash

Printed in Great Britain
by Amazon

41324754R00239